Feathers of Ash and Hope

FLAMEBORN SERIES I

K.J. ALTAIR

Copyright © 2025 by KJ Altair
All rights reserved.

No part of this book may be reproduced in any form or by any electronic or mechanical means, including information storage and retrieval systems, without written permission from the author, except for the use of brief quotations in a book review.

This is a work of fiction. All names, characters, places, brands, media, and incidents portrayed in this book are either products of the author's imagination or are used fictitiously. Any resemblance to actual persons (living or deceased), events, places, buildings, and products is entirely coincidental.

Editor: Jenny Sims (Editing4Indies)
Book Cover: Lennox Tocororo (@tocororoart)
Map and Graphics: KJ Altair

ISBN(ebook): 978-1-967591-00-8
ISBN(paperback): 978-1-967591-01-5

First Edition: June 2025

*To anyone who's ever felt they don't belong — you are not flawed, just brilliantly different. Don't dim your light to blend in.
And to my husband, my anchor and spark — this story breathes because of you.*

Feathers of Ash and Hope is the first installment in the Fireborn series and is set in a military academy in an unforgiving, fantastical world with magic, vicious creatures, gods, and high stakes. It includes elements of battle, violence, perilous situations, injuries, blood, self-harm, death, grief, PTSD, implied threat of rape (not graphic), and sexual activities that are shown on the page. Readers who may be sensitive to these elements, please take note and prepare before starting this journey.

CONTENTS

Chapter 1	1
Chapter 2	16
Chapter 3	24
Chapter 4	33
Chapter 5	40
Chapter 6	50
Chapter 7	56
Chapter 8	67
Chapter 9	75
Chapter 10	81
Chapter 11	93
Chapter 12	100
Chapter 13	111
Chapter 14	116
Chapter 15	126
Chapter 16	137
Chapter 17	148
Chapter 18	157
Chapter 19	165
Chapter 20	176
Chapter 21	186
Chapter 22	195
Chapter 23	203
Chapter 24	214
Chapter 25	223
Chapter 26	228
Chapter 27	238
Chapter 28	244
Chapter 29	252
Chapter 30	263
Chapter 31	275
Chapter 32	284
Chapter 33	288

Chapter 34	294
Chapter 35	304
Chapter 36	313
Chapter 37	318
Chapter 38	324
Chapter 39	334
Chapter 40	343
Chapter 41	354
Chapter 42	360
Chapter 43	367
Chapter 44	372
Chapter 45	380
Chapter 46	391
Chapter 47	403
Chapter 48	407
Newsletter	412
Acknowledgments	415
About the Author	419

BELARRA

STRUCTURE OF THE AERIE

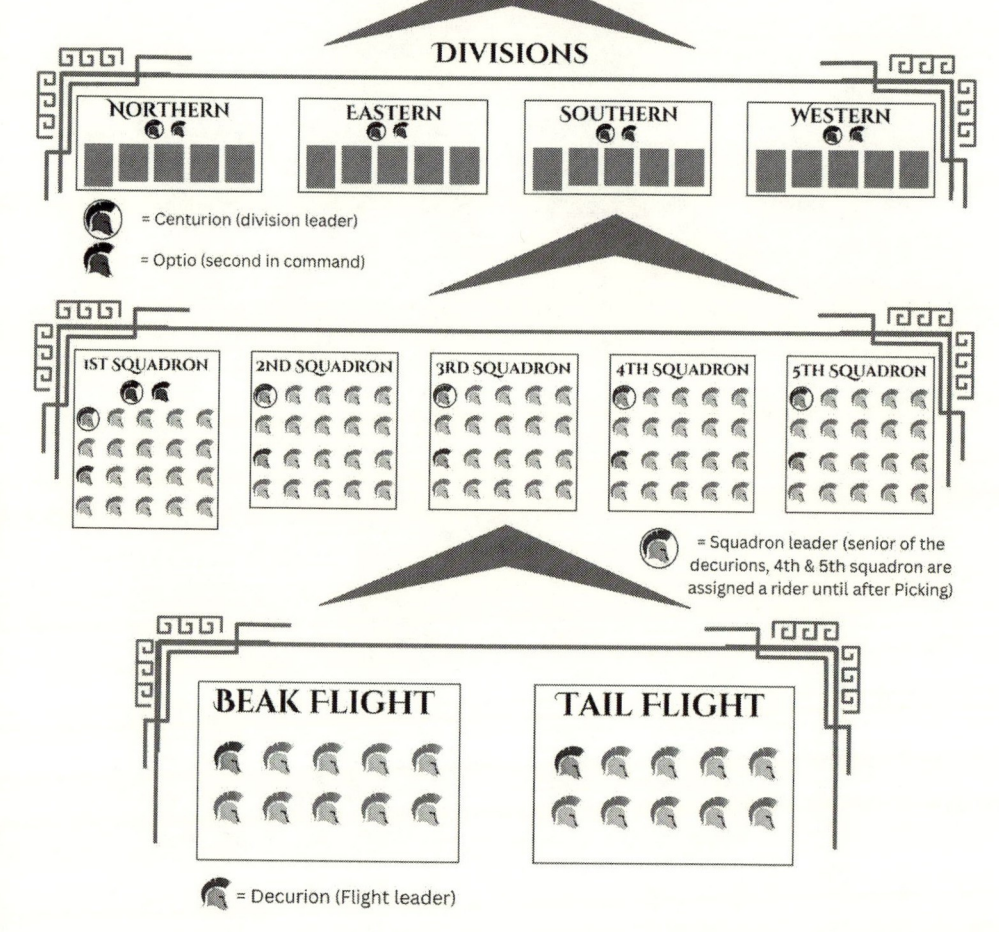

Aerie

DIVISIONS

NORTHERN | **EASTERN** | **SOUTHERN** | **WESTERN**

- = Centurion (division leader)
- = Optio (second in command)

1ST SQUADRON | **2ND SQUADRON** | **3RD SQUADRON** | **4TH SQUADRON** | **5TH SQUADRON**

= Squadron leader (senior of the decurions, 4th & 5th squadron are assigned a rider until after Picking)

BEAK FLIGHT | **TAIL FLIGHT**

= Decurion (Flight leader)

CHAPTER ONE

ARA

Three months earlier

It didn't work. The marking is still there and even darker than before, its edges harsh on my pale skin.

Gods, what now?

I fall back onto my bed, covering my eyes.

But when I open them, I stare right at that damn black mark in the crook of my right arm again. What if this means the king is right to fear people like me? What if I truly turn into something evil? And how am I going to hide it?

If scraping off my own skin doesn't work, nothing will. I'm plain and truly fucked, which means my family is too, and I'm once again the disaster ruining their lives.

I'll have to tell them.

I groan.

The handle of my door jiggles and is followed by a knock.

"Why is your door locked?" my brother asks.

"Go away, Ben. I'm not alone and naked," I shout.

He chuckles at that. Ben and I share not just our birthdays but also our humor, and thankfully, he gets my sarcasm.

He knocks again.

I get off my bed and check that my sleeve hides the mark before opening the door. My brother saunters in and throws himself on my bed in much the same fashion as I have before.

"Hey, you're in your armor," I protest.

"So are you," Ben replies, looking pointedly at my training gear of form-fitting black leather armor over a dark tunic and soft boots.

"Yes, you're lucky I'm dressed," I quip, and he snorts.

"You care too much about the fate of others to put anyone under Ian's or Dar's command in that position. But if it had been Ian and not me..."

"He would have kicked in the door." I finish his sentence and sit down next to him. We look at each other and grin. Darren and Ian, our oldest brothers, have many strengths, but sarcasm and humor are not among them.

"What are you doing here?" I ask after a while of companionable silence.

"I just wanted to see my favorite sister," Ben replies, playing hurt.

"I'm your only sister," I answer dryly.

"Okay, my favorite sibling, but don't tell the others I said that."

"You have to say that since I'm your twin"—I poke his side—"and I don't think they would be surprised to hear it." His grin mirrors mine.

Despite not being identical twins, we look very much alike. We both have our dad's changing bluish-green eyes and our mom's blond hair, only his is short and mine is long and currently braided up. When we were little, we were often confused for each other, but Ben is much broader and a hand taller than I am now.

My eyes catch on the markings running down his right arm. All gifted have them since magic marks its wielders.

"Did your markings spread up and down equally?" I ask. He gives me a quizzical look but humors me.

"No, they started down the arm first and then up until I reached my full potential."

"How long did it take?"

"About a year?" He shrugs.

"Did you ever hear of someone covering up or losing their markings?"

"No. What are you getting at?"

"Oh nothing, I was just wondering... Does your gift feel like a living thing?"

"What's with the hundred questions today?" I have his full attention now. "Have we all been mistaken, and you are suddenly gifted instead of cursed?"

I slap him, careful to hit his armor instead of his bare arms. "Thanks for reminding me. I totally forgot I risked your lives by simply existing," I snark.

"Shit, Ara, you know I didn't mean it like that," Ben says, sitting up.

"No need to dip it in honey. I'm the monster in the wardrobe, and everyone would be better off if I didn't exist." I jump up and shrug. I've grown up with this knowledge, so I have no idea why it affects me like this all of a sudden.

My mind taunts me by replaying the black mark on my skin.

"Fuck. You know I don't think that," Ben says. "If the fates had twisted the threads, it would have been me born cursed instead of gifted. It isn't your fault."

"Let's see if you still think so once I start drinking down magic like water and go on a killing spree," I reply dryly.

"Those are stories to scare children." Ben shakes his head. "There's no reason to be afraid of your immunity to magic unless you are a greedy old man who fears what he can't control."

"I don't think the king would be pleased about your description." I grin, trying hard to convince myself that Ben is right.

But there are things he doesn't know, things I'm too scared to admit out loud, even to my twin. Like every time my bare hands touch his skin—or anyone else's who has a gift—something within me reacts. There is a whisper, a sliding, a movement of something that shouldn't be. A pull. It terrifies me.

"So why are you here?" I ask, attempting to change the topic.

"I went to see Mom and Luc and—"

"You were hurt?" I round on my twin now and scan him from head to toe. Mom and my brother Luc run the infirmary at Fortress Blackstone, an active outpost in the Barrier Mountains, and the only home I have ever known.

Ben would only seek them out during the day if he was hurt during training or combat. Since I trained with Ben this morning, I know it wasn't the first.

"Nothing big. A little poison splattered over my hand when—"

"Where were you? And why weren't you wearing gloves?"

"If you would let me finish my damn sentence, you would know all of that already!"

I gesture for him to go ahead.

"We escorted Master Chapman over to the Ice Coast's bridgepoint. He swears they have the best fur, and he can't get anything like that from the hunters around here..." He sees my pointed look. "Well, anyway, we were attacked on our way back by some of Arachne's maidens, and poison splattered on my skin when I beheaded one." He shrugs. "Mom fixed me back up, and now it's like nothing ever happened."

That's another reason being immune to magic is a curse. Healing magic doesn't work on me either.

"What were those nasty, eight-legged monsters doing so close to the road during the day?" I ask.

"The days are getting shorter. Today is the equinox. The offerings will be moved soon..." Ben shrugs. "Maybe they were hoping to get lucky?"

"Do you think they plan like that?" The thought of monsters and demons actively planning their attacks is troubling. Ben shrugs again.

"Who knows what or if they think at all," he replies. "Dammit, now you derailed me again, what I meant to say is that Mom wants you to come over... something about measuring and ordering dresses."

I groan.

The two-toned blare of a horn sends adrenaline shooting through my body.

Heads-up!

A high-pitched screech, then a single tone follows.

All clear!

Ben and I hurry over to the window. My room is on the third floor, so we have a good overview of the courtyard, the gates below, and the gray and bluish-green sea of mountains surrounding us.

My gaze is instantly drawn to the majestic shapes of three huge birds descending in slow circles: two brown, one white—two Rukh, one Strix. They share the characteristics of predators, with curved beaks, short necks, and sharp talons, but unlike ordinary hawks or eagles, they are big enough to carry off a pony, maybe even a horse, and their breastplates and harnesses gleam whenever they catch the light.

They are too high to make out their riders yet, but skyriders circling the fortress can only mean one thing: Darren is back.

"Whoever is last to hug Darren has to do the honors at the offerings tonight," I suggest, and Ben grins at me, the dimple in his right cheek coming to life, mirroring the one in my left.

"Deal," he says, and I throw open the window. "Not fair." Those are the last words I hear before he crashes out of the door, his steps thundering down the stairs while I climb out the window and over to the rainspout. I'm in the courtyard within minutes, standing back while I watch the birds approach.

Rukhs are about the size of a war horse but stand taller and take up much more space with their wings spread. The Strix is even bigger, about one-and-a-half times their size. They look fierce with their breastplate, the chanfron to protect their head, and the weapons—spear, bow, and crossbow—strapped to their harnesses.

The three birds set down as one in a triangular formation, the Strix taking point and bearing two riders instead of one—one of them my brother.

A door bangs open behind me, and I grin when Ben stops next to me, his breath labored.

"That was cheating," he accuses.

"No, we never specified how we would reach the courtyard," I say while I watch the riders dismount. "And you could have climbed as well."

"We both know that no one climbs as fast as you do," he replies, and my grin widens.

Dar walks over to us, and as soon as there is enough space between him and the birds, I launch myself into my brother's arms with a delighted squeal. He catches me like he has done all my life and chuckles.

"Aren't you too old for that, little sparrow?" Darren asks, and I roll my eyes.

"Only if my goal were to appear dignified, which it isn't," I answer. "You're alright, aren't you?" I demand to know while holding on to him. Ever since he took Dad's place as the king's commanding general two years ago, I'm worried we'll lose him, too.

"I'm fine," Dar reassures me softly.

The skyriders step up behind him, two men and one woman. All of them wear the dark gray uniform of the skyriders—a form-fitting body armor, helmets with a black feather crest, and greaves and bracers protecting their forearms and shins. Winged swords, the emblem of the skyriders, are etched in silver on their chest.

"Has the infantry finally realized it's more fun to have women around?" one of the skyriders asks, his gaze wandering over me.

"Eyes off my sister, rider," Dar barks, making the rider's eyes widen and flinch away from me. His companions chuckle.

"My apologies, General Blackstone," he replies, his voice suddenly all business.

"That was some impressive climbing." The female skyrider steps up to me, her eyes wandering over my braided hair, leather armor, daggers, and down to my soft boots. "Ever thought of joining the skyriders?" she asks.

My eyes dance over the markings on the skyriders' arms. *That ... is actually ... a brilliant idea.* While gifts are mostly hereditary, skyriders receive a gift when bonding their birds, whether they previously possessed magic or not.

"Don't put such thoughts into her head, rider. My sister comes up with enough nonsense on her own." Dar turns to me. "That is a no to that thought."

"I didn't say anything," I protest.

"I know you well enough, so no!" He shakes his head, then embraces Ben. "How far along are the preparations for tonight? And where is Ian?"

Ben answers while I watch the stablehands relieve the birds of their harnesses, breastplates, and chanfrons.

Dar is right; the suggestion keeps playing through my mind.

"You can go over if you want to," the female skyrider offers and pushes a strand of dark hair out of her face. My gaze catches on the markings running down her arm to the back of her hand.

Would it work for me, too?

Then I notice the markings on everyone around me. Gifted people surround me, and I forgot my gloves. *Great.*

I place my hands behind my back.

"I would love to," I answer the rider's question, and she accompanies me over to one of the Rukhs, who bends down to greet her. She lovingly runs her hand over its beak.

"This is Neven, my Rukh. Rukh and Strix are the most common

and most approachable of the birds. As long as you treat them with respect, you'll be fine." She smiles at me.

"He's beautiful," I whisper. So close, the Rukh looks even more majestic and more than a little intimidating, his intelligent blue eyes fixed on me. I approach cautiously and only dare to run my hand along Neven's chest after his rider nods encouragingly. The feathers are sleek and far softer than I ever thought possible on such a fierce-looking creature. I keep the contact short when something inside me reacts to the Rukh's magic.

"How long do skyriders train?" I ask the question that has bugged me since her first comment.

"Only two years, as all candidates come already trained in combat." My chest becomes heavy. I don't have two years.

"And you bond with your birds at the end of that?" I fight hard to keep the disappointment out of my voice. I really hoped for it to be an option.

"Gods no." She laughs. "Picking is after three months." I perk up.

Three months could work.

"Do skyriders start in winter?" I ask. "Like infantry?" The woman throws a cautious look in my brother's direction, but he's talking to Ian.

"Yes, Assessment is two weeks earlier, which gives the ones who don't make it the chance to join the infantry instead."

Maybe that is where the rivalry comes from. I grin to myself, suddenly feeling giddy. Maybe if I talk to Dar and Ian and explain the situation...

"Are there many women in the skyriders ranks?"

The woman snorts at that.

"No, only one or two out of ten recruits are female. That's why I mentioned it earlier." Her gaze flies to my brother again, and she falls quiet when she sees him watching us with narrowed eyes. Thankfully, his wife, Elena, and my niece come flying through the front door, drawing Dar's attention.

"Thank you for letting me meet Neven." I smile at the bird and its rider before taking my leave and heading to the infirmary.

Giving my mother what she wants is an excellent excuse to get out from under my brother's watchful eyes.

The infirmary is at ground level and easily accessible from the courtyard. I hurry past a group of soldiers on horseback, getting ready to head out. The horses dance around, nervous because of the three huge birds launching into the air.

The soldiers are probably going to help with the preparation for the equinox festivities down in the village. The voices, bellowed commands, and clacking of hooves on paved ground fall away as soon as I close the door behind me. The scent of herbs permeates the air, and the soft murmur of my mother's voice guides me to the back room, the one she uses to prepare medicine.

I find her and my brother with their heads bent over a big leather-bound book, probably working on improving the recipe of some salve or whatever else is cooking over the fire.

"Mom, you wanted to see me," I say by way of greeting, but they keep on talking. I tap my fingers on the wooden worktable, waiting. They'll ignore me until they finish, so I save my breath.

My eyes wander over the drying bundles of herbs and the meticulously neat workspace around me and end on the copper cauldron hanging over a flickering violet flame. Magic flames are more efficient since they need much less fuel and burn without sooting.

"Tamara." My mom turns and smiles at me. "Perfect. I need to take your measurements. It's only half a year until your birthday, and I want a whole new wardrobe for you by then."

"What's wrong with what I'm wearing now?" I ask, and my mother laughs.

"No, none of your dresses will do when you are in Avina, and I will not send my daughter off to court wearing fashion from ten years ago."

"Mom, we talked about that. We don't think—"

My mom cuts off Luc's quiet objection with a wave of her hand.

"Wait, you have been talking about me and didn't think I should have been present for that?" I ask.

"Your brothers are just being ridiculous. We're not going back on our promise. Tamara will marry Frederick, and that is that," she states. My stomach sinks, my thoughts returning to the marking on my skin. There is no way I can head off to court if I develop markings without having any magic. And what if the markings of a cursed one don't look like those of a gifted one?

Are they linked to anything else? I think of the way I sense magic now and become a little faint.

I'm not looking forward to marrying a stranger, but disappointing my family would be much worse.

"Go over to room two and get out of that ghastly armor," my mother demands, and I do as asked.

I'm in my tunic and pants while she takes measurements. She runs the measuring tape down my arm and rubs over the still tender skin on my elbow during the process. I wince, and of course she notices.

"Did you hurt yourself during training? Let me see." Mom reaches for my sleeve, and I pull my arm away.

"I'm fine, Mom. It's just a scratch, and I'm quite adept at tending to my wounds by now, thank you."

"Are you still prickly that we didn't ask you to join us?" she asks.

"What do you think? Would you like it if we discussed your future without informing you?"

"It was by no means a planned meeting. Your brothers ambushed me... They think it isn't safe for you to be at court, but I think once your intended cares, there will be no place safer."

I have to tell her.

"But, Mom—"

"Don't start," she snaps. "This is important ... for you ... for us. If we pull out of this arrangement, there will be questions. With questions comes attention, and I hope I don't have to explain it. That is the last thing we want." Her chest heaves, and she turns away to note down the last measurements with angry strokes. "Simply do what you are told for once. Now go change, and I want to see you in a dress for the festivities."

"Yes, Mom," I sigh. I can't disappoint her. I have to make this work, and the only thing I can think of so far is to become a skyrider.

The wind starts picking up when I leave the infirmary and head back to my room to change. I look up at the fast-moving clouds. A storm is moving in.

Two guards hurry by, ignoring me, but otherwise, the courtyard is empty and quiet, a strange sight since someone is usually always around.

Four riders pass through the gate. I don't recognize them, but their uniform declares them part of my brother's forces. One of them spots me and shouts something, but the wind sweeps his words away before they reach me.

The horses' chests and flanks heave, their coats are slick with sweat, and steam rolls off their bodies.

Someone was in a hurry to get here. Poor horses.

The man who spotted me is marching in my direction now. He seems to be about Dar's age and not much taller than me. His dark hair is short, and his face is in a scowl. He is broad-shouldered and fit like all the men here.

"Didn't you hear me, boy? Our horses need to be tended to," he snaps before his gaze travels down my body. He draws to a stop, realizing his mistake.

Maybe it's my angular face or that nobody expects to see women in leather, but it's not the first time someone mistook me for one of the stable boys. Not that I'm dressed like them.

I smirk while his slanted eyebrows relax, then wander up in surprise.

"Are there female soldiers in the army now?" the man asks playfully. Why are they all asking that today? The way I dress doesn't even come close to their uniform.

"Not that I know of." I smile.

"Well, that's a damn shame." His gaze wanders over my body again. "They would look much prettier in our uniforms than we do."

I laugh. "Thanks for the compliment."

"Who said I was complimenting you?" He sends me a wicked grin.

"Your eyes." I wink at him and earn a rumbling laugh. "Come on, I'll show you the way to the stables. I have no idea where everyone has gotten to."

They follow me to the stables, and I enjoy the distraction.

"Don't get them into trouble, lass," our gray-haired stable master admonishes me as soon as we step through the door, and I roll my eyes at him.

"Damn, and here I was thinking about dragging them right off into the hay," I say dryly. That earns me five sets of round eyes, making me laugh.

"Ara." The growl comes from the stall next to me. A moment later, my brother Ian appears at the door. He doesn't look happy.

I roll my eyes at him. "Relax, I'm just kidding."

"I wouldn't mind..." one of the new men says, but his voice fades off when my brother sends him a death glare. He includes the other three for good measure.

"To be clear here, I'm Ian Blackstone, commander of this fortress, my brother is General Darren Blackstone, and this is our baby sister." I see all four of the newcomers swallow. Guess there won't be any more flirting. "We can use all the manpower we get up here, but if one of you as much as breathes in her direction, you are dead. Am I clear?"

"Relax, Ian, they didn't do anything." He searches my face, and his body relaxes. He nods at the men, then leaves the stables without another word. I send them an apologetic smile and hurry after him.

"You can't go around saying shit like that, Ara," he seethes. Yep, he's still in a mood. Great. I open my mouth to say something, but he goes on. "I don't want to dispose of another body."

I flinch. Hurt, guilt, and anger bubble up, creating a maelstrom of feelings I don't know what to do with.

"Really?" I laugh, but it sounds bitter, and Ian is the one flinching this time. "Sorry for being such a damn inconvenience to you," I croak out, my throat so tight I can barely breathe.

I turn around and walk away, not stopping even though he calls after me. I hate that I'm a burden to them. That they treat me like I need protection from everyone, including myself.

My feet carry me to the one part of the fortress no one will follow. A big part of the southern tower was lost in a landslide years ago, and now the only way up is to scale the wall.

Once at the top, I sit down, letting my legs dangle over the mighty drop. The mountain ends abruptly here, giving me a perfect view over the valley far below with its fields and trees, and the river snaking through. The ground is so far below that my stomach somersaults whenever I lean out too far, and I wonder if this is what flying feels like. I untangle my braid, and the storm whips the long blond strands around me, cooling my heated cheeks.

Dar, Ian, and my mother will never agree with my plan. After Ian's words, I'm sure of that. But what other option is there?

The rain is a grayish-blue curtain coming closer, washing the world away. It soaks me to the skin as soon as it reaches me, plastering my hair to my face and neck. The raindrops pelt my skin like needles of ice and break through the chaos of feelings burning inside me.

I have no idea how long I'm sitting there, my mind running over the problem again and again, but I only see one solution.

I have to prove I'm capable of solving problems on my own so that they don't have to worry about me.

"You are quiet today, little sparrow," Darren says later at dinner, looking at my fidgeting leg. "And restless." He searches my face. We sit in the dining hall with everyone else at Blackstone, and my eldest brother is a damn bloodhound if it took him less than a day to catch on that something is troubling me.

Not for much longer. I just have to find a way to execute my plan.

"I'm fine. Just tired." I reassure him, but he doesn't look convinced.

"Why don't you take a break?" my mother chimes in from the side, handing me a plate with eggs. I help myself before passing it on. "You train as hard as the boys, and there is no need for that."

I bristle out of habit, but ... that is perfect.

"Maybe I do need a break," I say, and Dar's eyes snap to me. I evade his gaze, my thoughts racing. "You know, I thought maybe I could visit Sloan for a while," I say. My mother beams at that while Darren's eyes narrow.

Sloan is my cousin, and they live in the south, close to the sea in Telos. A small town that just happens to have one of the four skyrider academies.

"You will have so much fun," my mother gushes. "Balls and parties," she goes on and on, and I nod along, smiling, but stop when I see Dar's suspicious gaze. "Dashing young men." Mom sighs, seemingly lost in memories. "That is how you should spend your days instead of this." She swirls her hand around in a gesture, indicating the fortress and its surrounding forests and mountains.

"Dashing young men?" Dar's voice sounds incredulous. "Mom, I don't think that's a good idea without one of us keeping an eye on her."

"Darren Richard Blackstone," my mom snaps, which makes all of us chuckle. "They are perfect gentlemen," she says, and all my brothers snort at that.

"Yeah, right," Ben murmurs under his breath.

"Mom, I think it would be better for Ara to stay here with us," Dar says, and Ian seconds that view.

"Darren, babe, I love your protectiveness," Elena chimes in. "But don't you think you're taking it a bit too far? You can't keep Ara locked up in this fortress all her life. She can take better care of herself than any other woman I know."

"She is also better at getting into trouble," Luc offers. My brothers exchange meaningful glances. Not even Elena knows about my curse since even hiding my existence is a death sentence, and Dar would never risk her like that.

"And who would accompany her?" Darren asks Mom. "You, Luc, and Ian are needed here. I can't either, and Ben..." He shakes his head.

"Come on." Ben throws his hands up. "I can look out for her."

"The twins in Telos. That even sounds like the title of a drama," Ian murmurs, and they all chuckle while I grin at Ben's mockingly outraged expression.

"No one needs to look out for me because I can kick ass all by myself," I throw in, which earns me Mom's leveling gaze.

"Tamara Summer Blackstone," she admonishes. "That is not something to feel smug about." Then she turns back to my brothers. "She won't be alone, and my brother and his family are capable of looking out for her, so I don't think there is a need for one of you boys to accompany her. Sloan is such a reasonable girl."

I do my best to hide my grin.

CHAPTER
TWO
TATE

I LEAVE THE SMALL DARK ALLEY AND HEAD TOWARD THE BIG street leading us back to the academy. I'm glad I wear all black today instead of my uniform. It makes the bloodstains much less noticeable.

"What the fuck, Tate? Are we really not going to talk about the reason I'll have to keep up this illusion until I'm back in my room?" Jared hurries after me. My best friend currently looks nothing like his tall, blond, and broad form but like a tiny redhead with killer curves, which makes hearing his deep voice out of her mouth even more bizarre, but that is not the only glitch. He matches my pace easily despite his seemingly shorter legs. Nobody's illusion is perfect if you're observant.

"You weren't invited, so don't whine if it bruised your sensibilities," I tell him.

"You can be such an ass," he grumbles. "How did you even know it was me?" he asks when he realizes I don't intend to say anything else. Not that this should be news to him.

"You still walk like yourself," I answer.

"And how do I walk?" he asks, exasperated.

I snort. "Not like a woman who looks like that," I tell him, which has him grumbling again and me hoping I avoided that conversation.

"What the fuck are you doing, man? That was a fucking shit show," he hisses, keeping his voice low since the street we just entered is much busier than the one before.

"I told you to stay away," I say dryly.

"Oh, and that makes it better?"

"What should I have done, Jared?" I round on him, dragging him closer to the houses to let a horse cart pass without getting run over. "Should I have let him slip his dagger between my ribs like he planned to? Should I have let him walk away after that?"

"No, of course not, but I can't believe you still won't let me have your back."

"It's my plan and my questions that got me into this. I will not drag you down with me," I hiss. A woman passes us and gives me a disapproving stare, probably because it looks like I tower over Jared's fragile form. *Fucking great.* I release him and step back before someone calls the guards. The blood on me might not be obvious, but it's still there, as well as its coppery scent.

"It pisses me off that you keep me out of this," Jared grumbles. "It's like you think you're the only one affected by what happened back then." He turns away from me, starting down the street. We've had more fights about this than I can count.

"Jared, you know that's not true," I say while I follow. "I just have to do that alone."

"Why? Am I not allowed to be affected because I wasn't there? Am I not allowed to want revenge?" He shakes his head. "Just stop fucking pushing me away."

"That's not what I'm doing. I ..."

"Well, it feels like it. You hurt Mom by staying away, too. You know that, right?" he adds without any heat or accusation, and somehow, that makes it worse.

"Jared, I'm sorry, I—" I start, but he cuts me off again.

"Are you coming with me to see her tonight?" he asks before I have the chance to recover from his verbal blows. He maneuvered me right into that one, the sneaky bastard. How can I say no after what he just said?

Still, I hesitate, not because I don't want to see her, but if she looks at me differently... I'm not sure I could take it. Jared feels my hesitation.

"If you don't come, she will soon show up at the Aerie and drag your ass home. You know that, right?"

Home.

I flinch at that word. I haven't yet stepped foot in the home Jared's mom has created here in Telos, yet Jared still includes me so naturally in that statement, as if it is my home, too.

Nan, Jared's mother, was my nanny when I was little, and even when she didn't need to keep an eye on me anymore, I saw more of her than of my parents.

Then I left court, and Nan and Jared packed their things and came with me like it was the obvious thing to do.

I've only seen her twice in the past three years, and always because she sought me out.

Jared is right. She gave me space, and I'm sure her patience is coming to an end.

"I'll come," I tell him. "But we need to change first."

Jared looks down at himself, grimacing at something I can only assume is blood since it's hidden behind his illusion.

"I don't have a problem with blood, man, but couldn't you have warned me that I would bathe in it," he complains. How I should have warned him when I didn't know he would come is beyond me.

"Do you need me to heal you?" I ask, but he shakes his head.

"Did you get any answers?" He wants to know instead.

"No." I shake my head. "But I clearly disturbed someone with the questions I already asked. I'll meet my contact tomorrow, so let's hope that goes better."

"I don't like it that you go to that meeting alone," Jared says, and I scoff.

"I would hardly call it alone. Daeva will be with me." Daeva is my Night Raven, a vicious and tenacious creature, bigger than a horse with mighty claws and a sharp beak.

"Tell that puny human I will show him what I do to creatures that disregard me," Daeva grumbles in my head, and I chuckle.

"I'm sorry, Daeva," Jared says, knowing what caused my reaction. "I'm just angry he still doesn't budge."

"Tell him I won't let him off this easy next time," she says, hearing Jared through me without me having to repeat the words.

"She forgives you," I relay her answer to Jared. "And no, I won't take you with me. It's bad enough that my contact knows my face and that I'm a skyrider."

"I could use my gift," he offers.

"And what about Zephyr? Do you want to disguise him, too?" I shake my head. To alter his bird's appearance for such a long time while Zephyr is flying would send him into exhaustion.

"But I will come to the next meeting in the city," he declares, setting his jaw, not even bothering to dress it up as a question.

I know a pointless argument when I hear one and stay silent.

"Hey, Trouble." I find myself enveloped in familiar arms as soon as I step through the door.

I don't know how she does it, but even though Nan reaches only up to my shoulder, she manages to give hugs that make me feel safe and cared for. I missed her hugs, missed her.

"Let me look at you." She cups my face between her hands, and her eyes aren't missing a thing while they travel over my face and body. "I worry about you," she adds.

"If you don't ease up, Mom, no threat will get him through this door next time," Jared teases.

"Oh hush, bug." She swats her kitchen towel at her son. "No such nonsense." She points her finger at me. "Enough now with the evasion. I won't tolerate it any longer."

I send her my sweetest smile. I have a lifetime of practice and know how to get on her good side.

"Don't you try to charm your way out of this one—I mean it, Trouble. I'm quite cross with you." She rests her hands on her hips, heaving out a breath. "Oh, come here." And I find myself in her arms once more, grinning at Jared over her shoulder. He shakes his head, smiling, and mouths, "Suck-up."

"Oh, and before I forget, your pay came in today. Trouble, yours is still coming to me, too. I already told you to clear that up, didn't I?"

"And who else should the money go to?" I ask, raising my eyebrows. "My parents?" Jared chuckles behind me at that suggestion. "And it's not like I need more than the bit I keep since the Aerie provides for us." Jared nods.

"Can you tell me what I'm supposed to do with all that money?" She glares at me and then at Jared. We both shrug, grinning at each other. This feels like old times. "It will be waiting for you," she declares, leading the way into the kitchen. Like I would ever touch that money after everything I owe her.

Another wave of affection and love washes over me when I step into the cozy kitchen and see the table set for three. Jared didn't have the chance to tell her I was coming. I would bet my favorite dagger that she had the third plate on the table at all the dinners Jared went to by himself.

"I had a feeling today was special." Nan bustles to the oven. "I made your favorite casserole and chocolate cake for dessert." I groan in pleasure, which makes her laugh. "That'll teach you not to stay away so long next time."

We sit down and dig in as soon as she sits as well. Jared sends me a mischievous smile before turning to Nan.

"Mom, I think some olives would have added a splash here."

"I don't want to hear a thing about olives out of your mouth, young man." She points her finger at him. "Every time the cook served olives, I knew there would be complaints about you two."

Jared and I look at each other and burst out laughing.

"Come on, you can't blame us. Those wineglasses made excellent targets, especially when people were mingling. And we were quite good at it, too." Jared smiles at the memory.

"Oh, I never heard the end of your 'accomplishments.' The maids had quite a headache getting those stains out," Nan scolds with a smile.

Jared and I earned somewhat of a reputation throughout the years, and many of the stories have Nan throwing up her hands in exasperation. But she laughs at them as well.

"You were always too curious for your own good. Your urge to get to the bottom of a secret or solve a puzzle drove your father crazy." Nan smiles at me.

"Do you remember the catacombs?" Jared asks.

"How could I ever forget that?" I ask.

"It was epic." Jared grins.

"It was terrifying," I disagree. "When my dad made everyone leave, I thought I would spend the night down there alone."

"You had no business being down there to begin with," Nan throws in.

"If the damn door hadn't slammed shut, no one would have known," Jared says. "And maybe we would have found a treasure. Who knows?"

I grin and shake my head.

"Good thing you were already on the other side. No one would have thought to look for us down there. Father was furious," I recall.

"Your mother pleaded with him, but he wasn't to be swayed," Nan says.

"But you got me out of there," I reply. "Mists, the relief when I saw the light coming back." I sigh, remembering my ten-year-old frightened self huddled in the dark.

"I planned to come back that night. I had already packed blankets, a lamp, and biscuits when Louis came back with you," Jared throws in as if I didn't know that.

I remember Louis's crooked smile and the words that had sounded like the best ones I ever heard.

"Let's get you out of here. I would rather not spend the night on this stone floor."

"And in the morning, he sneaked me back down there. I rubbed a little dirt on myself, and no one was the wiser."

We all chuckle.

Louis had been the best.

As if he senses my shifting mood, Jared launches into the next story, determined to keep it light and easy. It is easy to laugh with them, and the longer I sit at Nan's table, the less solid my reasoning for staying away becomes.

Nan is not one for throwing around accusations, even if she has every right to do so.

Nan looks at me, her expression serious. We arrived at the moment I dreaded all along.

"His death is *not* your fault," she says, and I look away. "Look at me." When I don't immediately react, she reaches over and places her hand on my cheek. I meet her gaze. "You are not to blame, and I need you to start believing it, or it will destroy you." Her gaze is unwavering, and there is truth in her voice. Only she is wrong.

My throat closes up, making it hard to breathe and even harder to speak.

"But if I hadn't..." There are so many ways to finish this sentence, but I can't force even one of them past my lips. I swallow. "Louis would still be here," I croak.

"He made his choices, and they led him right to that moment. Who am I to question that or the fates? Maybe it was his time to go."

She gives me a sad smile. "Yes, I miss him. Yes, I'm angry sometimes. But not with you. Never with you." Her hand runs over my cheek, catching slightly on the stubble. Then she focuses on her plate, her eyes suspiciously bright.

I'm glad Jared doesn't push for a conversation on our way back. My mind is stuck on repeat while I go over that day three and a half years ago and every possible outcome, trying to find the point that would have made a difference.

CHAPTER THREE

ARA

"They're going to kill me," Sloan mutters for what feels like the hundredth time since we started for the academy. A small miracle, considering it's not more than ten minutes on foot—and we are only halfway there.

Telos is a small town at the foot of the Malvada Mountains that borders the sea. Its biggest buildings are the academy, the arena, and the temples. Everything else is modest in comparison and ranges from sprawling villas and townhouses to the huts of the poor.

I arrived three weeks ago, so I thankfully had time to get used to the overwhelming number of people and noise. Despite Telos being a small town, it is big compared to what I'm used to.

Sloan pulls me aside when a cart loaded with vine barrels swerves to the side to let an oncoming cart pass.

"I'm as good as dead," Sloan mutters. My uncle thinks she is accompanying me to the carriage station and that I'm heading home today, while my family assumes I'm staying for three months. So I'm on my way to the academy.

"My brothers are not that bad." I roll my eyes at my cousin's dramatics.

"They kill for a living," she counters, making me snort a laugh.

"They are in the king's army, not assassins." I shake my head at her.

"Same difference," she mutters. "And now you want that too? Kill and be killed?" Sloan's family consists of merchants and has nothing to do with weapons and fighting.

"It's not half as bad as you make it sound," I tell her, trying to keep the annoyance out of my voice. We've had similar arguments at least a hundred times.

"Is that why you slinked out instead of telling them?" She raises her eyebrows.

I don't answer that. Since she doesn't know I'm cursed, I can't tell her about the marking. But she knows my brothers well enough to have a solid idea of how telling them would have worked out.

"Look, all I need is for you to post those letters for me. As long as they keep coming, no one will ask questions. You won't even have to lie for me." Those letters are the only reason I told Sloan about my plan. She will cover my ass by forwarding them since I won't be allowed to leave the premises until after Picking, which is three months away. Sending my letters with the military postal service simply isn't an option.

She stops and stares at me like I've lost my mind.

"Ara Blackstone, stop acting like this is not a big deal." She throws up her hands. "Applicants die in there!"

"Accidents happen everywhere." I shrug. "It's not like someone is trying to kill us off."

"Oh no, they kindly wait with that until after you're done and you get sent on patrol."

"Relax, I won't have any accidents, and I won't be on patrols until at least next year."

The hurried clatter of hooves on stone ricochets off the houses around us, and I tense.

"Right, that's why they call them accidents, because people plan them." Sloan's words drip with sarcasm, and I laugh.

"You worry too much. I'll be fine." I wave off her objection while the riders pass us and continue down the street.

You only have to survive Assessment, I think. I'll worry about the rest once I get there.

Sloan hurries to catch up with me. I see her eyeing me and know what's coming next even before she plucks on the tunic that peeks out from under my sweater. Both are new and represent the local style.

"I still don't see why you are dressed like a boy. They do let girls join, right?" Sloan looks affronted on my behalf, which makes me smile.

"It's less suspicious. I will be one of many instead of the one exception." Guilt swirls in my stomach. I hate lying, but Darren, as the commanding general of the king's army, gets regular updates on all the military posts. If he hears about a girl who climbs like a squirrel and just started training at the Aerie in Telos—the same place I happen to spend my 'vacation' at—he will be here to drag my ass back home before I even have the chance to try on the uniform.

"And what happens once they find out you lied?" Sloan voices the worries I've stubbornly ignored so far.

"I guess I have to hope that being bonded and my connections will be enough to keep them from doing something drastic."

Like executing me.

My smile falters for a second. Well, it's not like that outcome would be different from what I'd face now if anyone finds out I'm cursed.

"You hope?" Sloan's wide eyes are locked on me.

I shrug. I'd rather have her think I'm crazy than endanger her by telling her too much.

My plan is easy: get into the academy, bond a bird at Picking, and become a skyrider. Boom, all problems fixed, and no one has to protect me anymore.

At least I can fight. Growing up in a fortress that's an active outpost with four older brothers as companions has its perks in that regard.

Sloan is quiet next to me, and I hope she doesn't regret helping me.

A shadow slips over me, and I look up, multiple dark shapes circle above us. Some are so far up they can be mistaken for ordinary birds, some so close, their shadows blot out the sun while they pass overhead. The riders on their back are not always visible from down here, but I know they're there.

That is what I'm going to become—a skyrider.

Seeing their dark shapes outlined against the blue sky above me transports me back to the day three months ago that sparked the plan to come here.

"They are so going to kill me," Sloan says, drawing me out of my memory.

I grimace. If my brothers find out what I'm up to, they will lose their shit for sure. Not that they would harm her, but I can easily see them dragging me back like a glorified prisoner.

A tall sand-colored building peeks out from behind the townhouses surrounding us, and I perk up—the academy. Suddenly, I can't wait to get this over with.

I like Sloan, I do. We are as close as you can be if you see your cousin only a few weeks every summer, but she's too good at worrying, and I don't see the point. It's not like it changes anything.

Big iron gates loom beside us, marking the beginning of the academy grounds. The gates are part of an equally imposing iron fence held up by intermittent stone pillars of the same sand-colored stone as the buildings behind them.

On my left, the fence gives way to a tall building. The buildings all have a similar structure to our fortress at home, but their walls are as light as the fortress is dark.

The compound is in excellent shape, not a blade of grass or a tree branch out of place, and the building's big windows sparkle in the light of the sun rising above the mountains in the east. They have the distinctive bluish glint of magically enforced glass, making them as durable as the walls around them.

Ian would approve.

The two guards operating the gates give us a cursory glance before ignoring us. More guards patrol the perimeter farther down, and there is a slight shimmer in the air around the gate too, hinting at magic.

The whole academy is a lot bigger and more impressive than I thought. The buildings are all at least four stories high, their pitched roofs and towers surrounded by a parapet walk.

I swallow, suddenly not so sure going in there pretending to be someone else is a good idea.

I hug Sloan, pull my shoulders back, and step through the gates before I change my mind.

The square in front of me is orderly. Not even a single weed dares to peek out between the nearly white gravel at my feet.

My eyes fly to the buildings again. Decorating stones on their facade, drain spouts, and windowsills create climbable paths up and down. Maybe I can use that to my advantage when I meet Sloan next month.

You have to get in first, I remind myself, heading to the long line of candidates snaking across the area in front of me. It starts at the massive gate of one of the buildings, which is its only visible entrance, the building acting as a massive wall for whatever lies behind it.

At least I can't get lost.

Nerves swamp my body, and I regret eating the breakfast Sloan heaped on my plate this morning.

Great timing for developing nerves, Ara. I grimace.

With my sweater and dark pants, I fit right in with the crowd. Nearly half the applicants are dressed like me, and I'm not the only one with a hat, either.

My clothes are loose, and my fortunately rather average breasts are bound tightly to hide my form. Touching my wool hat to make sure my hair is still covered, I step behind the last in line, settling in for a long wait.

Maybe I shouldn't have let Sloan talk me out of cutting my hair. The long golden strands are braided in a tight crown above my head. Thankfully, it's already cool enough to justify the hat, and the uniform comes with a cap as well.

I size up the others in line, and many of them look very ... built. They have broad shoulders and strong arms, and most are taller than me. I release a nervous breath. There is a real chance I will have to fight some of them during the sparring part of the Assessment.

The applicant in front of me looks as nervous as I feel and regrets breakfast too, if the slightly greenish tinge of his face is any indicator.

Gods, I hope he doesn't throw up, or I'll probably join in.

I turn. The candidate behind me looks more red than green while his mother bids him a tearful goodbye. Our gazes collide, and he rolls his blue eyes. Dark brown curls stick out in every direction on his head as if his mom just ruffled through them. I grin.

As soon as his parents leave, he steps closer. He's broad and tall and easily dwarfs me even though I'm not small for a woman.

"I thought I would have to do Assessment with her hanging on my neck," he says and clasps my hand in his. "I'm Calix, by the way."

I chuckle at the image of his petite, perfectly coiffed mother dangling from his shoulders while facing an opponent in a sword fight.

"You'd think she's used to her kids moving out by now, with me being the last one to leave the house and all." He still looks slightly embarrassed.

"You're the youngest? Me too." I smile at him. "How many siblings do you have?"

"Four, all older. Let me tell you, they are..." He shakes his head.

"Insufferable?" I suggest, making him grin.

By the time Calix and I make it to the front of the line, my nerves are gone, and we are fast friends. Both of us having four older brothers, even though Ben only by half an hour, sped up the bonding process and made for a whole lot of good stories to share.

"I think we'll have a lot of fun if we manage to stay alive," I tell Calix.

Like Sloan earlier, he looks at me like I've lost my mind.

"What?" I grin. "Don't you have the feeling this is going to be our lucky day?" I tease him. "Don't worry, most of us will survive today."

"Are you always that optimistic?" He sounds like that isn't necessarily a good thing.

"Would it help to be pessimistic?" I grin. "Besides, worrying is not my thing," I say, making him laugh.

The applicant in front of me is still pale as he approaches the two men guarding the entrance. The dark gray uniforms and the insignia on their chests match those of the skyriders three months ago.

The blond skyrider on the right is writing down names and handing out numbers while his dark-haired counterpart seems to be guarding the entrance.

"Well, he doesn't look very welcoming," Calix comments, and I follow his gaze to the dark-haired skyrider. He wears a constant scowl, his golden eyes burning into the poor candidate in front of me like he has offended him. I swallow.

I grew up around gifted and well-trained men, but that one—despite his scowl—has to be the most beautiful man I've ever seen.

My eyes wander over him. He has dark hair, golden skin, and a hint of stubble on his cheeks. Long, dark lashes frame his piercing gaze. My mouth runs dry.

"Not one I would want to run into in the dark," Calix muses, and I nod even though I disagree. I wouldn't mind in the least.

When the dark-haired skyrider turns his head to look at the other one, I see the hint of a scar on the right side of his neck. This intrigues me because scars are rare.

Healing doesn't leave any scars unless the wound is severe, and many healers are capable of erasing even those. So wearing a scar that obvious is unusual.

Maybe I'm just intrigued because I have so many scars of my own.

Yeah, that's it. I laugh softly at myself, shaking my head.

"What?" Calix asks.

"Nothing," I say, while my eyes are still on the skyrider. His markings cover the backside of his right hand to the fingertips, and I can't help but wonder just how far it stretches across his body. While the blond skyrider is a little on the bulky side, this one is well-honed perfection.

Get a grip. Ogling handsome men should be the least of your worries right now.

My gaze flies to Calix to see if he caught me staring, but he seems to be in thought, looking up at the birds circling above us.

My eyes wander back to the handsome face with the golden eyes. I see the muscles in his jaw working and wonder what or who pissed him off. Maybe he's simply a moody bastard, that would compensate for his looks.

It's my turn to step up, and I can't help but regret my decision to pose as a boy. I train my eyes on the one with the scroll. He fights a smile.

Is he the reason the other one looks so pissed off?

He looks at me expectantly, his pen poised.

Right, he waits for me to give him a name.

My eyes flit to his dark-haired companion, and I find his eyes trained on me now. That only increases the flutters in my stomach. I force my eyes back to the one with the scroll.

Originally, I planned to give Ben's name. Posing as him seemed logical, but now that I think of it, it's a bad idea. That would catch Dar's attention for sure.

I have to come up with something else. Now.

"Summer," I blurt out my middle name. The one with the scroll lifts one eyebrow over gray eyes, clearly waiting for me to finish.

"Gray...Grayson Summer."

That doesn't sound too bad.

I hold my breath. Have I been too obvious?

"Too nervous to remember your name?" the guy whose eyes inspired my new name asks, chuckling. I shrug.

"Nope, just intimidated," I lie. Telling him that I was busy drooling over his friend seems a bit too honest, even for me.

"Have you two looked in a mirror lately?" I continue. "You guys are huge!" Gray Eyes is laughing now.

But the guard with the golden eyes is not even smiling. The way he watches me makes me feel exposed. Like he sees the missing pieces in my puzzle.

He can't know I made that name up, right?

Gray Eyes writes down my new name. My eyes follow the short tunnel in front of me and go on to the other candidates milling around in the inner courtyard.

Anything to stop me from looking at the man to my left again. Gray Eyes hands me a slip with a number. It will be used to track my results.

My gaze flicks back to his companion like he is a damn magnet that draws me in. Those honey-colored eyes are still trained on me, meeting mine, probing. His eyes remind me of someone... but I can't put my finger on it. My gaze wanders to his mouth.

Gods, I bet his smile is devastating.

I nearly groan.

What is wrong with me?

CHAPTER
FOUR
TATE

I STAND IN MY ROOM AND GLARE DAGGERS AT MY BEST FRIEND. I didn't sleep well, and my scars sting and itch. We got back late from Nan's last night, and since we have no duties today, my plan was to get up, help set up the inner courtyard for Assessment, then spend my day in the air. Now, Jared single-handedly let that plan fly out the window.

"Oh, come on, Tate," my best friend pleads while I get dressed. "It's not that bad." I only glare at him.

Assessment is once a year, at the beginning of winter. On that day, all academies open their gates to anyone who wants to try their luck in becoming a skyrider—like we did three years ago.

Belarra's natural borders are mountainous. Patrolling them on foot would be time-intensive and require a lot of staffing. But it is manageable from up in the air.

So it is our job as skyriders to keep the borders of our kingdom safe. Most of us are stationed in one of the four Aeries, and some are at the bigger outposts scattered along the border.

Becoming a skyrider is hard work, and for a good reason. The downside of getting easily where the infantry can't follow is that we are often the first and only line of defense against the creatures spilling out of the mist until they get there.

I still scowl at Jared while following him out of my room, closing the door with more force than needed.

We walk down the corridor, our steps on stone echoing off the bare walls.

"Couldn't you at least ask before signing me up for this?" I huff out a breath.

"Why? You would have said no." Jared evades the elbow I aim at him and snickers.

"Guard duties instead of a free day," I grumble. "What a hard choice," I say sarcastically. "Just for the record, I'm pissed."

"Aw, no. You love me too much to be pissed at me." He widens his eyes comically, followed by a goofy grin. He's right. I do love his crazy ass, but that doesn't mean I won't do my best to stay mad a little longer. I send him another glare.

"You may be my brother in everything but blood, but that doesn't give you free rein over my time." I'm actually closer to him than my brother and I will ever be, especially since I don't plan to ever go back home.

"No, free rein is what you handed your brother, and I don't envy him," he teases.

"Good one." I fight a smile. "Now shut up. I'm still mad at you."

He chuckles while we continue our way down to the main gate.

That Jared became a skyrider is on me. The stubborn bastard is too loyal for his own good and simply refused to let me slide off the deep end after I left my old life behind. Since his stubbornness rivals three Night Ravens, I often give up pushing before he does.

He bumps my shoulder, and I glower at him before I hurry down the last set of steps and push open the small door that leads into the inner courtyard, the atrium.

"Oh, come on, Tate, lighten up already. It will be fun. We get to see all the candidates first and can earmark the ones we would like in our division," he says as if it is the most obvious thing to do.

"Yeah, right." I snort, drawing a few gazes from other riders.

"Why not? Not having to put up with the worst of them later is an appropriate compensation for standing at the main gate for hours, don't you think?" Jared gives me a mischievous grin.

"Like they would let you handpick our runners." I shake my head at him. Runners—the new recruits who can't fly yet—will be distributed between the divisions, squadrons, and flights by drawing their numbers, trusting that the fates will have a hand in their selection.

Every Aerie has four divisions, named after the cardinal points.

The new runners will be split into flights of ten and will make up two squadrons in every division. After they pass Picking and bond a bird, they will fill up the flights here at the Aerie, while more seasoned riders will be sent off to supplement the borders.

That way, new riders can gather experience alongside more seasoned riders during patrols in their second year of training, after which they will graduate and enter full service.

We cross the atrium, which is seamlessly surrounded by buildings. This creates an easily defendable place for landing and takeoff since the big main gate is the only direct entrance from the outside.

Today, the space is separated into two main areas. Temporary barriers have been set up to help retain order once hundreds of candidates flood the space.

We greet other riders as we pass them. They are busy setting up targets and racks full of weapons and marking down areas for archery, swordplay, and hand-to-hand combat.

Jared is the one who draws the smiles, while the greeting I get is more reserved.

I'm not here to find friends. Coming here was a strategic decision.

I watch the riders bustling around us.

Once they finish setting up, they are free for the day unless they volunteer for additional duties. I give Jared another glare, but he ignores me.

"You are going to do all the talking, jotting down their names and handing out the numbers," I grumble while we continue toward the gate.

"Deal. It's better if I do the talking anyway. But try to rein in your charming personality, or you'll scare them away." He smirks.

I bare my teeth at him in a mocking smile. I don't see the benefit in trying to play nice. My reputation will make them wary anyway.

"Yeah, you have to work on that," Jared tells me, shaking his head.

"If they annoy you, I'll come over for a snack and abduct you when I leave," Daeva tells me. Her version of she has my back.

"I'm fine. Jared is here with me."

"Tell him I'll slice him into tiny pieces and feed him to the chicks next time he changes plans without consulting us." Bloody pictures accompany her words.

I chuckle. *"Very creative."*

Her pleasure floods me. Daeva is a constant presence in my mind unless I consciously block her out.

"What did the menace threaten me with?" Jared asks, then holds up a hand. "No, wait, I don't want to know. Zephyr wasn't happy either, and he is not half as bloodthirsty as your bird."

That is not surprising since Night Ravens use fear to establish their social standing.

We enter the short tunnel connecting the atrium with the outer courtyard and stop at the main gate. The heavy and iron-enforced wooden door is closed, a rare sight that casts the tunnel into darkness. It seems no one deemed it necessary to light the magic-fueled lights along the wall since it's a sunny day.

I hear shuffling and muted voices from the other side of the door, where candidates are waiting for sign-up to start.

"Let's get this over with," I say, pulling back the gate's heavy iron bar. I use my gift to open the door with a blast of air, but I overestimate the force needed, and the doors hit the stone walls with a bang.

"Show-off," Jared mutters and grins before he faces the first in line, ready to take the candidate's name.

Jared's gift of Illusion leaves him with fewer chances to use it for everyday tasks than commanding air. Unlike me, he didn't have a gift before bonding.

I lean against the wall, facing the unbelievably long line of mostly men ready to risk their lives for the slim chance of becoming a skyrider. Only to risk their life some more as soon as they are.

The coldness of the wall seeps through my clothes, another occasion when commanding air comes in handy.

Since Jared took over the tasks concerning sign-up, my only job is to make sure no one passes without entering their name first and to keep an eye out for trouble.

At least we don't have to check the candidate's age since Professor Myrsky wards the gate so no one can enter Assessment unless they are old enough.

Time creeps along slowly, and I shift my stance for what feels like the hundredth time. We have been at it for hours, and the candidates still keep coming. Daeva circles above and sends me her view of the line, the people no more than little dots. It is getting shorter but only marginally, and it's already close to noon.

I curse Jared under my breath, but he hears me and grins, keeping his eyes on the boy in front of him. The boy's pallid skin makes me doubt his desire to be here. Jared sidles up to me.

"If you keep up that face, this poor kid is either going to run or piss himself," he whispers.

"If a certain someone wouldn't have signed me up for this, he wouldn't have to worry about that," I reply dryly.

Jared snorts and gets back to work.

I feel eyes on me, but I can't see anything unusual. I guess standing in front of a row of people will account for a few eyes finding their way to me.

The candidate with the sickly color leaves, and the next one steps up. The kid is slim and doesn't look old enough to enter, but passes the warded threshold without a problem.

He moves well but looks like either one of us can push him over with a deep breath. His thin frame and carefree smile remind me of Leo. I slam down the metal shield in my mind as soon as the thought comes up. I'm not going back there. It's bad enough that he and the others keep popping up in my dreams.

Eyes of an unusual blue-green meet mine for a second, and I suck in a breath. I have no idea why this kid affects me that much or why he seems familiar. I push down my curiosity. I don't want to know.

"Summer." He fidgets. "Gray...Grayson Summer," the boy mumbles. His voice is warm and husky.

I instantly know the first name is false, but the last name sounds correct.

Truth-telling is one of my gifts. Lies are dissonant, like someone playing out of harmony, and make my skin crawl if I have to listen for too long.

It is not like I instantly know the truth, but it gives me a hint that something about a sentence isn't right.

That the kid stated his names separately is the only reason I'm able to make the distinction here, and it piques my interest.

Why would he make up a different first name?

I watch him closely. His voice sounds more relaxed now, and he jokes with Jared about how intimidating we are, surprising a laugh out of Jared in the process.

The kid's gaze flicks back to me. He has big eyes with long lashes, freckles dust his nose and cheeks, and strands of straw-colored hair peek out from under his woolen hat. His cheeks are smooth. He looks not a day older than sixteen and unaffected by the bad this world has to offer.

Why the fuck did he end up here?

Our eyes meet for a second before he looks away again.

Summer takes his number, and while I want to say something to change his mind and send him home to safety, I don't.

His eyes meet mine again. I can't read his expression, but he doesn't seem cowed by my glowering. Maybe there is more to this wisp of a boy than is apparent. He claims us to be intimidating, but clearly, that isn't true.

CHAPTER
FIVE
ARA

Assessment is a well-coordinated affair. I guess it has to be since they want to weed out the candidates until the best one hundred and sixty recruits are left—forty for every division.

When I step into the inner courtyard, the sun stands high, stealing all the shadows and making the air too warm for a winter day. It's like I stepped into a massive arena. Tall buildings surround the space, the ground is sandy, and the fighting in one half of it emphasizes the impression. Not that I have been to one of the big arenas to watch a fight, but I've heard of it, and this looks just like I pictured it.

I walk past temporary barriers and get in line for the first test.

Candidates in front of me whisper about recruits willing to walk over bodies to get in. I hope that is an exaggeration, but the seriousness of what I'm about to do registers.

Two men face each other with swords in one of the sparring

areas. Several shallow cuts decorate the arm of one of them, while the other's right cheek promises to be a proper shiner in the morning.

This is different from a simple bout of training with my brothers.

My gaze flicks to Calix, who is right behind me in line, but we are both quiet. The test has three parts. The one we currently stand in line for is called the mountain run, an obstacle course that tests agility, balance, and tolerance of heights.

Sparring will be the second part of our test.

The sound of colliding metal and the dull thump of arrows flows over the constant chatter of voices around me. I look over just as a big blond girl buries her sword in her opponent's gut.

Well, that answers my question.

I swallow and turn away while the guy sinks to his knees, blood coloring the sand at his feet. The wound might not be deadly for him with all the healers around, but it certainly would have been for me.

Despite all that, the test I fear most is the one for magical gifts—the questioning. If they find out I'm cursed... Acid floods my mouth, and my stomach rebels against the food I ate this morning.

I take a deep breath and examine the obstacle course in front of me to distract myself. Beams protrude from the wall of the building and hold a variety of wooden structures designed to test our balance and strength.

A candidate hurries over a tree stump suspended in the air by ropes two stories from the ground. Its surface reflects the sunlight, worn smooth by the feet that have passed it over the years, and it wriggles and moves with every step. He stumbles, and I involuntarily suck in a breath when he goes down hard.

His face slams into the wood before he slides off to the side. Thankfully, I can't see him landing, my view blocked by a partial wall that belongs to the course as well, and the clinking of swords and the murmur of voices around me cover up any sound he might have made. I'm not sure he'll get up again. Two healers hurry over to where he landed.

My gaze wanders over the buildings surrounding me. Their light color and big windows make them seem less massive and more elegant than our fortress even though the structure is very similar. Rows of columns form an open walkway that runs around the entire inner courtyard—the atrium, I heard others call it—a reprieve from the glaring sun and a way to reach everything dry-footed should it ever rain.

I turn back to the sparring area, where every station is operated by a rider who seems to call out the points. Two candidates face each other in hand-to-hand combat.

Back home, we don't practice fighting without weapons much, so I'll have to improvise, especially since my brothers refused to punch me, even for training. Taunting them didn't help either and only made me perfect the art of pissing them off.

Something is oddly satisfying about cracking someone's control, but I doubt it will help me here.

A whistle blasts me out of my thoughts, and the candidate in front of me shoots off into the obstacle course.

I focus on him and not on the lifeless figure of the one who slipped as they carry him off on a stretcher. I'm not sure if he is only unconscious or worse, but I don't want to dwell on it. Instead, I use the chance to watch the man in front of me move, noting all the points he struggles with and planning a route in my mind.

The obstacle course is higher than the one I'm used to from home and has a lot more moving parts, but I guess that makes sense if they want to test us for flying.

The candidate makes his way through the last part of the course, and my focus goes back to the beginning.

There are two possible routes. I can go around, take the path that is easier but thrice as long, or I can go straight up.

I shake out my arms. I never was one for taking it easy.

Anticipation surges through my body while nerves hum through my veins and turn my palms moist.

I bend down and pick up a handful of sand, spreading it between my hands and letting it run through my fingers, vowing to myself that touching the ground again means I made it through.

The whistle sounds, and adrenaline zings through my body. I charge at the vertical wall in front of me.

The blocks are stacked nearly seamlessly, leaving only small bumps and crevices to work with. But fortresses don't build their walls with scalability in mind either.

I pull myself up to the top, jump up and run over a narrow beam, then fling myself at the rope that will bring me to the next level instead of playing it safe.

Jumping off saves me another few seconds. I roll over the wooden platform and bounce up just in time before it ends.

I climb up a net, the ropes rough under my fingers, then another rope, bars, and then the tree stump.

While I'm used to climbing, it is mostly trees, walls, and wooden obstacles, and the big difference is that they don't move.

Like the sheen indicated, the tree stump is smooth, and dust and sand make it even more slippery.

Don't think. Don't hesitate. Just move.

I step onto the wood and try not to think of the candidate I saw falling earlier.

My next step is not completely centered, and my foot slides to the side. There is a collective intake of breath from the crowd below that seems to suck all the air from my lungs. I bring down my other foot, praying to all the gods that could possibly be interested in my fate to find my balance again. I wobble, and it's probably pure defiance that keeps me from falling, but I take it. The sigh from below lets my lungs expand again.

I keep going and increase my tempo. Going slower only gives me time to hesitate, and that hasn't worked out for any of the other candidates I watched.

My body knows what to do. My job is to keep my head from interfering.

Jumping, climbing, balancing, repeating over and over.

My muscles burn, the air rushes past me, and my body pulses in the rhythm of my heart, my breath. I'm alive.

Suddenly, I'm at the end of the course. I jump down and roll again to compensate for my speed, and the moment my hands hit the sand, a smile splits my face. I did it.

I hop up right in front of the wide-eyed rider, stopping my time. He scribbles it down next to my number, shaking his head all the while and copies it to a stamped slip of paper. One of three I have to turn in at the end.

Since it is a round course, I end up only a few steps away from the starting point, so I exit the same way I came in.

I walk past the line of candidates who will go next. Calix is the first.

"Watch out for the tree stump. You have to hit the middle or pray," I whisper to Calix while passing. The whistle sounds behind me while I make my way to the next test.

I'm standing in a line again, waiting for my turn, this time for sparring.

My eyes wander to the area dedicated to weaponless combat, where a red-haired girl takes down a guy a head taller than her with apparent ease. I'm fascinated and desperately try to understand how she did it.

Calix cuts in right behind me, ignoring the grumbling candidate he stepped in front of.

"Damn, Gray, you flew through that course! I have never seen anyone move that fast." Calix nearly knocks me over by slapping my back. "The rider taking the time was still stunned when I made it through. Thanks for the tip, by the way. That would have cost me otherwise."

I watch the male candidate surrender to the redhead before I turn to Calix, who grins down at me.

So much for evading attention.

I smile back. I'm glad about my decision to hide between the men. If my time was that fast, it would have probably caused even more attention as a girl.

"You practically ran up that wall." He shakes his head in wonder.

I shrug. "I like climbing."

"Yeah, no kidding." His gaze wanders from me to the shooting range behind me. "Will you excel at that, too?" He inclines his head toward the targets. "Or is there something you're not good at?"

"I'm good with a sword and a bow, passable with knives, but I have never even seen something like that." I gesture to another pair of candidates fighting with their bare hands. "So I'll probably get my butt kicked." I shrug again.

I better make sure I don't break something.

I watch as one of the candidates flips the other on his back and wince in sympathy at the impact. "Strength is not my strongest suit either."

Calix turns to me again and sweeps a glance over my shoulders, which are nearly half the size of his. "Yeah, you are a bit scrawny, if you don't mind me saying so. But speed and technique can make up a lot."

"Did you train with your brothers?" I ask Calix.

He laughs.

"No, I begged our neighbor to train me. He is with the city guard. I had enough of always getting my ass handed to me since I was the little chubby brother."

"Chubby?" I give his athletic body a once-over. "Well, I would say that worked out well for you," I say.

"I'm not complaining." He smirks. "Did you train with your brothers?"

"I joined my brothers' lessons as soon as I was able to hold a blade ... and they dragged me back to our mom. But I was right back ... so they gave up eventually," I say, and Calix chuckles. We both watch two candidates go at each other with swords, their movements fast and so fluid it looks like a dance.

Damn, they're good.

"I tell you what, if we get in ..." Calix's gaze returns to me. "We'll train together. I'll show you some tricks on the mat, and you can help me get better at that climbing stuff. My time was shit." He smiles, self-deprecating.

"Sounds perfect to me!" My smile widens. Maybe becoming a skyrider isn't as cutthroat as everyone tries to make me believe.

Half an hour later, I'm ready to take that thought back. I'm armed with a dagger and face a brutish-looking man. I didn't like him when we started and loathe him since he tried twice now to slip his knife between my ribs.

He has a calculating look in his eyes, is bigger and heavier than me, and fights as dirty as it gets. Sweat trickles down my temple and already soaks my tunic. I lost my sweater long ago. The cuts on my arm from deflecting his blade throb in time with my heartbeat.

Good thing I'm not above fighting dirty too, if needed. His chest is heaving, and he looks like a bull ready to charge. Being good at pissing people off has come in handy, after all.

I incline my head, giving him a sweet smile.

"Are you alright over there? You look a little ... constipated," I say, and the rider, who acts as the referee and stands behind my opponent, makes a choked noise, coughing to cover his laughter.

I think the rider's laughter, more than my words, makes my opponent snap, and he charges in a rush of fury.

Distracted by his rage, he forgets to monitor all my movements.

I wait until the last moment, then drop low and slide to the side, swiping my blade over his legs right under his kneecaps.

We fight with our own daggers, and I always keep this particular one very well-honed. He goes down like a tree.

The referee's eyebrows jump up, and he notes me down as the winner while a healer rushes over. They will fix him up easily enough; fixing two tendons is much less work than a complicated chest wound.

"Sneaky but effective," the rider says while he hands me the slip with all my sparring results. Weaponless combat was a loss, and I'm sure I will look the part tomorrow, but I won the rest.

I smile at him and nod my thanks while ignoring my opponent, who is cursing me to the mists and back.

Calix is already waiting at the side. We went through all the sparring stations together but, thankfully, never had to face each other.

I'm exhausted. My body is a mess of bruises and superficial scrapes, and the shallow cuts on my forearm burn every time the stiff fabric of the blood-soaked sleeve rubs over them. Calix, on the other hand, is sweaty and a little ruffled, but apart from a bruise forming around his left eye, he's completely unharmed.

No major injuries. That is all that counts.

Questioning is the only part of Assessment held inside the academy, so we follow the string of candidates heading inside.

The stairwell we enter is cool and dark after being in the full sun. Or maybe it is just the sweat cooling on my skin.

The dark stone floors are smooth beneath our feet, and the bare walls are made of the same light stone as the outside.

We drudge up a flight of winding stone steps and are greeted by another line of waiting candidates running along a corridor with the same stone combination as before and high, arched ceilings. Big windows let in enough light to make additional lighting unnecessary.

The light space reverberates with chattering voices. The atmosphere is relaxed, but I'm terrified.

"Do you know what happens in there?" I incline my head toward the door we stand in line for.

"Oh, it's just a physical examination and a few questions. Nothing big." The guy behind us chimes in before Calix can answer. "My brother is a skyrider, and he said it's more about them wanting to know our potential and if we already have a gift than a real test."

"Well, that doesn't sound too bad. Better than getting our asses kicked by a gifted. That's what I feared would happen." Calix grins at the man, introducing himself. All I hear is "physical exam."

I'm going to be sick.

"Are you alright?" Calix looks concerned. If I look how I feel, I can't blame him.

"Be right back." I leave the line and rush down the corridor to the toilets without looking back.

I'M SITTING ON THE CLOSED TOILET, LOOKING DOWN AT THE crook of my right arm. The stain on my skin is too dark for a bruise, and there is no way they will overlook it in a physical examination.

This small dark blotch of bluish-black started it all, and I refuse to be stopped by it now.

What does it even mean?

I know gifted people have to learn to control and wield their magic. That's how it was for my brothers. Without a controlled release, magic accumulates until it either poisons the blood or erupts out of you. The thought makes me shudder. But what about cursed ones? *And how can I control something I don't have?*

Despite all the questions, I'm sure of one thing. I can't let them see the mark. It will be my certain death, and my family's for hiding me all those years.

Cuts and scratches dot my skin. There is only one way. The wound has to be shallow enough that no one will heal me, but bloody enough to hide the darkness beneath. I draw the dagger from the sheath on my belt, set it on my skin, and pause.

Shit, this is going to hurt.

I take a deep breath and scrape it over the mark.

My skin turns lighter and rougher in texture. Two small beads of blood pop up—not nearly enough.

Someone pounds against the door, making me flinch, which opens up a shallow slice on my forearm.

Dammit.

I growl in frustration. One more scar on my skin when I already have too many of those. Gods, what would I give to be able to be healed? It is the most common way cursed persons are discovered. My luck was that Mom was the one who tried to heal me.

And nearly died trying.

I was unconscious and too small, so I have no memory of that day, but the guilt stays.

Another pounding. I start again, remembering where I am. At least I had enough space between my skin and the blade this time.

I'm doing this not only for me but for them.

"You okay?" It's Calix, his voice muffled by the door.

I take a deep breath.

"Yeah. I'm fine. I'll be out in a minute."

My skin is clammy, and my insides roil. I grit my teeth, set the blade on my skin again, and drag it over the stain, harder this time. I release my breath in a hiss—still not enough.

I have to repeat it two more times. The pain increases with every go. By the time my smooth skin is raw and bloody—finally hiding the mark from sight—it's a constant burn.

I have to take a few deep breaths before my stomach settles, then I pull down my sleeve and clean my dagger over the sink.

When I exit, Calix looks me up and down but doesn't say a word. Despite the pain—more of a pulsing now—I feel much better. Now, it takes more than one hard look, and if I avoid being healed, I might even get through this alive.

CHAPTER SIX
TATE

The obstacle course is deserted, and only a few stragglers are left sparring in the low afternoon sun and shooting at the targets. Most candidates are now waiting for questioning. It's the same every year. Everyone wants to get the most life-threatening parts out of the way first.

I turn back to Jared.

"Have you heard anything about how many died this year?" I ask.

"I heard Sanders say we had thirty-two unlucky ones."

"Not too bad." According to the numbers Jared handed out, there had been close to four hundred applicants to start with.

Hopefully, that means we have fewer people of the I-walk-over-bodies type among the recruits.

This year is my first as centurion of the southern division, and I'm not sure I have the patience to deal with that in a way leadership would approve of.

While killing each other on purpose is frowned upon and severely punished, there are always some who try to frame getting rid of their opponents as an accident.

"*I could accidentally drop them,*" Daeva offers, and I grin.

"*Not sure they would believe you about the accident part,*" I tell her. "*Are you on your way?*"

"*There in three.*" She lets me know, and I leave Jared, who is talking to a few members of our squadron, and head out the gate to meet up with Daeva.

The whooshing and rustling of wings behind me tells me the patrol is back. Perfect timing. Now the air is clear for at least an hour. Plenty of time for a meeting without drawing too much attention.

Daeva is harnessed and ready to go in record time, and she launches as soon as I'm seated. Her mighty wings come down on the next heartbeat, causing a cloud of dust below us.

Daeva quickly wins on height, and I watch the landscape pass under her wings. Flying is always freeing, even with body armor and a helmet.

I enjoy the wind on my face. That's why I disabled the protective charm on my helmet as soon as I had enough control over my gift. It is needed during rain, snow, or heavy wind. Otherwise, flying in such weather becomes even more miserable, but I can always shield my eyes with air if needed.

The sun is low, casting the valleys into darkness. Telos is a small town, and the academy, with its light buildings and sprawling grounds, stands out even from up here. Then there is the round form of the arena and the group of temples on the temple hill. The rest of the buildings are much smaller, often family homes adjoining one another, only visible as brown-red shingled squares from up here.

Some of the mountains are forested, but the area around Telos is dry, and there are always bald areas between where wildfires have raged. Water, fire, and air gifts help to contain them quickly, but they still leave their marks on the landscape.

Now, during winter, the highest peaks of the mountains are

capped with snow, looking like giant versions of the waves crashing against the shore in the south of Telos.

Telos is the most southern and remote of the four academies that take in candidates for training. It is also the farthest away from Avina, our capital. Not much danger of running into any acquaintances from my former life.

Daeva's shadow slips over the ground below, rising and growing on the mountain slopes and plunging down the other side.

Daeva circles a few times before starting elaborate maneuvers. The straps of my saddle dig into my legs on a sharp turn. She pulls out of a dive, and gravity pushes me hard into the leather under my ass.

"You are such a show-off. And you aren't even sure anyone is watching," I tease.

"Someone is always watching. Who wouldn't with how dazzling my feathers look in sunlight?" She sounds smug.

"Now I can't decide if you're paranoid or arrogant."

"Confident is the word you are looking for, human."

I snort, and Daeva clicks her beak in warning before plunging us into another dive.

If anyone is watching, it will look like we're practicing. An hour of practice can go a long way to keep anyone from getting suspicious.

Once I am satisfied it's safe, Daeva drifts toward the mountains, taking it a little farther with every turn until we dive out of sight behind the first peak.

My contact is already waiting for me, close to the bridge point to Muntos, the neighboring kingdom.

Bridge points look like normal bridges but are magically forged connections between two physical locations spanning the magical mist beneath. The mist separates all five kingdoms on Sortu from one another, making bridge points, portals, and sea routes the only connections.

Walking through the mist until you reach the other border may be a way to get there, too, but people who ventured into the mist rarely return, so no one is keen to try that.

I loosen the straps around my legs before Daeva even touches the ground and jump off as soon as she does. She takes off immediately. Daeva is still a daunting opponent while on the ground but at a severe disadvantage compared to her abilities in the air.

She will circle above and keep an eye out for trouble while I do the talking.

I eye the man I came here for while I take off my gloves and tuck them into my belt. He is pale and has white hair, which stands out against the forest behind him. His gaze flits over our surroundings before it comes back to me. I don't know him well enough to trust him, and he seems nervous, even more so than last time.

"*Anything suspicious?*" I ask Daeva.

"*Nothing so far, but anyone could use the trees as cover,*" she answers. She's right. I stay where I am, wide out in the open, where Daeva can swoop down and grab me.

My contact hesitates, his eyes flicking up to Daeva, but he finally comes to me when I don't move.

"I'm not doing this anymore," he blurts out as soon as he reaches me. "They know someone is asking questions." He looks over his shoulder like he expects someone to jump out and catch him talking to me.

"We have an agreement," I reply. My voice is cool and composed, but I want to yell in frustration. He's the third one to back out in the past two years.

"Find someone else to do it. You found me, didn't ya?" He squirms under my scrutiny. "Alright, alright." He searches the pouch on his belt and slaps three gold coins into my palm. "Here is half of what you gave me. I did half of the time we agreed on, so we're even."

At least he didn't just vanish like the first two men.

One is dead, and the second may be, too. I pocket the money. I don't blame him for wanting out after six months, even if it is inconvenient for me. At least he has the decency to tell me.

I nod, and he sags in relief.

"There have been six more raids on travelers and hunting parties. Same course of action as the rest," he says. "Only high-ranking members of society and good connections were spared and released against money or maybe information, but the families are very tight-lipped about it." He shrugs. "Not one of the victims breathed a word of recognizing crests or colors."

Disappointment and frustration simmer inside me. The icy blue of the Mras Family should be easy to identify.

Why can no one remember something important like that?

"*You can't expect prey to remember the fur markings of its attacker. They may do many things, but thinking or being observant is rarely one of them.*" Daeva tries to appease me.

"How come I can remember then?" I grumble.

"*You are no prey and never have been.*" That's her simple answer.

I turn my attention back to the man in front of me, gesturing for him to go on. I know it makes him uneasy to witness my conversations with Daeva, if he even realizes this is what I am doing. His gaze catches on the lines of my markings, visible beneath my sleeve.

His eyes come back to mine, and he swallows. "In one case, the attackers were forced to retreat in haste, and they left the body of one of theirs behind." I perk up at that. "He was stripped down, so I don't know what crest or colors he wore."

"What happened to the body?" I ask, holding my breath. Maybe I finally have the breakthrough I'm waiting for.

"He supposedly was handed off to one of the healing houses," the man answers, pushing his hair out of his face. "But when I asked for him, no one knew who I was talking about." He shrugs. "My guess is, his people found a way to get the body back."

I curse. A part of that man in the right hands could have gotten me some answers. Three and a half years since the attack that turned my life around, and still no progress.

They'll pay for what they have done.

"But a guard of the armed party that broke up said attack close to the Barrier Mountains found this at the site." He pulls a crystal out of his pocket, about the size of my thumb. It's a smoky gray, the hexagonal form pointed at both ends and tipped in gold. I reach for it, but the man quickly closes his hand over it.

"I paid him five silver for it," he says defensively. Nice try. I simply wait, and he fidgets under my stare. Daeva caws, amused.

The man flinches and hands over the crystal without another word. I turn it over in my hands.

"Any thoughts on what this is for?" I look at him, and he squirms, evading my gaze.

"You're the one with a gift, not me. It's not the stopper of a decanter and looks too fancy for a tent peg." He shrugs.

"Anything else?" I ask.

The man shakes his head.

"All of the raids still happen close to the border, and still nothing outside Belarra, right?" I double-check.

"Like I said, nothing changed." He looks longingly at the bridge point behind him.

I continue to ask my questions, but it soon becomes apparent he has nothing new to tell me. We go our separate ways. The crystal is the only reason I don't feel this meeting wasted my time and money.

CHAPTER SEVEN

ARA

We wait for what feels like forever in the line for questioning. It seems everyone chose to keep this part for last. We spend the time talking and joking, and the small group we formed allows us to wander out of line without losing our spot.

The last time I checked, the scrape I inflicted on myself had dried into a scab, hiding every sign of what lay beneath.

Calix excused himself a few minutes ago, and I'm listening to two other candidates talking while trying to stay calm. My nerves get worse the closer I get to the door.

A rider walks down the corridor, lighting the torch-like fixtures on the wall. They have a steady golden glow, nothing like the violet-bluish flicker of magic flames. Since Ian is fire gifted, we use a lot of magic flames at the fortress. According to him, anchoring his gift to an object—charming it—is easy, making it accessible even if he's not around.

Lighting a whole building like this solely with magic seems excessive, but not surprising, considering how many gifted live in these buildings.

A tall blond girl walks down the hallway like she owns the place. She strides forward, pushing two candidates out of her way, heading directly to the front of the line. I step to the side, letting her pass, but glare at her back when a red-haired girl, who didn't see her coming, stumbles over someone else and falls after being pushed aside. The arrogant bitch simply keeps going, not even sparing a backward glance to see if she harmed her.

I help the girl up, still staring in disbelief. The bully arrives at the front, going straight for the skyrider guarding the door. He shakes his head at her while he points at the end of the line, and she starts to argue.

I turn away from the pending drama to assure the girl I helped up is unhurt.

She is rubbing the wrist she landed on, her eyes on the bully.

"That's Livia Vaccari," she mutters. Seeing my inquiring look, she gestures to the girl who pushed her. "If you look up the word entitled bitch, I'm sure you'll find her picture."

I snort. "Which one 'entitled' or 'bitch'?"

She grins. "Both. I'm Mariel, by the way."

"Nice to meet you, I'm A..." I stop. *Shit.* "I'm Grayson." I try to cover up my fumbling with a smile.

That was close.

I have to be careful until I'm used to my new name. While Mariel seems nice, I'm still troubled by my near slipup and head back to the people and the conversation I abandoned before.

"My brother is bonded to a Strix. When he visited us, his bird stared like he wanted to take a bite out of me. Thankfully, he didn't." The speaker chuckles, and others laugh with him. I'm searching my brain for his name but come up empty.

"They say their scream can kill a man if he isn't healed in time," he continues.

I hope not. Otherwise, I'm fucked.

"Night Ravens are great, and they have night vision. How awesome is it to be able to fly at night, too?" a candidate says.

"Good luck with that." Another snorts. "They're incredibly picky. No, you better go for a Rukh or Strix. Rukhs are a little smaller, but they are unbelievably agile."

I listen to their arguments, but it isn't like we have a choice in the matter. The birds will choose us, not the other way around.

A person steps close, drawing my attention away from the discussion next to me.

"Hey, darling, you don't mind if I slip in front of you, do you?" I find myself face-to-face with the bully and recognize her also as the blond girl who buried her blade in her opponent earlier. She is currently invading my personal space and drags a finger down my neck, batting her eyelashes.

What the fuck?

I'm caught between irritation about her earlier behavior and being stumped as to why she comes onto me and not one of the men around us.

Ah fuck. I'm Grayson now. I forgot again, but at least it means my ruse is believable.

My eyes wander over her while I decide how to handle this situation. She is pretty—I have to admit—and she knows it. Her cold, calculating look also tells me she's used to getting her way, no matter the cost.

She picked the wrong target this time. I suppress a smile.

"Actually, *darling*, I do mind." I pluck her fingers off my skin and point at the end of the line. "The end of the line is back there."

We have more than one pair of eyes trained on us by now.

She pouts. "You really want me to walk over there? Instead of staying right next to you?"

"Yes, please." I try not to laugh at the indignation on her face. The candidates around us snicker while a flush creeps up her neck, and her eyes turn hard. She doesn't like to be told no, it seems.

"Do you know who I am?" Sounds like someone's family is mighty important around here. I know I shouldn't, but I can't help but poke a little.

"My, my, that must have been quite a hit you took." I give her my best innocent smile. "Don't worry, being confused can happen after severe head trauma." She rears back as if I had hit her.

"You think I have a head injury?" she screeches, looking insulted. I have an inkling she took what I said as an insult to her looks, which hadn't been my intention.

Laughter ignites around us. Her face turns red before she huffs out a breath and storms off, heading to the end of the line.

I may have made my first enemy before the first year even started.

Maybe backing down would have been wise, I contemplate as Calix walks up to me.

"What was that about?" Calix looks at the blond girl's retreating back.

"Apparently, I should have known who she was and fallen to her feet." I shrug. Calix chuckles and looks over at the girl. She now stands at the end of the line, sending me a death glare. He winks at her, and she looks ready for murder.

"Not one for charming the ladies, eh?" Calix bumps my shoulder.

I hide my laugh by coughing. "No, can't say that I am."

About an hour later, we reach the front of the queue. My palms are clammy, and I force myself to take deep, even breaths to calm my racing heart.

My hands graze the dagger on my belt, but I stop myself before checking the slim knife hidden in my boot. I'm always armed and not only to defend myself. Any trace of magic vanishes when a person dies. I swallow, and my mouth is suddenly dry. Not that it will change the outcome for me, but at least my family would be safe.

"Hey, you're next." The rider's voice jolts me out of my thoughts.

I take another deep breath and open the door in front of me.

I'm startled when I find myself in another hallway.

"Room four," a voice says right next to me, and I whip around. A girl a few years younger than me smiles up at me, sitting behind a small desk. "Undergarments only, you can undress behind the screen and leave your things there as well. A healer will be with you shortly."

I nod and walk over to the wooden door with a small four on eye level.

The room is a warm yellow, its window overlooking the atrium below. A wooden desk sits right beneath the window, and a dark leather-coated bed occupies the other side of the room, right next to the screen the girl talked about.

I'm just placing my clothes on the stool behind the screen when the door opens.

"Are you ready in here, or should I start with someone else?" a cheery voice asks.

"I'm ready," I say, stepping out from behind the screen while the healer places a thick, leather-bound book on the desk with an audible thump. The middle-aged woman is dressed in the typical dark red color most healers favor. With laugh lines around her eyes, she doesn't look the least bit intimidating, but I'm terrified.

She walks around me, inspecting my skin, while I concentrate on anything but the fact that her fingers and her healing magic are too close for comfort and that only a little dried blood covers my secret. This is it. This is the moment I dread.

I take a deep breath, fighting the urge to run.

"Quite a few scratches you've got there." She eyes my right arm. I squish the urge to hide it behind my back.

Calm and collected, no fidgeting.

"Happens when your opponents are bigger and stronger." I shrug, trying to keep my breaths slow and even.

"I can heal them for you," she offers.

"No, that's fine," I say.

She looks at me skeptically.

"Maybe they scar, and I have something to remember this day by," I add.

Her facial expression tells me she's not a fan of that concept, but at least it will explain the rest of my scars.

She shrugs and turns toward the desk. I release my breath, conscious of not being too obvious about it.

She picks up two objects and carries them over to me. Two balls made of a bluish-gray stone. She hands me the first; it's cool, smooth, and heavy in my hands. She watches me closely like there is more to it than holding a stone ball.

Is this some kind of test?

She takes it back and hands me the other one.

The hum in the air is the only warning I get before it hits my palm. Pain pulses through my hand, and I fight to keep my face passive.

The stone ball is loaded with magic. Something inside me stirs, like a snake uncurling, reacting to it. I struggle to maintain my stoic expression while the magic seeps into me, and the thing inside me rises and drinks it up.

It's only a small trickle, but I know it will get stronger the longer I hold it until there is no more magic left to take.

She reaches out to take the ball back. I can't wait to be rid of it, but I put it down slowly, just like the other one. I hope she can't sense the magic lessened, but I've never heard of anyone being able to gauge the amount of magic an object holds.

"Anything?" she asks. I shake my head, not trusting my voice right now. My hand still tingles and is slightly numb. The healer laughs under her breath. "I don't see the use either. It's not like a cursed one would be so bold to walk in here." She shakes her head. "Probably a relic from times when they weren't hunted yet."

This tidbit of information throws me off balance, and I'm glad her back is turned while she puts the stone globes back on the cushion they lay on before.

When they weren't hunted yet? There was a time when cursed ones were free to live in the open?

She is still at the desk, signing something. "We're done here.

Good luck." She hands me the slip with my number, gives me another smile, and leaves the room.

I made it.

It feels unreal, and I'm so giddy a laugh bubbles up. I clamp a hand over my mouth and look at the stamped and signed slip she handed me. It confirms my health and that I carry no markings.

With a big grin on my face, I hum while getting dressed, and any fatigue is momentarily forgotten. Even my secret of hiding among the male candidates is still safe because I am only a number to her.

My hand still tingles as if I slept on it while I make my way back outside and hand over my slips to the skyrider collecting them.

After a short wait, we are separated into two groups, and my grin widens when Calix walks over to me, looking incredulous and happy.

We are both officially part of the academy now.

The sun starts to set behind the tall mountains as we are ushered back into the courtyard. It looks different now. Only the obstacle course remains. Everything else is cleared away, leaving only a big open space.

I'm standing next to Calix in front of a big double door leading into the surrounding buildings. Four steps lead up to it, creating a small stone platform. The buildings cast the courtyard in shadows. Only the roofs and the towers of the academy and the colossal mountains behind them are still painted red-golden by the evening sun.

My mind goes back to the magically charged balls during questioning and what the healer said.

"...from when they weren't hunted yet."

It hadn't always been that way? When did it change? And why? Would I be able to find answers in the academy's library?

A group behind us is obnoxiously loud, bragging about how they eliminated their opponents in sparring.

I turn around.

There are four of them, all trying to outshine the other three. The way they go on, you would think they slayed a dragon, not bested another candidate. My eyes fall on a familiar face. It's the brutish man I cut down with a dagger. I snort out a laugh and shake my head.

My movement catches his eye, and he scowls at me. I smirk. His friends notice our exchange, and he takes a threatening step toward me.

"You think you can take me?" He puffs out his chest. I let my smile widen.

We both know I can.

For a second, he looks like he is going to attack me, and my hand slips to my dagger, but he stops short.

"He doesn't have to." Calix's voice rumbles next to me. The recruit gives me another glare before he turns back to his friends.

I give Calix a thankful smile before commotion at the front draws our attention.

A tall, stern-looking man with salt-and-pepper hair strides through the door, his piercing gaze gliding over us.

"Welcome, runners," he booms, and his words are greeted with a cheer. "I'm Legatus Janus, the Aerie commander," he continues once we all quieted down again. "I know today was hard, but believe me when I say you haven't seen anything yet." He crosses the platform and seems kind of disappointed that we don't make a sound at that declaration. "In this academy, we expect you to go above and beyond. Not only physically but in your studies as well." He gives us a stern look.

"Every one of you had to prove you are a warrior to be accepted. We expect you to be a weapon that needs to be sharpened and not a hunk of metal in need of a forge." He pauses. "Everything aims at making you the best version of yourself and preparing you for battle." He takes his wandering up again.

"We skyriders are the best weapons our kingdom has to keep our borders safe and to reach even desolate areas quickly and effortlessly, no matter the terrain. This also means that you are on your own in a fight—only you, your birds, and the brothers and sisters you see around here." He makes a sweeping gesture encompassing the whole academy, but I'm reminded of my brothers at home.

"Trust and loyalty are not given. They are earned, and you will have the next two years to do it," Janus continues. "You will have many opportunities while you interact and mingle with the active riders on assignments, during strategy meetings, and in everyday life. You will live and eat next to them, but..." His gaze roams over us. "Until you are done and fully accepted as one of us, every active rider is higher ranking than you, and you will follow their commands. And while you live and eat next to them, I don't want to catch a runner in a rider's bed." He pauses. "And by that, I don't mean that intercourse in any other place is fine." This earns him a few chuckles. "No fraternization. See it as your test of self-discipline and obedience. Any of you failing will be expelled. Have I made myself clear?"

Calix pouts next to me, and I stifle a laugh. Since I don't plan to let anyone close enough to discover I'm a woman, I don't see the problem.

I nudge Calix's side.

"Don't look so crestfallen. It's only three months, not a lifetime." I bite my lip to keep from laughing out loud when he gives me a look that says he has an entirely different opinion.

"So remember, do your best, value trust, loyalty, discipline, and obedience, and you will succeed here." He looks to the side, and a rider jogs up the steps and stops next to him. It is the same blond rider who wrote down my name this morning. They speak quietly before the rider turns to us, and the commander leaves.

"Congratulations, everyone. I'm Jared Venti. Professor Myrsky charged me with handing out assignments and giving you an overview of what your life here will look like since he is needed in the coop, our version of the stables, housing the Strix." He grins at us. "You all look exhausted, so I'll make it short. You will have theoretical classes over there"—he gestures to his left—"all first years together. You will start with subjects like history, geography, magical creatures, magic and flight theory, and strategy meetings. Then there are practical classes like all the physical training and flight classes, and you will be split into smaller groups. Until you have earned your wings during Picking, you are runners. Just like with riders, ten of you will form a flight, and two flights make up a squadron. A division is formed from five squadrons or ten flights, with four divisions in an Aerie. Clear so far?"

The numbers dance around in my tired brain, but I nod anyway. Venti looks us over and laughs.

"Doesn't matter. You'll get the hang of it. Every squadron was assigned a rider who will keep an eye on you and will be your contact for...everything, your squadron leader. You will meet them tomorrow." The twinkle in his eyes makes me think there is more to it than just meeting them. "And then there are..." He looks off to the side of the crowd, and when I follow his line of sight, three men and one woman in skyrider uniform are striding over to us. "Perfect timing. I was just about to start." They ascend the steps and stop next to Venti.

"Your division leaders," he announces. "Centurion Allard, northern division." A stocky woman with short-cropped brown hair nods at us and walks over to the left side of the stage. "Centurion Vega, eastern division." A man with the dark complexion of the southern isles steps up a few steps next to her. "Centurion Kyronos, southern division." My eyes stop on the dark hair and golden eyes of the man I admired during sign-up.

I blame my tired brain for missing the rest of the introductions.

I end up in the southern division, squadron 4, tail flight, together with Calix, which means Kyronos will be my centurion. Great. Now, I'll always risk drooling whenever he addresses us. It can't get much worse than that.

The stairs, hallways, and rooms we are shown afterward blur together, and I'm resigned to the fact I will get lost a few times over the next days.

At least everything is located in the buildings around the courtyard.

A grumpy-looking, gray-haired man, introduced as Prefect

Ovidius and in charge of the buildings and supply of the Aerie, oversees the issuing of bedding, towels, and our uniforms, as well as weapons, a backpack, and a healing kit.

With filled backpacks and armed with two short swords, a spear, a bow, a filled quiver, and a knife each, we reach the room our flight is assigned.

I'm not the only one who dumps everything rather unceremoniously on their bed, only to have the boy who led the way assure us he would wait until we put everything away.

I guess discipline isn't even to be neglected when you're tired enough to drop.

Sitting down in the warm refectory, filling my rumbling stomach with fish, cooked vegetables, olives, and salty white cheese, has the same effect as if Egin, the god of sleep and healing himself, was singing.

Exhaustion crashes over me, and the memory of walking to our room is only vague.

CHAPTER
EIGHT
ARA

A dull, deep pounding jerks me awake, and for a moment, I don't know where I am. Then everything comes back.

It's dark, and the deep rhythmic breathing around me tells me I'm the only one awake.

I planned on showering as soon as everyone was asleep, but that obviously didn't work. So I'll remedy that now.

I wince when my bare feet hit the cold stone floor and hurry past the row of bunks to the big wardrobe, taking up one wall of our room. I collect everything I need from my compartment, and rather than risking waking anyone by putting on boots, I stay barefooted while I hurry down the hallway to the washing rooms.

The hot water and the familiar scent of the soap I brought with me are so relaxing that I start daydreaming. Steps and a door closing snap me out of it.

Shit.

The person who came in is getting undressed behind one of the screens while I scurry over to the one where I left my clothes and hurriedly rub myself down with a towel.

My racing heart only starts slowing down once my breasts are wrapped and my clothes are back on.

I braid up my still-wet hair and grimace when a few drops run down my neck, but there is nothing I can do about it.

I'm on my way back down the hallway, my feet still bare since I didn't bring my boots and socks, when I pass Centurion Kyronos, and of course, he notices. Great.

Our room is dark and quiet when I return. I put everything away and sit down to put on my socks and boots when the door to our room flies open.

A person charges over to the window, throwing it open. A blood-curdling screech makes me and everyone else jump.

"Good morning, everyone. I'm Joel Cassius, your squadron leader," the shadowy figure exclaims, and my stomach dips. I was wrong yesterday. This is so much worse.

"Welcome to your life as a runner. Get up and dressed. We'll meet outside in the courtyard for a quick run when the drum strikes six."

The door slams shut behind him, and I can only stare.

Shoot me now. Didn't Ben say Joel went to the Aerie in Avina? What is he doing here?

It's still dark while we gather in the atrium. Apparently, every runner got the same wake-up call we did because the crowd seems to be the same size as last night. A dull, deep pounding starts, and I count six strikes. This explains what woke me and how the academy keeps time.

Joel—now Squadron Leader Cassius to me, I remind myself—calls out our names to check attendance while the same procedure goes on everywhere around us. We leave the courtyard through the big gate in an easy jog, and I do my best to stay in the middle of the crowd and away from Joel.

"Why the fuck do we need to run when we will fly soon?" a runner grumbles in front of me.

"To get away if necessary," a rider answers dryly.

"Can't our bird simply pick us up?" the runner whines.

"Have you ever paid attention to the streets in the center of Telos?" the rider asks.

"They are too narrow for a bird to land or get you," another runner answers, realization in his voice.

"Exactly, and that is why you need to be able to run. There will be areas your bird can't get to."

The grumbling stops after that, at least for now. We run along the fence bordering the academy grounds and soon pass a big tower with multiple arches on different levels. It's made from the same stone as the academy.

"What building is that?" I ask the rider closest to us.

"The coop," he replies. "There is one at every corner of the property. This one houses all the Strixes raised here."

"But I thought the birds always grow up wild?" Mariel, the red-haired girl I met during Assessment, asks.

"The bonded ones do," the rider agrees. "But if we confiscate eggs from poachers, they have to be raised by hand, and since they never bond or leave, they stay at the academy. You will have your flight lessons with them."

"Why don't they bond?" Mariel asks the question I had in mind. The rider shrugs.

"That's a question for Professor Myrsky. You'll have Magical Creatures with him."

I watch in awe as two of the white birds take flight the moment we jog past the tower. They launch from one of the arches, in short succession of another, and, swooping down, pass over us so closely that the wind of their wings whips around us. All runners cower instinctively, and the riders laugh.

"You'll get used to it," the same rider from before assures us, but I doubt it. How could you get used to something as magnificent as that?

By the time we get back to the main building, all runners are huffing and puffing, while the riders only show a sheen of sweat and seem fine otherwise.

We still have a long way to go.

At breakfast, we find the same crisp bread, olives, olive oil, and white cheese that we had with dinner the night before, but also a variety of fruit, cold meat, and fresh vegetables.

The food here seems as good as what I had at Sloan's, which is a welcome surprise.

Right afterward, we are back in the courtyard.

The Aerie in full formation is a sight to behold. The dark gray of our uniforms, the way we stand in straight lines and blocks. We can almost be mistaken for marble statues in the dim lighting, except for the occasional movement and whisper, which is much more pronounced in areas occupied by us first years.

The sky still barely shows signs of the coming sunrise, or maybe the sun just hides behind the hulking mountains to the east. Our breaths forming clouds, the dark morning and the snow-capped mountains remind me that it is winter, even if the days here are much warmer than I'm used to from home.

I know I will be thankful as soon as the sun is out, but at the moment, I wish our uniform was thicker, like the one designed for flying worn by the riders in front of us.

There would be no way to hide my curves in that one, though.

Their uniform consists of body armor fitted to minimize air resistance, worn over a tunic and leather pants. Those that seem to head out right afterward also wear bracers and greaves to protect their lower arms and legs, helmets, and next to two swords, their bow and quiver, a shield, and a spear.

Next to them, we runners look like civilians. Only the dark gray of our uniform matches.

While we listen to centurions address matters for the day for each division, the sky brightens slowly from gray to yellow-orange.

By the time the sky is a vibrant blue, only the first years and our squadron leaders are left.

After the surprise this morning, I chose the space behind Calix's hulking figure for formation. While I'm not short for a woman, I'm still one of the smallest in my flight, enabling me to hide in the back.

Joel is laughing about something one of the other squadron leaders said, and my stomach flips.

Joel Cassius is the son of the weapon master at Fortress Blackstone, Ben's best friend, and two years older than us. Needless to say, we spent a lot of time around each other growing up. He had been a good-looking boy with brown hair and warm eyes and was always nice to me. I had a major crush on him as a teenage girl.

His grin is the only thing boyish on him now. Joining the skyriders only made his shoulders broader and his movement more confident.

Shit.

I'm not surprised to see him climbing the ranks already—he soaked up as much of my father's lessons as my brothers and I did—but why here?

He hasn't seen me for three years, and I look nothing like my usual self. That has to count for something, right? *Instead, you look like a younger version of his best friend,* my inner voice taunts me.

With four brothers as study objects, my gestures and gait are spot-on, so normally I would say playing a boy for three months is easy, but now?

I peek around Calix. Joel separates from the others, and I hold my breath, still hoping this morning was somehow a mistake. I will him to go somewhere else, but he is heading in our direction. I bite my cheek to hold in a string of curses.

How am I supposed to accomplish my plan if the fates laugh at me by sticking me in his damn squadron?

Is there a chance of changing?

We head over to the temple of Otero, the god of power and war, and I do my best to hide between the others by staying in the middle of the crowd.

A huge likeness of the god dominates the temple, his head nearly grazing the ceiling. Otero is depicted as a powerful man in his prime, in body armor and with a spear and sword, the helmet under his arm, and his shield leaning against his leg. His eyes are crafted out of blue stones glowing with magic and fixed on a golden bowl in front of him.

I wonder if they have to charge the stones regularly.

The riders leave us in the care of the temple priests, their attire as warlike as their gods.

One after another, we prick our fingers and let the blood drip into the golden bowl. It instantly goes up in smoke while we pledge our allegiance to the skyriders and the crown, repeating the words the priest speaks over and over.

I somehow expect to feel different now, but I don't. My left shoulder burned for a second, and my body tingled like something brushed against me. The snake in my core shifted, but that was it.

Classes start right afterward, and our schedule is tough. We start with sparring. My body still hurts from Assessment, but since I'm the only one who refused healing, I can't complain.

My aching muscles slow me down, earning me a nasty hit to the hip, and my ribs and arms sport new bruises. If that streak continues, I'm sure my skin will be all blue and purple at one point.

I sigh in relief when the sparring is over, not only because my body gets a break but also because Joel hasn't shown up again since the temple. I know this charade won't last, but I can still hope, right?

Next, we have the lore of the sky, which seems to be a fancy name for skyrider history. Professor Etario fits the name of the class since he uses extra words wherever possible. A habit that drives me crazy within minutes.

Etario is a small man with thinning, cropped dark hair and a bouncy step who uses a lot of hand gestures.

He currently bounces from one side of the room to the other, telling us about the founding of the skyriders about three hundred years ago.

"While there have always been riders not unlike today, the skyriders as a military unit formed relatively late in the history of our realm. Can one of you tell me when that was and what caused it?"

"To finally eliminate the threats born from the mists, as well as the damn cursed ones, and these abortions of half beasts," says Gorgon, the brutish guy I faced during Assessment.

"That would be wrong," Etario answers. "Please raise your hand next time—Foley, was it? You wouldn't happen to be related to our deputy commander, would you?"

"He's my father," Gorgon replies proudly.

"I see," Etario answers in a way that has me overthinking my earlier opinion of him.

Maybe I can overlook his wordy habit after all.

"Anyone else?" Etario asks. And I know I shouldn't, but my hand is already up.

"Professor, I was just wondering, was there ever a cursed one, shifter, or fae bonded to a bird?" I ask, unable to pass up this opportunity.

"As if we ever would have trusted one of them to protect our back," Gorgon scoffs, causing agreeing murmurs throughout the room.

"Runner Foley, you have hands. Use them." Etario admonishes before turning to me. "There are no occurrences of that in the records, but they probably wouldn't have made it widely known since their social standing was already strained at the time the skyriders formed."

"So there was a time when that was different then?"

"I like your enthusiasm to learn more about our history, but may I ask what triggered your questions?"

"The healer, during questioning, mentioned something. It just made me curious," I answer as casually as possible.

"Our records don't mention any singling out or persecution of one or more magically gifted groups during the rule of the gods or the rule of the demi-gods, but they don't mention the mists either, so it is hard to say if it didn't happen or simply wasn't mentioned."

What a complicated way to say I'm not sure.

But if it is true...what changed?

I'm still marveling at that question while walking down the corridor next to Calix when I hear a familiar voice in front of us. I slip behind Calix, skirting around him so he is always between me and Joel. I release my breath once we pass, and Calix looks at me quizzically.

"I ... uhm ... just ... never mind," I mumble, having no idea how to explain *that*.

Calix shakes his head and grins at me.

He will either start asking questions soon or decide I'm crazy.

I'm sure of it.

During two other near misses, I duck behind Mariel, pretending to tie my shoe and slip into an empty classroom when Joel comes down the hallway.

The fact that I managed to avoid him so far should calm me down, but it doesn't. It's like I've already heard the thunder and am waiting for the lightning to strike. I know it'll happen. I just don't know when and how.

Two days later, I run out of luck.

It happens while I hurry down an empty hallway. A door opens, and someone steps out right in front of me. I look up.

Dammit.

"Ara?" Joel's eyes widen.

CHAPTER NINE

ARA

Considering he's my squadron leader, I guess I have to be proud I made it this long without coming face-to-face with him. And the hope he wouldn't recognize me was more wishful thinking.

Joel Cassius blinks his beautiful brown eyes at me as if he hopes I will disappear if he keeps it up. He pulls me into the room he just stepped out of. It seems to be some kind of storage room. Rolled-up maps and boxes fill the shelves that occupy all the walls and are even piled on a small table, which makes it a rather cramped space.

He closes the door behind him and leans against it, effectively trapping me in the room with him.

"What are you doing here?" His eyes travel from my boots up my body and end at the cap on my head. I'm very aware of just how unflattering this uniform is.

"Uh, you pulled me in here," I joke, but he doesn't seem to appreciate my humor. His eyes linger on my hair.

"What have you done to your hair?" He sounds shocked. His fingers graze my neck when he grasps the short strands that always escape my braid.

I'm suddenly too aware of his closeness and of just how broad his shoulders have become. The place his fingers touched is still tingling.

Dammit, not helping.

"Just braided up." I shrug. "Sloan stopped me from cutting it."

"Thank the gods, she was always the reasonable one," he says.

My gut twists. So that makes me the reckless, stupid one. The annoying little girl who always ran after her brothers.

I cross my arms and take a step back.

"I should set you on the next carriage home," he grumbles, and I can only stare. Is he serious? Does he think he can get rid of me that easily?

"Since you've made the vow, they'll count it as desertion, but you're here under a false name..." he goes on, ignoring my glare. "No one will be looking for a girl, or better yet, we'll write Dar—"

"What? No!" I shout.

"Ara." He sighs. "This isn't a game." He says it like I'm a little kid who decided to play soldier for a while. I grind my teeth.

When he sees my face, he throws up his hands. "You could get hurt, and Ben will kill me if he finds out..." His eyes grow even wider. "Wait, where do your brothers think you are?"

"In Telos." I give him a sugary smile.

His eyes narrow. "You want to tell me they know you're with the Third Aerie?"

I scoff.

"Ara," he snaps.

"Do you think I'd be here if they knew?" I place my hands on my hips and look at him incredulously. He knows my brothers as well as I do, so I don't know why he even asks.

"Fuck." He runs a hand over his eyes. "Okay, let me think. We could..."

Stay calm.

"I'm not leaving, Joel," I state.

"Ara, you can't ..." He steps toward me, shaking his head.

Okay, that's enough. My fists clench.

"You have no idea what I can or can't do." And he has no idea what's at stake for me either. "I'm not a child, Joel! You can't just send me home," I hiss.

Joel opens his mouth to reply when the door behind him opens, and another rider pokes his head in.

"There you are. We're waiting for you, Cassius. Kyronos is getting impatient."

"Fuck. Right, I'm coming." The rider leaves, and Joel turns back to me. "This conversation isn't over."

Oh, it is so over.

Joel shakes his head at my stubborn silence and leaves.

At first I'm worried that he'll make good on his threat to inform Dar, but when he still hasn't shown up two days later, I start to relax. Joel's eyes are on me whenever I cross his path. He's probably still plotting how to get rid of me. I ignore him, but make sure I don't run into him alone. I can do without a repeat of our nice little chat.

If he thinks I'll change my mind, he'll be waiting forever.

I only have to face two riders in the Aerie regularly. My squadron leader, Joel, and my division leader, Centurion Tate Kyronos.

The fates have a cruel sense of humor.

I'm sitting next to Calix in the strategy meeting. The room is filled to bursting even though some riders are out on patrol, and it is the biggest of the classrooms—the one referred to as the theater because of the little podium at the bottom of the swooping rows of chairs.

All four division leaders stand in front of a big map of the southern part of Belarra. Red lines indicate what I can only guess are the patrol routes. Little symbols of crossed swords appear along some of them, and I blink. One of them has to be gifted with Illusions.

Centurion Vega steps up.

"We had increased activity all along the mist line over the past week. I expect it to get increasingly worse, like every winter. There were already some coordinated attacks, seemingly focused here and here." He points out two places close to the border with Muntos, with nothing but farms and villages around.

Coordinated attacks?

Since when did nightmares and monsters coordinate their attacks? I'm looking around, but everyone else just nods along like that's nothing new. Are the mist creatures so much different in the South than ours in the North?

"One rider and his bird were wounded by arrows, no casualties."

Arrows?

I try to remember when anyone was shot by an arrow during an attack at our fortress but come up empty. Bites, stings, and slashes from abnormally sharp claws, shattered and broken bones, burns from fire, poison and acid, even damage by hurled rocks and trees— my mother and brother deal with all that regularly, but arrows?

However, the other reports are very similar to the first one, except that the northern division lost a rider.

I'm still trying to make sense of everything I heard while we walk to magic theory.

"You look troubled," Calix comments. "What is it?"

"I ... grew up at an outpost in the north ..."

"Oh, so you are legacy military?"

"Uh ... yeah, I guess you could say that."

"Are your brothers skyriders as well, then?" he asks.

"No ... they're infantry."

Calix laughs.

"You've gotten a lot of shit for joining the skyriders then?" he asks.

"Something like that," I answer, since the rivalry between skyriders and infantry will be the least of my problems if they find out. *When* they find out... I'll have to tell them eventually. My insides twist and I push the thought away. "We've never had coordinated attacks as far as I can remember."

Calix chuckles at that.

"What ... did you tiptoe into leadership meetings? Of course, you wouldn't hear about coordinated attacks at an outpost because they never get that far, and it's not like they would share that information with everyone."

I open my mouth to tell him that I overheard quite a few of those, but that would lead to questions I can't answer. I snap my mouth shut.

Could it be that I never heard about it? But the arrows... I would have heard about those for sure, right?

"But those mist creatures are animals ... how are they armed with bows and arrows? And how have I never heard about it?"

"Not the creatures." Calix laughs. "The titans are shooting the arrows."

"Titans?" I gape at him. "You mean like in the stories? But they don't exist, they are just ... myths."

"Every child knows that you don't leave the city walls at night or wander too close to the mists because titans will snatch you up and feed you to their monsters."

"That's what I'm saying." I roll my eyes. "Those are stories to scare children so they stay safe."

"The monsters are real," Calix objects. "And the titans sound real enough to me, if they shoot us out of the sky. Who cares what their actual name is? Titans works for me."

I ponder that statement for a while.

Of course, I have heard stories about titans—godlike people, stronger than any mortal and wielding powers anyone could dream of. I have also heard of the mist court ruled by the demon king himself, biding his time to smother our world in darkness ... and no one is taking that for the truth. Right?

The thought that there might be truth to these stories scares me. Because what does that mean for me? What about the stories they tell about cursed ones?

Even if people live in the mists. That doesn't make them titans or demons, I scold myself. *And it doesn't make the stories real.*

"Calix? Why do you think the attacks get heavier during winter?" I ask.

"Because there is less light, and the mist is thicker. It makes it easier to hide."

"Yeah, maybe ..." But something about it bothers me.

CHAPTER TEN
TATE

Jared and I lean against the wall in the sparring hall and watch our runners face off against the eastern division. The sparring hall is a big, open room with hardwood flooring. Tall windows run down one side, making it look even larger, giving us an overview of the atrium, a story below. Mirrors cover the opposite wall of the room. Twelve square mats in dark gray are spaced evenly throughout the room, currently occupied by twelve pairs of runners, one of them Summer and another runner about the same height.

"Why did you put Summer in our division?" I look at Jared, who stands next to me.

"I don't know what you're talking about." Jared tries to keep a straight face, but the corner of his mouth twitches.

"Don't play stupid. The second I saw you up on that stage reading off names, I knew you had a hand in selecting them," I reply.

He chuckles before shrugging.

"Be grateful, or we would have had her," he says, inclining his head toward a tall, blond girl who is seemingly agitated and talking to Professor Arkwright. I have heard other riders complain about Livia Vaccari all week. Her daddy seems to be someone important in Telos, and she acts the part.

I snort. "Okay, thanks for that. But why did you pick him?" I look over at Summer, who stops and seems to follow whatever is going on between the bossy blonde and the prof.

"I like Summer's humor, and he practically flew through the mountain run." He shrugs.

I watched our runners on the obstacle course yesterday. While Summer took the course with ease, he was far from flying.

"You sure about that?" I look at him skeptically.

"Yeah, I'm sure. Boko couldn't shut up about it. He was the one stopping the time. He said he had never seen anyone go through that course so fast."

"He is one odd duck, that's for sure, but I'm not so sure about the flying," I say, looking at the boy we're talking about.

Arkwright, a fair but demanding man responsible for the physical training of the recruits, is calling him over.

"She's right," Arkwright says, "and you don't do yourself a favor either by going easy on your hands. I want the gloves off for all fighting." Summer grumbles but removes his gloves.

Now that I think about it, I've never seen him without them before, even during lunch or dinner. Strange.

I decide to keep an eye on him. He lied about his name, after all. I let it slide because I've done the same, and frankly, he looks harmless, but now I wonder if I should have said something.

"Why do you think he's odd?" Jared sounds curious, and I can't believe he asks that.

"We haven't been around much the last two weeks, but this guy" —I nod toward Grayson Summer, who is getting into position against another first year—"was hiding behind his buddy for the first few days. But he didn't seem shy or scared when you signed him up."

Jared shrugs, so I continue, "He wears those gloves all the time, and if it's true what Boko told you, he dragged his feet in the obstacle course deliberately because his time was mediocre at best." I raise an eyebrow at Jared.

He shrugs again. "I like him," he states. I shake my head. That is typical Jared. He makes such decisions in the blink of an eye as easily as ordering a beer.

"Not everyone shares your affection," I reply dryly, eyeing the runners in front of us. Vaccari is openly gloating about her win with the gloves, and a brown-haired brutish guy glares at Summer, who doesn't seem to notice, fully engaged in his sparring.

"Who is he?" I point him out to Jared.

"That's Gorgon Foley," he says.

"Deputy Commander Foley's son?" I ask and whistle quietly when Jared confirms. I'm not surprised Jared knows their names already. He seems to know everyone. Summer, on the other hand, has a knack for making influential enemies.

I learn something else about Summer that afternoon. He's good with a sword and knives but awful without a weapon. He's fast, aggressive, and a bit reckless in his swordsmanship, but his technique is solid. Despite looking like a child, I would bet he has years of training under his belt. The incongruence is intriguing.

Maybe I was too quick to tag him as harmless. After all, big eyes and a sunny personality are no proof of good intentions.

He smiles and laughs a lot, and the professors and first years seem to like him. Frankly, he would be the center of attention if he did not always keep to himself. But he does, and I can't help but wonder why.

The more I watch him over the next few days, the more I get the impression that he tries to go unnoticed, not that he is very good at it since he draws attention like a flame in the dark.

During the next strategy meeting, Summer sits on his hands, like he tries to make sure he doesn't raise them on accident. I often see him early in the mornings while most others are still sleeping. He never ends up at the weight room or sparring hall, though, and he is scarily chipper for the time of day, which is suspicious all on its own.

His smile never falters despite my scowl. It seems as if nothing can spoil his good mood.

Nothing but Joel Cassius. Summer seems a little cool around him —another puzzle. Cassius is his squadron leader, and I have never seen him being unfair or unreasonable and not hotheaded, either, so what is Summer's problem?

At the moment, I stand with my division's two squadrons of runners in the inner courtyard. I look up at the big clock gracing the wall over the gate. We still have a few minutes.

Today, it's our turn to head out and up the mountains for camp training. Every division gets those five days to prepare our runners for Picking.

Only four riders will be on this trip. Next to me is Jared, who unknowingly volunteered this time—payback is payback, after all— and the two squadron leaders, Cassius and Flavius.

Jared and I scouted out the location for our final camp two days ago, making sure we picked a place with easy water access and enough shelter so we wouldn't be exposed to the wind. All of these are things we will teach our first years during the next five days.

A flight of riders is getting ready to leave for a long patrol on the opposite side of the courtyard. I catch Summer eyeing them and their birds longingly.

I would prefer a flight over the daylong hike, too. Sure, we could take out the birds that live on the academy grounds, but that would defy the purpose since this trip is meant to prepare them for Picking, and they won't have their birds until after that.

My eyes fly over the four orderly rows of runners in front of me. We are finally complete.

My attention is drawn to Summer when the runner beside him turns his head to face him.

"You've never been camping?" His shocked voice carries easily. "But ... how did you spend your summer?" He's focused on Summer, not on us. I glare at them, then look at Cassius, allowing him to handle it.

Being the squadron leader for runners— more of a babysitting job than active leading—is the first step on the way up. He has to prove himself if he wants me to appoint him as squadron leader over active riders next.

Cassius fights a grin and exchanges a knowing look with Summer. I frown. Maybe my squadron leader has more information about our new runner than he has led on so far. When he catches my look, he instantly sobers.

"Ilario, Summer, quiet," he snaps, and I can finally start.

"While we're out, I want you to get used to wearing armor. I won't make you don full armor—we are not headed into battle after all—but I expect you to wear these." When I point behind me to the helmets piled on a cart, I expect a protest, but I'm only met with silence.

"They limit your perception, and once you are full riders, there will be times you fight, rest, and even sleep in them. Wearing them nonstop for five days will help you get used to it and the extra weight of carrying a shield. Those two items are also the only things you will be allowed to take with you to Picking. So feeling comfortable with them is advisable." Everyone files in two rows while their squadron leaders distribute the armor parts.

That went better than I thought, so I'm cautiously optimistic while we head out the main gate.

WE LEAVE THE PAVED ROAD RIGHT AFTER THE CITY WALL, AND the ground is reddish-brown and dry beneath our feet, loose rubble making it treacherous for anyone not watching their step.

Orderly rows of silvery olive trees, orange trees heavy with fruit, cork trees, as well as vineyards line the first part of our walk before the wild beauty of the mountains swallows them. The morning air is heavy with the scent of herbs like thyme and sage.

I order the first stop after we have been walking for six hours. We are slower than I anticipated since most runners are not used to the mountain air. At that pace, we won't reach our final destination until tomorrow.

"Well, who doesn't enjoy walking up a damn mountain if he could fly instead," Jared grumbles next to me. "And with a helmet on my head so far off from the mists. You know how to serve payback, I have to give it to you."

I try to stay serious, but the corner of my mouth pulls up.

"You even enjoy seeing me suffer, you bastard." When I raise an eyebrow at him, he adds, "Sorry, Centurion Bastard, those are even worse than regular bastards." I catch a runner throwing Jared an incredulous look and shake my head at my best friend.

"Sorry, I know, not in front of the kids," he says before turning to the runner who heard him. "I've known him since before he knew his own name. If you try something like that, we'll have one less runner to worry about." The runner pales and turns away. "There, all cleared up."

I grin. Even bad-tempered, Jared is fun to be around. But Jared's speech about knowing me so long reminds me of the look Cassius threw Summer. I scan the forty runners resting in the shade and find the other two riders talking close to Summer and his flight.

"Cassius." I beckon him over.

"How do you know Summer?" I ask once he reaches us. He looks taken aback.

"I ... I mean, we grew up together, sir."

"Is he a safety hazard?" I ask the question that has bugged me for a while now.

"No, sir." His answer is immediate and truthful.

"That is all. Thank you, Cassius." He nods and leaves.

"What was that about?" Jared asks.

"I told you Summer is behaving oddly. Now, I know he is not a safety risk, or at least Cassius doesn't seem to think so."

"You're turning paranoid," Jared comments.

"I got things left to do before I go," I answer.

"What Mom said the other night—" Jared starts.

"Leave it," I snap. When Jared opens his mouth again, I shake my head. "I mean it, Jared. Leave it," I say softer now. He grinds his teeth but stays quiet.

It's already late into the next day by the time we make our final camp. Quizzing our runners throughout the march showed that some are ahead, clearly prepared by their parents or instructors before coming to the Aerie. Others seem clueless and will have to make up for it.

Everyone is tired from the long walk. Some even look ready to topple over, and their heavy packs are not helping.

Once again, Summer sticks out of the crowd. He's not fidgeting, and while he looks as beat as the others, he's smiling and joking with Ilario instead of grumbling and brooding or falling asleep sitting up.

I'm not the only one watching him. Cassius sits a few places to my right, and his gaze is also fixed on the two.

"Okay, everyone." I clap my hands. "I know you're tired and hungry and ready to drop, but during Picking, you will have to provide for yourself with the things you find out here. Gather into your flights, please." They do, and their squadron leaders take charge.

"Who is well-versed in edible plants?" A few hands are raised at my question. "Well, enough not to poison us by accident?" A few laugh at that question, but we soon establish that the two flights of squadron five are up for the job.

One flight of squadron four is going fishing, and the other one will look for game. The squadron leaders head out with them.

Jared and I stay back at the camp.

"You're heartless to make them look for food now. They're ready to collapse." Jared grins and shakes his head. "We could have used provisions tonight."

"Why didn't you take on a leadership position? Then you could have coddled them." I raise my eyebrows at him.

"Nah, if I would've wanted power or responsibility, I'd have made you keep your position and make me an adviser or something," Jared drawls.

I snort out a laugh. "Yeah, right." I don't know what's funnier, envisioning him in such a position or thinking he could have somehow made me stay. He grins at me.

"I'm not interested in authority or responsibility, you know that. So I stick with what I do best, let you shoulder the burden while I throw in my five copper whenever I feel like it," he says.

"I don't know." I look at him thoughtfully. "You showed excellent leading qualities while you talked me into at least half the shit we did as kids. I don't know how I earned that nickname from Nan instead of you," I tease.

He snorts out a laugh. "You caused even more trouble on your own before they let me join you in those boring functions." He grins.

"I just knew how to play it right." We both laugh at that.

When Summer's flight gets back from the stream, the tension between him and Cassius is nearly visible. Summer is no longer smiling but stomps around, growling like someone insulted his mother or something, and Cassius is in a huff too.

"Cassius, get over here," I call.

"Centurion." He stops in front of me, his brows drawn, his muscles tight with tension.

"What's going on?" I ask.

"Nothing, Centurion." The denial is so dissonant it hurts my ears.

I raise my brows. "Don't insult my intelligence here. You couldn't be more obvious if you waved a red flag."

He huffs. "Summer pulled some risky moves over at the stream. I called him out for it."

Truth.

"It can be hard to command someone you've known since childhood," I say, curious if he will open up. Cassius takes a deep breath, and when he releases it, some of the tension leaves his body.

"I don't like it when ... people take unnecessary risks," he mutters.

"You're worried about him?"

"Not for safety reasons. I meant what I said yesterday," he says. "But ... he just seems too ... young to be here," Cassius says, and I nod in understanding. But this dispute could bite us in the ass later and cause serious trouble.

"That's all?" I ask.

He nods.

"Fine then. But if I have the feeling this causes trouble, I will reassign Summer to Flavius's squadron. Do you understand?"

Cassius nods, his face grim.

"That won't be necessary, Centurion."

It's nearly noon the following day when everything goes to shit. It starts when squadron four reports a runner missing. He was the last on guard duty and can't be found when it's time for shift change.

I don't know him well enough to know how serious he would have been about his job. They are still recruits after all. Maybe he just wandered off or even decided that the skyriders weren't for him. If someone considered deserting, now would be their best chance. Still, the uneasy feeling in the pit of my stomach stays.

Jared is looking for him with Zephyr because there is also the possibility that an animal attacked him. We didn't hear any commotion, but the mountains are home to a variety of wild animals—some magical, some not—and it wouldn't be the first time one attacked a lone person.

A few others are out gathering firewood and some roots and herbs to complement the game that is up for lunch, while a runner from squadron four volunteers to cook.

"We're under attack."

Daeva's warning and her screech reach me at the same time, only seconds before the first attacker breaks through the wood around us. The heavy forest around us served them well and hid them from our birds' eyes.

Still, there is no mist and no bridgepoint close enough to surprise us that close to the Aerie without a patrol spotting them first. They must have used a portal.

All of our attackers are fair-skinned, their armor dark and mismatched, missing any signs of recognition, and apart from the sound of their bodies breaking through bushes, their attack is silent. It reminds me of another place, another attack in the woods.

The memories are so real that for a second, I hear the shouts of "Protect the heir" reverberate across the clearing. I shake my head to clear it.

Memories, nothing but memories. I blink, and slowly, the images playing in front of my eyes fade.

"We're under attack," I shout, repeating Daeva's words, then rush to intercept the closest attacker, who moves toward the runner standing next to the pot with water hanging over the flames. The runner only has the knife he used to prepare the food to defend himself, and he will be at a serious disadvantage against the sword his opponent swings.

He proves my assumption wrong by grabbing the pot and dosing his attacker with boiling water, splashing the fire in the process. When he follows through with his knife, I realize he doesn't need me.

I don't have time to look for who else might need help because two attackers are zeroing in on me. Okay, now there are three. This is one of the moments I'm happy I'm fighting with two short swords and that I have magic to wield as well.

Air gathers under my command, protecting my back, no more

visible than a ripple in the air, but it will prevent anyone from stabbing me from behind.

One of the attackers makes a guttural sound that I take for a curse when he realizes that his blade is deflected by my shield without doing harm. The distinct sound of steel against steel rings over the clearing.

Worrying about Jared and how our recruits are holding up lets me slip into Daeva's view for a second. She is right, though, with her complaints earlier. The visibility is shit from up here. Dark shapes flash between the foliage, often too short to make out friend or foe, and the missing overview makes it impossible to get a count on the attackers or a take on the situation.

"*I will come down.*" Daeva sounds determined.

"*You will do no such thing,*" I disagree. An arrow slides off the air protecting me. "Someone is shooting, too. You stay up there as long as I'm not in danger."

"*Three against one sounds dangerous to me,*" she snaps but obeys. I bury my blade in the throat of the one to my right.

"Only two now," I correct her.

"*I can see that for myself,*" she grumbles, using my eyes to keep track of the situation down here.

The third attacker takes the place of his fallen companion. He is abnormally fast. Maybe he has magic enhancing his speed. Fighting fair is for tournaments or sparring, so I simply cut off his air supply. He chokes, then stumbles. His fingers claw at his throat, but he won't find anything tangible there.

"*To your left,*" Daeva snaps, and I block the sword coming down. My attacker comes at me hard, doubling his efforts of cutting me down. I feint a weakness in my defense, hoping he will go for it. When he does, I use the opening it creates, and he scrambles back to evade my strike, aiming at his shoulder.

I make him stumble by solidifying the air around his feet and while he is off balance cut his throat without hesitation.

One look confirms that the attacker I suffocated with my magic isn't moving anymore, and I release my hold.

Two more men are rushing me. The three bodies littering the ground probably drew their attention. A big shape dives down, snatching up one of them, and his cries fade into nothing.

"*I told you to stay up there,*" I grumble.

"*Can't let you have all the fun.*" A screech accompanies her words, sounding victorious. I chuckle. My opponent takes a step back and seems unnerved. I watch him contemplating. Maybe I'll be able to get information out of him.

His gaze darts around, and I do the same, taking in the change. There are numerous people on the ground, but only a few in gray. All the riders are engaged in sword fights. Some runners have assembled into groups, and we have the upper hand now. Jared eyes meet mine over the clearing a vicious smile on his face, while he tugs his sword free, the man who faced him sinking to his knees.

I tackle the man in front of me to the ground, and send his sword flying with my gift.

"Who sent you?" I ask.

He shakes his head, his eyes wide. "Easssy tarrrget, they sssaid..." He sounds incredulous. He rolls his r, and his s is more of a hissing sound.

He is not from Belarra but could be from the Ice Coast. I curl my hand, the air mimicking my gesture around his throat, letting him feel the pressure without harming him ... yet. His eyes meet mine. "Brrring you back alive ..."

Not again.

White-hot fury burns through me, and I end his life before he can say another word. Those words only make sense if he knows who I am. Therefore, questioning him is off the table.

CHAPTER ELEVEN

ARA

I'm walking down a small path with a bundle of firewood in my arms. It's quiet around me, the trees swallowing the noise of the camp in the distance. The ground is spongy beneath my feet, and the air is fragrant with the scent of pine trees and eucalyptus. I look up when a shadow flits over me and watch Daeva's dark silhouette vanish behind the canopy of trees.

A screech and then the harsh sound of metal hitting metal shatters the silence, followed by a shout. I drop the wood and start running before my head catches up with what I hear. The shouts and clanging come closer, and with them, the hum of angry voices and shouted commands.

I might be new to the military, but I'm pretty sure that's not a drill. I push myself to go faster, and when I rush into the clearing, chaos greets me. I stumble to a halt.

Other runners break through the underbrush next to me, their faces a mix of horror and confusion.

Tents are turned over, people are jumping over discarded bags. Smoke wells up from the firepit, the pot that soaked the flames lies empty beside it.

Everywhere, runners and riders are fighting off pale, rough-looking men in mismatched armor.

Three fight Kyronos, who is the closest to me, and I am about to help him when he buries his blade in one of them, and another stumbles away clutching his throat. His blades are swirling through the air so fast that I have a hard time following, and he advances on his third opponent with a grin. I guess he doesn't need assistance.

A cry for help draws my gaze over to a runner whose right arm is limp, red staining his sleeve around a protruding arrow. I sprint to his side, drawing my two daggers, and meet the blade swinging for his neck before it connects. The runner doesn't hesitate. He rips the arrow from his arm and, angling upward, drives it through the attacker's upper belly into his heart.

I stay next to him, guarding him until he finishes wrapping his arm in a makeshift dressing and retrieves his sword. A dark shape dives down and grabs one of the attackers, his scream fading when the bird wins height.

There are shouts and screams all around me while I turn and look for my squadron and especially Calix and Mariel.

Calix's big frame is easy to make out even in this chaos, and I head his way when an assailant intercepts me.

"Summer, watch out!" The shout has me evading the strike the attacker meant to impale me with. I spin away, and he follows. He is fast, and I barely manage to get my blades up to stop his next maneuver.

Leaving my sword at the camp when I gathered firewood was a mistake I'll never make again.

Joel shouting my name in the distance registers dimly, but I'm too busy dodging the blows coming for me to react to that.

I evade more than I block and have nearly no chance to strike back.

My attacker is a bull of a man with reddish-blond hair, his chest protected by a chest plate. He comes at me hard, slashing, hacking, one strike after the other. I have to evade and retreat again and again.

The sword arcs down, and I step back again. Only to bump into something hard—a tree. I bumped into a fucking tree.

I shift sideways and stumble, my concentration faltering for a second, but that is all it takes. My curse turns into a hiss when my attacker slashes across my chest. I bring my leg up and kick him off before he can do any more damage. He stumbles back, right into Calix's sword.

I send Calix a relieved smile before looking down at myself and assess the damage. I prod at the red line that starts to color my tunic along the ripped edges and hiss.

The layers of wrap I used to hide my breasts provided some protection, but I already feel it give and slide.

"You okay?" Calix is in front of me, looking concerned. It has become quieter around us. I look around. Only two are still engaged in battle, and the attackers are either dealt with or flee as I watch. The tide turned quickly, not a given, considering we are mostly runners.

"Yeah. Thanks to you, I'm fine." I heave out a breath. "I will just put something on that." I gestured to the slash on my chest.

Calix winces and nods. "I'll see how the others are doing." The clearing is too quiet after the commotion. What happened seems unreal, like a bad dream. But the bodies, the blood, and the chaos surrounding us say otherwise.

Only when the first bird starts chirping again do I realize the animals around us have been silent, too.

I head over to our tent, relieved when I find my pack and sword where I left them.

In the safety of the tent, I quickly slip out of the bloodied and torn tunic and knot together what is left of the wrap beneath. The curved cut travels from my left collarbone in the direction of my rib cage on the right side, ending between my breasts. The most damage is close to my collarbone, with barely a scratch on the bottom end.

It doesn't seem deep enough to have severed muscle, which means one more scar for my collection. It will hurt like a bitch, but it won't restrain me too badly in case of another fight.

I guess I'll have to wear high-necked dresses from now on.

Cleaning the cut with the water I carry and dousing it in something from the healing kit that smells like the cleansing stuff my mother always uses is all I can do for now.

I manage to clean and bandage the wound and slip into a fresh tunic before anyone comes looking for me. The wound would probably be better off with stitching, but I'm not sure I'd be able to stomach that even if I had the time. It would take a lot of stitches.

I get back to the others without anyone noticing my absence. Once I come closer, I realize why. Centurion Kyronos, Joel, and the other riders stand beside four unmoving bodies, looking grim and talking in low voices. We have lost someone.

When I step closer, Gaius and Clay are the only ones I recognize for sure. They were in my flight. Next to them lie two more runners, so we lost at least four of our division today.

We pack up silently while a few decorate the bodies. The birds will bring them up into the mountains. Skyriders don't bury their fallen. They offer them to the birds, a start for new life to come. A practice I'm still getting used to.

While runners die at the academy too—sharp weapons, dangerous obstacle courses, vicious creatures, and learning to wield magic do take their toll—this feels different.

Kyronos's gaze rests on us until the last murmurs subside.

"We honor the memory of four brave souls," he starts, and I'm instantly mesmerized by his warm, deep voice. "They were more than runners; they were brothers-in-arms, ready to lay down ... everything for those beside them. In their brief time among us, they served with loyalty. They lived with honor, and their loss reminds us that protecting each other is the truest form of service." I watch him while he speaks. He doesn't wear his helmet. His dark hair is ruffled, and the stubble of his beard, the intensity in his eyes, and a streak of blood on his cheek make him look rough and dark, a stark contrast to the eloquent way he speaks.

"May they find peace and watch over us as we honor their memory through our actions." He takes a deep breath. "Their journey is finished, but we continue." For a second, pain flashes in his eyes, but his voice stays steady. "We carry them with us in each breath, in every step, assuring their sacrifice was not in vain." Gods, this man is beautiful, and the way he speaks ... He knows loss. I'm sure of it. That knowledge forms a connection, and the aching need to comfort him unfurls in my chest.

"We consign their souls to Elet, the mother who gives and takes. We will honor their gift and let it reinforce us whenever the path is dark and the cost heavy." Kyronos closes, and I draw in a shuddering breath.

Damn him. That glimpse of pain beneath the perfect facade draws me in and makes him more intriguing.

Why does my centurion have to be so damn attractive?

I do my best to smother that attraction while we runners bide our time. The birds take the bodies away, and our centurion and the other riders discuss how we proceed. Normally, we would have spent another day up here, but now...

"We should fly. We could be ambushed on the way back," the other squadron leader, Flavius, says.

"No, that would leave a small group vulnerable for hours," Kyronos objects. "We are one unit. We'll march back together."

We walk in silence, only stopping to make camp when dusk is well upon us. The cut on my chest itches and burns, the fabric of my shirt chafes, the pack pulls on the skin around it, and the sweat seeping into it doesn't help either.

I try to ease it by pulling my shirt away from my body, drawing Joel's gaze in the process.

"You're hurt," he barks out, standing in front of me in two quick steps. His shout draws everyone's attention. *Great.*

I follow his gaze down to my chest and see two dark stains on my once clean tunic. The bandages must have slipped or soaked through during the walk. Joel grabs my shirt like he wants to pull it up. I swat his hands away.

"I'm fine," I hiss.

"Let me look at it." He is anything but calm. Probably envisioning how he has to confess to Ben that I bled out on his watch.

"No!" I glare at him, trying to convey without words that he has to shut up. Now.

"Summer, you are hurt?" Kyronos stands next to Joel now.

Fuck me. Not him, too.

His eyes sweep over me, assessing the obvious bloodstains. "Come with me."

He turns and strides away, and I glare some more at Joel, contemplating if ignoring them both is an option while dread coils in my gut.

This is not fucking happening.

Kyronos snapping my name impatiently when I don't follow tells me it is.

Shit. Can I somehow convince him that it isn't worth his time?

I hurry after him.

"It's barely a scratch," I say while we pass Calix, Mariel, and Simeon, who are stacking wood for a fire.

"One of those buggers tried to filet him before I got there," Calix butts in.

Way to make it sound even worse. I glare at him. He just shrugs.

Kyronos glances at Calix before his gaze comes back to me. "Then you won't mind me assessing that for myself, will you?" He turns and walks over to a tree where he had placed his pack and bedroll.

"I'll take care of it." Joel is coming after us, finally realizing the problem he caused.

"Do you have healing abilities I didn't know about, Cassius?" Kyronos sounds bored.

"No, but ..." Joel tries to come up with something to say, his mouth working soundlessly.

"Well, I do. So get back to the others and start a fire." When Joel doesn't immediately react, he snaps, "That is an order, Cassius."

Shit, shit, shit, if he can heal, I'm in even bigger trouble than I thought.

Joel sends me a look that tells me he feels bad for putting me in this position before he follows the centurion's orders and leaves.

"Sit." Kyronos gestures to his bedroll. I plop my butt down because what else can I do now but play along. "Take off your shirt, Summer." He goes over to his pack, rifling through it. He glances over his shoulder when I don't move, pinning me with his golden eyes.

"I'm not gonna eat you." He turns back, shaking his head, while he pulls out a healing kit that screams healer since it is far more extensive than the one we carry.

My palms turn sweaty, and my heart accelerates. I take a deep breath and remove my helmet. No point in hiding my hair if he'll see me without a shirt.

I glance over at the camp, but everyone is busy setting up, and no one pays us any attention. Kyronos is still turned away from me, and I release the breath I've been holding. No point in delaying.

I wince as I pull the shirt over my head. It has gotten stuck on the two places the blood seeped through. My head comes free, and I look up into the stunned eyes of my division leader.

CHAPTER TWELVE

ARA

He doesn't say a word. His gaze is intense as his eyes travel from my boots upward. Slowly, he catalogs every detail.

There is no way to miss the curve of my hip or how my body tapers at the waist, and while my breasts are wrapped so tightly they are nearly flat, the placement of said wrapped material is obvious, too. I've never felt this vulnerable before. My palms are sweaty, my heart races like it has to be somewhere else, and I fight to keep my breath even.

Finally, he stops at the braid winding around my head before his eyes meet mine. His stoic face doesn't tell me anything.

I bite my lip to keep myself from blurting out nonsense. I want to cover myself, but I keep my hands by my side. He knows now. Nothing I can do will change that, and I refuse to show him how much his perusal affects me.

He keeps holding my gaze.

Why doesn't he say something?

My back is to the dark forest behind us, and his body blocks mine from views from the camp.

At least no one else can see me.

Time stretches unbearably. I don't want to be the one to break the silence, but if he doesn't say something soon, I will. I wiggle the toes in my boots. I'm always a twitchy person, and this is nerve-wracking on more than one level.

He exhales.

"Didn't see that one coming," he says. I feel my eyebrows jump up.

That's it? That's all he is going to say?

His eyes are already on the slash.

"A scratch, huh?" Kyronos shakes his head, his golden eyes flitting over my body again. "But I guess I know now why you didn't want anyone looking at it." He takes in my rigid posture, and his face softens a bit before he sits down next to me.

"May I?" His voice is softer now, too. Our eyes lock while he waits for my answer. I nod.

Tate's calloused hands tickle my skin with his light touch. I flinch.

"Sorry, I'll try to be more gentle," he says, his eyes on the wound.

"Gods, no," I blurt.

His gaze snaps up to my eyes, and he raises one brow. "You would prefer me being ... less gentle?" My cheeks heat. Shit, that doesn't sound right when he says it like that and brings up a whole lot of wrong ideas on my part. Does he have to be so ridiculously handsome?

"No, I mean ... It's fine. I'm fine," I stutter.

Kyronos's mouth twitches, but the smile is gone so fast I may have imagined it. His face relaxes, and he nods once while he goes on examining the cut as if I'm not making a total fool of myself. He selects a vial from the healing kit, and the familiar smell alerts me seconds before the burn draws a soft gasp from my lips.

I try to look at anything but him, but my eyes always find their way back. He pushes my skin together, securing it with little sticky strips from the kit.

His fingers gently scrape over my skin, sending out electric sparks. I get goose bumps all over, and the way his gaze flits over my skin tells me he notices. Hopefully, he thinks it's the cold causing this—not that I feel cold at the moment.

Ugh ... a hole in the ground would be nice. One that gobbles me up, like right now. Why can't he be less ... just less? At least if he would make dumbass comments, I could give some snarky remarks back—dispel this tension. But noooo, instead the silence seems to make it worse. My body feels like a furnace, and tingles run over my skin wherever he touches me.

I hate my body right now for being so aware of him. It's like he's the only thing registering with my senses—the sound of his breath, the heat of his body when he comes closer, his gaze, his touch. I swear my skin will erupt in flames any minute.

I clear my throat. "I'm just ticklish."

He nods as if that is a reasonable explanation for my behavior, and thankfully, he starts to talk.

"Didn't reach the muscle tissue. This should be quick." His voice is low, husky, and curls around my body like a caress. He places his fingers next to the cut, and a tingling warmth seeps from his fingers into my skin.

That is when I realize it's his magic. He's healing me, and I was too distracted to stop him. I flinch.

Kyronos's eyes jump to mine. I scootch back, trying to put distance between his hands and my skin, and fall backward. I forgot I'm still sitting on his rolled-up bedding. He grabs my arm, steadying me.

At least he stopped healing me.

He inclines his head, watching me like I'm a puzzle he has to solve. Curious, intrigued, searching.

"Are you scared of healing?" His voice is soft, probing.

I shake my head and immediately wish I could take it back. That would have been a good reason to decline being healed.

"Just me, then?" His eyes crinkle, and a smile tugs at one side of his mouth. "Hmm." There is too much resonating in that little sound for me to catch it.

Yes, I'm scared ... I'm terrified of what I could do to him. This whole situation is my worst nightmare, and on top of it all, my brain stops working around him.

I need to get out of here. I can't deal with this if I can't think. So I go for the most obvious course of action: ignore the problem. I grab my shirt.

"Thank you. Like you said, nothing serious. It will heal on its own." I flash him what I hope is a reassuring smile. "No need to drain your gift for that." I shrug and wait for him to release my arm, but he doesn't. The eyes examining my face look stormy, but his voice is calm and cool.

"I never said it wasn't serious. And I will heal you, even if I have to hold you down to do it." He doesn't sound like he's joking.

"Why?" I ask.

"I already lost enough recruits on this trip. I will not add another one because of an infection I can prevent." His determination would be admirable if it weren't so damn inconvenient.

"You doused it in enough cleansing stuff. Just bandage it, and I'll be fine." I try again.

"Cleansing stuff," he repeats. "That certainly sounds like you're the expert here." I open my mouth, but it's not like I can tell him I'm familiar with letting wounds heal on their own. My mother or Luc would never accept that on anyone but me. So I stay silent.

"Sweat seeping into it, movement, the bandages rubbing, your pack pulling it apart. Even if you don't get an infection from that, it will scar. Why risk it if I can fix it in minutes?"

And just like that, I can't argue against it without sounding stubborn or stupid, and he doesn't look like he'll back down either. Why does he even care?

I eye the trees around us before I slump and nod.

I'll deal with it. If I have to run, I run.

His fingers are back on my skin, and the tingling warmth seeps into me, gaining intensity.

Something inside me responds to the warmth, and I close my eyes—afraid he will see what is going on. A coolness snakes up inside me, slithering around his warmth and smothers it like an unwanted fire.

I can't let him deplete himself. Once he gets weaker, I'll push him away, and the connection should snap.

I will get away.

The curse is expanding, growing, drinking up the golden warmth Tate pours into me. I'm furious at this part of me that has overshadowed my life, endangered my family, and now takes my freedom and choice as well. I will be hunted. I will have to hide and run all my life. And what if the king goes after my family as well?

The silvery coolness grows and grows, winding so tight around the golden light that it's barely shining through by now.

Realization hits me. I can't spare him. Everyone will know what I am if I leave him weakened and drained.

Desperation and anger course through me, so potent I can nearly taste it, and I direct it at the silver beast responsible for my misery.

It strikes, and the beast falters.

I gasp, my eyes flying open. Kyronos looks at me questioningly. Shit. I close my eyes again, concentrating on the fight waging inside me, hoping he won't ask questions I can't answer.

I picture the coolness as a snake, grabbing it behind its head, I squeeze, demanding it to let go. Having an image turns it from something slippery and evasive into something I can hold onto. It fights and tries to wriggle away, but I clamp down tight and tug. Pulling it away from the warmth, I push it down into my core, where it can't touch his magic. It resists like a living thing, slips away again and again, but I catch it before it can reach Kyronos's magic. Letting it win is not an option.

I won't kill him.

Once I have control, I hold on and open my eyes, afraid of what I'll find. Can he sense what's going on?

He frowns at my wound. It still looks the same.

Come on, I pray silently.

Sweat forms on my brow, and my breath comes fast and shallow. It is hard fucking work to hold on to the slippery beast, to keep it contained. It thrashes against my hold, trying to wriggle free.

I watch him. Expect him to look at me any minute now with accusation or fear in his gaze. A quiver runs through my body, my strength fading quickly, and I lock my muscles to hide it. My tensing earns me another questioning look. Hopefully, he still thinks I'm afraid.

Time stretches into eternity. But I refuse to give up because it will likely cost both of us our lives.

The heat of the healing magic intensifies and spreads through my body.

Then, eventually, there is a change. Slowly, the cold beast relents, calms, and curls up, becoming a shimmering orb floating inside me, harmless and content. My mind struggles to match it to the raw and vicious thing I felt before.

And then ... it's over. His magic leaves my body, and his fingers my skin.

Holy mists, I did it. We did it.

Kyronos healed me, and it didn't drain him. I didn't drain him. I look at my flawless skin, still streaked by a few sticky stripes, and then up at him, stunned.

"Have you never been healed before?" he asks, puzzled. "It must have been worse than it looked." He huffs out a deep breath but doesn't elaborate. I'm sure healing me took more than a slash this size should have.

I should say something, but the enormity of what just happened floors me. Maybe there is a chance that no one will find out after all.

"Or was that not fitting your picture of me? You called me intimidating if I remember correctly," he goes on.

What is he talking about?

I realize my mouth is hanging open and snap it closed. I probably look as stunned as I feel.

Nope, just intimidated. Have you two looked in a mirror lately? You guys are huge!

The words from our first encounter dance through my head. Wait, he remembers that?

"But you were nervous for another reason, right?" He scratches his neck.

My heartbeat picks up, and my stomach sinks to my feet.

No, no, no.

He must have somehow caught on to what happened. But what can I say in a situation like this?

"Grayson isn't your real name, right?" he asks, pinning me in place with his golden eyes.

Oh, he means me being a girl.

Hope blooms in my chest. Maybe he didn't catch on to what happened with his magic after all.

Say something. I clear my throat.

"No, I made that up," I confess.

"What is it?" he asks.

I only stare at him, my gut clenching again.

"Your name," he clarifies. His lips curl into a smile. Something flutters in my belly. Which has nothing to do with his smile and everything to do with nerves, I assure myself.

I clear my throat again.

"My friends call me Ara."

He inclines his head to one side.

"And given how concerned Cassius seemed and how he tried to butt in, he is one of your friends?" I can't read his expression.

"Yeah, we're close." I shrug.

"I see," he says, and his expression shutters and my stomach sinks.

Get a grip. He is not your new best friend but your superior.

"Get dressed so we can grab something to eat," Tate orders and gets to his feet. I tug my tunic back over my head, fumbling with the buttons, when I realize he's watching me. Dammit. He must think I'm the most awkward person in the whole kingdom.

Once I'm done, he offers me his hand. I take it and realize my mistake as soon as he pulls me up. An electric spark shoots up my arm, and I snatch it away. Only to stumble over my own feet. His arm shoots out to steady me.

Gods, I'm turning into a clumsy, fumbling idiot.

I all but jump away from him, my face growing hot.

Fortunately, it is quite dark next to the trees, so I hope Kyronos doesn't notice when he offers me my helmet.

I put it back on my head, grateful for the cover it provides. My secrets once more hidden, I turn to my centurion.

"What are you going to do now?" I try to sound relaxed, which is laughable after my display of nerves a few seconds ago.

"I'm going to eat something and wish for a shower, but I guess that has to wait until we are back."

I roll my eyes before I remember that he is my division leader. I hope he didn't see it.

"I mean ... about me," I clarify.

"Nothing." He shrugs and starts walking toward the others. I hurry after him.

"Nothing?" Even I can hear the disbelief in my voice. Kyronos laughs softly, and damn if I don't like that sound even better than his smile.

"You earned your place the same way as everyone else. If you prefer to be a boy"—he shrugs—"that is your decision. But you'll have to reveal it at some point. You know that, right?"

I nod.

"Why did you go through all the trouble?" He sounds genuinely curious, and something about him makes me want to trust him. But I can't.

"I didn't want the attention." I shrug.

He nods. "I get it." We are nearly back with the group when he adds, "If you are hurt again, you come to me, okay?" When I don't respond, he grabs my arm. "I mean it, Summer. If you aren't at full capacity, it can endanger everyone around you."

I nod, stunned by his intensity.

Joel comes over to me as soon as we reach the campfire.

"Summer, eat something and then rest," Kyronos orders from right behind me. "I think your friends are already waiting."

He's right. Calix is already waving me over. I use the excuse he provided and walk past Joel, who probably only wants to lecture me anyway.

"Summer is excused for tonight, and Cassius, you and I will talk about why I hate lies once we are back."

Shit. I hope Kyronos doesn't punish Joel for keeping my secret.

THE WHOLE NEXT DAY IS JUST ONE NEVER-ENDING, GRUELING walk. Kyronos is in a bad mood and doesn't even let us stop for lunch, so we are forced to eat while walking.

The sky has only the barest hint of bluish-green light left, and my only hope is that we have to stop soon so we don't risk our necks.

I stumble over loose rubble, and only Calix grabbing my backpack keeps me from falling flat on my face. Someone dissolved the bones in my legs, leaving only a jellied mess unable to support my weight much longer.

"We will stop soon, right?" Even my voice isn't much more than a whisper.

"By Elet's mercy, I hope so." Calix sounds as bad as I feel. I stumble again, and the steadying tug on my backpack tells me he caught me yet again.

I groan with relief when, only minutes later, Kyronos signals us to stop. My butt hits the ground, and I sprawl awkwardly on top of my pack. I don't care how it looks. I need a minute.

Calix slumps down next to me, leaning against me and my pack. I close my eyes and concentrate on relaxing all the muscles that are screaming bloody murder at the moment.

"Shit, I could sleep just like this. No need for bedrolls," Calix groans.

"I know what you mean. I would do anything if it means I don't have to move again." I sigh longingly at that thought.

The heavy steps of booted feet stop right next to my head. I blink my eyes open, and I'm greeted by an upside-down version of Joel glaring down at me. Since our centurion excused me from my duties last night, I evaded him by retiring early. He doesn't look happy about it. I close my eyes, hoping he'll go away if I ignore him.

He coughs—no such luck, then.

I open my eyes again. "What?"

"Get up. I want to talk to you," he growls, his gaze wandering to Calix next to me. "Alone."

"Is that an order? Otherwise, it's a no thanks from me." I yawn.

"A..." He closes his eyes. "Summer." He looks at Calix again. "Ilario, set up for the night." He pauses. "That is an order." I snake my arm around Calix's chest to prevent him from rising and glare up at Joel. I'm pissed.

"So that is how you want to play it now?" I hiss out, trying to keep my voice down so as not to draw attention.

Someone stops next to my feet.

"Is there a problem here?" A tingle snakes up my body at his voice, and my head snaps up, meeting Kyronos's gaze, who stands next to my feet. His gaze wanders over Calix and me, stopping at my arm around Calix's chest. I let it fall away. Kyronos looks at Joel, his eyebrows raised.

"No, no problem, Centurion." Joel's voice sounds stiff and formal.

"Glad to hear that." Kyronos's lips twitch, then he points at Calix. "Now, Ilario get settled. I doubt Summer wants to play your cushion all night. Cassius, do your job and appoint guards for the night. Summer, come with me." He rattles the commands off in one breath, and I can't help but notice that giving orders suits him.

And why the fuck do I think that's hot?

Calix and Joel hurry off, leaving us alone.

Kyronos extends a hand to help me up, and I take it. Tingles shoot up my arm, but they are better than the awkward shuffle I would have done otherwise with the weight of the backpack holding me down. He pulls me up with ease. I smile my thanks, ready to snatch my hand away as soon as I take in his magic, but it doesn't come. I look at our hands, stunned. That has never happened before.

Then I realize I'm standing in front of him, still holding his hand, and I drop it.

His lips twitch again, then he turns and leads me off to the side, away from the others so that no one can overhear our conversation. He turns to me. His uniform nearly melts into the darkness of the forest behind him. The light is so low now that I can't read his expression.

"This is now the second time I find you in the middle of an argument with your squadron leader. It's inappropriate." I open my mouth, but his raised hand stops me before I get out a word. My eyes follow his hand, and my gaze is drawn to a strange bluish glow behind him. It floats at the height of my chest, unmoving. "I don't know what is going on with you and Cassius, but—"

My mind catches up with what my eyes see. The blue glow comes from the hands of a person barely illuminated by it. Magic.

I grab Kyronos, using my momentum and the added weight of my backpack to turn us and push him away before the sizzling bluish-white light hits me. Engulfs me. Drowns out everything but the pain. It is everywhere and everything, burning, all-consuming, smothering ... worse than anything I've ever felt before.

CHAPTER
THIRTEEN
TATE

"We have to stop soon," Jared states the obvious, shouting to be heard over the lashing wind. The sun is setting behind the mountains to the west, and the slope we walk down is already cast in shadows, which makes the freezing wind even worse. Emphasizing Jared's observation of us needing to make camp.

The winding path we are on skirts the edge of a mighty drop, which forces us to go single file.

"I would feel much better knowing all of them were behind the academy walls for the night," I yell back.

"Falling to their deaths will kill them as surely as another attack would," Jared teases, glancing at the forested valley far below us. "And Zephyr starts complaining about the wind. It costs them too much strength to keep circling."

"Why didn't you tell me the wind is getting too much?" I ask Daeva.

"It's not. Zephyr is just complaining," she answers, insulted. Admitting weakness is not her strength.

"*Because I'm not weak,*" she huffs.

"Fine," I tell Jared. "We should reach a suitable place within the next half hour." I shake my head when Jared raises his arms and lets his head fall back, thanking the gods for my decision.

About half an hour later, we reach the place in question. Trees surround a medium-sized clearing, holding off the wind that has lashed at us constantly for the past hour or two. I don't like that the trees can be used to sneak up on us, but the light is already low.

As soon as I declare we stop for the night, most of the runners simply plop down where they stand. I did push them hard today.

"They are not the only ones. If I can't go off to hunt something soon, you can decide which runner you'll miss the least," Daeva gripes.

I chuckle even though I'm not sure she's joking.

"It's fine. Go off, feed yourself, and take the other birds with you."

Out of the corner of my eye, I see Cassius glowering down at someone. Even if I can't see the person on the ground, I know who it is.

"Have a good hunt. I have to take care of something," I say, already heading in their direction, not in the mood for whatever is going on now.

"*If you kill someone, tell me so I can abandon the hunt,*" Daeva teases. At least I think she's kidding.

"Will do."

"*Don't have too much fun without me.*" With those parting words, she veers away from me.

"So that is how you want to play it now?" Summer asks, and she sounds pissed.

"Is there a problem here?" I ask, taking in the picture in front of me. Summer is sprawled out on the ground like she fell over where she stood. It doesn't look comfortable. She's lying on her pack, which is still strapped to her back. Her head is lifted now but has been tilted back before, exposing her throat, with Cassius standing over her.

Anger explodes through me, but I stifle it.

Is this what all this tension is about?

If all of this is simply a lover's spat, I will rip Cassius's fucking head off.

Summer is beautiful, I'll give him that, but damn, he should know better. Now that I know, I notice the telltale signs of her feminine form, like her slender waist, even if her loose shirt conceals most of it.

How have I missed it before?

Ilario leans against her. It's as if they are very comfortable in each other's presence, accentuated by the arm she has thrown over his chest.

Summer looks at me and drops her arm, freeing Ilario.

Otero, give me strength and patience.

No one has answered my question so far. I raise my eyebrows at Cassius.

"No, no problem, Centurion." His voice sounds as rigid as his posture.

"Glad to hear that," I answer dryly, even though it's a lie. This situation is ridiculous, and since talking to Cassius doesn't seem to do the trick, I'll have a word with Summer. I point at Ilario.

"Now, Ilario, get settled. I doubt Summer wants to play your cushion all night. Cassius, do your job and appoint guards for the night. Summer, come with me," I command.

Cassius and Ilario hurry off. I pull Summer to her feet, and she first stares at my hand, then drops it like I burned her.

I decide to let it go and stride off to the edge of the camp, ready to get this over with.

I turn, facing the camp, keeping an eye out for anyone who comes close enough to listen in. It's nearly dark by now, and the rest of the division is only moving shadows. Like yesterday, I limited us to one fire for the night.

"This is now the second time I find you in the middle of an argument with your squadron leader." Summer opens her mouth like she wants to argue, and I raise my hand to stop her. "I don't know what is going on with you and Cassius, but—"

That is as far as I get. Summer's eyes widen, and she catches me off guard when she rushes me. Grabbing my elbows, she pushes me around and down.

I stumble back, and Summer lights up in a bluish-white light. Her body twitches, then bows back, her face a picture of pain.

She groans in agony. Her eyes start to glow from within, and light dances over her skin in little sparks.

Lightning.

I jump up, drawing my blades, but I'm blinded by the bright image of Summer's silhouette dancing in front of my eyes. Cries of alarm ring through the camp, and I move, closing in on the source connected to Summer by a stream of light.

"What is going on?" Daeva screeches, alerted by my turmoil.

I relay the images while I keep moving. My eyes slowly adjust, and I hurry the process along with my healing gift. I start to make out my surroundings.

No one jumps out at me, and the lightning wielder's gaze is fixed on Summer, who is still engulfed in light. His magic is a strangely constant stream flowing into her, and he looks horrified.

A trick of light, surely, since I doubt he will lose a night's sleep over killing the wrong person. Because there is no doubt in my mind that this attack was meant for me.

I creep closer, but the lightning wielder still doesn't spare me a glance, seemingly transfixed by Summer. He doesn't even move when I attack, and my short sword slips between his ribs without resistance.

The lightning stops the same moment the light leaves his eyes, and he crumples at my feet.

I stare down at him.

That was strange.

Jared appears next to me. I still hear shouts and voices from the camp but nothing else indicating an attack. My eyes fly to where Summer stood only seconds ago, but there is only a slumped form on the ground, and other runners gather around her.

"Guard him," I snap.

"Sure thing," Jared murmurs while my gaze is already fixed on Summer.

I'm furious. What right does she have to step in front of me, to offer her life for mine without even knowing me?

There are already too many deaths on my shoulders without adding her to that list.

CHAPTER FOURTEEN

ARA

My body twitches as little sparks run over my skin and sear their way to my core. The coldness inside me rises with a vengeance, drinking down the lightning running through my body. And damn, it *hurts*. My already sore muscles are so tense that they are about to crumble to dust. A point of unbearable heat at the base of my neck sends power down a burning path straight to the beast inside me waiting to be fed.

I would scream if I could, but the muscles in my jaw aren't budging, clamping my mouth shut. I groan.

I want it to stop.

Everything hurts, only ... the coolness inside me is unaffected. I dive for it, huddle into it, tug it up around me to give me some relief, and ...

It works.

I keep tugging and pulling, and as it covers more of me, the pain becomes ... bearable and concentrating easier, which makes the beast more compliant.

I slowly regain control of my muscles, but they are still cramped and rigid, and the adrenaline coursing through my body makes it hard to relax.

The bluish light stops, plunging the world around me into darkness, and I collapse to the ground. All that is left are orange spots dotting my vision, blinding me to my surroundings. I concentrate on breathing.

Gods, I'm happy I'm still breathing.

Shuffling and voices penetrate the buzzing in my head.

"She's breathing."

"Is she burned?"

"Was that lightning?"

"What the fuck is going on?"

"Are we under attack?" The voices sound far away, too soft to recognize.

"Gray, can you hear me?" Calix says right next to my ear. "I don't know where I can touch you." I try to sit up. The weight of a hand settles on my shoulder, only to be snatched away again when I grimace. "Don't. Just breathe for a minute." He sounds worried. "Where does it hurt?"

"What happened?" Joel demands with underlying panic in his voice. Great, just what I need right after Kyronos wanted to talk to me about it.

As if I summoned him with that thought, I feel Kyronos coming up next to me.

Wait, what?

I have no idea why I sense his magic without touching him, but that is unmistakably the warm presence I felt when he healed me.

Great.

I groan.

As if I need to be even more aware of his presence.

"Make room. Give me some space to work here," Kyronos barks.

"Have them search the surroundings and double the guards, Cassius." His voice sounds clipped and angry.

Steps are leaving, and the murmurs become muted as everyone hastens to comply.

Calloused hands frame my face. "Where does it hurt, Summer?" His clipped and harsh words are a stark contrast to his gentle touch.

"I'm fine," I croak out.

"Are we back to that again?" Now he sounds exasperated on top of angry. "Are you going to make me check?"

I blush at the thought of him undressing me. Thank god it's dark enough that he can't see it. I hope my warm cheeks don't give me away.

The spots in front of my eyes slowly start to fade, and I can make out the dark shape of his head above me.

"You wouldn't be able to see a thing," I mutter while Kyronos helps me out of my pack and to sit up. My voice still sounds pathetic, and the thought of him using his hands to search for injuries makes breathing difficult.

What is wrong with me?

I survived a lightning attack, successfully used my curse to protect myself, and all I'm thinking about are his hands on my body?

I clear my throat.

"I'm fine, I promise. Maybe you could just help me up?"

He takes a deep breath before releasing it in a frustrated huff.

"Alright. If you insist." His grasp is firm and steady, his palm rough and calloused. The world around me makes a slow turn when I rise, and I steady myself against Kyronos's arm before I face-plant into his chest.

Once I'm sure I'm steady, I take a few steps, clenching my teeth to keep from wincing. My muscles are not happy, not happy at all.

I use the movement to put some distance between us. That I still sense his magic freaks me out, but the sensation lessens a bit with distance.

"See, I'm fine." My voice is hoarse but steady.

"But how?" He sounds incredulous. The shock of seeing me walk away after being grilled by lightning seems to have overpowered the anger I sensed before. Shit, that's the part I haven't thought through.

How much has he seen? How long have I been exposed to the magic? Where is the attacker?

My gaze flies to the darkness around us. Now that my eyes have adjusted, the moonlight is enough to make out shapes. Is one of them moving? Tate seems to guess where my sudden distress is coming from.

"He's dead," he reassures me.

"Are you sure?" It's a stupid question. I doubt he would say it otherwise. The white of his teeth flashes in the dark when he grins. My stomach flips, and I regret that I can't see his face more clearly.

"You want to check for yourself?" He's probably mocking me. But I take the chance it provides to get out of answering questions I can't.

"Yes, please." He chokes back a laugh.

"Sure, doubt my abilities to kill a man, why don't you?" He snorts. "Let's go. I need to search him anyway." He sounds like he's humoring me, which seems out of character.

He probably thinks the lightning addled my brain.

Kyronos walks slowly, staying next to me. I'm sure he expects me to fall over, but I don't, even if it's mainly pride holding me upright. Gods, I'm tired.

My muscles hurt, but it gets better with movement. By the time we stop again, it's more like a severe case of sore muscles—not unlike what I'm used to after heavy drills the day before.

Jared Venti stands next to a motionless figure on the ground, guarding it.

There is no movement, at least as far as I can see. Kyronos squats down, lays out something next to the body, and starts rummaging through the pockets of the person's long coat.

I lower myself next to him, much less gracefully.

Light hair and a short beard frame a very pale face that sticks out against the darkness surrounding it.

"Have you seen him before?" Venti asks.

"No," Kyronos and I answer simultaneously.

"You think he's connected to the attack?" Venti goes on, and I have a feeling he would say more if I weren't around.

"What else? Coincidence?" Kyronos snorts. "Not likely."

"If they—"

"Let's not waste time on theories." Kyronos cuts him off.

My eyes fly from him to Venti and back. What is going on? And why did someone try to kill him?

"Dead enough for you?" Kyronos snaps at me, and I nod numbly.

How did he die?

My eyes fly to the body, searching for injuries. He's dressed in black, and the light is low, but what if there aren't any? The curse had been eager to suck in his magic and had protected me. What if I killed him—the curse killed him—without me even noticing? I managed to control it while Kyronos healed me, but ... shit, if I killed him, they'll know what I am.

I need to know, but I'm afraid to ask.

Kyronos gathers up all he found and gets up, striding away.

"Keep up, Summer, unless you aren't fine after all."

I rise, sucking in a breath when my body protests.

"You need help?" Venti asks.

"No, I'm fine," I grumble and follow Tate, only to realize he waited for me a few steps away. Ass.

Venti, Kyronos, and I make our way over to the low fire someone started in the middle of the hastily thrown-up camp.

Now or never.

"How ... how did he—" I stammer.

"Die?" Kyronos completes the sentence I don't seem able to. He stops and turns to me.

I nod.

"I killed him."

Sure, doubt my abilities to kill a man, why don't you? His earlier words come back to me.

I freaked out for no reason at all. I release the breath I have been holding and catch Kyronos still watching me.

"Good," I answer, breaking the connection by walking past him and over to the fire.

Two runners tend to the flames, but apart from them, only Joel and the other squadron leader are present.

Where is everyone?

"Update," Kyronos barks, and all persons present snap to attention.

"We are still searching the perimeter, Centurion. Guards were doubled as ordered, and the rest have set up the tents for the night," Joel reports.

"Check on the guards and the search," Kyronos orders, and Joel sends me a worried glance before he and the other rider hurry away.

Kyronos and Venti squat down next to the fire, and my centurion opens a bundle, laying out its contents and looking through them.

The things he found on the attacker.

No one is paying me any attention, and I'm curious. I get closer, peering over Kyronos's shoulder. My gaze catches on a small two-pointed crystal. I gasp, and Kyronos's head whips around, leaving only a few fingers of space between us since I'm still leaning over his shoulder. I swallow and ease back.

"Sorry, I'm ... ah ... is one of the birds around?" I whisper even though I know this crystal only transmits location, not sound.

"Why?" Kyronos and Venti ask simultaneously.

"This crystal is called a Tracer." I crouch down between them and run a finger over the smooth surface. "They are from the Ice Coast, I think." I look up, my gaze jumping from Kyronos to Venti and back. "They come in pairs, and one is used to track the location of the other."

Venti curses up a storm while Kyronos goes completely still.

"How do you know this?" Kyronos's voice is laced with suspicion. It's true, Tracers aren't common knowledge.

"My father told me. He once met two mercenary brothers from

the Ice Coast. They used them to find each other during battles." What I can't say without giving away too much is that they had been spies sent to infiltrate my father's forces and harvest information.

Kyronos gets up abruptly. "Let's go then. This will be a long night after all."

"Douse the flames and break up camp." Kyronos's orders ring out over the clearing and are taken up by other voices. The camp erupts into a flurry of activity, and despite some people grumbling under their breath, I don't hear any open objections. But then, Kyronos is not a man you openly deny.

Faster than I would have thought possible, we line up and are ready to go. Ropes tether us together to prevent us from falling to our deaths, and we march.

The darkness seems to stretch on forever, and time loses all meaning. Even though the moon provides some light, the ground stays treacherous, and I stumble along, fighting to keep my balance and thankful for the quiet support of my flight around me.

By the time the sky lightens, all of us are more stumbling than walking, and I sigh in relief when I spot the giant silhouettes of the birds circling above Telos. Strange how something so fierce can be so comforting, so homey.

Soon, I make out the pale towers of the academy, and when we finally arrive, the academy lies silent around us in the early morning hours.

"Leave the ropes and tents and use the day to get some rest," Kyronos orders once we are in the atrium. "Well done, everyone."

The riders walk over to their birds, and we do as we are told.

We are quiet while we stumble to our room and fall into our beds, ready to sleep the day away.

THREE DAYS HAVE PASSED SINCE THE GRUELING WALK BACK home, and I can still feel it in my bones, or maybe it's the lightning attack still bothering me.

But currently, I don't have to move. I sit in class and listen to Professor Myrsky, who teaches Magical Creatures, as he tells us everything we need to know about our future bonding partners.

The classroom slopes downward, and I'm sitting next to Calix about halfway up, which brings us on eye level with the elaborate drawing that occupies nearly all of the wall above the blackboard. Five birds are captured mid-flight, all of them majestic and beautiful in their unique way.

"Night Ravens are stubborn and vicious creatures but extremely loyal and fearless. Any of you lucky enough to be a match for one of them can rest assured that they will be with you no matter the threat." Professor Myrsky paces along the front of the class.

The Night Raven on the painting is black, the darkness only interrupted by streaks of azure and indigo to show the colors sunlight can bring out in their feathers.

"If they inspire fear in you—run." Myrsky's gaze wanders over us, his expression serious. "Can someone tell me what their strength in battle is?"

A guy two rows in front of me raises his hand before anyone else. "Next to their fearlessness, they have exceptionally good night vision, the feathers on the tip of their wings are poisonous, and they are very tenacious. They will keep coming until they either win or die trying."

"Excellent." Myrsky nods. "Can anyone tell me more about their poison?"

"It isn't a poisonous substance, but more like a poisonous magic. A strong one. Only magic wielders with strong shielding can withstand it," a dark-haired girl from the western division answers.

"Yes, and that is the reason you should keep a healthy distance. Only their bonded riders are immune to it." He wanders over to the other side of the room. "Let's talk about the Phoenix. Most of you will probably never see one in your lifetime, but that doesn't mean I won't test you on this, so listen closely." He taps the wall behind him, and my gaze wanders to the image of the fiery bird. He's depicted in gold, yellow, and hues of red and orange. Is a Phoenix actually burning, or do its feathers just match the color of fire?

"Like Lightning Birds, they are rare, and since the treatise of the guardians, only four bonds to a Phoenix have been recorded." He holds up four fingers. "Before that, it's said they were more common, but since those records were destroyed ..." He shrugs.

"I heard there were sightings of a Phoenix during the last summer solstice," the dark-haired girl from earlier throws in, and Myrsky nods.

"There have been, but we can only speculate about the meaning of that," the professor replies.

The Phoenix has always fascinated me, not just because of its striking colors or magic abilities but also because of the thought of going up in flames and being reborn. Do they feel invincible? They still can be killed for good by beheading or submerging them in water long enough to kill their inner flame, but who would manage to get close enough for that?

"Phoenixes are very secretive. We would love to know more about them, but even their riders were unwilling to divulge much information." Myrsky looks longingly at the image.

"They select the most powerful riders, which makes sense since their rider needs a vast amount of magic to hold a shield against their flames and wield their gift at the same time without getting burned."

Charming. Maybe I'm not too eager to meet a Phoenix after all.

"Riding a Phoenix has to be great in winter. I bet you would never get cold," Calix murmurs next to me.

"As if you even know what winter looks like," I tease. "But I think riding a Phoenix has to be great no matter the season or temperature," I whispered.

"True." He smiles. "I would take any of them." He gestures at the painting. "I would ride anything with wings if it meant I got to see the world from up there."

"Gross, man, with your reputation, that sounds all wrong." I make a gagging motion, surprising a laugh out of him. He smothers it when we receive a warning look from our professor.

"Not my fault if you have such a filthy mind." He grins at me, and I look away. His words remind me of my thoughts about a certain centurion, who my gaze finds far too often whenever he is around.

Kyronos, on the other hand, doesn't seem to have a problem keeping his eyes off me.

That is a good thing, I remind myself, *I don't want eyes on me.*

The low rumble of the drum marks the end of class and pulls me out of my musings. We grab our books and notes.

"Seriously, I can't wait for flight practice to start next week," Calix says with a longing look at the images on the wall.

"Me, too." I agree, and we make our way to the refectory for lunch. Maybe the new challenge posed by flying will help to keep my mind from wandering.

CHAPTER FIFTEEN
ARA

The trip changed us. Maybe the reality of our lives as riders set in and made us realize we had to work as a unit. Perhaps it was fighting side by side or enduring the grueling march back that welded us together.

No matter what triggered it, our squadron dynamics changed. The current situation is a clear sign of that.

"Just a little farther. You got this, Mariel," I shout, and I'm not the only one. Our whole squadron has been shouting encouragement and whooping loudly since we started our drills at the obstacle course, and since I peeked at the list Joel keeps, I know our times show the extra push.

My experience in the mountains was also a much-needed reminder that I have too much I can't share or even explain without landing myself in hot water, which makes our group becoming tighter a double-edged sword.

Feeling the support is incredible, but keeping up my ruse and lying to them becomes harder and harder, especially to Calix. He's the most open and likable person I've ever met, so I feel like shit for deceiving him. But he flirts constantly, and I can't see him treating me the same once he knows I'm a girl.

The other problem is that suddenly, everyone wants to know where I'm going when I try to creep off.

"She's getting so much better," Calix comments next to me, his eyes on Mariel.

"Yeah, she's incredible," I say and earn a knowing look from Calix.

"What?" I ask.

"So you're into her?" he asks while he watches Mariel balancing over a beam, his mood suddenly somber.

"What? No, of course not."

"I mean, I wouldn't blame you. She has serious fire and a hot figure on top of it." He grins. Whatever is bugging him is seemingly forgotten.

"No, I'm not into her," I protest, but stop when he only smiles.

This argument will get me nowhere. Thankfully, Calix is up next.

"Who's caught your eye, then?" Calix continues the same discussion over lunch, and I nearly choke on the sip of tea in my mouth. He pounds my back while I cough.

"Don't break him," Simeon jokes while plopping down in the seat next to me. Ever since we got back, our squadron has been sitting together during meals without losing a word about it.

I'm thankful for his interruption. My gaze darts to the other side of the room, where I spot Kyronos grinning at something Venti said.

When I snap my attention back to what's going on around me, the guys are roasting Simeon about his crush on a girl from the northern division.

"How do you intend to charm her?" one of them asks.

"You mean how he'll charm the pants off her," another throws in.

"Assuming he hopefully knows his way once he has," I joke, and Simeon groans next to me before he begs us to stop.

"I take it you do then," a voice asks right next to my ear, startling me. I look over my shoulder and meet the gaze of a girl from the eastern division, her hand resting on my shoulder.

"Hey, Trina, looking good," Calix pipes up next to me. That is another problem I didn't anticipate when I stepped in front of our centurion. I fight down a groan.

How does getting nearly fried make me more desirable?

Since flirting is his second language, I have no guilt over leaving Calix to deal with Trina.

"Nice meeting you, Trina," I say, my eyes on Mariel's plate, who just sits down opposite me. "Oh, Mariel, those cookies look great." I jump up.

"Yeah, I know you like them. I brought one f—" I don't let her finish before I grab my plate and hurry away.

Crisis averted.

I grab two cookies because they really are delicious, and when no one is watching, I rush out the door and head to our next class early.

It takes a while before Calix sprawls into the chair next to mine. He stares at me, shaking his head.

"What is wrong with you?" he asks. "You ran away like your pants were on fire."

"I don't need distractions," I grumble. "And she's only interested because she makes me into something I'm not."

He bumps my shoulder with his fist. "Who cares? Loosen up. We could die any day. One wrong step on that damn squirrel path you like so much ... and your body makes its last journey." He shakes his head. "And you throw away a chance like that." He gestures to the door. "Live a little."

His encouragement makes me think of our centurion and the way he looked this morning, his hair still wet from a shower while he sat down for breakfast.

Damn, this is getting ridiculous.

I huff out a breath.

"I'll happily let you do the living for me," I say.

Calix smirks.

"Don't even pretend you didn't seize that chance." I raise my eyebrow at him.

He shrugs, still grinning. "I had to boost Trina's confidence after you brushed her off like that."

I snort. "Yeah, right. How utterly selfless of you."

"I do what I can." He sends me a wolfish grin, and I burst out laughing.

Two hours later, after Geography and Lore of the Sky, we find ourselves in the courtyard.

Arkwright decided the sunny day is perfect for drills outside. I'm facing Mariel, and she's as good with a sword as she is without it. Her bright red hair is braided back, a fiery splash of color whenever it catches the sun.

She is one of three girls on my squadron, four if I count myself, but the only one in the same flight.

"Switch partners." Professor Arkwright's voice cuts through the clear winter air, giving us a short reprieve while Mariel's side shuffles up to the next runner. The sun has nearly reached its peak, stealing all the shadows and turning the air far too warm for a winter day.

I roll up my sleeves but undo the last turn of the right when my mark becomes visible.

It is growing. When I marred my skin to hide it, it was the size of my thumb. It's three times the size now, like an ugly, dark caterpillar crawling down my skin, and I've been so occupied with everything else that I haven't even started my research on that.

Godwin, who occupies the bunk above mine, smiles down at me. "Ready to get your ass whooped, Gray?"

I grin. "In your dreams, Godi." He grimaces at the nickname and charges when the whistle sounds.

This is something I know, something comfortable. I push away everything else and sidestep his attack before going on the offensive.

I get lost in the simple dynamics of charging and retreating, acting and reacting. My muscles go from warm and loose, past burning and aching, into protesting and screaming while we change partners again and again.

Two hours later, I limp back to our room, covered in sweat, dust, and bruises. Calix slings his arm over my shoulders, bumping into a bruise on my right arm, and I hiss.

Thank the gods Simeon twisted his blade in time and hit me with the broad side, or I would have needed Kyronos's help again. A shiver goes through my body. The thought of getting healed still freaks me out, and who says it will work again? And that I'm attracted to him... it's madness.

I dive out from under Calix's arm and shove him playfully. "Get away from me. You are disgusting."

He laughs. "As if you look any better."

I grin up at him. "I still don't have the desire to get your gunk all over me, too."

He laughs again. "Too late for that, Gray."

"Oh, so you are all over me now?" I ask, waggling my brows.

"Stop it, or you'll ruin my reputation." He laughs while lunging for me and trying to get me into a headlock.

I dance out of his reach, throwing mock punches to keep him away.

"You have to do better than that," Calix says, coming at me again. I jump back, my injured shoulder colliding with something hard. I stumble forward, hissing in pain when that brings all my weight on my right leg, which is still tender from a nasty hit yesterday. A hand grabs my arm, and I nearly jump out of my skin.

I look over my shoulder into a familiar pair of golden eyes.

Dammit. I step away.

Despite multiple steps between us, I still feel the golden glow of his gift pulling me in. Great, now I can sense it from over here? And even worse, I feel drawn to it.

What is wrong with me?

"Sorry, didn't see you there," I mutter.

His gaze lingers on my leg for a second before it wanders back to my face. For a moment, I think Kyronos is going to say something, but he just nods before stepping around me. He's already halfway down the hall before he looks over his shoulder, catching me looking after him.

"He's right. You have to do better than that."

I watch his retreating back and hear Calix exhale next to me. "Well, that was anticlimactic."

"What?" I look at him, confused, while a little tingle of panic ignites in my belly.

Does he know about my crush?

"Why?" I ask.

"Haven't you heard what they say about him?" He looks at me incredulously and shakes his head when I only widen my eyes in question.

I don't pay attention to gossip. I'm busy enough with my own shit and have no inclination or time to dig into someone else's.

But Calix failed his calling as one of those chatty old women who spend all their time at a window commenting on the neighborhood. I grin at the image of Calix leaning out a window in a dress and headscarf.

"Well, then listen up," Calix tells me, and to my mortification, I do. I'm simply too eager to learn more about Tate Kyronos.

"He and Jared Venti showed up here for Assessment three years ago, and no one knows where they came from." He gives me a meaningful glance, which doubles my discomfort since he could say the same about me. "They say he escaped a prison up in the north since he has this scar on his neck, and they were dressed in northern fashion when they got here." I snort at that.

Of course, the only reason someone with healing magic didn't heal himself is that he was suppressed. I shake my head. Suppressants are shackles used in prison to subdue gifted people, but that is by no means the only possible explanation. I do wonder about that scar myself, though.

"He is also disgraced and still doesn't seem to mind showing his chest openly."

Tate Kyronos shirtless—now that is a thought to dwell on.

"And he supposedly has three gifts." Calix has my full attention.

Three?

He has to be from a powerful family if he already came with two gifts, which would explain the way he speaks.

"But no one can tell me what the third is. Do you think it's classified?" Calix looks at me, waiting for my reaction.

I shrug.

"Oh, and he's ruthless in a fight. In his first year, another runner had to stay in the healing quarters for days after Kyronos was done with him. After that, no one dared to mess with him again."

Well, I have seen him fight. He has a certain vibe, and I don't doubt he can be lethal, but ruthless? I simply can't get past the way he treated me while tending to my wound. Soft and careful.

A healing gift alone is a hell of a reason to stay away. Never mind the fact that any rider is officially off-limits.

I know how misleading rumors and reputations can be. Dar, for example, has the reputation of being fair but hard and cold at times, and he's the biggest softy of all my brothers.

Or the rumors that went flying two years ago after the incident with the officer. I shudder just thinking about that man. I'm not sorry he's dead, but I'm sorry Ian killed him. That encounter is one reason I keep my daggers sharp and always on me.

We sit at dinner, and my thoughts keep wandering.

"Are you alright?" Calix asks. I realize I've zoned out on him again, and for the life of me, I can't remember what we've been talking about.

I give him a nod while chewing and then look around the room to evade any more questions.

Across the room, Gorgon rests his arm on the back of Livia's chair and leans in to whisper something in her ear, which makes her laugh. The bully and the brute? My eyebrows jump up. *What a fitting match.*

Something draws my eyes to my left, and I find Kyronos looking at me, who sits two tables over. A jolt zips down my spine, and tingles erupt all over my skin. I force my eyes back to the plate in front of me.

He is off-limits, I remind myself.

Maybe my disguise is a good thing after all. It isn't like I can openly flirt with him without sparking questions. Otherwise, I might have been tempted.

Let's be real: you would have thrown yourself at him no matter the risk. The voice in my head sounds suspiciously like Ben's.

Are they glad I'm not around to cause chaos?

"You are one odd fish, Gray." Calix chuckles, watching me. "You know that, right?"

"You are one to talk," I quip back and smile at him, but Calix's teasing makes me miss my brothers even more, especially Ben.

Better get used to it. You won't see them much once you're married anyway.

Maybe I should have stayed at the fortress for good like Dar proposed. I could have worn high-necked dresses and gloves like Grandma used to and played the crazy aunt for Dar's children. I grin at that thought, but then I would never have come here.

I watch my friends squabble.

No. Whatever happens, I don't regret my decision to come here.

I LIE FLAT ON MY STOMACH ON THE ROOF OF THE HOUSING building, peeking down. A guard patrols the perimeter of the academy grounds below me.

With divisions constantly out for camp training and the doubled patrols to prevent another attack, the academy is much quieter. Doubling patrols is all the reaction we see concerning the attack two weeks ago. Most runners and riders agree that the attack must have come from the titans, but I find that hard to believe. Why have we never had any trouble with them at home? And the attackers were nothing like the people from the stories.

Fewer runners and riders make it easier to get around without being seen, but being part of a group does not. I have never had the companionship of anyone apart from my family, so it's comforting and irritating at the same time.

Screeching and the rustling of wings tell me the last patrol just returned. It's already dark, but I still freeze and hold my breath.

There are no Night Ravens in this flight, and they don't pass over me—the only reason I'm up here despite knowing they'll come in. Strix and Rukh might not have the exceptional night vision Night Ravens do, but they're still good at detecting movement.

My cheek rests against the cold stone shingles beneath me, but I can picture the perfect V-formation swooping down so synchronized that they seem like one creature. My lungs start to burn with the need to breathe, but I resist until creaking leather, steps, and voices confirm they have landed. I can't help but wonder how long it will take until we become one entity like them.

The guard moves below, undisturbed by the arriving patrol. I take deep, even breaths, and my heartbeat slows.

In a few days, I'll meet Sloan to supply her with new letters, and I have a plan for how I'll get out of here unseen. I wait for the guard to wander out of my sight to check my timing. With nothing to occupy my thoughts, they wander back to my centurion.

Apart from our run-in a week ago, I haven't seen him much, and while that should make it easier to push him out of my mind, it doesn't. He acts as distant and cool as before the healing incident, making me question everything. Maybe I imagined his warmth?

The guard vanishes around the corner of the building, and I

count under my breath until he returns. After nights of watching the guards, I found the perfect way to sneak out.

Our room's window overlooks a small street following the borders of the academy, and because there is nothing to hide behind on this side of the building, the guards spend much more time monitoring the front. There is not enough time to sprint the distance from one corner to the next, but it'll be ample time to slide down the rain pipe and climb over the fence. From there, I can melt into the shadows of the houses across the street, and nobody will be the wiser.

Scrambling back up could cut it close, but I'll worry about that when I get there. I also hope they concentrate on the ground and don't look at the building too closely.

I wait for the next turn before I climb back down and through the window. Thankfully, our room is still empty. The common room is much cozier than the sleeping quarters, so normally, everyone hangs out there.

I'm closing the window behind me when the door opens.

"There you are." Mariel stands in the doorway and gives me an odd look. Okay, I have to admit standing alone in a dark room does look strange.

"Where were you? You simply vanished on us."

"Oh, I only aired the room a little," I say and step back from the window.

"For the last hour?" She sounds skeptical.

I laugh, shaking my head. "No, I took a walk before that."

"You are not so into big groups, are you?" she asks.

"I'm just not used to it." I shrug. "Sometimes it's just—"

"It can be a bit much. I get it. No need to defend yourself." She crosses over to me and puts the lamp she carried on the table in front of the windows instead of lighting the other lights. "I think it's great that you can admit it. I'm not much of a people person myself." She smiles at me, and there is a moment of companionable silence.

"If you feel up to it, we're about to start a game of cards..." She watches me, waiting for an answer.

"Why not?" I return her smile. Sitting close to a roaring fire for a game of cards sounds pretty good after the cold, and hanging out with my flight, too. Even the riders from Joel's flight tend to join us.

Ever since our trip into the mountains, he seems to have taken a different approach—or maybe Kyronos talked to him, too. He hangs out with us whenever he's around, probably to keep an eye on me, and he has stopped talking about sending me home. He's more like the guy I used to know back home.

I follow Mariel down the corridor to the common room of our division; voices and laughter reach us despite the closed door. Now that my plans for visiting Sloan next weekend are set, I have nothing left to do but throw myself into classes and training and banish a certain centurion from my thoughts—not that it's working. But I do have our first flight lesson to look forward to.

CHAPTER SIXTEEN
TATE

Today is one of those days it sucks to be up in the air. Telos is located so far south that winter is hardly noticeable most days, but today, a sharp and icy north wind creeps into even the tiniest gap in our uniform, and the drizzle that accompanies us for the better part of two hours makes being up here simply miserable.

Since I have to draw on my body heat to warm up the air around me, I gave up on it ages ago. The damp, cold air leeches any warmth so quickly that it would send me into hypothermia in no time, defying the purpose.

We fly in the typical V-formation, rotating who takes point to distribute the strain evenly between our birds. A wind like today makes taking the lead over longer periods noticeably more tiring.

My fingers are stiff from the cold, and I can't wait to get close to a fire. The rest of the flight is not any better off, except for Zaza, who uses her fire gift to push her body temperature into toasty regions. The steam coming off her body is a foolproof sign of that.

I bury my fingers deeper into Daeva's feathers for warmth and keep my eyes open for anything moving below us.

The threat we encounter most at the borders is not an attack from neighboring countries but from creatures of the mist. The mist that separates the five kingdoms from one another.

We pass over a little village that sits right at the border. In my opinion, it's too close to the mist on a sunny day, but today, the ominous white even seeps into the streets.

How can people live like that?

Avina, located in the north, is too far off the border to interact with the mist, its people, or its creatures. So I had no contact growing up. Now, I know them much too well.

The dark clouds make night fall early.

"Movement at nine o'clock," Daeva warns only seconds before the first arrow flies past us.

I slip my bow over my head and curse when the first arrow I retrieve nearly slips out of my stiff fingers.

"Way to make a miserable day even worse," I mutter.

"It's a full-on raid on the village," Daeva says. I slip into her view, the contortion of color and view so natural to me by now that I acclimate quickly. Through Daeva's eyes, I can easily count ten human shapes moving in the mist. She's right. This is a coordinated raid of the titans instead of a random creature attack.

Fuck.

I have Daeva relay the information to Tanner, my flight's squadron leader and second-in-command, and have him take over so I can concentrate on shielding us. He has us draw a tight circle and takes point. His arm is raised, and the wet air gathers around his fingers, coalescing. A dive brings us into shooting range, and his arm comes down.

A volley of hailstones the size of hen's eggs accompanies his movement, and the whole flight loses their arrows.

FEATHERS OF ASH AND HOPE

They multiply in the air, thanks to Jared's illusions, making it hard for the enemy to distinguish the real ones.

Three of our enemies fall, but that means at least seven are left, and maybe there are more waiting in the mist. Tanner's hailstones took our enemies by surprise, and they didn't have the chance to retaliate, but that won't work again.

Sure enough, they all took cover on the next sweep, and we can't get a clear shot. They lose their arrows, which fall back harmlessly, stopped by my shield.

I manage to hit one more on the next one, but with the darkness, the rest of the flight is at a severe disadvantage. We're on our fourth pass when a sudden flare of light blinds Daeva and me since I shared her sight. She caws in outrage, and her unease at flying blind floods our bond.

I'm momentarily disoriented. The bluish-white dots dancing over my vision remind me scarily of the lightning wielder's attack.

"*It's fine. You've got this.*" I try to calm Daeva, but how am I supposed to shield us when I can't see where the threat is?

"Everyone pull up," I shout, but I don't think anyone hears me over the wind, so Daeva relays the message as well. I have no idea how close we are.

The sharp pain in my leg hits me the same moment Daeva's cry pierces the air. We are hit.

Daeva pulls up, but her movements are labored.

"*Where is it?*" I demand to know.

"*My right wing,*" she says, and I find the exact location easily once I slip into her perception. It sits between her elbow and wrist. Thankfully, it missed the tendon, but it moves with every beat of her wing, a stabbing pain radiating outward. I curse.

"*Can you land?*" I ask her.

"*In a moment,*" she tells me. "*But I'm not sure it's safe around here.*"

"*Could you bear my weight on your wing if you glide?*" I ask her, and she snorts or a sound as close to that as a bird can get.

"Jared and Zephyr are on their way over. I told them what you are up to. They will follow our movement from below," Daeva informs me. They'll catch me in case I fall is what she leaves out. Not that I plan on that. My vision clears with every passing second, and Jared and Zephyr close in on us.

Despite the pain, Daeva wins on height, using the air currents to her advantage. The air turns even colder. I'm focused on Daeva, caught up in her perception, and only remember I was hit, too, when bending to loosen the straps, jostling the arrow in my thigh. Fuck.

I grit my teeth and yank it out unceremoniously. No time to be careful. I roar in pain when it takes a good chunk of my flesh with it, thanks to the barbs. The blood flows freely, and I concentrate on healing it.

Healing myself is harder than healing others. Maybe because concentrating on whole and healthy tissue isn't easy when the pain tells you it's quite the opposite of well, and a nagging headache always accompanies it that ironically, I can't heal myself from, no matter what I do. It isn't like that for everyone, but frankly, healing myself sucks.

We are high above ground by the time I'm done. I free myself from the saddle, and Daeva goes into a glide. Lying down on my stomach, I slide onto her motionless wing, distributing my weight as evenly as possible.

"The arrow went through. I'll cut off the fletching to pull it out," I inform Daeva about what I'm doing. Using my magic, I sever the arrow below her wing. She caws at my jostling. I grip the tip, protruding on the top, and a screech accompanies the moment I dislodge the arrow. Relief floods me once the arrow is gone. I slip my hand over the wound, and it closes easily.

Sliding back into my seat is harder than getting here since I have to slide backward, and my armor catches on her feathers, ruffling them. Daeva complains about it.

"You're welcome, beautiful," I tell her dryly.

The fight is already over by the time Jared and I join our formation. No more arrows or movement from the mist, and the fire is contained as well. Infantry is on its way from a watchtower nearby, so we head back to the Aerie.

When we land, Zaza is slumped in her saddle, and Boko grimaces when he hits the ground, the broken shaft of an arrow sticking out of his leg. Zaza is close to exhaustion since she battled not only the fire our enemies set to one of the houses but also the wielder who did it.

"We have you," Jared murmurs. We loosen the straps holding her in the saddle. Zaza refuses to let him carry her, so we take her between us, setting off for the healing quarters. Miller helps Boko by lending him a shoulder to lean on, and Tanner heads for Legatus Janus's office to make a report while the rest of our flight sees that our birds get the care they deserve.

It's two hours, a good meal, and a hot shower later that I find myself at the library, continuing my research on the Tracers. I prefer the always empty back part of the library. None of the books needed for classes are back here, and not many runners or riders spend their free time hanging out in the library.

I sit at a table with four chairs tucked between tall bookshelves. To one side is a little nook with two big and dusty armchairs and a little side table. Other than that, there is nothing but bookshelves around me, creating an area that can't be seen until you turn the last corner.

I warm the air around me. I have had enough of the cold, and the library is rather drafty and cool, so air magic does come in handy. My head and leg still throb, too little to seek help in the healing quarters but enough to be irritating. Heat seeps from my body into the air around me, and I stop once the temperature is comfortable.

I picked up some books from the library, and I'm now eyeing the tomes in front of me. *The Ice Coast and Its Minerals*, *Ice Coast: Customs and Traditions*, and *Great Minds and Their Inventions* are spread out around me, but Summer's words are still the only information I have. I open the book *Ice Coast and Its Minerals* at the back, checking the glossary. Heaving a breath, I get to work, starting with the promising first entry.

I pull out the Tracers to compare them to an image of another crystal and leave them on the table for reference. Only Jared and Summer know about the Tracers and their connection to the attack.

Maybe I should have gotten rid of the crystals since I suspect the one my contact handed me might have led those men to our camp.

We were too high up in the mountains and too far away from the mist for the titans to attack us. Even if the silent advance would fit their approach, the man's accent didn't.

Brrring you back alive... those words, combined with the lightning wielder's attack and the fact that we were far from any bridge point, leaves me with the suspicion that they targeted us specifically.

Their attack resembled the one I survived three and a half years ago, and the option of them stumbling over us by accident is also out. No one lurks around so close to an Aerie just for the chance to run into someone. The risk of being discovered by one of the patrols is simply too high.

I have to face the possibility that my contact double-crossed me and set up a trap by handing me the crystal.

And he had the gall to ask for payment, too.

Now, the Tracers are usually stored in my room, but I had the first one with me all the time since I was trying to figure out its use.

Once more, the deaths are on me.

The scrape of a boot sounds behind me, and with the attack and thoughts of double-crossing and traps fresh on my mind, I'm out of my chair, my dagger drawn before I even think about it. I grit my teeth when the sudden movement causes the pain in my leg to flare up.

Big blue-green eyes meet mine, and I see concern in them while the corners of her mouth tip up into a guilty smile. Summer.

"Sorry, I didn't mean to startle you." Her eyes fly past me and widen before they flick back to my face. Following her gaze, I see what caught her attention: the Tracers. Fuck.

Her eyes wander over the Tracers and the books scattered on the table before stopping on the leg I favor.

"Are you alright?" she asks, her eyes returning to mine, and I'm startled to see genuine concern there.

"Yes," I tell her. Her lips part on my brusque tone, drawing my gaze, and all I can think of is how damn beautiful she is and the soft skin and slender curves hidden beneath her baggy clothes.

She looks up at me. "Do you want help with that?" In combination with my thoughts, that question is anything but harmless. Desire slams into me.

"No," I snap, the word much harsher than intended.

I shouldn't think about her that way.

"Alright then." She sends me a strained smile, shrugs, and turns. Summer disappears around the next shelf in a heartbeat. I stand there frozen until her footsteps fade, only then realizing I never thanked her for saving me.

I sigh and slump back into my chair. Maybe Jared is right, and my social skills are severely lacking these days.

Granted, gratitude wasn't my first reaction when I realized what she had done; more like horror and disbelief.

Her action still puzzles me, just like the concern I saw in her eyes minutes ago. Apart from Jared and Nan, I'm not used to seeing anyone worry for me.

I'm respected as a centurion, and we have each other's backs within our flight, but to take a hit for me like that without knowing me?

I don't know if that makes her brave, stupid, or simply reckless. The image of her being struck by lightning still haunts me, and the fact that she survived unscathed still baffles me.

I'm fine, I promise.

Her words make no sense. How can she be fucking fine after being roasted by lightning?

I sigh. She doesn't deserve to be brushed off like that, especially since she didn't even try to dig for information concerning the objects lying on the table. The least I can do is thank her and act less like an ass.

The following day, we're in the sparring hall while the runners have a break between classes. Half of the room is shadowed by one of the Aerie's towers, while the other half is bathed in gold by the afternoon sun. I lean against the wall, my eyes on Summer, who spars with Ilario.

The room is alive with the sounds of curses, grunts, and things colliding, either bodies or steel or both. Again, I find myself wondering about her. Who else knows about her disguise? She practically admitted that Cassius knows. But what about Ilario? I remember him crouching next to her after the lightning attack, looking worried.

Just how close are they?

Ilario demonstrates for the hundredth time how Summer has to put her body behind a punch to make it count.

"What's up with you? You look like someone puked in your breakfast or something." Jared strolls up to me.

"Nothing," I mutter.

"Yeah, I know that *nothing*. Want to hit the weight room? I would offer to spar with you, but I'm not a masochist." He bumps my shoulder.

"Sure," I say, but my eyes are still on her. Her punch is still shit, and the only thing Ilario does is go through the movement again. "What the fuck is he doing?" She surely won't get it from watching him again. Otherwise, she would have mastered it by now. I stride over to them.

"If one way of teaching isn't working, trying another is no disgrace," I grumble. I place my hands on Summer's hips, and she flinches at my touch. I ignore it and try very hard not to think of her soft skin beneath this tunic.

"Do it again. Slowly," I instruct, and she complies. I twist her hips in time with her movement. Her gasp when her knuckles connect and the "umpf" from Ilario tells me they both felt the difference. She laughs in wonder before apologizing to Ilario.

Her smoky laugh and the wide smile on her face when she looks at me over her shoulder make my stomach flip. Her joy feels infectious, fizzing through my blood like thunderbolts, and I smile back. The air between us charges, and I catch my thumb, tracing tiny circles on her lower back while my hands still rest on her hips.

What am I doing?

I let my hands drop to my sides and step back. I get my face back under control and take another step back before I nod at her.

"That's it. Do ten more, then change sides." My gruff and clipped voice reestablishes the needed distance between us. I turn and stride off, but the warmth of her smile lingers in my chest.

"Thank you," Summer calls behind me, causing heads to turn, but I resist and only raise my hand in acknowledgment.

Maybe being nice is not such a good idea, after all. It's too easy to get sucked in by her light.

Another reason to stay away is Cassius. I saw him in the weight room this morning, pounding away at one of the targets like it was his mortal enemy. I always perceived him as reasonable and even-tempered, but since Summer arrived, he's all over the place.

Yes, keeping my distance is important.

"What was that?" Jared looks confused when I get back to him.

"What? I just helped him out. He didn't get the hang of it, and Ilario was doing a miserable job of teaching him."

"That's not what I meant. You smiled." He looks at me suspiciously.

"Don't worry. I won't do it again," I deadpan. "Summer did save my life, though. Maybe I was trying to be nice."

"There aren't many around who can say that," he agrees.

Because they're all dead.

He probably didn't mean to imply that, but the thought sours my mood.

"My point exactly." I slap his back. "Let's go hit something."

THE COMMON ROOM IS CROWDED THIS EVENING, MAKING THE big space seem much smaller. Apart from a few riders on courier duty, all squadrons of the southern division are in at the moment, and it seems most of them opted to stay in since the weather is still icy.

A few second and third squadron riders have a friendly competition of throwing knives at the target in the corner, and most chairs and couches are occupied. People are chatting and playing card games. Zaza is at the fireplace, casually placing wood right into the violet flames. The flames dance over her hand while she's chatting with Tanner. Thankfully, she bounced back quickly after the run-in with the titans.

I sit next to Jared on one of the couches, balancing a book on my knees while I work on the patrol plan for next month. I have to hand it in tomorrow, and working around granted leaves and even distribution of all the squadrons can be a headache, even without the commotion going on around us.

I lift my head when the door opens. Summer walks in with another girl from her flight, and I nearly groan. Just what I need: another distraction.

The girls are both grinning like they shared a joke just before entering. Summer's smile falters for a second when our eyes meet, and she looks away. They walk over to the rest of their squadron, sitting at one of the tables, animatedly discussing something. There is a bit of shuffling to make room for the newcomers, and Summer ends up on a bench between Cassius and another seasoned rider.

Since when do they hang out with riders?

I let my eyes wander over the group again and recognize the riders as being part of Cassius's flight.

I turn back to the paper in front of me. This is exactly why I keep my distance.

"You can't put squadron three on that." Jared taps on the paper, criticizing my last entry.

"And why the mists not?" I ask.

"Because that one takes about eight days, and Jenna has leave coming up after five." I curse when I see he's right.

"How about you take over the planning?" I ask dryly, but shake my head when a wicked smile spreads across my best friend's face. I know how Jared's mind works by now.

"No, you can't partner us with the second squadron of the eastern division for the whole month just because you're sleeping with Nadja." His smile morphs into a pout.

"Oh, come on, have a heart," he pleads, "and I know for a fact that Stina would love to have you in her bed." He grins at me. "You seem a bit stressed lately."

Stina is a pretty redhead and Nadja's friend, but all I can think about are those goose bumps popping up under my touch and a warm, smoky voice asking me not to be too gentle.

Holy mists, this girl is fucking with my head without even trying.

That she's such a puzzle isn't helping either.

"What?" I ask when I realize Jared must have asked me something. He gives me an odd look.

"Something is up with you." He studies my face.

"Nothing is up," I deny and try very hard not to look at the table across the room.

CHAPTER SEVENTEEN
ARA

"I want to make sure you understand me here." Professor Sanders pauses. "They are not pets," he emphasizes the last four words. "Those Strix were raised and trained by humans, are far gentler than their wild brethren and any other kind of bird raised here. They will tolerate you on their backs, but"—he lets his gaze wander over us—"and this is important... they have no connection to you, they are not invested in your welfare, and they couldn't care less if you fall to your death. So, under no circumstances are you allowed to loosen your straps. You will follow my instructions and those of your squadron leader to the point. No shenanigans. No excuses. Understood?"

We all nod. The thought of falling to death is savage enough to cow us into silent obedience. We stand in front of the stables, or coop, which is what the building housing the birds is called. It's an impressive tower, not too far off the main building, with countless open arches on various levels for the birds to come and go as they like.

But it's not the building I'm looking at. My eyes are on the seventeen harnessed Strixes waiting in front of it. They are massive and majestic, their white and gray feathers sleek, their intelligent eyes on us as we approach.

Sanders gives us the go, and I head to the last one on the right. The violet streaks adorning his head indicate he is male. Like we have been taught, I lock my eyes with his, my posture straight and proud, not hesitating in my advance but not rushing either.

Slowly, I lift my hand to his beak and nearly sigh in relief when he rubs it against my palm. The strong beak feels smooth and surprisingly warm against my skin. There is a short spark when magic starts to transfer, but I quickly stifle it. I'm getting better and better at suppressing it.

"Hey, beautiful. You ready to soar through the sky?" I whisper.

He makes a clicking noise that sounds like agreement to me.

"You two seem to get along well." His caretaker, a giant strawberry-blond man with more freckles than I have ever seen before, smiles down at me.

"How could I not adore a beauty like him?" I grin at the creature next to me, letting my fingers slip through his soft feathers.

"Oh, stop complimenting him, or his ego won't fit into his nest tonight." The man laughs. "Let me help you up and show you how the straps are tightened so you are ready to go."

We have just finished when I hear him mutter a curse and rush off toward the building the birds are housed in. Another group of Strixes and one Night Raven are led over to another group of recruits. I guess we aren't the only ones starting flight lessons today. I'm confused by the Night Raven, though. Didn't Sanders say unbound Night Ravens are nearly impossible to handle? Did someone borrow a bird from another rider? Is that even possible?

There seems to be a disagreement because the helpful man who was all smiles with me only minutes ago is facing off against another caretaker, both shouting.

Joel lands with Asta, his Rukh, right next to me, drawing my attention.

"Are your straps tightened?" he asks.

"And good morning to you, too, Joel. Yes, I have slept very well, thanks for asking. How are you today?"

He stares at me, not amused by my antics. "I'm serious," he says and looks around, but everyone's attention is on the arguing men. "If I have to tell —"

"You don't have to tell anyone anything," I snap. "And yes, they are tight enough. I even let the caregiver check. Satisfied?"

"No need to get pissy." He gives me a hurt look. "I'm only worried about you."

Great, now I feel bad.

"Yes, and that is very sweet of you." I heave out a breath, trying to curb my irritation. "But please tone it down a little," I plead. "I'm fine," I reassure him with a smile. "I'll even let you check again if that will make you feel better, but you'll have to check everyone else, too, or they'll think I get special treatment." I wink at him, making him laugh.

Joel raises his hands in surrender.

"Okay, I'll back off if you promise to leave those on no matter what." He points at the two pairs of thick leather straps securing my legs. "And I mean for all flight classes and not just today."

I crinkle my nose.

"I hate promises like that. They are so absolute. No wriggle room."

His face is serious. "That is exactly why I want one from you."

I shake my head. "How about I'll leave them on unless I have no other choice?"

He looks at me, contemplating my offer. Then he huffs out a breath. "Okay, fine. I'll take it." He holds my gaze expectantly.

I groan. "You are going to make me say it, right?"

He nods. "You seem to forget that I know you."

"Fine." I sigh. "I promise I'll leave those straps on unless I have no other choice. Happy?"

"As happy as I'll ever be as long as you are still here," Joel responds.

"Ouch," I wince, "great way to give me a complex."

He laughs. "For that to work you'd have to give a shit about other people's opinions." That comment stings a little. Does he really think I'm that callous?

Sanders clears his throat at the front. He sits on a Strix too. The big male with a scar across one eye is probably his bondmate.

"Okay, you are about to take your first ride. Just a little reminder: These birds are not horses, so don't dig your legs in or do anything like that. Most of the navigating is done by shifting your weight. If you need more, you tap the bird's neck. Everyone should know the commands by now, I hope. Also, they do understand you, but wind and other weather conditions can make it hard to communicate up there. Of course, you won't have that problem with your bonded birds."

Then it's time for take off. When the Strix catapults off the ground, I'm very happy about the straps keeping me in place. I nearly topple over backward, and my stomach visits my knees, thanks to the sudden acceleration, but I know one thing instantly: flying is awesome.

My Strix climbs, every powerful stroke of his wings vibrating through my body. Then he tucks them close and dives, and a mix of whooping and laughter bubbles out of me. This is incredible. I have never felt so alive before. Gravity claims me again when he flares his wings, and up we go again. Faces flash past us, all of them with the same wide smile.

Calix raises his hands over his head while his bird does a hard bank, his laughter infectious and carefree. Mariel's Strix shoots up in the sky, and she throws herself forward to keep upright. This is so worth all the risk and sore muscles.

I'm so grateful to this wonderful creature carrying me that I throw myself forward and hug him. He makes a few clicking sounds, and I hope he understands what I'm trying to tell him. With the wind whistling past us, a conversation is impossible, but he reacts so sensitively to weight shifts and taps on his neck, there is no need for words.

I'm so caught up in my bliss that it takes a while for the sound of shouts to register over the wind whipping past my ears. Above me, I find the cause for it. A Night Raven attacks one of the Strixes. Sunlight catches in bright red hair, and I realize the attacked Strix is Mariel's.

I get closer. The Night Raven's rider is Gorgon. His frantic gestures and commands don't seem to faze his bird.

Why is he riding a Night Raven?

The Night Raven climbs higher, ready to strike from above. Mariel's Strix tries to evade the attack, twisting and turning faster than I have ever seen a bird move. Mariel is tossed around like a rag doll, only the straps holding her in place.

Joel gets closer, shouting something. His Rukh dives in, hacking at the Night Raven, trying to drive him off. But the black bird only evades and goes for the Strix again.

The Strix twists, trying to evade the beak striking for him, then tumbles when they collide. Mariel cries out in pain, and I see a dark stain spreading on her left shoulder. If we don't do something, this will end badly.

Professor Sanders is now on it as well. He and Joel hover over the fighting birds.

They try to force them to land.

The fighting birds are descending, but slowly, too slowly.

I guide my Strix closer. He obeys, his feathers bristling.

"Mariel," I shout, trying to draw her attention. I have to yell her name a few times until she looks at me, her face tight with fear. The Night Raven attacks again.

Gorgon clings to the harness, his face pale, while his bird ignores his frantic commands.

"Watch out," I scream a warning. Mariel ducks, the Night Raven's talons missing her face, when her Strix dips hard to the right, evading the attacker.

Mariel is jostled around, clinging to the harness for dear life.

"I'll get you out of there," I promise even though she can't hear me.

My Strix is reluctant, but I steer him closer. Only two wingspans separate me and Mariel. Joel and our professor are still above us, slowly forcing the two birds to go lower.

"You'll have to jump," I shout. I start gesturing when she looks at me helplessly.

Mariel finally nods and starts loosening the straps on one side of the saddle. She leans over to get the ones on the other side when the Night Raven barrels into her Strix. Both birds twist in the air, and my bird dives to avoid a collision.

When I look back at the fighting bird, my breath catches. Mariel slides sideways, her form limp and slumped over. Only the strapped-in leg keeps her from falling.

"Mariel!" I shout, but she doesn't react and makes no move to right herself.

Shit, shit, shit.

Another collision. Her body slides farther to the side. With only one leg strapped in, I'm not sure how long she will stay in the saddle.

I make up my mind in a heartbeat, silently apologizing to Joel. I steer my Strix closer and slightly above the fighting birds, right next to Joel.

I look at him, let our eyes meet, and I see the moment realization hits him. He starts shaking his head, drawing in a deep breath. I already undid the buckles on our ascent, and I don't give him the chance to react before I jump.

My landing on the other Strix is rough, and only grabbing the saddle with one hand and Mariel with the other keeps me from sliding off right away.

I slide into the seat behind Mariel and secure the buckles around my legs while freeing her. I grab her waist with both arms, holding on for dear life when the Strix goes into a dive, trying to outmaneuver his attacker. With two of us weighing him down now, his movement is strained and slower.

"What the fuck are you doing?" Joel roars at me, his bird hovering next to me for a second before he attacks the Night Raven, trying to turn him away. When he gets close again, I motion toward Mariel.

"Can you catch her?" I yell.

"We can take both of you. Just jump with her." He lets his Rukh lose height, getting slightly below us.

I shake my head. "Too much weight," I shout back. I'm also not ready to give up the Strix, but I'm not going to tell him that. Streaks of bright red color the white and gray feathers of the bird beneath me, and the movement of his wings is labored.

Joel doesn't look happy, and I'm sure his moving lips mean he is cursing up a storm, but he nods.

"I'm coming back for you, and then you'll jump."

I smile reassuringly and give my consent. His Rukh loses height. Once he is below us and gives me the go, I heave Mariel over the side, letting her go before the fighting birds can move again. She tumbles through the air, and I lose sight of her when the Strix twists.

Joel will catch her.

The next time the Night Raven collides with us, I meet Gorgon's frightened eyes. Right. I forgot about him.

"You have to jump off," I scream, but he shakes his head. "This won't end well." I try to get through to him.

He sets his jaw. "I'll be fine," he says. "The Night Raven will win." My jaw drops. How can anyone think of winning at a moment like this?

I shake my head and concentrate on the bird beneath me instead. I stroke his feathers soothingly, getting ready to implement my plan.

The Night Raven breaks away to gather momentum. I give the Strix the signal to dive, and he does. We turn and swoop, making it harder for the Night Raven to catch us, masking my plan in the process.

We head straight to the cliff behind Telos. It is steep and wide, like someone chopped off a part of the mountain to make room for the city below. We come closer, and I spot the flaw in my scheme. The Strix is too tired to pull up at such an angle with my added weight on his back. I'll have to get off to give him a chance to make it.

"Head straight to your nest and caregiver," I shout, hoping he hears me, before I pull the dagger off my belt and slash the straps on both my legs. I swing a leg over his side, and when we pass the city wall, I jump.

I misjudged the effect speed has on my body. The Strix's right wing clips my shoulder and sends me tumbling. My body's right side hits the top of the city wall, the impact rattles my bones, and my whole side goes numb for one blessed second before the pain hits. I curse wordlessly, and the world goes black.

I'm back home sitting in a tree, and I'm momentarily disoriented. I look down at my legs; they are much shorter than I'm used to. My brothers are searching for something or someone below me.

I remember this moment. I was around eight and hid in the forest after a fight with Ben. My brothers had been shouting at each other, and I fled so no one would see me cry.

I watch them and see the growing concern on their faces. I don't want them to worry, and I don't want to get them into trouble either.

So I call out to Dar when he starts to head back home. His gaze flies up, relief washing over his handsome face once his eyes find me.

I grin down at him.

"I'm still better than all of you at climbing," I brag.

A small smile tugs on the corner of his mouth, like he's trying to suppress it. He nods.

"True. How about you come down here without breaking your neck?" he asks.

"Okay." I push off the branch I'm sitting on and see Dar rushing forward.

"*Ara!*" he shouts. *I land on a thicker branch below me and jump off. My hands grab another branch, and I swing back and forth for a few seconds before I let go and slam into Dar. He wraps his strong arms around me, grumbling.*

"*I would have landed just fine.*" *I smile at him.* "*But thanks for catching me.*" *I kiss his cheek before I wriggle out of his arms.*

I hear a voice and feel arms tighten around me, lifting me. My body hurts.

"I think I landed wrong this time, Dar," I mumble. "No wings after all."

I groan when I am jostled. My cheek stings when it hits something firm. There is a rhythmic sound beneath my ear—a heartbeat. Someone is carrying me, but it isn't one of my brothers; the smell is wrong.

Breathing hurts.

Wait, what? Why does my body hurt so much?

There is something important I have to remember. I flail, fighting the darkness around me, and someone curses.

"Stop fighting, Gray, or I'll drop you."

Calix? Why is Calix carrying me?

"You'll be fine," he continues while relief floods me. Calix is safe. I relax, drifting off. "I'll get you to the healers real quick. They'll fix you right up," he says while I fight the blackness closing in.

CHAPTER
EIGHTEEN
TATE

I face Jared in weaponless combat, anticipating his next move. He's damn fast, and since we know each other's movements like our own, it's always challenging. One moment of inattention can make all the difference.

We alternate in our attacks, the movements fluid like a dance. Punches meet blocks or air most of the time, so Jared's grunt when I sneak past his defense is satisfying.

"*Your first year needs help again,*" Daeva chimes in, making me stop mid-swing.

"Summer?" I ask, while I keep my attention on the fist going for my chin, dodging it.

"*She has guts.*" Daeva sounds approving, and that has never happened before.

Commotion spreads from the doorway, and someone calls my name. I catch Jared's arm before I search for the source.

It's one of our first years calling me over—Calix Ilario. He's hard to overlook and draws murmurs in his wake, with what Daeva just told me... I turn in his direction, releasing Jared.

"What the fuck did she do?" I ask Daeva the moment Ilario steps through the crowd surrounding us, carrying someone. I don't need to signal for a break because Jared is already with me. We both reach him in a few quick steps.

I curse under my breath when my eyes land on Summer.

"Damn. Someone got you real good." Jared whistles through his teeth.

"She jumped off a flying Strix," Daeva says.

"You jumped off a Strix?" I step closer, taking in the mess that is Summer's face, fighting the urge to check her over right here and now.

"Yeah and still fought me like a demon until I agreed to bring him to you instead of the healers," Ilario says, gazing down at his friend like he still doubts that decision.

"I'm fine. Let me down, Calix." Summer winces. The right side of her face is a swollen purple mess, her skin torn in places like she slid over something rough, and the split on her lip opens back up while she speaks.

He growls down at her. "I'm not setting you down, Gray. You weigh nothing, and you'll only fall over again." He sounds exasperated. "You didn't even know who I was in the beginning. Called me a collection of names that weren't mine and apologized for not having wings."

Shit, that doesn't sound good. I look her over, but her loose clothes hide everything but her face.

"I'll take over from here." I hold out my arms to take Summer. Ilario looks at me warily, hesitating before handing her over. Once again, I'm wondering how close they are.

"Get back to classes and just...keep it quiet, okay?" I order Ilario.

He nods. "Not sure there is a way to keep that quiet, but I'll do my best." His gaze wanders to Summer, who is now nestled in my arms and sends her a crooked smile. "No more jumping off flying Strixes, alright?" he admonishes and gives me another nod before he leaves.

"I can walk by myself." Summer glares up at me, daring me to disagree, but the effect is spoiled by her battered face and the one eye that is nearly swollen shut by now. She definitely took a hit against the head, and if Ilario is right and she's disoriented and can't stay upright, I better get to work.

"I'm sure you can. But I haven't got all day," I say and ignore her grumbling while I stride out of the room.

She jumped off a flying Strix? What the fuck?

Calix is right to admonish her, but he's also right about something else: she's ridiculously lightweight.

"What was that about jumping off Strixes?" I ask.

"He wouldn't have been able to pull up otherwise." She winces. Speaking clearly pains her, so I'll hold off on the questions for now.

"*Can you get me the whole story?*" I ask Daeva instead. If birds were involved, she could get me answers quicker than anyone else.

"*Sure,*" Daeva caws. "*This is how it ended.*" She sends me a memory. Summer on the back of a Strix, his movements labored, his feathers streaked with blood, going straight for the cliff right behind Telos. My breath catches in my throat. They are never going to pull up in time.

He wouldn't have been able to pull up otherwise. That had been her words. I watch helplessly as she throws herself off the Strix, tumbles through the air, slams into the top of the city wall, and doesn't move again. The memory stops. I pull in a stuttering breath.

Holy mists.

I look down at the woman in my arms to assure myself that she still lives.

The hallways to the living quarters are empty at this time of the day, and my feet carry me to my room without thinking. I open the door with my gift, and Summer stiffens in my arms.

Is she uncomfortable being alone with Jared and me? I chose

privacy because of her lie about her identity, but maybe she isn't okay with that? That reminds me that Jared isn't in on her secret.

"How bad is it?" I look down at her and try to convey my other question with a look. *Is it okay if Jared knows?* She shakes her head. So I will have to find something for him to do. But if this is going to be something regular, I'll fill him in, with or without her permission.

"My head hurts, I can't move my right arm, and every time I try, it feels like someone is burying a knife in it. My ribs hurt when I breathe. My leg hurts too..."

"Can you get us a healing kit and something to clean Summer up a little? I can't see shit like that," I ask Jared. It isn't the best excuse, but I can't think of anything else at the moment. Jared simply nods and leaves.

I put her down on my bed and lock the door. "We don't have much time, so strip, Summer."

"I would be happy to oblige, considering I'm sitting on your bed and all, but I think I need a hand." I fight a smirk at her sass, relief coursing through me. Her attitude must mean she already feels better. The other part—well, it's hard not to let that affect me.

Maneuvering her shirt, I help Summer get out of it, freeing her bad arm last.

There is purple discoloration and swelling all over the right side of her body.

Her right shoulder looks asymmetric compared to the other side and is probably dislocated. I go over her collarbones to rule out any breaks and encounter a bump on the left side, but she doesn't flinch or make a sound. "Does that hurt?" I ask.

"No, that's old." Her voice sounds raspy. The implication hits me a second later, and I still. This broken bone healed on its own. She must have been in pain for weeks. Who lets anyone go through that when healers are so easy to come by?

The urge to deal out pain to anyone who let her suffer like that rushes through me.

She avoids my gaze, and I swallow the questions lying on my

tongue since I have the feeling she would rather walk out than answer them. But I will get to the bottom of this once she's no longer in pain.

I assess her ribs and am relieved to find them intact. Her skin is so soft I could skim over it for hours, but I resist the temptation and try even harder to ignore the goose bumps popping up all over her skin. She's so damn responsive to my touch.

There are no signs of damage to her spine either, and I'm relieved. I can handle bruises, cuts, and even tears and simple breaks. But for more complicated things, I would have to get her to a healer. Given Ilario's words and her reaction, I'm not sure that would go over well.

Seeing the extent of her bruising makes me grit my teeth. My emotional response to seeing her hurt unnerves me.

I notice scars, too many of them. Some even show signs of stitching.

I swallow. No wonder she's wary of letting anyone look at her wounds. Who would do something so savage?

I'm careful while assessing her shoulder, but she inhales sharply as soon as I touch it, and I find my suspicion confirmed.

"I have to pop your shoulder back in," I say, resenting that I have to hurt her again.

"Just do it." She sounds resigned.

"Can you lie down on your belly, the right arm over the edge of the bed?" I help her out of her boots and position her, using one of my shirts to cushion her shoulder. "Now relax." She seems a lot more at ease around me than last time. Maybe she's starting to trust me. "Just like that." Slowly, I pull her arm down. My gaze catches on a dark line in the crook of her arm. That wasn't there last time, was it?

Her shoulder pops back in as soon as I move the arm slightly forward. Her breath hitches, and she sighs in relief.

"Better now?" I ask.

She nods.

"Let's get you on your back." I guide her arm while she turns, draping it across her belly. My gaze is drawn to the dark marking again because that is what it is. She sees me noticing but evades my gaze. "There are a few things we have to talk about," I say. My eyes lock on her.

"No, we don't," she answers, her jaw set.

"Yes, we do," I disagree. When she doesn't react, I let it slide—for now. "Let me see your face so we can start with the healing."

She closes her eyes, nodding to let me know she's ready. Her lashes are dark against her pale skin, and she looks softer and vulnerable. I skim my thumb over her cheek and brush some loose strands out of her face.

"Do you trust me?" The words are out before I even realize I'm going to ask that. Her eyes fly open, the wariness loud and clear. She doesn't, and it irks me. I want her trust.

I shove down my ridiculous feelings. She's not mine. I have to remember that.

When I stay quiet, her eyes flutter closed again.

She doesn't make a sound when I use my magic to straighten out a fracture in her cheekbone, but twin tears streak down her battered face, vanishing in her hair, slaying me.

I avert my gaze before I give in and wipe them away.

What is it with this girl?

I place my hands gently on the bare skin of her shoulders and let my magic flow. Just like last time, she stiffens. But she doesn't jerk away this time, so I count that as progress. I pour in even more magic, unbearably aware of my fingers on her bare skin. My eyes roam over her face, looking for change.

Her breathing becomes easier, her body relaxes, and the bruises fade. The cut on her lip closes, and the swelling goes down until only the dried blood remains. Summer exhales slowly, her eyes fluttering open when I lift my hands.

Sweat beads her brow, and she fights a yawn. The hand resting over her chest trembles, but she hides it when she sees me noticing.

Our eyes lock. Little flecks of gold hide amid the blue and green, like sunlight playing on the ocean's depths. I could drown in those eyes. Her pupils widen. Awareness gathers between us like a bowstring snapping taut.

The jiggling of the door handle, followed by a knock, snaps me out of my trance. Jared is back.

"Just a minute." My voice sounds husky, and Ara shoots off the bed like we have been caught red-handed. I grab the shirt next to me and pull it over her head.

Only realizing it's mine when it falls to her thighs. It's the one I used to cushion her shoulder. She winces while shoving her arms in the sleeves, seemingly not caring that it's the wrong shirt. She avoids my gaze, and there is an awkwardness between us I don't like.

"You may be sore for a few days," I say in an effort to dispel the tension, gesturing to her arm.

Ara rolls her shoulders, wincing a little, drawing my gaze to her mouth.

"That's what a girl wants to hear coming out of a man's bed," Summer says. Her eyes widen, and her hand flies to her mouth, covering it.

She looks up at me, heat sparking between us.

The knock sounds again.

Impatient jerk.

I go over to the door, still trying to get rid of the images Summer just planted in my mind. Her voice husky with want, her skin slick with sweat against mine...

I take a deep breath, but her scent, invading my senses like she has wrapped herself around me, does not help.

A knock sounds again, jarring me out of my fantasies and stopping me from doing something stupid like exploring that statement with her.

I unlock the door and curse under my breath, tempted to slam it shut again. Jared is not alone. Cassius is with him.

"What are you doing here, Cassius?" I snap.

"Don't be an ass." Summer steps next to me.

"Did you just call me an ass?" I glower down at her.

"No, I told you not to be one." She grins up at me. She's enjoying this.

Cassius does a double take when he notices my shirt on Summer, and I smirk.

"What were you thinking?" he hisses, pulling Summer into his arms, and she lets him.

Not your girl. I take a deep breath, try to relax my hands that have curled into fists, and stop grinding my teeth.

I can't knock out a squadron leader for hugging a runner, can I?

Summer frees herself and takes the water from Jared, thanking him and striding back into my room while Cassius glowers at her back.

"You drown in that shirt. What is wrong with yours?" he asks.

Summer snatches her shirt off my bed and holds Cassius's gaze while dipping a clean part into the bowl, then cleaning her face.

"It's wet and bloody," she answers.

Jared snickers.

Damn. She sure loves ruffling some feathers. I feel a little sorry for that brother of hers they mentioned, and maybe even for Cassius...okay, I don't.

Life can't be easy with a girl like that—but not dull either.

"You missed a few spots." Cassius beckons her over and takes the shirt from her, cradling the base of her head with one hand while he cleans the blood off her face.

I take a deep breath since beating the shit out of him isn't an option. Holy mists...I need to harden myself against this...attraction. Against her. Reestablish the distance between us.

CHAPTER NINETEEN

ARA

I just returned to our room and changed into a new uniform when I'm summoned to Professor Sanders's office. The rider accompanying me gives me a pitying glance.

I'm in trouble.

I haven't seen anyone after Kyronos healed me. Tate. I silently let his name roll off my tongue and decide lying half naked in his bed justifies using his first name—even if it's just in my head.

The room I share with the runners of my flight was empty when I came back, which puts me on edge, too. They should have been back by now.

It won't be too bad. I only helped another runner. Having each other's backs is the basis of being part of a flight, right?

All the reassurance I pull from that thought evaporates when I enter the office. Not only is Sanders waiting for me but also Legatus Janus. My stomach drops. *Shit.*

Their faces are grave, and their eyes pin me in place as soon as I enter.

I swallow.

The door clicks shut behind me like a trap.

"Summer, your actions today go against everything I taught you," Sanders says. I want to object, but his eyes let me know that would not be wise, so I clamp my mouth shut.

"However," the Professor continues, "you acted with good intentions, and you are not solely to blame for the tragedy. The Night Raven should never have been up in the sky with us."

Tragedy? What is he talking about?

"But even if not intentional, your action led to the death of—"

A knock on the door interrupts him. My stomach turns.

Oh gods, did Joel not catch Mariel? Did I kill her by throwing her off the Strix's back? But he didn't say anything.

I'm caught between demanding answers and clapping my hands over my ears. I need to know, but I'm not sure if I'm ready to hear it.

I don't turn around, but the warm glow of his magic tells me Tate just entered the room, and someone else is with him, the gift not as bright as Tate's.

"Centurion Kyronos, Centurion Vega, I'm glad you can join us," Legatus Janus's booming voice greets the newcomers while he had no more than a glare for me. He gestures for Sanders to continue.

I really am in trouble.

"You were informed what happened?" Sanders asks the centurions.

"Yes, Professor, we were informed," Vega answers. I glance at Tate, and he nods in agreement, his eyes fixed on Sanders.

Great, so everyone knows but me.

"We decided on a punishment for Summer's action—"

"Punishment for what?" I ask. I really tried to wait it out, but not knowing is killing me here. Four gazes lock onto me, and I try not to squirm. If I'm going to be punished, I want to at least know what it's for.

"Are you serious?" Vega explodes behind me. "Is taking a runner's life not punishable in—"

"Summer was hurt." Tate's voice interrupts him coolly. "He doesn't know." That cuts off the rant.

"Right, Ilario said you bumped your head," Sanders says.

Tate coughs, but he doesn't say anything.

"I trust you're all healed now?" Legatus Janus asks.

I nod and hastily add, "Yes, Legatus," when I see his eyes narrowing at my informal answer.

"Great. Then I don't see any reason to delay," Janus says. "You need to learn to follow orders, runner, and until I know you can, you are banned from flight classes. The only reason I don't throw you out right now is because Sanders is convinced of your good intentions and because you also saved a life today." Janus turns to Sanders. "I trust you can take it from here. I have a lot to do, consoling a grieving friend being one of them." He sends me another glare and strides out the door.

"How about I start with a short explanation so we're all on the same page," Sanders says. "Gorgon Foley used his father's influence and money to get his way of riding a Night Raven instead of a Strix. The responsible caretaker, my assistant—who was overseeing his class—and Gorgon's squadron leader, are seeing disciplinary actions as well. But Gorgon paid the ultimate price for his actions, as did the stubborn bird."

I'm lightheaded, the blood rushing from my face.

Gorgon and the Night Raven died?

"That bird should have never been up in the air during flight classes," Sanders states. "Summer disobeyed orders, but I do not doubt that it's only due to his unquestionably reckless behavior that Mariel Tethys and the Strix are still alive."

I release a breath, which earns me a glare from Vega.

I'm allowed to be glad about Mariel being okay, aren't I? Yes, it's shit that Gorgon died, but I did what I could when I warned him.

"And Gorgon Foley dead," Vega cuts in. "Everyone knows Night

Ravens don't break off an attack, and I heard this one"—Vega nods in my direction—"had a feud with Gorgon going."

"I did not," I protest. "I even told him he had to jump, or it wouldn't end well for him."

"He tells the truth," Tate tells Vega when the man doesn't look convinced. That seems to do it because his glare toward me softens.

"I watched Summer jump onto the back of another Strix to save one of the runners of his flight. I think that alone speaks for his character," Sanders adds. "However, Legatus Janus decided that it would be best for Summer to experience reality as a rider to drive the importance of obedience home."

"You mean to tell us Summer will join us for training, right?" Tate asks sharply.

Sanders looks uncomfortable at that but meets my eyes when he says. "I'm afraid not. He wants you to join one of the active flights for... everything." The way he says it makes it clear he doesn't agree with that decision.

"What?" Tate calls out. "Since when do we use runners as target practice for our enemies?"

"Excuse me?" I turn to him.

Is he calling me useless here?

"I can hold my own with a sword." I challenge him with a glare, but Tate simply waves me off. My face heats in anger.

Oh no, I don't fucking think so.

"He is as good as dead out there," Vega declares.

Are they being serious right now?

Vega sees my look and adds, "No offense, kid, but Foley is Janus's right hand, and this is nothing but a veiled execution."

That does kill my indignation.

I look at Sanders, but he doesn't meet my gaze, so I guess Vega is right on the money.

Shit. They don't expect me to get back from this?

"We'll see about that," Tate grumbles. "Summer is in my division and under my protection." He looks at Sanders and Vega like he expects one of them to contradict him.

"That won't win you any favors," Sanders says.

Are we still talking about me joining Tate's flight here?

"It really doesn't matter at this point." Tate shrugs.

"Well, then Summer is with Kyronos." Sanders nods and looks at Vega.

Vega nods. "If he came with us, he would be dead after the first night." He looks at me. "Gorgon was one of us and had a lot of friends, but you don't seem as bad as I expected." *Is that supposed to be a compliment?* "So yeah, I think that is the best."

"Well then..." Sanders claps his hands together and turns to me. "You are, until further notice, under Centurion Kyronos's and Squadron Leader Tanner's command. You are expected to attend class whenever you are free and to make up anything you missed during your free time as well. Other than that, you will be part of the first squadron for the time being and train, eat, and fight with them."

"But I don't have a bird." I point out the obvious.

"Yes, I'm aware of that. That is why Kyronos will assign you a partner for patrols."

It seems like I will be seeing a lot more of Tate Kyronos in the coming weeks, and that while needing to stay focused so I don't get myself killed. I huff out a breath while I follow Vega and Tate out the door.

Vega gives us a wave and strides off, and I grab Tate's arm just as he intends to do the same. He goes rigid under my touch and glares at me.

Have I offended him somehow?

"Wait, I just wanted to thank you for having my back like that," I say.

"It's the least I can do, considering what you did for me, isn't it?" he replies, his voice harsh. Yes, he's angry.

"Listen, if I did—"

"I will get the patrol schedule to you by tonight." He interrupts me. "And I expect you to be up and in the weight room at the fifth hour tomorrow. See you then." He walks off without a backward glance.

Okay then, I guess at least one of us is not happy to see more of the other.

I make my way back to our room, ignoring the looks and whispers I receive on my way there. Damn, I have to work on keeping my head down. Otherwise, I will blow my cover long before Picking.

Or I will be dead by then.

The latter seems more likely at the moment.

I only let my shoulders slump once I step through the door of our room and find myself immediately enveloped in slender arms and lots of red hair.

"Gray! Thank Elet, you're all right." Calix's voice booms through the room before he throws his arms around Mariel and me and squeezes until we both gasp for air.

"I'm not sure it's for long, though," I tell them once I have detangled myself.

"Vega thinks I got Gorgon killed on purpose," I say, unable to meet their eyes.

"What?" Calix shouts.

"But the stupid bird flew into the wall," Mariel says. "You didn't make him do that."

"He really did?" My eyes go wide. "I just thought the wall would slow him down so the Strix could escape."

"It's not your fucking fault," Mariel seethes. "Putting that on you is unfair!"

The rest of my flight seconds that thought, and their outrage about the accusation makes me feel better, especially since the stares in the hallways have been less than friendly.

I brace myself to share the real news. "Janus banned me from flight classes. I'm assigned to Ta— Kyronos's flight for training, exercise ... everything."

"You mean while here at the Aerie, right?" Mariel asks.

I shake my head. "No, I get the patrol schedule tonight."

There is only shocked silence.

"Shit. Well, we have your back, Gray," Calix declares.

"We can help you make up the classes you'll miss," Mariel joins in. Every runner in the room nods in agreement, and my throat closes up. They are unbelievable.

The following morning starts early for me, and while the time is nothing new, the amount of training I undergo by the time we stand in formation is staggering. I'm ready to go back to bed.

My flight surrounds me while we attend Gorgon's funeral, a friendly barrier against all the hostile stares. If I had any doubt left about his father's position, it's moot now. The funeral for Gorgon is far more elaborate than anything we have had so far.

It is definitely more than just saying a few words and giving us time to slip into the temple between formation and the start of classes.

Even the start of classes has been delayed for half an hour, and they expect us all to attend. I stay in the back of the temple, far from anyone close to him, like Livia.

I'm still not sure how to feel about Gorgon's death. It's not like we were friends or he was a likable person at all, but was it my fault? Am I to blame for his death?

Livia stands in front, right next to Gorgon's decorated body. Tears keep pouring down her face, and she sniffles. I have seen her and Gorgon together, but I didn't know it had been that serious between them.

When she catches me watching, she glares at me. I huff out a breath.

At least I tried to do something.

Livia's glare drew attention, and quite a few unfriendly stares are aimed my way now, most of them from runners and riders of the eastern division.

It's not like I've seen them rushing to his help. I didn't intentionally harm him. They have to realize that at some point, right?

"Ignore them," Mariel whispers from my right. My gaze wanders back to Livia. An older man in a rider uniform follows her gaze, landing on me. He leans over to her, and they exchange words. His gaze hardens, and his jaw tenses. Whatever she said seems to have gained me another person who isn't fond of me.

"Who is next to Livia?" I lean to my left and into Calix to get his attention. His gaze searches the crowd until he finds the one I'm talking about. He exhales.

"You mean the one glaring at you?" he asks.

"Probably." I keep my gaze averted, trying not to be too obvious.

"That would be the deputy commander, Gorgon's dad," Calix whispers.

"I'm officially garnering enemies in executive positions." I sigh.

"Yes, you have a polarizing effect on people. Maybe it would be good to keep your head down for a while?" he suggests.

"That's what I was doing all along," I grumble.

"I hate to tell you, but you're not doing a very good job of it," he answers.

No, it doesn't seem like I am.

Joel is still angry with me. I don't blame him, but I don't feel bad for what I did, either—despite the consequences.

Mariel is still alive, after all. She expresses her gratitude by being practically glued to my side whenever I'm around. With the extra training, keeping up with classes, and everything else that shifted in my daily routine, it's hard to find time to keep up my research, but not being in his squadron makes it easier to evade Joel.

Yes, we are back to that.

Oh, I'm aware that he tries to catch me by myself. I'm also aware that he will probably shout at me and start planning to smuggle me out again. It's just easier to avoid him altogether.

I slump down into the soft cushions of the well-used armchair and just sit there for a moment, enjoying the quiet of the library. It's only been two days since I joined the riders of the beak flight of the first squadron, and I'm already exhausted. I was paired with one of the female riders, Zaza, and she took me on a training flight today. It was only a couple of hours, but my back and thighs made themselves known. I have no idea how I'll survive being on a bird for the better part of a week soon.

I open the book I retrieved from its hiding place and continue reading where I left off. The fable is dark, all doom and gloom just like all the others. It's about a cursed girl who leaves her village to find someone to teach her. But one sentence catches my attention.

And while she grows into her power, magic etches patterns into her skin.

It's the first mention of markings on a cursed one, but the story ends in death and destruction, like always.

Even if I try not to, it's starting to trouble me. Is it her curse that taints her? Is it the master she chose? Is it her revenge? Is the story only designed to scare, or is there truth to it?

I haven't found any mention of a time when cursed ones weren't hunted, either. Calix is already teasing me about all the history books I check out. I keep the more obvious ones hidden behind other books until I'm done reading instead of checking them out. It's not the only thing I'll get in trouble for if I'm caught. I look guiltily at the honey cookies I smuggled in, sitting next to a flask of hot tea. I pick up my steaming mug and take a sip. The library is quite chilly, and I'm thankful for the warmth.

I dive into the next story. It's about a cursed man hunted down by the king's men for killing innocents. I sigh.

Why do we have to be the bad guys in all of them?

A throat clears, and I know who it is even before I look up. Tate leans against the bookcase opposite the armchair I'm curled up in. His gaze is on the cookies and the steaming mug of tea in my hand.

"You look comfortable. Do you plan to stay longer?" he asks.

I nod toward the cookies.

"Want one? I charmed them off the kitchen staff." To my surprise, he comes over and settles down in the chair next to me but declines the cookie.

I scan the titles in his hand. They are all about the Ice Coast again. So he's still researching the Tracers. I want to ask him about it, want to know why he had a pair of them with him the last time I met him here, but I don't. I want him to stay, so I go back to my story and smile to myself when I hear him rustling through his books next to me.

We stay like that, both reading in comfortable silence.

I only realize the warmth once I step out of the little nook, the cool air pebbling my skin.

I look back at Tate, but he doesn't look up. I spot a slight glimmer in the air around the armchairs.

He must have a gift for air.

Knowing he shared his warmth with me ignites a glow inside me.

The same repeats the following evening. We spend it in comfortable silence. Not exchanging a word, just smiling and nodding at each other as a way of greeting. No questions asked even though I see his curious looks, and I'm sure he notices mine. It's like both of us know the other might bolt if pushed.

The evening after that, I find a blanket on the armchair I normally use, which makes it cozy even though Tate doesn't show up.

Guilt coils in my gut at his thoughtfulness, knowing I won't be here tomorrow because I'll meet Sloan despite everything Tate did to keep me out of trouble.

Not going just isn't an option. If my letters stop coming, at least one of my brothers will come down to check on me, and I can't have that.

CHAPTER TWENTY
TATE

Since she's going to be around me all the time now, I gave up on avoiding Ara. I enjoyed her company in the library so much that I deliberately stayed away yesterday. I want to ask questions she's not ready to answer.

My gaze wanders over to her, where she's currently training with Zaza. She's good with a sword and has no problem holding her own against the woman who has at least five years on her. I wonder who trained her because her form is excellent.

It's six weeks since the recruits started, and while we are still deep in winter, today feels more like spring. It's much warmer here in the south than what I'm used to from home, not that I'm complaining. The windows toward the atrium are open, letting in a fresh breeze, but the sparring hall is still too warm.

We have been training for over an hour, and all the men of our flight have lost their shirts by now. Even the women stripped down to their undershirts.

Only Summer is still fully dressed. And I'm wondering if I'm the only one noticing.

Today is a holiday, and unless we have guard duty, we are free, but that is no reason to slack off on training.

"I will drag you out to a bar tonight." Jared grins and jumps back to avoid the grab I make for him. "No need to get violent."

I chuckle, shaking my head. "Should have figured you'd fill my free evening for me. How come I don't get a say in this?"

"Because I want a beer with my best friend. How's that for a reason?" I hear other voices as another flight enters the sparring hall that, up until now, we had to ourselves. I keep my focus on Jared, not paying them any mind.

"I'll tell you what," Jared continues. "The best out of three, and whoever wins gets to decide about tonight. I'll even hang out in the library with you if that is your idea of fun these days," he teases, and I agree.

I win the first round, and we are well into the second when I hear a snide voice next to us.

"Maybe we should take our training outside," a female says. "I'm not in the mood to rub elbows with scum and murderers." My eyebrows jump up, Jared bristles, and we both turn to see who said that. "What do you expect when they let someone like him lead a division?" a tall, blond girl states, seemingly uncaring that she has everyone's attention now.

Rumors and hostility started when I was a runner, and someone spotted the mark over my heart. A few busted lips and broken bones cured people attacking me openly and earned me a certain reputation, but there isn't much I can do about the rumors without revealing my past, so they stick around... but murderer, that is a new one.

"And if manners and common sense could be bought, some people would actually be pleasant to be around." I know that voice. Summer's comment makes our whole flight crack up.

Is she picking a fight to defend me?

She and Zaza continue sparring like nothing happened, Zaza chuckling, and Ara grinning. Completely unaware of or ignoring the glares of the small group of people standing close to our mat.

I recognize the tall one now, Vaccari, the one Ara never gets along with, whatever the reason.

Another group of people enters the room, riders of the eastern division, this time. I tense.

"She humiliates me after everything she did," Vaccari whines, instantly addressing Vega.

"Centurion, get your runner under control," Vega hisses, and I turn to him to give him a piece of my mind, but Ara is faster.

My eyes widen when I see her stepping up to Vega, somehow managing to look down at a man who is not only taller but also outranks her.

"How about you get your runner under control?" she asks. "She comes waltzing in here throwing around accusations aimed at me and my centurion, while I simply stated facts. So if she feels addressed by 'someone without manners and common sense,' the boot seems to fit, doesn't it?"

"I'm not sure if I should congratulate him on the size of his balls or tell him to grow some sense," Jared whispers next to me, clearly awed. I agree, but my gaze is glued to Summer. I'm sure the situation will escalate in a second, so I throw up a shield between her and the eastern division, molding it to her to keep it from view. We are not allowed to use our gifts on other runners or riders unless it's an officially declared training bout with gifts or in case of an attack. I count this loosely to the second group.

Summer's eyes wander to me. Did she somehow see my shield?

The whole flight steps closer. Ara is one of us, even if it's temporary.

"What did you say?" Vega demands to know from Vaccari, and she hems and haws, clearly not willing to repeat herself.

"It was: I'm not in the mood to rub elbows with scum and

murderers and what do you expect when they let someone like him lead a division?" Ara replies helpfully. Vaccari stares daggers at her, then crosses her arms in defiance.

"I'm not wrong, though. He's a murderer," Vaccari points at Summer and then turns to me. "And he wears his disgrace stamped on his skin."

Jared tenses next to me, his normally pleasant face murderous. But before either of us has the chance to react, Summer does.

She laughs.

Vaccari whips around, her glare once again on Summer.

"What are you laughing at?" she barks.

"You." Ara chuckles.

"You think I'm funny?" Vaccari seethes.

"Either that or delusional." Summer shrugs.

"It says dishonored right there," Vaccari snaps and dares to point at the mark on my chest.

"You know that's where you are wrong." Summer strolls over to me, and lays her fingers right over the two parallel lines that make all the difference, her fingers now resting right above my heart.

My pulse jumps, and her gaze comes up to meet mine. Her eyes widen, and her lips part slightly. The awareness on her face burns through my veins. I've touched her body a few times by now, but this is the first time her fingers rest on mine, and we both know it.

She snatches her hand back like she got burned.

"He gave up a position out of his own choice," she says, her eyes still fixed on me. Gods, a man could drown in those eyes.

She turns to Vaccari and walks back, stopping right in front of her.

"Get your markings right before you throw around accusations."

I don't like the look on Vaccari's face, so I once more throw up a shield between them.

Vega shakes his head at Vaccari.

"Your father's position doesn't do shit for you here," he warns her. "You better work on your attitude. You'll help out with breakfast for the whole week. I'm sure the kitchen staff will be grateful, and I hope you learn something from it."

Vega and his riders wander over to the free mats at the end of the hall, and the rest of our flight goes back to their training as well, leaving only Vaccari and her friends, Summer, Jared, and me.

I step closer. I don't trust Vaccari. She leans in and only my gift lets me listen in.

"Watch your back, killer." There is ice in her voice, but Ara doesn't seem perturbed.

"Your boyfriend got himself killed. I didn't have anything to do with it."

"You killed him," Vaccari hisses, and when her hand goes to her blade, I move.

I step behind Summer, fighting the urge to pull her behind my back.

"Careful or you'll find out how fast you can trip and fall onto your own blade." My voice is low and quiet, but Vaccari gets the warning, taking a step back, no longer so sure of herself.

"Maybe you should ask someone in your division what happened to Flaccus," I tell her, and she turns and leaves the hall without another word.

"What happened to Flaccus?" Summer asks.

"I beat him to within an inch of his life," I tell her.

"Well, then he must have deserved it." Summer smiles and goes back to her mat like nothing happened. I don't know what reaction I expected, but that hadn't been it.

Jared and I exchange a look.

"I knew I liked him for a reason." Jared smirks.

I nod, but my thoughts are hung up on two things—she hadn't judged me, hadn't even flinched when I told her I nearly killed another rider, and she displayed knowledge only common in circles carrying high positions. They are the ones who need to know the difference between someone being stripped of their rank and someone giving it up willingly. And that circle isn't too big.

There is no way we haven't met before if she grew up like I suspect she did.

And the no judging part...yeah, I'm not going to analyze why that warmed my chest from within. But I'm distracted, which gives Jared the advantage he needs to beat me. So I'll have plenty of time to contemplate those thoughts over a beer tonight.

ARA

I should have kept my mouth shut. From the moment Livia Vaccari opened hers, I knew she would only spout shit.

Seeing Tate without his shirt had been enough to make me stare, smooth golden skin over devastatingly cut muscles, the markings running up the whole length of his right arm and spilling onto his chest and down his right side until they vanished into the waistband of his pants. My fingers had itched with the need to touch him, trace the black lines, and slip over the ridges of his abs. But it had been the mark on his left chest that had snapped me out of my reverie. It looked like an ornate X set over his heart, and when my eyes landed on the two parallel lines beneath, I was stunned and angry.

Dishonored, my ass. Whatever he had given up had been willingly. True, it wasn't common to see someone give up a position out of choice, but how the fuck did anyone dare to give him shit about that and why didn't he say something?

I had still been fuming about the injustice when Livia started spewing shit and I couldn't stay quiet. I couldn't. If that earned me more enemies, it was well worth it. Who was counting at this point, anyway?

"You know what, Summer? I like you," Zaza declares while we are heading to lunch.

"Me too." Jared comes up from behind us and throws an arm around our shoulders. Zaza tenses for a second before she relaxes. She sends me a wide smile, her teeth startlingly bright against her dark skin. I wonder if she and Jared have a history.

Jared congratulates me on the way I dealt with Livia before flitting off when someone calls him.

"Is there something between Jared and you?" I ask Zaza as soon as Jared is out of earshot.

"Nah, I'm not his type," she tells me.

"Why? You are beautiful, kind, and funny, and really good with a sword," I tell her honestly. She looks at me like I am a little puppy before biting her lip.

"That is really cute of you to say, Summer, but...unfortunately, you are a little young for me." She gives me an apologetic smile.

She thought I was coming on to her?

"No, I...uh..." I stammer. Fuck, how do I get out of this without offending her or making an even bigger fool of myself? To my horror, my cheeks grow hot.

"Gosh, you are adorable, Summer." Zaza giggles. "Much too sweet to hang out with a flight of cynics and commitment phobes like us." Her eyes go over to Jared and Tate, walking in front of us, and I can't help but wonder if she meant to include both of them in that statement or just Jared.

"So no one in this flight is seeing someone long-term?" I ask.

Zaza snorts. We reach the dining hall, and even though I can see my flight over at the far side, I decide to sit with Zaza for the moment, too interested in what she has to say.

"Jared is flighty like a butterfly, and Tate doesn't get attached at all." Zaza ends her report about the men in her flight.

"What are you talking about?" Jared asks while he and Tate sit down opposite us.

"I told Summer that he shouldn't copy any of your behaviors concerning women," Zaza tells him sweetly.

"What? I'm good to women," Jared protests.

"And a lot of them," Zaza interrupts him dryly. "No, seriously, if any girl asked me for my opinion on dating anyone in our flight, I would tell her to look elsewhere."

"Excuse me?" Jared looks affronted while Tate watches for my reaction without giving anything away.

Damn, why is he so hard to read?

Jared and Zaza start bickering after that while Tate and I do what we do best, sitting in companionable silence.

After lunch, I join the other runners in geography since no duties or patrols are planned.

We have been handed little squares of a map. Apparently, they represent the average overview we will have from a bird's back at a comfortable travel height. We are in teams of three—I partnered with Calix and Mariel—and are now supposed to locate the areas on a bigger map.

"That could be anywhere." I turn the square in my hand and squint at it from a different angle. "If I ever lose the rest of you, I might as well land and wait for you to find me," I mutter.

"Oh no, you'll be fine. Let me see." Mariel takes the square from me. "Oh, that is over at the eastern border, see, the way these villages are placed is very distinct." She points it out for me, and I nod, but as soon as she takes it over to the map, I can't remember their placement. I hate memorizing, mainly because I suck at it.

Looking at Calix, who gazes quizzically at the square in his hand, turning it this way and that, makes me feel a little better.

I pick up the next one, but that doesn't look any better. I should have spent more time looking at the maps instead of playing with my father's figures placed on top of them. I smile at the memories flooding my mind.

My five-year-old self, curled up in my father's lap, enjoying the way his rumbling voice vibrated next to my ear, the voices around me a comforting buzz in the background while my eyes get heavier and heavier... Ben and I sitting beneath the big table in my father's study playing out epic battles while deep voices talk above us...and our teacher, Mr. Tennet, complaining because I played outside instead of studying like I was supposed to.

Yeah, it's safe to say I did not spend much time looking at the maps I was always surrounded with.

"Oh, come on, both of you. It isn't harder than doing a puzzle," Mariel chides, shaking her head at us.

"I just don't see the point," Calix complains. "First, our birds will probably be better at it than we are, and second, landscapes look completely different from these boring signs on a dull background."

I nod enthusiastically, and Mariel snatches up the rest of the squares, placing them on the map in quick succession, muttering to herself about being surrounded by simpletons.

The others have flight classes after that, and I go back to our room, distracting myself by finishing the letters I'll hand Sloan tonight, trying very hard not to think of the rest of my squadron having fun in the air right now.

I'm finishing the last one when my flight gets back.

"Hey Gray, you up for a game of cards tonight?" Calix appears at the end of my bed, and I suppress the impulse to hide the letter I just put into its envelope.

Relax. You're just writing your family. Nothing wrong with that.

"Are you alright?" Calix asks, eyeing me carefully. Damn, I hate lying to him. Maybe I could tell him about meeting Sloan tonight?

Godwin leans down from his bed above mine, reminding me this isn't the place for a heart-to-heart.

"I'm in. When are you meeting up?" Godwin says.

Calix replies, but his eyes are still on me, waiting for my answer.

"I'm fine," I say. "I'll have to skip tonight, though. I have to catch up on studying." Which isn't a lie. I still have to memorize the map for geography and go over Mariel's notes from yesterday. So I will sit down and study until everyone is otherwise occupied, then sneak out.

"If you say so." Calix is still looking at me like he knows something is up, then turns to Godwin and they continue talking while we head to dinner.

I nod along to whatever Mariel is telling me, while my thoughts are on tonight. Sloan's parents will be out at a premiere, giving us the time to catch up without being interrupted. I just hope nothing has changed since I haven't heard from Sloan, just like we agreed.

Mariel stops, and I look at her, confused as to why we stopped just outside the refectory. She looks at me expectantly.

Did she ask me something?

"Uhm...could you repeat that?" I ask her.

"I asked you if you'd like that idea?"

What idea? I blink. *Damn, I haven't heard a thing she said.*

"Uhm...sure?" It seems to be the right answer because she grins and skips through the door in front of me. I shrug and follow.

CHAPTER
TWENTY-ONE
ARA

Sloan said she would meet me in the parlor, overviewing the gardens. Climbing the walls surrounding Sloan's house is a breeze, and since it's winter, the garden lies dark and deserted before me, surrounding a picturesque two-story villa, its weathered stone walls adorned with creeping ivy and bathed in the warm glow of windows and lanterns. The villa has a terracotta roof and arched balconies with wrought-iron railings.

I crouch behind the fountain in the center of the garden—its statue depicting Ura, the goddess of sea and trade—and watch the house for movement.

The scent of blooming winter jasmine drifts over from the pergola, the only sounds are distant crickets, the burbling of the fountain, and muted voices on the other side of the wall.

Sloan sits in front of the fireplace, stitching what looks like a border of little flowers onto a pillowcase. I never had the patience for that kind of work, and my mother gave up trying after I declared I wanted a sword for my ninth birthday. So if my future husband hopes for something like that, he will be sorely disappointed. Sloan's movements look precise and elegant, not once stopping to undo a stitch she made.

I knock softly on the windowpane. Sloan looks up, a relieved smile splitting her face before she jumps up to let me in. She hugs me as soon as she closes the door behind me.

"Thank gods you are alive and well." She pushes me back. "You're alright, aren't you?" Her gaze wanders over me like she'd be able to see anything through the layer of clothes. "You really look like a boy." She crinkles her nose. "We can't let them see you. You would cause all kinds of gossip meeting me like that."

"What? Don't you feel like having a secret affair with me?" I wiggle my eyebrows. She swats at me, laughing.

"Stop it," she admonishes. "I would never hear the end of it. Let's go up to my room, and you can change into one of your dresses. I hid them all in my closet."

"Ooh, you're living dangerously, taking me up to your room." I chuckle.

She shushes me and checks the hallway before ushering me up the stairs. We are giggling like little girls by the time we shut the door to her room behind us.

Nelly, Sloan's maid, nearly caught us on the way up.

Sloan collapses on her bed, wiping the tears from her eyes.

"Nelly's face," she gasps. "She totally thinks I lost it."

"I nearly pissed my pants when she tried to sound all nonchalant about you enjoying the *view*," I giggle and flop down next to her. I give my cousin's hand an affectionate squeeze. "I'm so glad I came over. I needed that!"

"Are you not having fun at the academy?" Sloan turns her head to look at me, one eyebrow raised.

"I am, but it's much more...serious, I guess." I look at her and shrug.

"Really?" Sloan widens her eyes comically. "And here I thought dying was fun."

"Smart-ass," I mutter, which makes her giggle again.

Twenty minutes later, Sloan is up to date with what happened in my life, with a few adaptations. I left out everything about me being hurt, the punishment, and also Tate. I don't want to worry her, and maybe I don't want to be grilled either.

My letters are safely stashed in Sloan's desk drawer and I stare at my reflection after changing into one of my dresses. I look both familiar and different.

The green dress matches my eye color. It hugs my body, revealing and highlighting my small waist, where my uniform is loose to hide it. I still wear my daggers, but the flowing skirt and sleeves hide them from sight. My hair is unbound, the golden strands flowing in waves down my back, nearly reaching my hips. I look softer and more my age.

Disguised, I resemble more a boy than a man, my body not as broad and rather gangly against most runners and riders. The missing beard growth and my big eyes emphasize the effect. I sigh.

Damn, I like being a girl.

Remembering the fun we had so far and the dangers waiting for me next week, I have the urge to enjoy this evening to the fullest and live a little, as Calix advised me.

"Let's go out tonight," I say, meeting Sloan's gaze in the mirror, with a big smile on my face.

"What? No!" She shakes her head. "What if someone recognizes you?"

"I'm just a girl enjoying a night out with her friend. Nothing suspicious about that." She still doesn't seem convinced. "No one will recognize me," I promise.

"Tamara Blackstone, have you officially lost your mind? No!" She shakes her head.

"They haven't seen me like this," I try to convince her. "and no one knows about me—well, except Joel and Tate." She still shakes her head, so I plead with my eyes. "Please?"

"I don't think that's a good idea." She narrows her eyes. "And who is Tate?"

"Please. Let me enjoy being a girl for one night before I go back to that." I gesture toward the clothes I piled on her desk, ignoring her question. I'm reluctant to share Tate with her. Even if there isn't anything to share.

She sighs. "Alright, but don't blame me if you get caught."

The night air is freezing, and my legs feel oddly exposed in a skirt, even if it nearly reaches the ground. It's been a while since I've worn a dress.

Bruce, their butler, looked at us strangely on the way out, but I hope he doesn't mention it to Sloan's parents. We pretend to take a stroll around the neighborhood and get away without taking anyone with us.

The streets are only sparingly populated because everyone is hurrying to get home. Not the best weather for taking a walk.

We pass three taverns before I feel like we are not going to chance running into anyone we know. The houses around us are simpler and smaller but well maintained. We are close to the docks by now and a good distance away from the academy, so we should be safe from run-ins with any riders, too.

Since it's my fault we are halfway across town, I promise Sloan to see her home later.

The taproom is a little darker and seedier than I would have liked, and Sloan steps closer to me. Turning around right away will send the wrong signals, so I drag a reluctant Sloan to the bar and push her toward the last two open seats.

"I feel like everyone is watching us," Sloan whispers, leaning into me. I look around.

"Maybe because they are," I tell her. Apart from a group of older women in one corner, we are the only women. "Relax, I'm armed, and I won't let anything happen to you. They probably only gawk because we are new here," I reassure her.

Half an hour later, we are still in the same seats. The glasses of wine in front of us are reasonably clean, the room is warm, and after sending three men on their way, we are left alone. Even Sloan relaxes.

She is filling me in on an accident at the last dinner party her parents hosted that ended with pudding in the elaborate hairstyle of a lady we both can't stand when I feel *him* enter the tavern.

I know his magic well enough by now to recognize it without a doubt, but I still pray I'm wrong. How can I sense him when he's on the other side of the room?

Fighting the urge to turn, I consider my options. Why did they have to pick this tavern... tonight?

There is shuffling and chairs scraping over the floor, clearly audible over the murmurs of the other patrons. After a few seconds, I chance a look over my shoulder. Yep, it's him and five of his flight—well, our flight at the moment—all of them settling in at one of the tables across the room.

Tate sits with his back to the wall, which puts me right in his line of sight. Awesome. I watch his lips move while he talks to Jared. He looks up, and our eyes meet. A jolt zings through my body, setting my skin on fire.

The way I react to this man is ridiculous.

I fight the urge to duck and instead turn slowly back to Sloan, cursing my stupidity and lack of restraint. The room is sparsely lit, and there is a sea of strangers between us. My hair is down and I'm wearing a dress. He didn't recognize me. Right? I groan.

"What is it?" Sloan looks alarmed.

"Some men I know just dropped in." I fight the urge to look over my shoulder again.

Her eyes widen. "Should we leave?"

I look at our half-full glasses. "Let's finish these, and then I'll get you home," I decide.

"My brother can accompany you back after you drop me off," she says.

I snort. "Yeah sure, because Bastian will be fine with me climbing back into the academy. No, I don't want an escort."

"I can't let you walk all alone in the dark." Sloan sounds concerned.

I raise my eyebrow at her. "I don't spend my day weaving, you know."

"You should have brought Joel."

I laugh at the thought.

"Yeah...no. I wouldn't be here if he knew about it."

"Why are you here, Ara?" A rumbling voice asks in a deceptively calm tone.

Shit.

I close my eyes and take a deep breath before I turn around.

"Hey, Kyronos. What a surprise to see you here." I give him a sweet smile.

His face doesn't betray a thing, but his eyes burn into mine. He raises one eyebrow.

"I didn't take you for the partying type." I ramble on. "Me and Sloan were just about to leave, so..." I hop off my stool, expecting him to step back, but he doesn't. My chest grazes his when I inhale, sending a shiver up my spine and I look up to meet his eyes.

Big mistake.

I'm acutely aware of how close his lips are and how little it would take to close that gap. My cheeks grow hot, and I drag my gaze back to his eyes.

"Ara." My name is a growl that ripples through my body. My eyes dart to his lips again. Well, I already know my restraint is shit around him, and who can blame me when he says my name like that? Gods, I want him to say it again.

I bite my lip, and his gaze drops to my mouth. For a second, I see something flicker in his eyes, too, then he blinks, and it's gone and he looks even more pissed than before.

Two things are certain: I am in a boatload of trouble, and it will get even worse if I don't put some distance between his delicious lips and me.

I give him one of the smiles that make my brothers go ballistic and pat his chest. "Nice meeting you." I grab Sloan's hand and, pulling her with me, squeeze past him. We weave through the tables, heading for the exit.

I need to get out of here, fast, before I do something reckless. Okay, even more reckless than having a drink with my cousin when I'm not allowed to leave the academy.

My thoughts jump back to Tate. How would he have reacted if I kissed him? I grin. Kissing him is such a bad idea, but gods, it's tempting.

I still pull Sloan with me, and we are nearly at the door, but stop short when a group of men comes in from the cold.

Traveling soldiers, by the look of them, maybe Mercenaries. They look like a whole lot of hassle, and not the good kind.

I pull Sloan aside, but we have already caught the attention of one of them. *Dammit.* Why is nothing going smoothly today?

His swaggering steps and broad grin have me guessing that he considers himself irresistible. I suppress a groan.

I try to relax, the feeling of the daggers under my wide sleeves and the one strapped to my right thigh a comforting presence.

"You surely aren't leaving, ladies. The party is just about to start." The man's voice is as oily as his hair, and the way his eyes roam over me makes me want to punch him in the face.

Play nice, I admonish myself. But after weeks of being nearly invisible—disguised as a man—it's even more jarring to be ogled like that.

"It's getting late." I do my best not to sound snippy and shift my weight, angling my body so I'm between Sloan and this creep and his friends. There are six of them, but two are already heading for a table, while three observe our exchange, grinning.

"Oh, come on, we will make it worth your while," he says.

Is he implying that they can buy us? My eyebrows creep up, and I clamp my lips shut. *I won't start a fight. Okay, maybe I am lying to myself now.*

His friends stand to our left. If I shove him in their direction, we should be able to slip out the door without anyone stopping us. But he will come after us, I'm sure of that. He seems too proud to let us go after embarrassing him in front of his friends. And that will leave us in a dark alley without anyone around. If it had been just me, I would have climbed the building and let him search himself stupid. But with Sloan, that isn't an option.

Before I can decide on my next move, I am yanked back into a very solid chest. I stiffen for a second; then I recognize the gift and his scent.

Looking over my shoulder, I meet the stormy depth of golden eyes, his hands settling possessively on my hips, and I relax into him.

Guess I don't have to fight my way out after all.

Oily loses his leering grin and quite a bit of color as he looks at the man standing behind me. He steps aside without Tate needing to say a word.

Damn. That is impressive. I wish I could do that.

"Jared." Tate waves his friend over. His voice rumbles through my body and does funny things to my core, distracting me so Jared nearly reached us before my brain kicks back in.

Shit, I can't let him see me.

I turn into Tate, burying my face in his neck, letting my hair fall around me. His scent envelops me, leather, pine, and something fresh and cool like a winter night. His arms tighten around me.

We could die here any day, and you throw away a chance like that...Live a little. Calix's words play through my mind. *Ah, fuck it.*

I lean in a bit more, running my nose along the side of his neck. He flinches. I have never seen him so much as wince before, that he jerks like that when I barely touched him...It's kind of addicting. I do it again.

What would he do if I explored his neck, his jawline with my lips, my teeth? His hand squeezes my side, maybe a warning to behave myself. I swallow the laughter bubbling through me.

"Escort Sloan safely back home, would you?" Tate's voice sounds rough, and I nearly hum in appreciation. "I need to talk about appropriate fight and flight reactions with this one here," he continues.

I hear Jared's affirmative and squeeze Sloan's hand before releasing her. I can feel her burning questions without her having to say anything.

I'll have to visit her soon. The door behind me opens, cool night air caresses my hot skin before it closes again.

CHAPTER TWENTY-TWO
TATE

She shakes in my arms, but she hasn't acted scared. The way she stepped between this brute and her friend, the way she shifted her body right before I grabbed her, told me she was about to fight him.

She ran from me, ignored my questions, patted my chest like I was some...pet she was rewarding, and then... Knowing we are here—that I am here—she would rather fight a guy twice her weight than ask for help?

Holy mists, this woman is driving me insane.

I still feel the burning line along my neck like she fried my fucking nerves just by touching me with her nose? Lips?

What is wrong with me? And what is wrong with her?

Her breath warms my skin in small puffs, and I'm caught somewhere between wanting to shake some sense into her and kissing her senseless.

That we are drawing more and more attention by just standing here isn't helping either. I should drag her back and report her for sneaking out but handing her over when Foley already wants her dead? Fuck. I can't do it.

What the fuck did I get myself into?

The guys of my flight—our flight for the time being—are already staring curiously, and one of them will come over any minute now. I have to get her out of here.

I take a deep breath, and my airways fill with her scent. Clean, soapy with a hint of something warm like cinnamon. I pull back and meet twinkling blue-green eyes full of mischief and laughter. I blink. She's laughing? Of course, she's fucking laughing. I scowl at her.

"Sorry." Her voice sounds breathless while she fights for control. "The look that creep gave you was priceless." She pats my chest, turning away, ready to dismiss me. Again. I trap her hand with mine, which brings her gaze back to me.

"You think that was funny?" I glare at her. Doesn't she have any concept of self-preservation?

"Immensely, I have to say you are quite handy to have around." She grins like all of this is one big joke. Irritation crawls up my throat. This could have had serious consequences. If the bastard hadn't backed down so quickly, I might have ripped him to shreds, and she thinks it's entertaining?

"I'm not some tool you can use how you please." My voice is dangerously soft.

"Pity, and I would have had so many good ideas on how to use...ah, never mind." She winks at me, and for a second, I'm stunned speechless. *Is she flirting with me? Now?*

"See you tomorrow." She sends me a smile, extracts her hand, and is nearly out the door before I catch her arm.

"Where do you think you are going?" I snap.

"Where do *you* think I'm going?"

"You are not going back alone." My voice is full of warning.

Her eyebrows shoot up, and suddenly, she doesn't look so sure of herself. Then her smirk is back in place.

"Is that an offer?" She lets her eyes roam over my body in an appraisal that leaves my skin tingling. Fuck, she's much too enticing for her own good, and that sassy mouth...

"Unfortunately, I have to decline," she continues, shrugging. "I need some shut-eye before that grueling training of yours." She heads out the door. And I catch it with my hand before she can slam it in my face.

"I'll walk you back." I follow her into the dark, and she grumbles something that sounds a lot like "overbearing men."

She sets out at a quick pace, her long legs eating up the sidewalk. It's cold tonight, but she doesn't seem bothered despite being only in a dress. A dress that hugs her body in a way that is impossible to overlook.

I watch her while we walk, but she does her best to ignore me. I expect her to speak, considering how she tends to become fidgety and rambling when tense, but she stays quiet.

A dog barks off in the distance, and a few people hurry along the streets, their eyes on the uneven cobblestone pavement. She turns into a smaller street, and the light spilling out of windows is the only sign of life around us.

"Why did you sneak out?" I start with the most obvious question circling in my head.

"Could I have gone openly if I asked you?" She looks up at me, sounding curious, not slowing her steps.

"No, of course not!"

"Didn't think so," she says. I take a deep breath, reminding myself that shouting will draw too much attention.

"Okay, why did you need to go out tonight?" I rephrase.

See, I can be patient.

She shrugs. "A yearning for a glass of wine with a friend." It's a lie, and I have seen her dedication in training. She may be reckless, but she's not careless.

"Bullshit," I tell her.

"If you say so." She sounds bored and marches on. We're getting closer and closer to the academy grounds, and I need answers before we get there.

I catch her arm, and she swings around, ready to clock me with the other one, so I grab the other one for good measure. She struggles, and when she tries to knee me in the groin, I back her against the next wall, trapping her between me and the hard surface.

"What the fuck, Ara?"

"In my experience getting manhandled in a dark alley requires fighting back."

"I just want to talk."

She huffs out a breath, donning a bored expression, but her body is still tense.

"Tell me why you left the academy tonight, and I will let you go," I tell her.

"I already told you I wanted to meet a friend." She speaks the truth but doesn't meet my gaze. Something is up.

Is she passing on information? Is she another trap?

The thoughts make my blood run cold. I don't know anything about her unless I count joining the academy under a false name and that Cassius grew up with her. I tagged her as harmless, but what if she isn't?

"And why is that?" The ice in my voice mirrors the one coursing through my veins. Our faces are so close that the clouds of our breaths mingle. She goes rigid at my tone but still doesn't offer any explanation.

Have I endangered my flight, my division by trusting her?

I watch her closely while I go through the possibilities. "You met up with someone," I reiterate. "Did you give her something?" Her eyes flare for a second, telling me I'm right on the mark. "What was it?" I ask. She lets her head fall back against the wall and I see the resolve in her eyes before she answers.

"Letters," she whispers.

"Are you spying on us?" I ask, my voice gruff. Her eyes go wide with shock, her head snaps forward and her pulse spikes under my fingers.

"No!" She shakes her head frantically. Truth.

"Well, Jared knows where your friend lives now. Do I need to visit her, or are you finally going to talk?" I push.

"Leave Sloan alone!" There's a fire in her eyes now, but fear, too, and seeing that emotion on her face slices me open. I don't want her to be afraid of me. "I'm not spying on anyone, I promise," she assures me hurriedly.

"And why would you sneak out letters in the middle of the night instead of posting them yourself?" I ask, my voice softer now that I know she isn't a spy.

She sighs, studying her feet before looking up at me again. "They don't know I'm here."

"Who?" I fire back. We're finally getting somewhere.

"My family," she answers, her shoulders slumping, her eyes back on her feet. I blink at that.

What?

That is not what I expected. Most want to shout it from the rooftops that they are a skyrider, not hide it like a dirty secret.

"Where do they think you are?" I duck my head to meet her eyes.

"Visiting Sloan." She shrugs. Well, that is kind of fucked up. My mind jumps to the scars on her skin.

"Are you hiding from your family?" The thought of someone hurting her deliberately...I grind my teeth, fighting for control.

"It's a long story." She sighs, and her eyes jump to my hands still circling her wrists... with more force than necessary. I relax my grip.

"You are not going anywhere at the moment, so try me," I tell her. Now that my focus is on her wrists, I notice the sharp edges under the soft fabric.

Daggers.

She may look harmless in that soft dress, but she's not.

And why the mists do I think that is hot?

"You're armed," I state the obvious.

Her eyes wander over my weapons before meeting my gaze. "So are you."

"Do you have more than those two daggers under your dress?"

"Now, wouldn't you like to know that?" She gives me a slow smile that makes me much too aware of how close our bodies are. The twinkle in her eyes tells me she knows exactly what she's doing, and damn if it isn't working.

I take a deep breath of the frigid night air and quirk an eyebrow.

She laughs softly. "Can't blame me for trying."

I'M STILL SHAKING MY HEAD WHEN ARA IS SAFELY BACK IN HER room, and I make my way back to the tavern. This woman is trouble in all caps. Who leaves her family for a "vacation" only to join a fight force known for decimating their applicants in droves?

I do buy her wish for standing up for herself and getting out from under her brother's wings, it even makes sense that she thought she would draw less attention by posing as a boy, but I would bet my life on it that there's more.

Four brothers ... no wonder she knows how to get under a man's skin. The thought of having a little sister like that is enough to give me gray hair.

And the way she shimmied up that rainspout like it was a damn ladder and in a dress... I have a suspicion she doesn't care to use the front door at home either.

I'll need to keep an eye on her.

"*Yeah right, that is the only reason you'll keep an eye on her.*" Daeva laughs at me.

"Oh, shut up," I grumble.

I push into the tavern, and I'm instantly enveloped by warmth and the smell of beer and food. The guys are already well into a round of cards as I settle back in my seat. My beer is warm and has lost its foam, but I take a big gulp nonetheless, trying to wash away the scent of her still lingering in my nose.

"That was quick. Didn't think we would see you back here, Centurion," Boko teases and laughs at my crude gesture. "Only Jared here was even quicker." That earns him a jab from the right.

"I would have taken my time with someone like that in my arms." Tanner winks at me.

"With you, that means all of what...two minutes?" Boko evades Tanner's punch, laughing.

"Careful with your teasing. I see a pattern there, Boko. Wouldn't want anyone to suspect you are lacking in that department, do you?" Howling laughter meets Jared's comment.

"Seriously, Centurion, how did you do it?" Miller, the youngest of our bunch, looks at me with something close to adoration. "You were gone for not even ten minutes, and the next thing I know, you have your arms around that beauty."

"Must be that face of his. It sure isn't his sunny character," Jared teases and nudges my shoulder. "I got the other girl safely home. But she was concerned for her friend. Who is she?"

With anyone else, I would have kept my mouth shut or made up a story, but it's Jared. My best friend and partner in crime since his mother let us out of her view. He knows all of my secrets. I hesitate for a second, then lean closer.

Boko claims this round of cards, the others swearing about their bad luck and handing over coins reluctantly. I use the commotion to fill Jared in.

"No way!" His shout causes all heads to turn in our direction. I give him a reprimanding stare, and he drops his volume to barely audible. "She turned into you before I came close enough to see her face. Now I know why. Damn." He chuckles. "Now what?"

I shrug. "I will keep an even closer eye on her, I guess."

"Not such a hardship, is it?" He only grins when I glare at him. There is a lot of teasing coming my way, I'm sure of it.

"That girl has trouble written all over her," I grumble.

"That was your middle name, last time I checked." He smirks. "So does that make her yours?" I'm shaking my head at my best friend. If I'm smart, I'll stay far away from Ara. She could make me lose my fucking mind.

I nod at Boko's silent question when he starts dealing cards for a new round.

"Seriously, if you aren't interested—" Jared leans closer and smirks. "I already liked her, but after the comment this morning and seeing her in that dress... I might just be in love." I growl at him, and he chuckles. "So you are interested," he concludes, and I realize provoking a reaction out of me has been his plan all along.

"Not sure that even matters. The way he acts around her, I'm pretty sure she's with Cassius," I answer even though the thought irks me.

Not for you, I remind myself. I have no place even thinking about her in that way, not while I have a target on my back. She's a runner, and I am her centurion, for fuck's sake.

And now I will be around her constantly for the next week, if not more. I groan at that thought.

"And Cassius is her squadron leader," Daeva comments. She's right.

"*I will have to have a word with him about that*"

"She will come at you swinging if she gets wind of that," Daeva adds her opinion and sounds gleeful. I guess she isn't over me telling her to shut up. "*She is fierce*," she continues. Together with her statement, *she has guts*, a few days earlier, this is the most approval Daeva has ever shown for anyone before.

I will stay away from Ara, I vow to myself.

I'm a risk for her, and if I let her in, she's a weakness I can't afford. I know what happens to people I care for, and her being so...reckless on top of that. I shake my head. I can't let her close.

CHAPTER
TWENTY-THREE
ARA

Dammit. I shouldn't have crept out again today. Two days in a row is madness, especially after running into Tate yesterday. I push against my window, but it still doesn't budge. Someone locked it, or it got stuck when it slammed shut earlier. I shift my weight, trying to press my body close to the wall.

This is the perfect ending to a shitty day. Tate avoided me all day like I had the plague. Disappointment and hurt course through me, remembering how he backtracked as soon as he saw me sitting in our place in the library. Our place...gods, I'm pathetic. He doesn't know I saw...well, felt him, but his magic signature gave him away.

The guard will come around the corner any second now. I hold my breath, fitting as much of my body into the nook of the window as I can. I'll have to sit it out until he's gone again.

My face is pressed against the windowpane, but there is no movement inside. I'm not sure if I'm relieved or put out about it. It would depend on who was moving, I guess.

Calix has been in a mood today, too, and even Mariel seemed subdued and monosyllabic, both acting like I should know what was going on when I asked about it.

I listen to the guard's footsteps, bracing for shouts of alarm and hurried steps, but nothing comes.

I just had to see Sloan before we head out. I can't leave her worrying about me, especially since there is the chance that I won't come back.

Now I just have to get back inside without being caught. The drizzle of rain and the wind make the situation even more uncomfortable. I go through all my options, but really, I can only think of two: knock on this window and hope it's Calix who wakes up and not someone else or climb to Joel's window.

Joel has his room to himself. Joel, it is.

He will be furious, of that I am sure, but he won't rat me out. I can weather a bit of screaming if it means getting into the warmth.

He is up on the third floor, so instead of going back down, I climb up to the roof. I lie down, making myself as flat as I can so I'm less visible. My front gets soaked by the wet roof, and I grimace.

I lean over the edge and search for the window that has to be Joel's.

I walk over the roof until I am right above it, only to realize there is no rain pipe close to it. I lean over again. I can get down at the next window over. There is no light, so whoever's room that is hopefully sleeps. With the windowsill as a foothold, I should be able to jump to his.

As soon as my plan is formed and the guard wanders out of sight, I set it into motion.

I hold my breath as I drop in front of the first window. I wear my uniform, and while the gray is great for hiding in the dark, I'm not naive enough to think my silhouette isn't a clear outline against the moonlit sky. No one stirs, and I pause only long enough to find my balance; then I jump.

In one fluid motion, I sail through the air, my feet touching Joel's windowsill. My right foot slips since the wet stone is slippery. I curse and thrust out my arms for balance, knocking into the window with a crash. My fingers grasp the frame, and I barely manage to steady myself before the window flies open, knocking my balance out of whack again.

Strong fingers grip my wrists before I slip over the edge, and I'm hauled inside by an at-first stunned and then furious-looking Joel.

"You gotta be kidding me!" He looks mad enough to spit fire.

"Sorry to bother you." I send him a sunny smile.

"What is wrong with you?" He still holds my arms but seems torn between pulling me into him and pushing me away in anger.

"Oh, I'm fine. No worries."

"Fine? Fine! I really should..." His volume rises with every word.

"Speak quietly, or we'll have an audience in a minute." I watch while he struggles to compose himself and only now realize that he's shirtless. Damn. Maybe I'm not fine after all if I missed that detail until now.

I used to drool over that sight when we were kids, and he's totally drool-worthy, but the zing of heat I'm used to feeling around him doesn't come.

Yep, broken.

He squeezes his eyes shut, visibly fighting with his temper, releasing my arms in the process. I inch slowly toward the door, then stop when his eyes fly open, pinning me with a glare.

"I should send you home, this minute." His voice is a hiss through clenched teeth. "Are you out of your mind? Why aren't you in your bed like you're supposed to be?"

"I thought we were through that already. The whole I send you home, I mean."

"That was before you climbed through my window in the middle of the night. Why?"

"Why did I come through your window? Mine was stuck this time." I wince at my slipup.

"This time?" He's shouting again but lowers his voice immediately. "Are you telling me this isn't the first time you disregarded curfew to bump through the night?"

"I had things to do." I shrug.

"Like what?"

I smile at him. "Sending letters to appease my brothers, of course."

"You do realize how fucked up that is, right? Risking yourself to tell them you are safe and fine."

I pat his chest reassuringly, knowing quite well it will infuriate him and test me at the same time. Having my fingers on his warm skin should do something to me. But there is nothing. I scrunch up my brow in confusion. This is weird. I've had a crush on Joel since... like forever.

I shake my head and hurry to the door. Joel follows, but I quickly slip out into the corridor before he can stop me.

"Good night," I whisper, leaving him standing in the open doorway. I turn and walk straight into a broad chest. Strong arms steady me. The smell of pine, leather, and night air as well as the warmth of his gift tell me exactly who it is before I lift my eyes. My whole body lights up like a bonfire. Well, shit. Why do I always have to run into him, of all people?

My gaze travels up and finds honey-colored eyes trained on Joel, looking ready for murder.

Tate blinks, and the emotion vanishes. His face relaxes. Then his eyes meet mine. No, I was wrong. His eyes aren't calm at all. A thrill zips through my chest and drips down, creating a dull pulsing heat that has me shifting.

I have the strangest urge to rush out an explanation for being in Joel's room at night, to make him understand.

Which is ridiculous. Nothing is going on between Joel and me, and I don't owe Tate anything.

I don't turn around, but I know Joel is still standing bare-chested in his doorway. I know exactly what this looks like. I'm disheveled and slightly out of breath, and Joel is only half-dressed.

Shit. Shit. Shit.

"Follow me, Summer." Tate's voice is clipped and emotionless, and he doesn't even wait for an answer before he turns around and strides away.

I'm not sure what to make of that.

I reassure Joel that I'm fine and send him a strained smile before I follow Tate down the corridor.

TATE

Seeing her step out of Cassius's room in the middle of the night, her cheeks flushed and her hair mussed, my first instinct is to fucking kill him. The reaction is so primal and raw, it shocks me. I am still rooted to the floor as she walks right into me. The smell of rain, night air, and simply Ara hits me at the same time her body does.

It is pure reflex that I catch her before she stumbles back. My hands meet cool, damp fabric before they snatch her waist, reminding me just how small it is under all those loose clothes.

My eyes lock with Ara's, and I step back, releasing her.

"Follow me, Summer." I turn around and stride down the hall, before I do something stupid like planting my fist into the face of one of my squadron leaders.

I hear a murmured reassurance addressing Cassius, and then her soft footsteps follow me. My bedroom is on the same level and would have been closer, but instead, I usher her into the common room a few minutes later.

She speaks as soon as I close the door behind us.

"It's not—"

"What I think?" I finish Ara's sentence, cocking one eyebrow. "I don't want to hear it."

She opens her mouth but shuts it without saying a word when I glare at her.

"The way you behave is thoughtless, reckless, and simply disrespectful regarding your flight, your squadron, your division." Hurt flashes over her face, but I ignore it and the twinge for hurting her.

"I get it. You don't care about rules or how your actions impact others, but let me make one thing very clear here. When we leave tomorrow, we'll patrol a region that is anything but hospitable. Our survival depends on us having each other's backs. You can risk your own life all you want, but if you risk anyone else's, that's it. That is my breaking point."

She nods, and I do everything to ignore the sheen in her eyes. Maybe I was a little harsh, but I'm so angry with her, so angry with myself for making it so easy for her. Perhaps she wouldn't have done half the shit if there had been consequences from the start.

Would I have treated her differently without the attraction between us? I hope not, but I'm not sure either.

"Get some sleep. The next few days will be hard on you," I tell her, my voice gentler now.

She nods and turns to the door, but stops again, turning back to me. She licks her lips, and my eyes follow the movement. Fuck. Even after catching her coming out of Cassius's room in the middle of the night, I still want her. And I hate myself for it.

She swallows.

"I visited Sloan tonight." Her voice wobbles slightly. "I needed to say goodbye in case...well, in case I don't see her again." Fuck. Her fighting her feelings while talking about the possibility of her death does me in. My chest constricts.

"My window got stuck, and well...Joel let me back in." So she didn't plan to end up in Cassius's bed tonight? My eyebrows rise.

She clears her throat.

"What I'm trying to say here..." She bites her lip. "I just want you to know that I'm not breaking all the rules."

"Okay?" I still have no clue where she's going with this.

"I didn't sleep with him," she rushes out. "I just wanted you to know that. Not that I think you're interested," she hurries to add, then huffs out a breath, looking at her feet. "Gods, this is awkward." She laughs embarrassedly. "Well, now you know, and... I'll do my best to ignore I ever said that."

A smile stretches my lips, and breathing becomes easier. She's adorable all flustered like this. It reminds me of how she acted the first time I healed her.

She slips out the door before I have the chance to say anything. Her steps are so soft she doesn't make a sound, like the night simply swallowed her.

I like this brutally honest, flustered version of her. It makes me think of the way she reacts to my touch.

I imagine her skin pebbling, her breath hitching while I trace her soft, soft skin. Her silky golden strands wrapped around my hand, her pouty lips swollen...

Fuck, now I'm turned on. I run a hand through my hair.

I have no idea how she can think I don't want her, but holy mists, I would be clay in her hands if she ever seriously tried to seduce me.

She is not with Cassius.

I hum when I head back to my room.

Not that it changes anything. She's still off-limits. But... I shake my head. *Don't even go there.*

I remember how she faced Vega. Recall the way her eyes widen sometimes, like the words spilling out of her mouth surprised her. Her silent laughter when she stepped out of my arms yesterday.

I grin. Something about the amused and unapologetic way she faces life is ... fascinating.

ARA

I'm on my way to meet my temporary flight in the courtyard. One thing I look forward to is that my being gone will give Joel time to cool down. I have no intention of letting him yell at me again, but that plan goes down the drain when he waits in the corridor ahead of me. Dammit.

He gestures to the open door of an empty classroom. I contemplate whether to keep walking, but the only thing I want even less is him making a scene in front of the whole flight, in front of Tate.

Joel shuts the door and leans against it, probably ready to start his spiel about smuggling me out again.

I sigh and hold up my hand to stop him before he even starts.

"It wouldn't work. Tate knows I'm a girl, and Foley took a personal interest in my demise, so there is no way you can get me out of the city before someone catches up to us."

"I don't like that Kyronos and you are so cozy," he grumbles.

I scoff at that. Cozy would be the last word I'd use to describe whatever is or isn't between Tate and me. Especially after my awkward rambling last night.

"We are not."

"You jumped to his rescue, getting yourself lit up like a bonfire in the process, and I saw his grin after helping you during training. What was that last night?" He challenges my words.

"And whose fault is it that he knows about me?" I incline my head, staring him down, ignoring what he said.

"Fine." He throws up his hands, agitated. "But you were hurt and didn't tell me."

"No, no, don't try to blame *me* now. I had it under control, and you overreacted." I point my finger at him.

"Just keep away from him, okay?" he commands. He tries to soften it to a question, but he's not fooling me. What is it with the men in my life always trying to order me around?

"That will be hard since I'm currently in his flight, and he's my centurion, and you know I hate when I'm told what to do," I hiss. What the fuck is his problem anyway? Tate has done nothing but help me so far.

"Even you wouldn't jump in his bed only because I told you to stay away." He scoffs like *I'm* being ridiculous.

I narrow my eyes. I don't like this side of Joel. I can't believe I was ever attracted to this cocky, demanding bastard.

"Is that a challenge?" My voice drips honey, daring him to say just one more word on this. He throws up his hands, anger written all over his face, and stalks toward me.

"What are you trying to prove here? That you can have him if you want to? Congratulations, no question there." He's seething now. "Just stay away from him. He's bad news and a coldhearted bastard who cares about no one but himself. He may be above me in rank, but believe me when I say it won't stop me from warning him off if you can't be reasoned with." He's getting in my face now, but I refuse to budge even an inch. When I don't react, he continues, "And if that doesn't help keep his fingers off you, I will write your brothers... all of them." I gasp, and his eyes lower for a second before they are back on mine.

How fucking dare he?

"That is such a low blow I won't even acknowledge you said that." I'm so angry I wouldn't be surprised if I burst into flames. "You have no right to tell me what I can or can't do." I drill my finger into his chest. When he snatches my arm, I resume with the other one.

He leans in. "I don't get it. You have a wonderful life in front of you. You'll have everything you could ever ask for, but you are out here risking all of it. Why?" He steps back, releasing my arms. "Just because you feel like it? For the thrill? Because you want to experience some adventures before settling down? Grow up already, Ara."

"Exactly. You don't get it, so keep out of it. Don't try to make decisions or pressure me into the ones you think are right for me."

"Then explain it to me!" Joel roars.

"I can't!" I shout back.

"Can't or won't?" he yells before continuing more quietly, "I thought we were friends."

"I don't want to be protected and cared for all the time," I explode, not letting him mellow me with the I-thought-we-were-friends crap.

That seems to take him aback. "Why would you not want that?"

"Every one of my steps watched, judged for everything I do or don't do. Not able to move without someone around me, keeping an eye on me." Disgust drips from every word. I laugh humorlessly. "Sounds like a dream. Or what about all the things I'm expected to spend my time on? Have you seen me do..." I wave my hands around, looking for the best word to describe it. "Girly courtly stuff, like... ever?"

He rubs his neck, the fight gone.

"Um, no?"

"Well, I'm abhorrently rotten at it," I tell him. "My five-year-old niece is better in most things expected of me. Do you have any idea how terrifying that is? How scared I am of disappointing all of them?"

"You don't want to live at court?" He looks confused.

"Oh, I absolutely *love* the thought of marrying a stranger and living in a strange place I have never seen before, away from my family," I say dryly. "What do you think?" I raise my hand before he can answer. "Forget I asked. The point is you all stamped me as irresponsible and reckless and can't see that I would hang the fucking moon for the people I love, even if it cuts me apart." I huff out a breath, fighting to keep my voice stable when I'm reminded of Tate's cutting words from last night.

"You always seemed to judge me less," I whisper. "Guess I was wrong."

FEATHERS OF ASH AND HOPE

I use his stunned silence to escape, and it feels like déjà vu. I'm glad I'll be gone for a week.

CHAPTER
TWENTY-FOUR
TATE

Ara crosses the courtyard, heading toward us. Her movements are tense, her smile looks forced, and she doesn't meet my eyes, which makes it hard to read the feelings swirling behind them.

I shouldn't have lashed out yesterday.

She hands me her pack but doesn't linger, and I keep my hands busy by securing it next to mine on Daeva's back instead of reaching for her. She will be riding with Zaza, and I'm thankful for that. There is no way I could keep this cold indifference up if I spend hours with her body pressed to mine.

My whole body already itches with the need to hold her, comfort her.

Ara walks over to Zaza and her bird Pax, a Rukh, waiting while Zaza checks all her straps.

When everyone is mounted, Tanner—who takes point first—gives the sign for takeoff, and our flight rises as one. Tanner is a good squadron leader and an experienced rider. If climbing the ranks hadn't been part of my plan, I would have been content with serving in his squadron.

The mountainous landscape, with its white peaks and forested sides, has been quiet so far. Hopefully, it will stay that way. I am not eager for Ara to see action while she's out with us. Not only because it's always dangerous to have someone as inexperienced as her in our midst but also because bearing two riders will slow down Pax, which makes evading attacks much harder.

"Maybe Ara should ride with Jared and Zephyr," Daeva suggests innocently. "Or Tanner and—"

"Enough," I snap, and she clicks her beak in amusement.

"*Just saying, Strix are bigger than Rukh, so if you are worried, it would make much more sense—*"

"I said enough," I growl. Daeva caws, clearly laughing at me now. Which makes Jared throw me a questioning glance. When his laughter wafts over only seconds later, I know Daeva spoke to Zephyr.

The mountains below us swell and ebb, the scenery lush and green so close to the coastline. Daeva perks up when we pass over a herd of deer, the animals freezing in place as they feel the preying eyes.

"Tonight," I promise Daeva. "You know there will be plenty of game around."

"*You sure we don't have time for a snack?*"

I chuckle at her hopeful tone.

"*You know we will barely reach the outpost before nightfall, even without delays.*"

"*I don't mind flying in the dark,*" Daeva says.

"Yeah, but it's not just us." I pet her feathers in front of me, reminding her of the fact that neither Rukh nor Strix have the night vision she does and wouldn't enjoy flying with impaired sight.

We reach the outpost just when the sun slips behind the surrounding mountains. We had a smooth flight without issues, unless you counted cheeky birds and annoying best friends. Jared loves the idea of Ara riding with him and tells me so repeatedly.

Ara winces after dismounting. The first part of this patrol route is always the most challenging since we don't make any stops. Her body isn't used to riding the way ours is. Her walk tells me her muscles are stiff and tight from holding one position for so long.

I'll offer to heal her later because tomorrow will be worse. We unpack and relieve our birds from their harnesses for the night. By the time I'm done tending to Daeva, there is no sign of Ara.

I catch her right before we sit down for dinner, but she declines my offer to heal her and quickly slips past me.

"I already helped Summer stretch out a little," Zaza comments. "He didn't complain once today, but it won't be pleasant tomorrow. As stubborn and proud as the rest of us." She grins up at me. "He fits right in."

"You are getting along well," I say, hoping for some information since they talked every time I looked in their direction, but Zaza only nods.

"You should have paired her with me," Jared whispers, passing me, clearly amused by my frustration. "I would have all the information for you by now," he says with a wink before he seizes the last free seat next to Ara. I glare, but that only makes his grin widen.

Ara is quiet during dinner, despite Jared's attempts to draw her into a conversation. She sends me a look I can't decipher before she rises and excuses herself for the night.

Jared gives me a questioning look, but I shrug. I have no idea what that was about and have no intention of telling him about my encounter with Ara last night.

The next two days are pretty much the same. Ara persistently declines my offers to heal her, and while she's back to her friendly and exuberant self with everyone else, she's bitingly polite to me, and it chafes. I don't even have the excuse to help her find her way since all outposts have the same build.

I'm sitting on the fortification wall, my legs dangling over the edge, while the rest of the flight sits in the common room. I heard her peals of laughter the minute I came close and changed direction.

It's dark, the light spilling out the windows behind me the only light source next to the stars. We are far from any other settlement, and nothing but wilderness surrounds us. It can get cold up here in the mountains, and I'm glad we have the outposts with their warm fires waiting for us each evening instead of spending the night in a tent, like on some of the other routes.

The rooms are not luxurious, but they do have a proper bed, a warm common room to hang out, and people to cook and maintain the base. No skyriders and only a handful of regular warriors are stationed here, but since many routes pass it, riders are nearly always around.

I take in the quiet around me, but my mind is still on Ara. Now that I spend so much time around her, I realize she isn't as open as she seems. She evades or deflects questions about herself with a laugh or a joke, and no one seems to notice. I wonder if she keeps Cassius and Ilario at arm's length, too.

"*She is protecting them in case she goes down,*" Daeva remarks.

I go over her actions and realize she could be right. Images of Ara throwing herself in front of me and her shifting in front of her cousin in the bar pop up. She even jumped off a Strix to save someone from her flight. And like Daeva says, keeping her ruse to herself can be seen as her protecting her friends from the consequences, too.

Great, now I feel like an even bigger asshole for implying she only cared about herself.

"*Awareness is the first step in betterment,*" Daeva consoles me. Sometimes she sounds like one of those sayings you would frame.

"*I heard that,*" Daeva retorts, and I chuckle.

"I've been an ass again, haven't I?" I ask her.

"*Don't worry, everyone who knows you is used to it.*"

"Thanks," I reply dryly, which makes her caw, laughing at me.

"A copper for your thoughts." Jen hops onto the wall and sits down next to me. She's two years older and with the third squadron of the southern division, tail flight. Our flights cross paths today since they head back to Telos while we go the other way. We get along well enough even though I wouldn't call us friends.

"Not much on my mind. Sorry to disappoint you," I answer.

She scoffs. "I don't believe you, but if you don't want to share, that's fine with me." She nudges my shoulder. "Since we're on the topic of sharing. The nights up here are awfully cold. I would be up to sharing a bed if you want to." She smiles at me.

Maybe I should take what she's offering. Perhaps it would help to get Ara out of my head.

She trails a finger down my arm, scooting closer. But there is no heat, no tingle of anticipation, and the thought of taking her back to my room settles unpleasantly heavy in my gut. All I can think about is long blond hair and blue-green eyes.

I am surely and truly obsessed with that woman.

I shake my head at Jen. "Sorry, I have to decline."

She pouts. "I'm sorry, too." She gets to her feet, then smirks. "Guess that answers my question about what is on your mind, though, or should I rather ask who?" She looks at me expectantly.

"I don't know what you're talking about," I lie.

"Sure you don't." She snorts. "You just declined all this." She makes a sweeping motion down her body. "For brooding alone out here in the cold." She shakes her head, her short dark hair flying with the movement. "If there isn't some girl involved, I will let Axar choose my dinner." Axar is her bird, and he loves his food bloody and still twitching.

She suddenly laughs, then shudders. "He is eager to educate my taste. I better not be wrong, Kyronos, or you will hold my hair while I throw up afterward."

I shake my head at her. Maybe I should nudge her in Jared's direction. I'm sure they would get along splendidly, and I know he just ended things with Nadja.

Knowing Axar is watching, too, I look up at her. "She is not wrong," I admit.

"Thank you!" She sighs and waves in parting, her eyes already glazing over in a way that tells me she's having a discussion with Axar.

Which leaves me alone with my thoughts or as alone as I can be when someone always butts in without being asked.

"*I heard that,*" Daeva states, and I chuckle.

ARA

We sit in the common room, but it's already dark. This deep into winter, the days are exceptionally short, especially here, where the mountains swallow the sun as soon as it dips.

My gaze wanders over the room, but Tate isn't here. I wonder what he's doing.

Jared plops down next to me.

"He's a broody bastard sometimes," he declares out of the blue.

"Huh?" I raise my eyebrows at him.

"Tate." I blink at him, and he laughs. "That's who you were looking for, right?"

I deny it, but his sparkling eyes tell me he doesn't believe me.

Does he know? How else should I take this comment? And Calix mentioned they go way back. *Tate told him about me?* I'm not sure how to feel about that.

While my mind flies away on that thought, Jared is thankfully roped into a discussion by Boko, another flight member. It has been going on for a while now between him and a rider of another flight about the advantages of Strix over Rukh. Jared joins in with glee since Zephyr is a Strix.

My attention is drawn to my right when I hear Tate's name. A dark-haired beauty is getting out of her chair, smiling at her friend.

"I'll go and see if Kyronos wants to warm my bed tonight. He sure looks like he could use a little help relaxing." She winks at the other girl, making her laugh, and strides out of the room. My stomach drops. The previously enticing aroma of food suddenly makes me queasy.

Jared nudges me with his shoulder, and I force a smile on my face. His brow creases, and he looks at me.

"Are you alright?" he asks.

I'll have to work on my fake smile.

"Just tired, and my body hurts all over."

"Yeah, the first patrol is always hard," Jared agrees. "Maybe you should let Tate—"

"No," I blurt. His eyebrows lift at my sudden outburst.

The last thing I want to think about right now is Tate and what he could be up to. Jared shrugs and goes back to the conversation. I try to relax and take my mind off Tate by listening to the guys, but it isn't working.

I wait for him or the girl to appear, but neither does. The thought of them coming back together—flushed and relaxed—is too much. I get up.

"I'm not hungry," I tell Jared and hurry out of the room before he can object. Back in my room, I stare at the wall because closing my eyes conjures images of them together.

Dammit.

I think about taking a walk, maybe to the stables. But there are enough dark corners around here.

Memories of Tate pressing me against the wall flash in my mind, the warmth of his body, the way he held my wrists captive between us. I groan.

I toss and turn, but sleep eludes me. At least I don't have to pretend otherwise. I'm glad I don't share rooms with anyone.

"You look like shit," Zaza tells me the following morning. I feel like it, too. I nod off during the flight again and again, and I'm glad I'm strapped in. Otherwise, I would have fallen off at one point.

We reach Platoria, a little seaside town, right as the sun is setting. The red-golden sunlight sparkles off the sea and the golden roofs of a castle-like structure that dominates the center of town. It also paints the mainly white buildings and the light face of the cliff in gold and copper hues.

To the west, the city descends in terraces until it finishes in a massive port. Ships of all sizes and flying various colors are anchored, coming in, or just leaving. All in all, the harbor seems bigger than the size of the city justifies.

"Stunning, isn't it?" Zaza asks me, and there is pride in her voice. "It's where Tanner and I come from," she lets me know, which explains her feelings.

"It's beautiful," I agree. And it is. The town rests on a cliff reaching into the ocean, escaping the mountains to the north. The buildings are of the same white stone as the cliff, which makes them seem one with their surroundings. Vibrant green dots the areas between the structures and surrounds the massive but elegant castle with its golden roof. Gardens, I realize.

Platoria is much prettier than any city I have seen before.

"What is that building?" I ask, pointing at the imposing one with the golden roof.

"The king's summer castle," Zaza answers.

Of course it is. I'm not surprised that he or his ancestors chose such a pretty place for it.

We land not far from the summer palace in a courtyard surrounded by white buildings. Caretakers hurry toward us, fussing over the birds as soon as we dismount, while a boy comes over, ready to show us our rooms.

This is much bigger than any of the outposts we've encountered so far, and we've never received such a welcome either. There is much more commotion, and the units of training warriors and riders we see off in the distance tell me this base is much better staffed too.

"We'll go out for dinner tonight." Tanner declares when we reach the corridor where our rooms are. "So take a shower and rest a bit. We'll meet back here in an hour."

Exploring the city does sound good, but I have no idea what to expect from an evening out with the flight.

...Tate doesn't get attached at all.

... see if Kyronos wants to warm my bed...

Zaza's words from days ago and the casual way the girl last night informed her friend...shit. Even thinking about sitting there quietly while another woman is all over him lets anger and something else explode in my chest. I'm also still confused about him telling Jared about me. What does that mean? Is he the only one who knows?

The thought of the whole flight knowing makes my insides heavy with dread. Surely someone would have slipped up if that were the case?

I bury my face in my hands, once again relieved that I have the room to myself. Shit.

Unease writhes in my gut like snakes, and for a second, I think about staying back. I could simply eat in the dining hall and go to bed early.

No.

I straighten. No fucking way am I missing out on seeing this beautiful city and having a great time tonight because of Tate Kyronos.

I get up and get dressed.

He made pretty fucking clear what he thinks of me the night he caught me coming out of Joel's room. Or the night before that, when he accused me of spying. And how fucking dare he spill my secrets to his friend?

I embrace the anger and feed it. By the time I leave my room to meet the rest of the flight, a nice glow warms my chest. Tonight will be fucking epic.

CHAPTER TWENTY-FIVE
TATE

We sit at a table wedged between all the other patrons. The Golden Boar is well-frequented, as always. Sturdy tables crowd the room, leaving only small trails of scuffed wooden flooring for the serving girls to wind through. Oddities from all over the continent decorate the whitewashed walls, and a bar takes up half of the back wall.

Music and the chatter of voices compete with each other in volume, so it's impossible to hear anyone outside a two-step radius.

I watch Ara, who, to my annoyance, sits at the opposite end of the table, wedged between Tanner and Boko, and seems to enjoy herself. She hasn't even once looked in my direction.

"You two are pathetic. You know that, right?" Jared asks me.

"I have no idea what you're talking about." I lie, which has recently become something I do quite often.

"Please tell me you at least had the decency not to screw Jen last night," Jared says, and I nearly spit out the sip of beer I just took.

"Excuse me?"

"Oh, you heard me." Jared leans in even closer. "I know you're in denial about this, but for me, it's as clear as day that you want her, and she wants you, aaand we are not at the academy at the moment sooo..." This time, I choke, and Jared laughs while he claps my back. "Unless you really aren't interested, then I could offer myself to help the poor girl—"

"Don't finish that sentence," I threaten. "How do you even know Jen approached me last night?"

"Oh, I heard the girls talking about it, and after I put two and two together, I realized so did Summer. It would at least explain her change of mood last night," Jared whispers.

Fuck.

"I would clear that up if I were you, or it will come back to bite you," he advises before he turns to Miller next to him, giving me time to mull over what he just said.

Up till now, staying away had seemed like a pretty good idea, but just thinking about her turning to someone else makes my thoughts murderous.

On the other hand, starting something with her would be utter madness.

I watch her talk to Tanner and realize Jared is right. The way she hangs on his every word raises my hackles and turns my mood sour.

What the fuck are they talking about?

Miller draws Tanner's attention away from Ara, and I relax. Yeah, I have to talk to her, but I'll have to catch her alone first.

When Ara excuses herself to the bathroom, I seize that chance and get up as well. Boko delays me by asking to get him another beer on the way back, and I swallow a groan. Now that I've decided to face her, I'm eager to get it over with. I wait in the hallway to catch Ara when she comes back out. It's darker back here, and the voices from the dining room are only a subtle hum in the background.

I have no idea what to tell her. All I know is I want but can't have her, and to the mists and back, I don't want anyone else to even come close to her.

Ara closes the door, and our eyes meet the moment she turns. A mix of hurt and anger flashes over her face.

Fuck.

She tries to hurry past me, but I stop her, using my body to cage her in against the corridor wall. My hands rest on the wall next to her head. Our bodies don't touch, but they may as well be because I am aware of her every breath. She could duck out, but she doesn't, and I decide to take that as a good sign.

Damn, she smells good.

She crosses her arms and leans back against the wall, her eyes blazing up at me, her mouth in a defiant little pout.

Shit. I want to kiss the stubbornness right off her lips.

I shake my head at the thought and try to form the words to make her see...

"This would get you into trouble," I tell her and fight the urge to lean in, her fiery eyes burning into mine. "I can't let you—"

"Oh, this is rich." If I thought her eyes were on fire before, they're now a fucking inferno. "I've had it with everyone telling me what I can or can't do," she hisses before she gets into my face. "Let me tell you something, Kyronos. If I decide to sleep with you or any other rider, it's my decision and my risk, not yours, so you can't let me... anything."

"You're not sleeping with anyone else," I growl.

"I'm free to do what I want, just like you." She sends me a false smile. "And thanks for informing me that you told Jared about me," she adds, sarcasm dripping off her words like blood off a killing blade before she ducks under my arm and hurries off.

Fuck.

I let my brow fall against the wall. This did not go as planned, and I haven't even said what I came here for.

By the time I make my way back to the table, Ara is back in her seat and not looking in my direction.

I curse under my breath. The chances of catching her alone again tonight are low, even if I didn't have plans of my own.

Maybe I'll give her a few hours to cool off and try again tomorrow.

I do my best to push thoughts of Ara out of my head while I leave the orderly part of Platoria behind, entering the area that borders the port. Platoria's port is an important trading point because of the mist. Nearly all trade between the five kingdoms takes place by sea. It's the perfect place to find answers or hire someone to find them for you.

The streets get darker and less frequented, and it always baffles me that this part of town is only a stone's throw away from the cliff where I used to go swimming with my brother and Jared. Those summers seem like a lifetime ago.

We spent many summers down here in the south. I smile at the memories that belong to a life I left behind more than three years ago.

Nan sits on a blanket reading, the now empty picnic basket at her side. Louis and two of his friends are our guards for today, which makes the afternoon much more relaxed than it would have been otherwise.

I watch my brother race his best friend Leo to the edge of the cliff, clearly enjoying the free day as much as I am. They shout in joy when they propel themselves off the ledge, spreading their arms like wings.

They're at that age when they have just started growing into their long arms and legs and seem a little uncoordinated and out of proportion, no matter how they dress. It's even more obvious now since, apart from Nan, all of us are dressed in dark cotton shorts and nothing else.

"Oi, wait, you little buggers," Louis shouts, running after them.

I remember our laughter while we jumped off that cliff, challenging each other to increasingly reckless jumps until Nan put her foot down and made us stop.

Louis was ten years older than his brother—about twenty-eight in that memory—but rivaled Jared in childish ideas even on a good day.

He was also the best at sweet-talking his mother. So after his pleading and our promises to behave, we're allowed to jump again.

We basked in the sun whenever our legs were too tired from running up the countless steps from the water below, just to do it all over again.

My smile slips when I remember why it's the last summer I spent that way. The last summer of Louis's and Leo's lives.

I haven't been back at the cliffs since. I haven't even been back in Platoria until starting patrols.

CHAPTER TWENTY-SIX
ARA

Two men at the table behind me talk about a dragon being in town, and I can't believe my luck. I tune out the riders around me and focus on the conversation behind me.

Based on the heavy silence that follows when one of the men drops the dragon's name, Lorcan, it seems his companion has heard of him.

"Lorcan was seen at the Dark Horse every night this week," the deep voice continues. "I wonder what he's waiting for."

"Probably just a lucrative deal," his friend answers. "Or maybe he got bored hiring out his services. I heard he fought on quite a few battlefields in the past century."

"Fuck, can you imagine being around that long?" the first man asks. "He probably saw more people die than we ever met."

"Forget seeing," the other snorts. "He probably killed more people than we ever met."

My mind whirls. Dragons are highly magical creatures, shapeshifters, and like the man said, they live a hell of a lot longer than humans do. So if anyone can answer my questions, it's a dragon.

I have to meet him.

I glance at Tanner to my right. Zaza said he grew up in Platoria, so he would know where the Dark Horse is, right?

I wait for him to finish his conversation with one of the serving girls, who he seems to know on a personal level, and then engage him in a conversation about growing up in Platoria. He makes it easy, and I soon know a lot about his family and the town around us.

"So what is the Dark Horse?" I finally ask, holding my breath when Tanner sits up straighter at that.

"What? Why do you ask?" He sounds alert.

"Oh, I just overheard some men talking about it and wondered what it is." I try to defuse his suspicion. He relaxes, and so do I.

"It's a tavern close to the port," Tanner answers my question, and I could have kissed him. "But not one you ever want to visit, kid. Believe me, there are more crooked things going on in one evening than you ever want to encounter in a lifetime."

"Oh, that doesn't sound good." I bite my lip. I'll have to be careful, then. He scoffs.

"No, nothing good ever came of it." Tanner shakes his head. "Not a place where anyone in uniform ever wants to show his face."

"What are you talking about?" Miller inquires, but Tanner waves him off. "Nothing good. Didn't you go home last weekend to help your brother prepare for the next assessment? How did that work out?" he asks instead, and I happily let them move on to a different topic. I won't get more information out of Tanner without raising suspicion, anyway.

I will need to change before I can head to the Dark Horse. But with the information that it's close to the port, I should be able to find it. I'm buzzing with nervous energy at the thought of finally finding answers.

I look up and catch Tate watching me. Guilt tries to overpower my anger at him and my excitement over this chance. I stomp it out like the last embers of a fire.

I will not feel guilty about doing everything to survive and save my family.

His gaze is probing, like he wants to figure out my thoughts. It's too much. I jump up and hurry off to the restrooms.

My thoughts jump around, trying to find the best way to meet the dragon. If I manage to slip away from the group before we get back, I would avoid having to sneak out later. Unfortunately, I think Tate will have everyone look for me once he sees I'm missing.

Why does he have to be so annoyingly observant?

I splash water on my face and take a few deep breaths to calm down. When I look in the mirror, my cheeks are flushed and my eyes are determined.

I will not blow this chance.

I step into the hallway and slam to a stop when I see *him* waiting for me. My feelings flash like the spokes on a fast-moving carriage, turning and turning until they are one big blur of chaos. Why do I always feel too much when he's around? I avert my gaze and try to slip past him, but he moves fast. Before I can blink, I find myself between him and the wall, his body blocking out everything else. My mind goes blank. The chaos inside me screeches to a halt. Tate leans in the tiniest bit, and for a second, I think he's going to kiss me. My heart picks up speed while I try my best to appear unfazed.

He shakes his head like he knows exactly what I'm thinking. Bastard.

"This would get you into trouble," he says, his voice rough. As if I would care about that right now.

"I can't let you—" He starts, and that pulls me back into reality. Oh no, he didn't. Not him, too.

Anger explodes in my chest, leaving it hollow.

"Oh, this is rich," I nearly spit the words. "I've had it with everyone telling me what I can or can't do." I get into his face. "Let me tell you something, Kyronos. If I decide to sleep with you or any other rider, it's my decision and my risk, not yours, so you can't let me... anything."

"You're not sleeping with anyone else," he growls, and indignation and triumph war inside me. How dare he tell me what to do, but ... is he jealous?

My common sense wins out. For all I know, he cozied up to another girl last night, and now he wants to tell me I can't do the same if I feel like it?

Fuck him.

"I'm free to do what I want, just like you." I bare my teeth at him. "And thanks for informing me that you told Jared about me," I add, escaping from the delicious cage of his arms and body to hurry back to our table.

The nerve of this man.

I slam my fist on the table while I slump back down in my seat, making all the drinks jump. All eyes land on me.

"A mosquito," I say dryly.

"A mosquito?" Jared raises his eyebrows. "In winter?"

I shrug. "I hate those buggers, drawing blood when they have no business even being there." I earn a few quizzical looks before everyone gets back to their conversations.

Jared looks unconvinced, but I don't care. I think I earned some major points since I neither slapped nor jumped my centurion. I'm not sure which urge would have won out if I had stayed.

Jared leans over the table like he wants to say something but is interrupted when the reason for my mood drops back into his seat. I turn away from them and give Boko my full attention.

I meet Tate's eyes more than once when I look up, but he doesn't try to talk to me again, and when he heads off on his own after we leave the Golden Boar, I ignore the twist in my gut and decide I'm glad the fates are making it so easy for me. It gets even easier to slip away when the group breaks up even more. No one pays me any attention when I fall back and then slip into a narrow side street.

I hold my breath for the first few steps, expecting someone to call my name, but no one does.

The city is as pretty from down here as it was from up in the air. Little shops line the street I find myself on, their big windows sparkling with the light spilling out. Some people bustle around, trying to finish their errands, while others stroll leisurely, laughing and talking in groups or pairs.

The streets are clean and well-lit, the people relaxed and well-fed. It seems safe to say Platoria is thriving with all the business that comes with having a big port.

I pass two pairs of guards within five minutes and no longer wonder about the absence of pickpockets. I guess a city with the royal family in attendance every summer must keep up its appearance.

I stop at a cute little shop that promises immediate delivery of all dress orders, and when I step inside, to the peal of a bell, a smiling woman the age of my mother greets me. She laughs when my jaw drops as soon as she starts working.

Under her administration, the fabric I picked splits, molds, and merges until I'm left with a dress that fits me perfectly without so much as a stitch in sight. I've never met someone with a gift like that before.

It costs me all the money I have with me, but the experience alone is worth it. She even agreed to hold on to my uniform after I told her I wanted to surprise someone.

Hopefully, I'll be able to recover it. Between this set and the one I left at Sloan's, I'll soon be short on uniforms otherwise.

Finding the port is easy. I just have to follow the streets downhill. Soon, I leave the well-lit and orderly district behind. The lights get dimmer and fewer until they stop altogether.

The streets are dirtier and in an increasing state of disrepair, just like the houses that frame them. It's hard to believe I'm still in the same city.

I take care to keep my walk easy and confident. Showing weakness should be the last thing I do in an area like this. Maybe coming here wasn't my smartest idea.

Something moves in a shadow ahead, and I change to the other side of the street.

My neck is tingling, but I don't turn around. Occasionally, I hear steps behind me, and all my senses are on high alert. But the closer I get to the water, the less reliable the magic around me feels. It flickers and jumps like something distorts the signal, playing tricks on my mind. I could have sworn I felt Tate behind me once, only for his warmth to vanish a second later.

Losing this sense of the magic makes me aware of how much I've come to rely on it already, and the lack of it blinds me in a way that makes me feel vulnerable.

I refrain from asking for directions to the Dark Horse after a seemingly harmless old woman I approach sizes me up like I'm a horse for sale.

I take a few wrong turns and once stumble to a halt at the edge of a cliff, the dark water swirling beneath me. But finally, I spot an askew hanging sign of a black horse on weathered wood.

The door underneath doesn't look much better, and the boarded-up windows make it seem anything but welcoming. I suppress the urge to turn away and step into the tavern that has to be the Dark Horse.

The room is only marginally better lit than the streets outside, but the air is decidedly more stuffy, filled with the smell of unwashed bodies and sour beer. Apart from being run down, it doesn't look much different from any other tavern I've been at—except for the massive cage in the back, where, surrounded by a cheering crowd, two people are fighting each other. The bad lighting makes it hard to see anyone's face.

After what Tanner told me, only a fool would think that this is any safer than the alley outside. I'm no fool, even if some might argue differently, considering I'm here to meet a dragon, something many would consider madness.

I shove Tate's face out of my mind.

My eyes are well-adjusted to the dark, so I have no problem spotting the dragon the minute I walk in. He looks like he's illuminated by a fire that only exists for him.

He's beautiful and terrifying at the same time. His eyes seem to glow an eerie orange, and his symmetrical face looks unnatural. After watching him for a moment, I realize he doesn't blink, and his movements are off, not human. No wonder everyone gives him a wide berth.

Not my best idea.

I square my shoulders, ignore the turning heads from the people I pass, and make my way over to him. This is my chance to get answers.

The closer I get, the stronger the raw power radiating from him. It's wild and barely controlled, like a vicious dog on a tiny leash.

Worst idea ever.

My heart pounds in my chest, nearly drowning out all the noise around me, and everything inside me screams to turn and leave. But the dragon's gaze is already on me, tracking my movement through the room, and everyone else turns away.

Dragons are said to be very greedy and possessive. No matter what happens, no one will step in. Not that the people here are the kind to step in for anyone anyway.

I shove down my rising anxiety.

Don't show fear. No sudden movements. No strong emotions. I recite every scrap of information I ever heard about approaching a dragon, desperately trying to ignore the rule above all. *Just don't.*

He moves his head sideways. A predatory move that belies his human form.

"Tamara Blackstone," he purrs when I reach his table, and my brows jump up. "I had the pleasure of meeting your brother," he continues. Well, that explains how he knows who I am. I have heard about their freakishly good noses and memory, but experiencing it is something else entirely. He inclines his head, sizing me up, the vertical slits of his pupils and glowing eyes even more unnerving from up close.

"Now, why would a pretty little thing like you approach a dragon?"

Here goes nothing. I take a steadying breath.

"Lorcan." I incline my head respectfully and hope my smile looks more convincing than it feels. He gestures for me to sit, and I position myself with my back to the wall, even if it means I sit right next to him. "Thank you for your time," I say, determined to stick to politeness, even if it kills me. Not doing so will kill me for sure.

"What is it?" he asks. It seems like he's as impatient as the tales say. I look around us, but everyone is out of earshot. Lorcan notices my glances, and I see something glimmer in his eyes. Interest maybe? Curiosity?

Shit, am I really going to do this?

Before I talk myself out of it, I lean on the table, reducing the space between us.

"I need information about cursed ones," I murmur.

He leans in, scenting my neck. I lock my muscles and make myself stay still even though I want nothing more than to jump away.

"And why would someone like you be looking for information like that?" he asks softly.

It's a trap. If I lie, I will never get my answers.

He is so close now that I don't need more than a whisper to reach him. "Because I am one."

His eyes roam over me. It feels like a caress, so sensual and private that I want to lean back. His voice is a purr.

"I can tell you all about your heritage and your magic," he says casually.

Yes.

"What do you need?" I try for a neutral tone even though he probably hears my heart pounding out of my chest.

Deep, controlled breaths. Relax.

With a smirk, he rises from his chair. I move without thinking and get up as well. He comes even closer, stepping way too much into my personal space. He wraps a strand of my unbound hair around his hand, tugging me closer, and there is no room to step back.

Maybe putting my back against the wall hadn't been a good idea. He leans in, scenting my skin again, and I hold my breath.

"I need to taste you," he tells me, his breath hot against my skin.

I recoil—as far as the wall lets me—and he laughs softly.

"Not so brave now, are you?" He sounds curious. "But you hold yourself better than I thought. I give you that," he continues, his eyes wandering over me before stopping at my face again. "Body fluids work well..." He does that head tilt again. A predator assessing his prey. "Blood being the most reliable."

Fuck. Fuck. Fuck. Dragons have a thing for blood? I've never heard of that.

"How much blood?" I press out.

"Oh, a scratch will do. Unless..." He licks his lips, and I don't want to hear what he'll suggest next.

"A scratch sounds perfect." My voice sounds too high, even in my own ears.

Hold it together, Ara. Get your answers, and then you can leave.

He laughs. "You sure?" He puts his finger on the pulse throbbing in my throat, and I grit my teeth.

Polite. I need to be polite.

I take a deep breath but release it instantly when I realize how it lessens the space between us.

"What do you want for it?" I ask with a thin voice.

"Oh, knowing your secret and a favor in the future will be fine, considering who you are." He winks at me. I don't like owing him, but backing out is not an option.

"I owe you a favor—not the sexual kind—" I add hastily when his gaze wanders over me again, and he smirks. "You will keep my secret, and you'll tell me everything you know about cursed ones in general and me specifically, and hold nothing back?" I ask to make sure we're on the same page.

"That's a deal then." He sounds pleased. Smiling, he clasps my hand in his.

"Deal." I exhale and suppress a yelp when I feel a burning sensation on the inside of my right forearm. Well, I didn't think it would be so...binding, but I guess that was naive. He leans in, and my heartbeat picks up even more.

"Wait," I say and put my hand on his chest to stop him from getting any closer. "I...could you just start with the general information?"

"Scared?" he asks, then laughs when I shake my head in denial. "Show me your mark," he demands, and I obey.

"So cursed ones always have marks?" I ask.

"Cursed?" He snorts. "The gifted have marks, don't they?" I nod. "So why would you think it would be any different for you? Magic marks its bearers. It doesn't care about the name you put on it."

Magic? As in gift?

He traces the mark, a wriggly line the length of my index finger, running down the inside of my arm. "Give me your hands." I place my hands in his, and the beast inside me snaps, eager to get to his power, but I hold it back.

"So much potential." He looks up at me. "And you learned to control it." His eyes wander to my neck. "Let me have all the information."

Blood. I take a deep breath and nod.

It's just a scratch. Nothing you haven't had a hundred times.

I squeeze my eyes shut, and my muscles tense in anticipation. The sting of a sharp talon runs along my collarbone. Then all hell breaks loose.

CHAPTER
TWENTY-SEVEN
TATE

I'm walking back toward the center of Platoria when I spot a familiar shadow hurrying around a corner. I don't linger on the thought of how truly fucked I am if I know her movements so well that I recognize her in such bad lighting.

Ara.

Does she never sleep? Or stay where she's supposed to, for that matter?

She will be pissed if I follow her.

But she doesn't know this city, and I remember how easily I pinned her to the wall in that alley in Telos. I curse under my breath before going after her.

Every thought of leaving her alone flies out the window when I follow her into the seediest area Platoria has to offer.

Doesn't she have any concept of self-preservation?

I lessen the distance between us. Staying hidden isn't my focus anymore because I see the gazes she draws. Anger burns through me —at her for risking herself and at the human predators assessing her from the shadows. If they so much as move for her, they are dead.

In all the time I follow her, she doesn't look behind her once.

What the fuck is wrong with this woman?

She ducks through a doorway, and I swear as I recognize the sign above the door. The Dark Horse is notorious for crooked bargains, betting, and illegal fighting. What the hell is she doing here, of all places?

I look down at myself. I'm wearing my uniform, so there is no way I can go in there looking like this and not draw attention. I slip into the shadows of an entryway, watching the door across the street while I contemplate what to do next.

She's made it pretty clear what she thought of being told what to do, but I can't just leave her here. The door opens and closes. Others go in and come out, but Ara doesn't.

She's a good fighter and probably has a lot of blades hidden under her dress, but ... I need to know she is all right. I sigh.

I will take one look, and then I'll go.

That plan goes up in flames as soon as I step into the room and see her. See them.

There is a man—no, a dragon—crowding Ara against the wall, much like I did earlier. He's talking to her. She shakes her head and says something back that makes him laugh.

My knee-jerk reaction is to go over there and rip off the hand currently playing with her hair.

"*Cool down. That is a fucking dragon,*" Daeva pipes in, clearly alerted by my turmoil. "*I'm coming your way.*"

"No. Stay," I tell her. "*I'm keeping my cool, I promise.*"

I have no claim on her, I remind myself.

But a dragon? Is she serious? Not that there is anything wrong with dragons—if you have a death wish.

I let my gaze roam over the other guests. They are all taking great care not to look in the direction of Ara and her fiery friend. They won't lift a finger, even if he decides to sample her right here and now.

Shit, I probably should leave, but my eyes find their way back to Ara. Like they always do.

Is he scenting her? What. The. Actual. Fuck.

She jerks back, and her head hits the wall behind her. She doesn't look scared and isn't fighting him off either, but her pulling back is enough to have me reassess what I see.

Her smile looks brittle and jagged, missing all the teasing and fire I'm used to seeing by now.

Holy mists, I don't know what game she's playing here, but she doesn't look like she enjoys having his hands on her. That's all it needs to have the beast inside me screaming for blood.

His blood.

When he trails a finger down the soft skin of her neck, I see red and start moving.

I wind around tables, people muttering in my wake when I shove past them, but my eyes never leave Ara's face.

She squeezes her eyes shut, bracing for something. His hand resting above her collarbone ripples. Scales form, replacing skin, and sharp talons appear, reflecting the light.

My daggers whisper against the leather of their sheaths when I draw one on each side. The dragon is focused on Ara now, not even looking up, showing no interest in the commotion I cause.

One black talon slices her skin, drawing blood.

Hell, no.

I throw both daggers, which come to a quivering halt on the wall next to his shoulders. That maneuver draws more than just the dragon's attention.

Chairs scrape over the floor. People jump out of my way while my steps eat up the room, bringing me closer to her.

My throw did what I intended. His attention is on me now. There is no mistaking him for human anymore. Scales replaced his skin entirely, and his face twists into a feral snarl.

The way he positions himself leaves no question about him considering Ara his for the moment, and I'm not okay with that. She is... not his.

I palm another dagger. Even with people getting out of my way, there isn't enough room for a sword in here. They move around me, careful not to come between us and hurry to the door, overturning chairs and tables in their haste. Smart.

I have no illusions. He will be spitting fire any minute now.

My gaze searches for Ara, meeting her wide eyes. The slip in attention nearly costs me. Her eyes widen a fraction more, and instinct prompts me to drop to the floor before heat cooks the air above me.

Well, shit. This is getting ugly fast.

I crouch, waiting for the blast to stop, and then propel myself across the room, seizing Ara and pulling her with me behind the next overturned table, throwing up a shield of air between us and the piece of furniture. Not a second later, another heat blast reduces the table to little more than cinders while we scramble to get away from it.

"What are you doing here?" Ara sounds breathless.

"How about we talk later?" I ask.

Continuous crackling dominates the room. The old wooden tables and chairs doused in wax, grease, and alcohol over the years burn better than kindling.

"Get over here." It's a snarl, nothing human in it—a predator commanding his prey.

Ara takes a step like she's about to obey him.

"Hell, no." I grab her, shoving her behind me. "Keep down and get to the door. And if I tell you to run, you run. Okay?" I turn to her when she doesn't answer, and it earns me four deep gouges across my shoulder. The dragon is upon us.

I whip around and use the gathered momentum to punch him in return. Thank the mists the nose is a sensitive organ, no matter the species. He stumbles back, and I waste no time. I grab Ara's hand, holding it like a lifeline, and race out the door.

We run down the street. Turning right at the next corner, we nearly collide with a drunken sod coming the other way. He curses when I shove him out of the way and keep going.

"That is not the way back to the base." Ara's voice sounds remarkably calm, and I'm glad about the daily training at the academy. Dragons are fast, and they have wicked good noses. So I have no hope of him not following us in a minute.

Maybe we'll be lucky, and the blood running down his nose interferes with his sense of smell, but dragons heal fast too.

"We are not going back. We need to get to the water." Water is one of the only things that can stop him from roasting us alive.

I snatched Ara from him and hurt him in the process. No matter how even-tempered he normally might be, now he's an animal out for blood, and he will shred us without a second thought if he reaches us.

There is a reason there are so few half-breed dragons; accidental deaths in a lovers' quarrel are unfortunately common. Other species are just too breakable.

This leads me back to the problem at hand.

"A dragon, really?" I ask and steal a look at Ara, who is running next to me. Fortunately, I know the way. The streets are dark down here, and there are many dead ends. One wrong turn and we are fucked. "Is sneaking out not enough of a kick anymore?"

She huffs in indignation. "That is not what it's about."

"Then do tell. Enlighten me because I can't see any reason you would associate with a dragon otherwise."

"Maybe I thought he was pretty?"

"Pretty?" I gawk at her before snapping my gaze back to where we are going. "Pretty lethal, you mean." I curse. We nearly missed our next turn. My shoulder protests when I skid and slam into a wooden wall. I turn slightly and catch Ara when she slams into my chest, making me grunt.

The whole building shakes, and someone starts shouting. We pick up speed again, but a roar behind us tells me the dragon found us.

"Run," I order.

We leap into a sprint, much too fast for these dark streets with uneven ground. I can already smell the sea, so we are getting closer.

I stumble but catch myself, and I grab Ara's hand to keep her upright when she does as well.

The last houses are behind us now, the pavement giving way to a smooth dirt road with the occasional weed and grass dotting it.

Our steps become more certain, our breaths getting choppy while we press our bodies for all the speed we have left.

I keep her hand in mine, making sure she doesn't slow down. She tries to tug her hand free, but I don't let her. I have a plan but can't risk her hesitating.

About a hundred steps in front of us, the world ends with only sky and waves beyond that. I can hear the dragon's steps behind us, gaining ground. It's good that he followed us on foot instead of turning fully and taking off for the sky. Otherwise, we would be roasted by now. There is nowhere to hide out here, leaving us completely in the open. That leaves us exactly one way out, and we're getting closer. Unfortunately, so is the dragon.

CHAPTER
TWENTY-EIGHT

ARA

We are running toward a cliff. Even in the dark, there is no mistaking the drop in front of us for anything else. The drop Tate is going for at full speed. I try to slow down, but he holds on tight, not giving me any chance to fight the momentum or his strength.

"We are... going to jump," Tate gasps, confirming my worst nightmare.

"No!" I struggle against his hold, but his grip is like iron. "I can't swim!" I try to reason with him. Our momentum propels us forward and keeps us moving.

"Do you trust me?" He glances my way but doesn't slow down and never lets go of me.

"No!" Well, not when he's about to hurl us off a cliff. My breath stutters from the view in front of us.

He snorts. "Well, you're gonna have to." He grabs me around the waist and jumps.

We fall for ages, tumbling through the wind and spraying water before we hit the waves. The impact rattles my bones and drives water up my nose. The cold hits me, surrounds me, stuns me.

The frigid water soaks my clothes, steals my breath, and pulls me down instantly. I can't discern up from down. Bubbles surround me, tickle my face, obscure everything around me. I panic and thrash around. I'm lost.

Slowly, I realize the bubbles are all going in one direction.

They're going up.

Finding my equilibrium and some sense of direction helps to wrestle down the panic. The relief is short-lived, however, because when I look up, the surface is a silvery shimmer far, far above me.

The water presses in on me, and there is no way I will get up there before I give in to the increasing need to breathe.

Kicking my legs, I fight against the weight of my clothes. The hem of my dress tangles around my legs, making it hard to move. I struggle, kick, and fight against the watery grave around me and make no progress at all.

I would have laughed about the irony of it all if I had any breath left. In my quest to stay alive, I gained the wrath of a dragon, was nearly burned to a crisp, and will now drown. Maybe I should have gone to bed after all.

A strong arm circles my waist and pulls me up toward the light. Sure strokes spur us upward, the beckoning ripple finally coming closer. Our heads break the surface, and I gasp for air.

"You infuriating, arrogant, crazy bastard." My hands hit Tate with every word. I gasp down another breath. "Drowning is not how I want to die. How could you..." He lets go of me, and my dress pulls me down instantly. My hands grab for him on instinct, holding on for dear life.

He uses the moment to adjust his grip, pinning my arms between us.

"Relax, Ara." His chest heaves against me. "I won't let you drown." Water trickles down his face, turning his long lashes into little spikes. The moonlight turns his normally golden skin a pale silver.

Damn, he's beautiful.

And I really have a problem if that's the first thing I notice after nearly drowning.

I avert my gaze and look up at the cliff instead. It seems to reach for the sky.

"You can't promise that." My breath still comes in gasps, cutting my words in small bites. "How are we going to get out of here? We can't climb like that, the wind will make us numb and clumsy in no time, and then we will fall back into the water and end up eaten by fish." My voice gets higher and higher, the words tumbling out faster and faster.

He looks at me and smirks. He simply *smirks* at me, like what I say is funny. I draw in another breath, ready to lay into him. But he cuts me off.

"You will not feed the fish today. Even though it's dark, Daeva would come for us before letting me drown. But...we will simply use the stairs over there." He motions with his head to his right. Now that he points them out, I can see the stairs cut into the stone.

I feel foolish and cringe inwardly about my panic. My brothers would have had some choice words to say about that...after yelling at me about getting into such a situation in the first place.

I would have blushed in shame, but my face feels like a mask of ice ready to shatter at the wrong movement. If there is any color on my face, it's probably blue or white.

"You knew there were stairs." It's more of a statement than the accusation I intended. My teeth start to chatter.

"We jumped off the cliff when we were younger." He smiles. "Do you want to take back anything you said before?"

"No." I send him a glare. He chuckles and starts for the stairs. Tate is frighteningly efficient, even with my body weighing him down. And maybe I admire the powerful strokes and the muscles working to save us both.

He pushes me toward the stairs, treading water behind me, waiting for me to climb out first.

I look forward to getting out of the water, but as soon as I drag myself up the first few steps, I take it all back. The cold of the water is nothing compared to the agony once the wind reaches me.

If my face felt like an ice mask before, I now feel like a cursed marble statue. My chattering teeth are joined by rattling knees. About halfway up, my whole body shakes so hard that I'm afraid I will tumble down at any second.

Tate is not much better off even though he tries to hide it. No one is waiting for us when we finally reach the ground above.

Maybe Lorcan didn't know about the steps or simply gave up waiting. I don't know if I'm relieved or sad about it. A little fire would have been nice, and I still want my answers. However, there is a chance he's still caught up in his rage, and I don't want to face that version of him right now.

Tate uses his gift to shield us from the wind, but it doesn't make much of a difference at this point, and when he tries to warm the air around us, he turns frighteningly pale.

"S-s...stop," I tell him, my teeth chattering so hard I'm astonished I even manage to speak. "N...n...not carry...y you."

He hesitates for a moment but then nods. "I'm calling Daeva," he says, his gaze turning distant.

"No!" I shake my head frantically. The only place Daeva can land close to the base is in the courtyard, which will draw attention I can't afford.

"Ara," Tate growls. But I shake my head again and start walking.

My actions are sluggish and stiff, but I keep moving. The warmth of Tate's gift is right next to me, calling to me, and I want nothing more than to snuggle into it, to draw the warmth in and let it heat me. I...*what?* My eyes widen in alarm, and I stumble. No, surely I meant to say I wanted to snuggle into him, his body right?

"Let me carry you." Tate looks worried, but I shake my head. I will not get close to him right now, not after that. Not when it's something I want so badly, and I'm no longer sure the reason is simple attraction.

"I'm...f-f—" I start, but he cuts me off.

"If you say fine," he threatens, stepping closer, "I will pick you up right now because then you are delirious."

I bite my tongue and start walking again. By the time we reach the edges of Platoria, it's painfully obvious that I will never make it back in this condition. My body is no longer just stiff but also numb. Thankfully, the shaking has stopped, but I'm more stumbling than walking, and it takes all my concentration to set one foot in front of the other. I'm so tired.

When I stumble again, Tate sweeps me into his arms, his eyes daring me to protest, but I don't. This is so much better: his arms, his warmth...I snatch my hand away from the skin of his neck, placing it on his uniform-covered shoulder instead.

My sudden movement earns me a raised eyebrow, and I look everywhere but at his face. I only now realize the houses around us look nothing like the ones we ran past while escaping the dragon. They are tall and proud, and the street is clean and well-lit.

"You didn't think I would walk with you in that state through the worst area Platoria has to offer, did you?" Tate asks. "This way is also shorter, and we can do this." Tate steps up to one of the houses and knocks.

That he wears his uniform does come in handy now. We are ushered in without a question and find ourselves in front of a roaring fire, covered in blankets and cradling cups of hot tea before we can utter so much as a question.

The shaking returns as if my body had simply been too rigid before and continues now that it can. The feeling in my feet and hands returns with a vengeance, and I bite my lip to hold in a moan. It hurts.

Gradually, the mix of stabbing pain and tingles gives way to my extremities feeling like they are on fire.

I drink three cups of tea, the hot liquid warming me up from within. The shaking finally stops, and my body no longer feels like it might shatter.

Apart from a few muttered thanks to our host, a matronly woman who, despite her curious glances, hasn't asked any questions so far, we sit in total silence.

I have to admire her for her restraint. I would have asked a lot of questions if two strangers came up to my doorstep soaking wet, uniform or not.

She is currently bustling in her kitchen, warming up the stew she offered us if the heavenly scent is anything to go by. I eye the room around us. It's cozy, with thick rugs covering the floor, a big fireplace, and multiple bookshelves, but clutter is everywhere.

My lips twitch at the thought of what Ian would say to that since he always gives me hell for leaving stuff out.

"How is it that I find you always in the thick of it when trouble is to be found?" Tate breaks the silence, and my eyes fly back to his face.

"I was doing just fine until you came charging in," I say.

"Which I did because you were cornered by a fucking dragon who looked like he was ready to devour you!"

I roll my eyes at his dramatics. "Lorcan was hardly going to eat me."

"Oh, you're on a friendly basis now?" His eyebrows jump up. "He sure as hell looked ready to take a bite out of you when I came in." The muscles in his cheek twitch. "And then he chased us!"

"Because you stormed in wearing your damn uniform and throwing daggers." My anger bubbles up. If not for Tate, I would have answers by now.

"It is a *damn uniform* you should be wearing instead of walking around in disguise." He glares at me.

"Then I wouldn't get any answers." I bite down on my lip as soon as the words are out.

"What answers?" Tate leans toward me, his eyes alert.

"It's personal." I put aside the empty teacup.

"No answer is worth risking your life." He holds my gaze, waiting for my consent, but I look away. All of this *is* about keeping me alive.

Will Lorcan talk to me if I manage to find him again? Will he honor our deal after this mess, or will he ask for something else as compensation?

"You're angry with me for stopping him?" Tate's voice sounds incredulous. He leans forward, getting in my face. "What the fuck were you hoping he would do? Fight you? Fuck you? Maybe even right there in front of everyone?" His voice brims with anger. "Please do enlighten me on why you thought getting close to a dragon was a good idea." He is furious, and I don't know what to feel.

I'm angry he ruined my chance at answers. I'm embarrassed he thinks I was looking for a hookup. And he willingly faced down a dragon for me—yeah, I won't even go there. My anger evaporates.

His face goes blank when I don't say anything, wiping away all traces of anger and replacing it with indifference. I blink.

"I was clearly wrong then," he says, his voice flat. "I'm sorry for ruining your evening."

My chest tightens at the cold look he gives me. He has never looked at me like this before. It hurts. My eyes prickle, and I try not to blink to keep the tears from falling.

"Please stop," I whisper. "Don't look at me like that. I'm just trying... to survive." My last two words are no more than a whisper.

He shifts closer, and my eyes snap to his. Concern replaces indifference. His gaze jumps between my eyes like he's trying to read me.

He opens his mouth, but I cut in before he can get a word out.

"I've already said too much." I shake my head. "Please don't ask," I plead because I want to tell him. I want nothing more than to throw myself into his arms, hide my face in the crook of his neck, and spill all my secrets.

It scares me, and it would be the biggest and maybe last mistake of my life. I look at the fire, biting my lip.

Tate comes closer, and I hold my breath. His thumb brushes my lower lip, tugging it free from my teeth. Sparks shoot through my body.

I close my eyes, my breath shaky when I release it. His palm is an exquisite caress sliding along my jaw, cupping my face. And I can't resist. I lean into his touch, savoring how his thumb continues to trace my lips. The subtle rasp of his calloused pad against my lips makes my hair stand on end. I shiver. My tongue snakes out, and I taste the ocean on his skin.

He groans.

I have never felt so drawn to anyone. And before tonight, I didn't doubt my attraction. But now...is it simply attraction or the curse... gift...whatever it is that pulls me to him?

"Look at me, Ara." His voice is gravelly, his words whispering over my face, and it doesn't matter anymore what pulls me in. All I can think of is how close he is.

Oh gods.

Heat pools in my gut.

My eyes fly open, following his command, and the same heat is burning in Tate's eyes. His focus shifts to my lips, and he leans in even closer.

CHAPTER TWENTY-NINE
TATE

"You make such a lovely couple." The voice of our host shatters the moment, and we jerk apart.

I release my breath and drag my eyes away from Ara's lips to the woman who took such good care of us.

"I didn't mean to startle you," she says, handing us each a bowl filled to the brim. I'm glad my hands have something to do because I want to reach for Ara.

I nearly kissed her.

I can't believe I came so close to stepping over that line. A line that looks more and more like it's drawn in quicksand instead of the stone it should be set in.

Discipline and self-control are second nature for me, but around her, I'm teetering on an edge, one nudge away from going down the wrong side.

We eat quietly, and the silence stretches and grows with every minute that passes.

Ara's words keep circling in my mind, waking an unease I can't shake. What does she mean when she says she's trying to survive?

I huff out a frustrated breath, which makes Ara look up. But she doesn't ask, and I don't explain. She's the first person I have met who has maybe even more secrets than I do. And I want—no, need—to know all of them.

Warmed up and our bellies full, we thank our host profusely, and she declines our offer of compensation. We head back to the post, the silence between us still intact. It seems unbreakable by now.

Ara's face is unusually somber, and she keeps so much space between us that another person could walk there without touching either of us.

I have a plan to get her in, and since I'd rather not have a knee in my groin or a dagger between my ribs, I decide that breaking the silence is the least painful option.

"Let me handle it and play along," I tell Ara gruffly before I wrap an arm around her and tug her into my side.

She stiffens at first but then relaxes and snuggles into me.

Fuck, she fits perfectly.

The guards operating the gate come into view. Thank the gods, no one here knows Ara, and we'll be leaving the following morning, so the chance of running into those two guards should be minimal.

The leather of my armor is still soaked and looks slightly darker, the surface a little rougher, but nothing overly noticeable. My hair is dry again, and my boots are no longer squelching with every step.

Ara is a different matter, though. Her dress is still wet and clings to her body in very distracting ways. Her hair falls down her back in damp strands, slightly ruffled from when she rubbed it dry earlier, and her cheeks are slightly pink from the cold.

She is beautiful, and I'm not the only one noticing.

The way one of the guards ogles her makes me want to punch

him, but since a scene is the last thing we need right now, I glare at him instead.

The one demanding my name smirks knowingly before he notes Ara down as "visitor female" without even asking.

That was easier than I thought.

I keep my arm around her until we reach my room, even if we don't run into anyone. I turn to her but don't have the chance to say anything before the door to my room flies open. Jared lifts his brows when he sees us, and his posture relaxes. His hair is even messier than usual.

He grabs our arms and yanks us inside, grimacing at the damp coldness of our clothes.

"Where the mists were you?" he hisses while he closes the door. "And what the fuck did you do with her?" He takes in Ara in her wet dress and shakes his head.

"He threw me off a cliff," Ara replies, which makes Jared's eyes go wide and look in my direction for clarification.

"I did not throw you off a cliff," I disagree.

"Okay, you grabbed me and threw both of us off a cliff, which is basically the same thing," she states, raising her eyebrows in challenge.

I grin, remembering how cute she had looked with water running down her face, her eyes blazing while she launched herself at me.

"Okay, that's a story I need to hear," Jared declares. "But first..." He levels a glare at Ara. "Never skulk off like that again. My heart nearly stopped when I realized you were not with us, and I was dreading telling this moody bastard I lost his...uh...runner. Which brings me to you..." Now, I'm the one in his focus. "Why didn't you let me know she was with you?"

"Oh, you'll understand as soon as you hear where I found her, but first..." I grab a set of training clothes out of my closet and thrust them at Ara. "Change."

"I'm fine," Ara protests.

"We are not having that conversation again," I tell her. "Once you are dry and your lips are no longer blue, we can talk about fine."

"Alright." She takes the clothes. "Turn around, both of you." We do, but I realize quickly that the dark window works as a mirror.

"Close your eyes," I hiss at Jared, who does as I say but shakes with silent laughter. I concentrate on my feet while trying to ignore the fact that Ara is undressing behind me and that I only need to look up to see her reflection.

Fuck. I've never felt so tempted in my life.

"All done," she announces finally, and I release a breath I didn't know I was holding.

When I turn, I find Ara sitting cross-legged on my bed, combing through her hair with her fingers. My shirt is too big for her, the soft fabric flowing over her curves and slipping down over one shoulder. I swallow.

She rolled up the sleeves a few times, and black lines peek out from under the right one. I reach for her hand, and the sleeve falls back when I lift it, revealing a pattern of black lines on the inside of her arm like vines winding around a line. That has not been there before.

"What is that?" I snap.

"A promise," she answers in a duh voice.

"I can see that. Whom did you give this promise to?" I demand to know.

What has she promised that is so binding?

Her gaze flies to my face, and she opens her mouth like she's going to answer, then her eyes fly to Jared, and she clamps her mouth shut, shaking her head.

"That is none of your business," she finally says, freeing her hand and smoothing the sleeve back down.

I keep staring at it. She didn't have it when I healed her, but during training? I would have noticed it, wouldn't I?

"I'm tired." Ara gets up and heads to the door. "Good night." She steps through the door, her expression shuttered when she meets my gaze, and I let her go. I won't get any answers tonight.

The door closes softly behind her, and Jared steps up to me.

"You are so fucked, man," he declares, slapping me on the back. I just nod because there is no use in denying it.

Even my reasoning of her being safer if I stayed away starts to waver after tonight. My life sure as hell was quieter before I met her.

Would it really be so bad to give in to my attraction?

THE FLIGHT BACK IS PURE AGONY. I'M AROUND ARA ALL THE time but never manage to catch her alone. By the end of the second day, I start to suspect she's avoiding me on purpose. She even chose to share one of the double rooms with Zaza, so catching her alone after everyone went to bed is out, too.

The only good thing so far is that we have seen very little action. Extraordinarily so. There was movement along the mist once, but they retreated as soon as we came closer to investigate.

One more day, and we will be back at the academy. I have no doubt it will be even harder to catch her alone than when she easily avoids me in the comparatively cramped space of the outposts.

I could order her to talk to me, but that feels wrong.

When I return from my shower, I glimpse her slipping outside and seize the chance.

She sits at the edge of the fortification wall, her legs dangling over it, seemingly lost in thought. When she notices me, she's instantly alert and ready to bolt.

"Please stay," I say.

She shakes her head, her eyes wide. "I can't," she whispers. "I can't answer your questions."

"I'm not gonna lie. I'm going to ask questions." I give her a rueful smile. "But would you stay if I promise not to ask them tonight?"

She hesitates but then nods, and I sit down next to her. The situation reminds me so much of my encounter with Jen that I realize I haven't cleared that up yet.

It seems strange to state something like that out of the blue, but then I remember her words after I caught her coming out of Cassius's room.

"I did not hook up with Jen or anyone else lately," I say, looking over to gauge her reaction. The smile that blooms on her face sparks my own.

"I didn't talk to the dragon for that reason either," Ara offers back.

"Why—" I stop myself. "Sorry, no questions. I remember."

Ara laughs at my pained expression. "It's killing you, isn't it?" she asks, and I nod sheepishly. "Too bad because I still won't tell you," she teases with a wide smile.

"Cruel." I can't help but return her grin. "So since I can't ask questions, maybe you want to just tell me something about yourself willingly instead?"

"That was a question." She grins. "I think I'll ask you some questions now."

"You can ask," I agree, "but I won't always answer." She snorts in indignation, and I laugh.

"What?" I ask when she simply watches me, smiling.

"Nothing." She shakes her head, but her smile widens.

"You want to ask me nothing?" I raise one eyebrow. She widens her eyes comically.

"You laugh, and you joke? Who are you, and what did you do with Centurion Grumpy?"

"Smart-ass," I grumble, and her laughter washes over me like sunshine on a summer day.

"How long have you known Jared?"

"Since before I can remember. I'm closer to him than my brother."

"So you have a brother. Where is he?" she asks, but I only shake my head. "Okay...how is it to be bonded?" she fires the next question.

"It's like you gain an additional part of yourself, if that makes sense?" I smile when she scrunches up her nose, but she nods.

We settle on the safe topic of the academy and becoming a skyrider after that.

"So the cliff," she suddenly says, and I tense. "You and your flight went swimming there before?"

I shake my head.

"You and Jared, then?"

"It was a lifetime ago," I answer. "I don't want to talk about it."

"You lost someone," she says, and that statement hits me like a punch. Images of Louis and Leo pop up in my head, of their last moments in life. Of the blood, the pain, the emptiness in Leo's eyes.

I swallow.

The happiness from moments before is instantly replaced by something darker, oozing like a wound never allowed to heal and festering with all the missed chances and unspoken words.

Ara's hand lands on my arm, a comfort, sunshine in the vortex of darkness that threatens to swallow me. Her touch grounds me and pulls me back into the here and now, away from the abyss of grief and rage.

"The only way to honor the dead is by living," she whispers. The words reverberate inside my chest like I've heard them before but forgot.

"It's what my father used to say." She smiles at me sadly. "So... that is what I'm trying to do... to honor him." Her breath hitches, and she looks out into the dark. "It's funny really how others gained a hero while I lost mine." Her voice breaks, and she bites her lip, her breath slow and deep, like she's breathing away her pain. And I feel it, feel the pain in my chest lessen marginally while I breathe in rhythm with her.

"When you held the eulogy after the attack...I knew then," she says, squeezing my arm before dropping her hand. I instantly miss her touch.

"I'm so, so sorry, Daddy…I hope you know that." She whispers so softly that I would have missed it if not for my connection to the air around us. "I'll make sure they are safe." I know those words weren't for me, but I can't help but wonder what she means by that.

My chest is a mangled mess of feelings, and I couldn't have talked even if I tried. Instead, I cover her hand with mine, where it rests on the stone between us, and I hope she understands.

We sit like that for a while until Ara extracts her hand and runs her fingers over the back of mine. A soft caress I feel in my soul. Her fingers are so light against my marked skin. She looks up at me with a sad smile before she leans in and brushes her lips over my cheek. I freeze, afraid to spook her.

"Good night, Tate." She jumps up and hurries off while I still savor the feeling of her lips on my skin and the sound of my name rolling off her tongue.

I'm stunned, rattled, and awed but also slightly less broken than before. Like Ara started to push the shattered pieces of my soul back together.

Never in a thousand lives would I have guessed that the same pain and regret lurked beneath Ara's sunny surface, that she would understand so completely without me having to say a word.

ARA IS THE ONLY ONE AT THE BREAKFAST TABLE WHEN I ENTER the dining hall the following morning.

"Good morning, sunshine," I murmur while dropping into the seat next to her. I relax when she smiles at me instead of shutting me out.

"Sunshine?" she asks.

"Your mood, your name." I shrug. "It fits."

"What fits?" Jared plops down next to me.

Ara and I share a smile.

"Finally," he sighs. "The tension between you was giving me anxiety just by watching," he whispers even though no one else is in the room yet.

"Why are you always up so early?" I ask Ara one of the questions that bugged me since before I knew her name.

"I hate braiding up my hair while it's wet," she confesses.

"Maybe you should date someone with air magic who could help you out with that," Jared suggests innocently, and I kick him under the table. "Ouch, what was that for?" he complains while Ara giggles. I glare at him. While we talked, I'm still not sure if my questions or the almost-kiss had her avoiding me for the past two days. And I will not risk pushing her away because my best friend thinks he's funny.

The next days are like a quiet dance between us, both of us unsure of the steps. We're back at the academy, which means we have to be careful of watchful eyes, and Ara is back with her squadron. Janus released her from punishment after we got back. He didn't have much choice since Tanner and I reported excellent behavior.

It's good for her, but fuck, I miss having her around.

Since she has classes and I'm on patrols, we often don't exchange more than a glance or superficial chitchat when we pass in the hallway. I catch her watching me during strategy meetings, when we are both in the sparring hall, or during lunch, and my eyes sure as hell find her whenever she's around.

Today, all riders from our division had a drill up in the mountains to practice handling large-scale operations. It made us late for lunch, so I haven't had a chance to see her yet.

I'm sitting opposite Jared, both of us quietly digging in, when her scent hits me.

"Why don't you like cake and cookies?" Ara's voice is teasing, and I find her standing behind me when I turn around. She holds a plate of cake, placing a big piece into her mouth, her teeth trapping the fork while she grins around it. She lets the fork glide out against her soft lips while holding my gaze, then moves right back to the cake for another piece.

I swallow.

"Sugar is not part of a healthy diet," I answer. I wouldn't have anything against the sugar clinging to her upper lip right now, though. Her tongue darts out, cleaning it off, and I nearly groan.

Fuck. Focus on something besides her mouth.

"Really, not tempted at all?" she asks, and I narrow my eyes at her. *That has to be on purpose.* But the look she gives me is pure innocence, like she just continues our game of simple questions.

"Nope." *Liar.*

I hear Jared choke behind me. His coughing is accompanied by the sound of a hand pounding his back. She smiles like she knows I'm full of shit.

"I, for my part, like to live dangerously," Ara says.

"Don't I know it," I mutter, replaying the encounter with a certain dragon in my mind. Another piece of cake disappears into her mouth. Yes, I'm definitely tempted.

"Come on. What is your favorite cake?" she inquires. "There has to be one you would make an exception for."

I don't think anyone has ever asked me such an innocent and, at the same time, loaded question before.

A smile tugs at the corners of my mouth. She is something.

"Chocolate cake," I answer. It was my choice for every birthday back home.

"Good one. Fits you," she declares, nodding.

I blink. How can a choice of cake be fitting? She laughs at my face and leans in until her breath tickles my ear.

"Dark, tempting, delicious, and much sweeter than anticipated." She sends me a devilish smile before she turns and vanishes in the group of runners at the buffet. Heat surges through my body, making my skin sing and turning my thoughts into mush. I shake my head, trying to clear it.

Holy shit. How did she manage to turn me on by comparing me to cake?

When I tear my gaze from the spot where she just vanished, my eyes meet a smirking Jared.

"What?" I ask.

"I would pay dearly to know what Summer whispered in your ear," he says. I scowl at him. I will *not* repeat that. The bastard throws his head back and laughs.

CHAPTER THIRTY

ARA

It's strange to be back, not just at the academy but also with my classmates, my flight, and my squadron. It's only been two weeks, but still, I miss training with the other flight. I miss the banter and joking at one of the outposts after a day of flying while we sat in a warm common room. Most of all, I miss being around Tate.

Gods, I wish he had kissed me because all I keep agonizing over is how his lips would feel on mine. Would he have kissed me softly or with the heat I had seen in his eyes?

I sit at lunch surrounded by my flight but don't listen to their chatter. Tate is on patrol today. I know that since I have their schedule, but my eyes still wander over the sea of runners and riders around us, looking for him.

It's undeniable that something changed between us since Platoria and our conversation at the outpost.

I abandoned the notion that it's only my curse pulling me toward him because damn, I notice a lot more than that. But that doesn't solve the puzzle of me being acutely aware of his gift and where he is at all times of the day unless he's too far away. Like right now.

I sigh, which draws Calix's attention, but his gaze goes back to his plate without saying anything.

Magic marks its bearers. It doesn't care about the name you put on it.

The dragon's words play through my mind, but what do they mean?

Despite being scared by how close I came to spilling my secrets to Tate, I wish I could talk to someone about it.

"Can you just talk to her?" Calix's voice draws me out of my thoughts. He's been in a strange mood lately.

"Huh?" I look at him questioningly.

"Talk to Mariel and apologize for whatever you did," he says. Now I'm completely thrown.

"What? What did I do?"

"You tell me." Calix is glowering at me now. "I know I told you to live a little, but ever since your date, she's off, and now she even avoids you, so you clearly fucked up somehow. I want you to apologize and stop acting like nothing happened." He throws up his hands, angry with me.

"What date?" His eyebrows jump up at my question.

"Are you shitting me right now?" he growls.

"No, I swear I'm not. I never went on a date with Mariel. Why would I?"

If all I want is to jump our centurion?

"Because she's a great girl—"

"I know that Mariel is great." I hold up my hands in surrender before he can go on defending her. "That's not what I meant. She's my friend. Why would I mess around with her like that?"

Now Calix looks confused, too. "But she said she was meeting you the night you didn't get back, so I thought..."

I huff out a breath. I'm fed up with all the lies and drama.

"No, I met up with my cousin that night. I didn't see Mariel at all. I promise."

Calix's shoulders relax at that. This seems to have bugged him more than I thought. I pat his shoulder.

"You know what? I'll go find her right now and clear up whatever this is," I tell him, and that's what I do.

It takes me a while to hunt down Mariel, but I finally find her in the coop, cuddling a little Strix after a runner told me he'd seen her head that way.

"Hey," I say softly, stopping at the door of the stall to gauge her mood.

"Hey," she answers, not looking up.

"Mariel, did I hurt you somehow?" I ask. No point in beating around the bush. "I'm sorry if I did. That was never my intention."

She looks up at that, but her eyes dart away again.

Fuck. I did hurt her.

I step inside, closing the door behind me carefully so none of the baby strix can escape. They are little black clouds of impossible soft plumes the size of a medium dog, their striking blue eyes nearly glowing between the dark feathers. They hop around me, chirping in hopes of a treat.

I go over to Mariel, carefully avoiding the fluffy feather-balls flitting around me. Crouching down, I settle one hand on her shoulder in comfort. At that, she throws herself into my arms, catching me by surprise and nearly toppling me over. I pat her hair and hold her while her body shakes with sobs.

Shit, what did I do?

"Uh, Mariel?" I ask tentatively, "What the fuck did I do?" This makes her laugh through her sobs, and she pulls back.

"I'm sorry. This is not just about you." Her breath is still choppy, and she wipes at the tears running down her face. "I just thought we had a connection, and you were the first I ever asked out after Scott... and that wasn't easy, and then... you didn't show up without any explanation..." She hiccups.

It takes a while, but I finally managed to coax the whole story out of her.

Mariel asked me on an evening walk with her the night I met up with Sloan, and because I was so preoccupied with my plans, it didn't even register.

Scott, on the other hand, had been Mariel's fiancé, who joined the skyriders two years before us and lost his life during an accident in training.

"In the beginning, training was just...a way to cope with the pain, I guess..." Mariel shrugs. "And then...with his death, all my life plans had gone up in smoke...so I decided to join the skyriders to...feel close to him." Mariel gives me a self-deprecating smile. "Pretty stupid...huh?"

"Fuck." I heave out a breath after Mariel's confession. "I'm so sorry you lost him, Mariel." I hug her. "And no, I don't think it's stupid. Everyone copes with loss in their own way, and there is nothing wrong with that. I'm just so sorry I stood you up without even realizing it."

She waves me off. "It's fine. We just got along so well, and then you risked your life to save me..." She shrugs.

I huff out a breath. I only see one way to say this without hurting her any more than I already did. I trust Mariel. What is one more person knowing?

"Uh, I only ever saw you as a friend," I tell her and rush on when I see her face fall, "because I'm kind of ... uh ... I'm a girl myself." Mariel's eyes go wide at my confession. Then her shoulders start to shake. Laughter bubbles out of her, and I can't help but join in.

That is how Calix finds us, collapsed into each other's arms, giggling. He shakes his head in confusion but seems visibly relieved.

We sit in the biggest of the classrooms—the theater. The rows of chairs rise in steps behind me since we first years always sit in the front. I snap my mouth shut when I realize it's still hanging open. Legatus Janus's mouth is still moving as he stands at the front facing us, but all I keep hearing are the words that are the end to my beautiful plan.

"*I have the honor to announce that General Blackstone and his staff will be visiting us at the end of the month...*" I should have known it couldn't mean anything good when Janus showed up at the end of the strategy meeting.

There is a ringing in my ears.

Fuck my life. Why does he have to come here, of all places?

It's been two days since my heart-to-heart with Mariel, and everything between us is good again. My secrets are still safe. Tate just got back from patrol today, and I got to see him, so the world looked great until a few seconds ago.

"That is so great." Calix bumps me with his shoulder. "Do you think we'll get to meet him?"

I give him a weak smile. *I hope not.*

"Just think about it. To meet General Darren Blackstone personally. He's the youngest general Belarra ever had, and they say..." Calix goes on and on, and it's very strange to listen to him hero-worshipping my brother when I would have described him so differently. I would say that Dar gives the best hugs, looks the happiest when he plays with his daughter or is next to Elena, and hates the cookies Mom makes for solstice but eats one anyway so he doesn't hurt her feelings. But none of that will help me when he finds me here.

The whole room is alive with excitement, and I want to throw up. I fidget. I need a plan. And there is only one person I can ask for help.

I try to catch Joel's gaze, but he avoids looking in my direction. It has been a little awkward between us ever since our confrontation before I left for patrol. Tate is frowning at me, and his gaze stays intense even when I try to appease him with a smile. He's too observant for anyone's comfort. I look at Joel again and nearly jump out of my seat when I feel a caress on my cheek. I turn to Calix, but he's in a conversation with Mariel.

What? How?

"What's wrong?" Tate's voice whispers next to my ear, and my eyes snap to him. He grins at me wickedly, and I feel like someone poured lightning down my veins.

"How?" I mouth to him.

"Air gifted, remember?" I see his lips move with the soft words that reach my ear. Then Jared asks him something, so he turns away, and my mind snaps back to the problem at hand.

I need to talk to Joel.

Instead of running to Joel as soon as the meeting ends, I wait next to the door, my fingers beating out a steady rhythm against my leg.

I grab his arm as he passes, mumbling a half-assed apology to the rider he had been talking to before dragging him into a niche down the hall.

"I can't be here," I whisper-shout.

"That's what I've been telling you for two months now," he says dryly.

"No, I mean when Da..." I look around. "Ah, the general comes."

"I know," he groans, his hands messing up his once impeccable hair.

"So you'll help me?" I ask, holding my breath.

Resolve runs over his face, and I could kiss him for it, but that would definitely lead to unwanted questions. My face splits into a smile.

"I do value my life, don't I?" he grumbles, but a smile tugs at the corner of his mouth as well.

"You sound like Sloan." I push against his chest playfully. "My brothers aren't that bad. You should know that. You grew up with them, and you're Ben's best friend, for goodness' sake."

"Oh, I do know them." He raises an eyebrow at me. "And I don't think being Ben's best friend will count for anything if Darren finds out I hid your whereabouts from him. Hell, Ben himself will murder me."

"I won't let them kill you. I promise." I smile up at him.

"Who wants to kill you, Cassius?" Tate asks. Damn. As much as I like that voice, I don't want to discuss this in front of him.

"No one...yet." Joel sends me a meaningful look before he walks around me, leaving Tate and me standing there.

"Thank you!" I call after him, but Joel doesn't acknowledge it.

"What is going on, sunshine?" Tate levels me with one of his no-nonsense looks. And a thrill goes through me at hearing his pet name for me.

"Nothing you have to worry about." I smile, but he doesn't look convinced.

"Why doesn't that ease my mind when it comes to you?" He ruffles his already mussed hair, making my fingers itch with the want to run them through his hair as well. Nope, not going there. I have much bigger problems at the moment.

"I don't know. Why doesn't it?" I try to look as innocent as possible, walking around him.

"How come I didn't bend the rules before you got here, and now I find myself with both feet over the fucking line all the time?" Tate growls at my back.

I send him a sunny smile over my shoulder. "Coincidence? Luck? Take your pick."

"I think it's more about the current company," he says, and I laugh at his resigned tone.

"No. I don't take the blame for that. I didn't drag you into it, not once. Actually, I do my best to keep you out of it, like right now."

Tate groans.

I chuckle and dive into the crowd of runners and riders still leaving the auditorium. I have no intention of giving him the time to question me or to figure this out by observing my reactions.

Livia leans against the wall next to the auditorium door, her eyes fixed on me, and I don't like the look of satisfaction on her face.

"Summer, a word, please." Tate's voice is all business when he calls out to me the following morning before I can exit the sparring hall. Calix looks at me questioningly, but I shrug and tell him to go ahead before walking over to Tate.

When I reach him, Tate holds out a letter to me, but I only stare instead of taking it. My eyebrows rise when I recognize my brother's painstakingly accurate handwriting. I even glimpse his seal now that Tate moves the letter in front of my face.

Shit, how does he know I am here?

"Where did you get that?" I look up at Tate.

"Jared met Sloan at the gate. She seemed anxious to get this to you," he says, I look around worried someone might listen in and realize we're the only ones left in the room.

Awareness gathers between us until the air seems to hum with it. My eyes dart to his lips and then to the letter in his hand. The letter I just know he will have questions about.

"Why, thank you for hand-delivering my mail." I snatch the letter out of his hand and step back, hoping it will dispel the tension. "Now, if that doesn't make me feel special," I joke and wink at him before shoving the letter into my bag.

"Don't you want to open it?" he asks. Is that disappointment I see in his eyes?

I shake my head. "No."

"It looks official."

"It looks like an officially annoying letter by my officially nosy family trying to make my business officially theirs," I joke. "So yeah, pretty official."

"It's stamped by the headquarters." He tries again. Damn his attention to detail.

"Well, I never said that my officially annoying family doesn't hold annoyingly official positions, did I?" My smile is a little strained now, and I turn to leave. I'm worried now—without even reading the damn letter.

"Didn't I earn your trust by now?" His quiet question makes me pause.

I do trust him. But enough to risk not only my life but also my family's? And if I'm honest, I'm afraid of his reaction, too. Most people grow up with us being the monster in their bedtime story. Gods, not even I am sure that I'm not.

"Are you ready to spill all of your secrets?" I play the ball right back. The way his jaw tenses is answer enough.

How can we ever have a chance together with all the secrets between us?

I smile at him sadly. Maybe it's foolish to even hope.

"See." I shrug. "And neither am I."

I hurry out the door and nearly run into Calix, who is hovering in front of it.

"You didn't have to wait for me," I tell him.

"I wanted to." He shrugs. "Just in case you were in trouble or something."

"Worried he would secretly dispose of my body?" I tease.

He shrugs. "There is a strange tension between you two lately. Don't blame me for assuming the worst with his reputation." I nearly laugh but realize he's being serious.

I stop him by laying a hand on his arm when he turns to leave.

"He won't hurt me," I promise. At least not in the way Calix fears.

His gaze is skeptical. "You sure?"

"Yes." I'm saying it with a smile and all the conviction I can muster, but deep down, I'm worried about that, too.

When we arrive at Flight Theory, I sneak my brother's letter between the pages of my notebook. It can't hold anything good. After yesterday's announcement, I can guess what it is—I hope I'm wrong.

Everyone's gaze is on the board in front, where Prof. Sanders sketches something that looks like a wing. His voice is only background noise to me. I need to know what is in that letter.

I pry off the seal and unfold it. My fingers feel clammy.

My gaze skims over my brother's neat handwriting before it finds the words I dreaded. *I look forward to seeing you...* Shit. Now I read the whole letter, and it keeps getting worse.

...didn't answer any of my questions... last letter...worried about you... coming home with me...

Shit, shit, shit.

Calix's concerned look tells me I said that out loud. I force out a smile, but it doesn't even feel convincing.

"What is it?" he whispers. Our gazes lock on Professor Sanders's face. He hates talking in class.

"One of my nosy brothers wants to visit," I whisper. He glances my way, the question plain on his face, before he turns back to the front. "Um..." I swallow. "They don't know I'm here." His head whips around to face me.

"What?" His question earns us a reprimanding look from Sanders. I wince. He lowers his voice to a hiss. "Where do they think you are?"

I bury my face in my hands, which makes my voice sound as hollow as I feel. "Visiting my cousin."

"Shit."

I peek up at him. "That's what I said. Isn't it?"

TATE HAS BEEN AWAY FOR EIGHT DAYS, AND I KNOW HIS FLIGHT returns from patrol today, but I haven't seen him yet. Avoiding being alone with Tate is one thing but not seeing him for days is another.

I'm on my way to the library and just crossing the small hall to the stairs when the door to the courtyard opens, drawing my gaze. Jared steps through it, and I gasp. He's covered in blood.

"What happened?" I hurry over to him.

"Not my blood," he answers, and my stomach drops. "Not his either," he hurries on when he sees my expression. "We came upon a full-on attack. It wasn't pretty, but everyone will be alright." I nod numbly.

I need to see him. Knowing they have been engaged in an attack... I need to see for myself that he's fine because I didn't miss Jared's wording that everyone *will be* alright.

"Where is he?"

"Reporting back to Janus. Where are you going?"

"I'm on my way to the library," I tell Jared. "And you should clean up before you make someone's heart stop."

He chuckles at my joke but seems weary, and his steps are heavy when he heads off to the sleeping quarters. This must have been one hell of a patrol.

I'm sitting in my usual spot, biding my time trying to read, and a smile steals on my face when I sense Tate's signature warmth coming closer.

I focus on the signatures around me and notice someone else heading in my direction. Something about the magic is strange.

I close my eyes and concentrate on it. It's heading in my direction, but I can't say I've encountered it before, and it's strong.

I open my eyes, expecting to see a light moving toward me. But there is nothing, only darkness.

A shiver runs down my back. Why is someone slinking through the library in the dark?

This is nothing but a veiled execution. Vega's words concerning my punishment run through my mind. Could it be?

The book drops from my suddenly numb fingers, and I don't care about the loud thump reverberating through the silence around me.

You're overreacting, I tell myself. But it does nothing to slow my erratic heartbeat.

My hands shake as I turn down the lamp next to me until it flickers and finally dies. Darkness surrounds me, and I feel like I'm floating in a void. The magic signatures are my only anchors. Like tiny stars, they move around me, two of them heading in my direction.

I jump up and use my hands and memory to navigate. Treading carefully to muffle my steps, I make my way to the bookshelves, but my progress is painfully slow.

Tate's magic is my focal point. Spreading my arms to touch the walls of books next to me, I hurry up my steps, going as fast as I dare while zigzagging blindly through small corridors.

My breath catches in my throat when I realize the signature is following me, coming closer.

How is that possible?

I abandon all caution and start running, no longer trying to be quiet.

Tate strides down one of the bigger pathways straight ahead. If I get to him before whoever is chasing me catches up, I'm safe.

I close in from the side and chance a look back before I hurl myself right into Tate's path.

I barely step out between the dark shelves before being slammed into the next one. The air leaves my lungs in a rush, and the pain in my back and ribs makes it hard to draw the next one.

Tate's forearm presses me into the books behind me, and the cool metal of a knife rests against my skin. He dropped his lamp when I rushed him, so we are standing in total darkness.

Shit, I didn't take into account that he didn't know I was coming.

Despite the pain in my back and the blade at my throat, Tate's closeness makes me feel safe.

I struggle to catch my breath while I search the area around us. The signature is gone.

CHAPTER
THIRTY-ONE
TATE

My thoughts are on Ara while I'm on my way to the library. Nothing new there, but I'm worried. Ever since I caught her talking to Cassius and then handed her the letter, she's seemed off and on edge.

It also pisses me off that she potentially spoke to Cassius about it but doesn't say a peep to me.

Eight days on patrol also gave me too much time to think about all the possibilities. We nearly lost Zaza today, and just the thought of what might have happened if Ara had been with us makes me sick.

I have had enough of tiptoeing around. I won't give up until she answers my fucking questions and spills whatever is bothering her.

The library is dark and quiet. I grab a lamp from the front desk, nodding at the librarian standing there, and head into the labyrinth of bookshelves, already planning how to coax information out of Ara.

The pounding of running steps is the only warning I get before someone jumps out of the shadows of a narrow pathway. I drop the lamp, swipe a dagger, and press the other person into the shelves without thinking twice.

Adrenaline floods my body, and I brace for a fight, but my opponent doesn't struggle. The lamp went out when I dropped it, plunging us into darkness.

The other person is slender and smaller than I am, chest heaving, heart thundering against my arm. My hold on the blade is steady, ready to strike if needed.

Then I register the scent, a scent that has been haunting me for weeks now.

"Ara?"

"I'm happy to see you, too," she answers dryly, sounding breathless, and I quickly sheath the dagger.

"Mists, did I hurt you?" I ask and start checking her over. I have been anything but careful since my mind instantly went into fight mode. My finger encounters wetness at her throat, and I curse.

"Fuck, I'm sorry. I didn't know it was you." I lean in closer, but it's too dark to see anything. "Here, let me fix it."

"It's fine, Tate. It's barely a scratch," Ara whispers, still breathless. Fuck, I love hearing her say my name.

"Say that again," I demand.

"I'm fine?" She sounds confused.

"No, my name," I growl, and her breath hitches, setting my skin on fire.

"Tate," she whispers and rests her hands on my chest, softly, questioningly. My heart picks up speed.

This is such a bad idea.

I should step away, walk away. But... I can't.

She fists my shirt, and I lean in, unable to fight the pull she has on me. I place one arm next to her head to steady myself, and my other hand finds her face, cupping her cheek.

She turns into my touch, her lips brushing the inside of my wrist.

It's such a small, barely there touch, but it sends fire through my veins.

Her lips touch the sensitive skin again, and then she places open-mouthed kisses right above my hammering pulse.

"Ara," I groan, barely holding on to my restraint.

Her tongue flicks over my skin playfully, deliberately, taunting, and unravels my control quicker than a sharp knife on taut rope.

I'm not sure which of us moves first, but her hands slide up my neck while I pull her into me, her body molding to mine.

Every thought of where we are is lost as soon as our lips meet.

I drown in her scent, her taste, the way she moves. Her lips are soft and demanding against mine, not surrendering but taking.

Her tongue slides against mine in sure, playful strokes and flicks, exploring without hesitation.

She tastes sweet, like the cookies she devours while reading. I pull her closer, angling her head to give me better access, and she nips at my bottom lip.

The sting of her teeth travels straight to my groin, stoking my need for her. The kiss turns from exploring to devouring in a heartbeat.

Steps come in our direction, and I'm so lost in her that it takes a moment before the information sinks in. I jerk back.

Fuck. What am I doing?

My chest is heaving, and I clear my throat while wrestling my control back into place.

"We shouldn't..." I croak. What was I thinking? Anyone could have seen us, and she would be in trouble, not me.

A light comes closer. Ara is silent apart from panting breaths. I can make out her form but not her expression.

I want to know her thoughts on what just happened, but a librarian comes around the corner holding a lamp.

I take another step away from Ara and turn to the grumpy old woman who eyes us suspiciously.

"The lamp slipped from my fingers," I lie, my steady voice a complete contrast to the turmoil inside me.

"I heard the noise," the librarian says in a way that tells us that that alone is an offense in her books. "I hope you didn't spill lamp oil all over the books." She lifts her lamp and moves to assess the damage with pursed lips. "Seems to be your lucky day. Follow me," she mutters, keeping the lamp she picked up, clearly not trusting us with it.

Ara doesn't say a word on the way back and rushes off the minute we step out of the library.

What did I expect? Only four weeks until Picking and she would risk everything if we are discovered. But fuck, it still stings.

The following morning, I'm called into Deputy Commander Foley's office.

I haven't slept much and haven't had breakfast yet, so to say my mood is not great to start with is putting it mildly, and it gets worse.

"Kyronos, change of plans. The eastern division will take over your patrols for the next five days, and we will send your division up Mount Albión." He looks up from what he's writing to glance at me. "An increasing supply of eggs is on the black market, and I need you to put a stop to this," he orders.

"Yes, sir." I nod. He returns to his writing, and I'm about to head out when he adds. "Oh, and I mean the whole division. Your runners missed out on mountain camp, so it will do them good to make up for it before Picking."

It takes everything not to outright ask him if he has lost his fucking mind. I know the man is grieving, but this is insanity.

"*Or revenge,*" Daeva throws in.

I take another look at Foley, and my stomach twists. He has a calculating gleam in his eyes, and if he seeks revenge for his son's death, Ara is his target.

Discouraging poachers from stealing eggs by spending a few days on Mount Albión or even catching them in the act is something I support wholeheartedly, but taking the runners with us? That is not the normal procedure.

I have a bad feeling about this, and it gets worse the more I think about it on my way to the refectory.

"What crawled up your ass?" Jared asks when he sees my face. I grab the apple next to his plate and sink my teeth into it.

"Hey, get your own food," Jared protests, but then looks at the big clock on the wall and gets up as well. It's only five minutes until formation. He sighs and hands me half of his sandwich.

"I'm only doing this because you are unbearable otherwise," he informs me while we leave the dining hall.

I fill him in on the way. Jared doesn't see it as bleak as I do, but he hasn't seen Foley's look.

"Don't you think it's strange to send the runners out with us?" I raise my eyebrows in question while I step aside and hold the door open for a group of runners rushing past us.

He shrugs. "Maybe leadership does try to give them a chance to catch up?"

"By effectively sending them into combat?"

"It doesn't have to come to that. There is no guarantee we will encounter anyone," he argues.

I snort. "True, but if we do..." I shake my head. "Do you think fighting an enemy who has nothing left to lose is a good way to ease them into things?"

Jared gives me a knowing look.

"The life of a skyrider is deadly," he says. "We all know that, and it's not like we can change anything about the orders. We can only try to make the best of it."

"That still doesn't mean I have to like it," I grumble.

We left the academy at first light, and the ledge we picked for our camp on Mount Albión is still cloaked in mist—or rather low-hanging clouds. The sun will burn them away quickly as soon as it rises, but for the moment, it only barely reaches the peaks of the mountains around us, the light still more blue than golden.

Our camp is bordered by a cliff on one side with a steeply inclining path as the only way in or out and the sharp drop of the mountainside on the other. Tall pine trees surround us, keeping us out of sight.

Most runners and riders are occupied with tents while a few key players stand before me.

Ara is one of them, and by the looks she throws me, I know she wonders why she's here since she's the only runner.

We are in my tent, which doubles as a meeting place for now.

We are high up in the mountains, and the mist shrouding our camp might not be magical, but it still creeps into your clothes, making you clammy and miserable in no time.

"Summer, you stay back and watch the camp," I order.

Ara lurches back like I've slapped her. Her eyes, still locked on me, narrow. I know that look by now—to say she isn't happy about the order is an understatement.

Well, that makes two of us who are unhappy about orders they still have to execute.

The only positive thing about this trip compared to the last is that the runners didn't have to walk up here, and we won't have a problem evacuating.

The negative is that we are about to face armed men, who will probably face a life in one of the arenas when caught, and the thirty-two runners with us have nearly no fighting experience.

And the thought of Ara between all of that or jumping in front of me again...I can't stand even the thought of that. There is no way I can concentrate on fighting or making the right decisions if I worry about her.

As soon as the meeting ends, Ara marches over to me. She stops about five steps away and taps her foot, waiting for the others to clear out.

Jared sends me a pitying glance before he leaves the tent.

"*I think I feel a storm brewing,*" Daeva throws in. "*I can nearly feel the wind ruffling my feathers.*"

Ara is especially good at ruffling feathers, and I enjoy watching her do it, but unfortunately, her ire is directed at me this time.

"Why are you keeping me here?" she whisper-shouts as soon as we're alone.

"Sunshine, you have no idea what we face out there." I try to reason with her. "It will be safer—" I don't get to finish that sentence and realize my mistake as soon as the word safer leaves my mouth.

"You have no right to make me wait here while everyone else risks their neck," she hisses. Her finger drills into my chest in a staccato rhythm, accentuating her every word. I capture her hand before she can hurt herself. I'm wearing armor, after all. When she resumes with the other one, I catch that as well. She glares at me.

"Actually, I have every right to make that decision." I glance at the markings on my uniform, and she huffs.

"I'm much better with a sword than many others, so what is your..." She stops tugging on her hands. "Is this about the kiss?" she asks, and I let her hands go. "If you think you can lock me away in the next belltower because of one little kiss," she seethes, "then it's a good thing you changed your mind because—"

"Little kiss?" I raise my eyebrow mockingly. She incinerated me with that little kiss. Seeing the fire in her eyes flare at my words, I want to claim her mouth right here and now.

Keep your cool, I admonish myself.

"*If that is keeping your cool...*" Daeva's unwanted comment nearly makes me snap at her, but one pissed-off female is enough. I take a deep breath and address the one in front of me, getting back on topic.

"No, this is about your tendency to act before you think. You throw yourself into danger without any thought about your safety. You don't take the time to think it through first."

"Well, that worked in your favor, too, if I remember correctly." She throws up her hands like she doesn't understand my fucking problem with that.

"You could have died," I roar, finally running out of patience and far past fucking caring who hears me.

"Well, you could have, too. But we're still here, aren't we? Both of us. And that is because of the tendency you just complained about."

"You didn't even know me." This time, I'm getting in her face. How can she not see my point?

"It seems like I still don't." She throws me a disgusted glance, turns around, and marches to the exit. I grip my hair in frustration because she drives me up the wall.

"You will guard the camp," I order, nearly expecting her to talk back.

"Do I look like I'm stupid enough to hand you or Joel an excuse to kick me out for disobeying orders?" She scoffs. "For my own safety, of course," she adds mockingly and flips me off before stomping out of view.

I huff out a breath. Now that went well.

Could have been worse. You wouldn't be bodily unharmed if you tried something like that with me, Daeva informs me sweetly.

Great. Why do I always have to pick the bossy ones?

Daeva caws in a way that sounds suspiciously like laughter.

You didn't. You were chosen. Be grateful for it, she informs me.

I bury my face in my hands.

"Charming. I love you too," I say dryly.

I know you do. But how would you feel if she left you behind and went out to fight? Daeva's voice chimes in again. I would feel like shit, but I'm not ready to admit that yet.

"That is not the same. I don't act without thinking, and I don't risk myself—" I'm cut off when Daeva sends me pictures of my encounter with the dragon.

"It seems to me that you are no better than her if she's involved. That makes you a hypocrite, doesn't it? Unfortunately, they don't have wings." She sounds smug.

Her amusement washes over me.

"You humans are just ridiculous. We always fly into battle next to our mate. Everything else is madness."

"Noted." I huff out a breath.

But I won't go back on my decision. She will be safer here, especially since I suspect Foley is planning something.

The camp holds no eggs and therefore no reason for poachers to come this way. She has an overview of the surrounding area so no one can sneak up on her, and the small path up the mountain makes it impossible for anyone to get to her without passing us first.

So even if Ara is spitting mad at me, my decision is justified.

CHAPTER
THIRTY-TWO
ARA

The first sign that something is wrong is the smell of smoke. It's faint at first but soon becomes stronger and hangs in the air like a cloying blanket, drifting down and wavering along the path the others took.

Unease tickles my back. We flew here, and as far as I remember, this path was the only way out of here other than climbing the steep wall while literally hanging off the face of this mountain.

I march over to the ledge, look down, and dread settles heavy in my gut. I have no problem with heights, but the drop in front of me goes on forever, the trees below looking as small as the seed of an apple.

Yeah, even I don't want to climb this without a safety line. A few ledges on the way down are occupied by dark brown spots that have to be nests. Whoever those nests belong to probably wouldn't be happy if I showed up, especially if eggs have been stolen lately. Great.

I turn away from the drop of doom and look up the mountain. Smoke forms a dark gray blanket over the forest, drifting between it like the earlier mist.

I am fine here, I try to reassure myself.

It surely won't come this way, right? I try to make out the direction of the wind, but our camp is too sheltered, and the smoke makes it hard to see anything. If I could just get a little higher, I should be able to feel it.

I don't think twice about it. Happy to finally do something other than sit around and wait, I start looking for the best way up the cliff.

I'm halfway up when I notice the bird circling restlessly above me. My hope that it's one of ours plummets when I realize there is no harness and no rider.

It's a female Strix, easy to identify by her white-and-gray color and the missing violet markings. *I hope she doesn't think I'm a threat.*

The wind correlates with where the smoke comes from, and while I know nothing about wildfires, I know that is not a good thing.

Shit, what do I do now?

The Strix keeps circling, and back in the camp, I watch the bird and the smoke, and I soon realize why she isn't leaving.

The nest blends in well, and I wouldn't have found it if the Strix hadn't landed. And in the nest is an egg.

She doesn't have a choice, I realize. The egg's shell is too smooth and slippery for her to carry away in her talons.

I sit literally on my hands on a boulder at the edge of our camp, unsure of what to do. I'm still pissed at Tate, but I would appreciate his presence right about now. I know nothing about dealing with a fire like this. Where I grew up, even thinking of anything going up in flames is laughable with the amount of rain we get.

My mind switches between stewing about the problem at hand— one I don't know how to solve—and the way Tate has gone all overprotective of me all of a sudden, reminding me of my brothers. Can't any of them see how frustrating it is if they demand the right to protect me but don't let me do the same?

My mind goes back to the kiss we shared. Tingles shoot through my body just thinking of it, but my stomach sinks when I think of the way he pulled away.

We shouldn't...

What in the mists had he wanted to say? "We shouldn't" isn't "I don't want to," right? Or is it just a polite way to say the same?

Cawing makes me look up, and the smoke is getting heavier.

Why is no one coming back? What if something happened to them? What if I'm stuck here?

Is there a chance I can get a better glimpse of what's going on from up there?

The Strix looks agitated. Her movements are jerky. She keeps unfolding and folding her wings and hops from one side of her nest to the other.

They are intelligent creatures. If I offer help, will she let me near her nest? Would she even carry me off while I hold her egg?

I decide to at least try talking to her. I can't just sit here and wait. What if they don't come back?

Tate will come back for me.

Will I really sit around and wait for him to rescue me when I just complained that I don't need his protection?

The stone is more corroded the farther up I climb. Soon, it takes twice as long to cover the same distance since I have to check for loose parts before going on.

I reach over with my left hand, my feet wedged into a tiny crevice. I tug slightly, and it seems sturdy enough. I swing my left leg over, and suddenly, the stone crumbles beneath my fingers. Because of the sudden shift of my weight, my right foot slips, too, and I scrape against the rough stone, the grip of my right hand the only thing that keeps me from falling. My legs scramble for purchase as I frantically look for something I can grasp with my hand.

There is a small crevice where the piece broke off. I grunt when I shove myself up with a push of my legs while pulling my weight up with my right arm. My left hand latches onto the place that nearly made me fall before, and I pray what lies beneath is sturdier. It holds, and after I find purchase for my legs as well, I take a second to simply breathe.

That was close.

I look up. I'm nearly halfway there. The cliff is only about as high as the fourth story of the academy buildings, and I could have climbed that at least three times by now. Going slow is not only annoying but also eating away at my strength.

The wind pouring down from above is getting warmer and picks up speed, ripping at my clothes. But that's not the worst. It's also heavy with smoke, stinging my eyes and nose, and itching my throat with every breath I take. My eyes water, and I cough repeatedly.

My progress slows to a crawl. My sight blurs with tears streaming down my face, and my arms start to tremble.

This was a fucking terrible idea.

My body is covered in sweat, the wind doing nothing to cool me anymore, and all I want is to rest, to sleep.

A violent cough shakes my body, and that's when it happens. I slip.

CHAPTER THIRTY-THREE
TATE

The smoke is already heavy when we get back to our camp. We followed the poachers' tracks and caught four in their camp. We confiscated two eggs, and squadron two flew the poachers and the eggs out and informed the academy of the wildfire that needed to be contained.

The camp hinted at there being more than just the four. That is why we took so long getting back. But the search has been fruitless.

Everyone has their orders, and there is a flurry of motion in the camp as soon as we land. We break down the tents and pack up.

I let my gaze wander over the commotion around me, looking for Ara. I don't think she encountered any troubles here, but I want her report nonetheless. I need to know she's okay.

The fire started during the fight in the poachers' camp when one of them grabbed a burning log to defend himself but let it drop and decided to run instead.

The area around Telos is always dry, and wildfires happen regularly. Since we haven't had much rain lately, the dry stalks of grass and bushes from last summer burn easily. We only got out in time because we hadn't been on foot.

Ara is probably helping with the tents.

I walk through the camp, taking in the progress. Ten minutes is all the time I gave everyone to finish packing. Everything else will stay here. I'm not ready to risk lives for stuff that can be replaced.

I can't find Ara anywhere, and unease creeps in.

You only missed her in this chaos, I reassure myself. But this is Ara, and I usually miss nothing if she's concerned.

I try to put myself in her position. Waiting down here with the smoke getting thicker.

Fuck. Would she go looking for us?

"Hey, Ilario," I call out. "Have you seen Summer since we got back?"

"No, I haven't seen him. Why?" he answers, looking around.

"Haven't got the report yet," I say casually. No need to worry him until I'm sure she isn't here. I go through the camp again, asking if anyone has seen Summer since we got back, but no such luck.

The tents are packed now, and most things are stored in packs. I inspect every flight that leaves, and once only our flight is left, there is no point in keeping the hope up. Ara is nowhere to be found.

"You head back. I'll look for Ara and come back as soon as I find her," I tell Jared quietly. He's reluctant to leave, but he has a runner to take back, and there is no visibility with all the smoke, so a search is pointless. But I can't just leave either. Jared nods.

"If you aren't back by tomorrow evening, I'll come looking for you." He holds my stare before he mounts behind the runner already sitting on Zephyr, and they take flight.

I get on Daeva, and we take off too.

I don't know what I expect to find. I don't even know where to start, but anything is better than doing nothing.

A feeling of urgency started the minute I suspected Ara was missing, and it grows and grows. She's likely in trouble, and not being able to do anything drives me insane.

"Where are you?" I murmur under my breath. The wind steals the sound of my words as soon as they leave my lips.

We circle above the area where the camp was. Ara is on foot, so she can't be far away. What prompted her to leave camp? Did someone kidnap her?

Now you are being ridiculous, I admonish myself. But her recognizing the mark on my chest means she probably has connections to someone in higher circles, and we are close to a border... But they wouldn't have gotten her out of here without us noticing.

"*We aren't the only winged creatures out here,*" Daeva reminds me, her voice surprisingly soft.

"I know that, but—you think the dragon came for her?" My eyes search the area around us for a flash of scales.

"*At least he wouldn't have had a problem with fire,*" she muses.

"True." But he couldn't have known that Ara would be on her own. No, she still has to be around here somewhere.

"Keep an eye out for him, just in case," I tell Daeva.

We continue flying rounds when Daeva perks up beneath me.

"*I found her,*" she swoops down, heading for the remains of our camp.

"But we already looked there," I tell her. I switch to her sight, and for the first time in a long time, fear grips me. It slams into me with a vengeance and leaves me reeling.

A small figure lies at the base of the cliff, the gray of her uniform one with the stone around her, her body partly covered by rubble. She doesn't move.

She doesn't fucking move.

My urgency prompts Daeva to pull out of her dive at the last second, landing with an impact that rattles my bones.

I'm out of the saddle before she even tucks in her wings, running over and falling to my knees next to Ara. She looks so still and pale.

I'm too late.

Her face and hair are covered by stone dust, and she looks nearly as gray as everything around us. She lies on her back, her eyes closed. And for one horrible second, all my fears come true. Then her chest rises, and I start breathing again.

I look at the cliff. Did she try to get out of here? Did she think we abandoned her?

I reach for Ara, and her eyelids flutter. Her pulse is weak and fast.

I call her name and rattle her softly when she doesn't respond, but it takes me a moment before I manage to rouse her. When she finally does look up at me, she seems confused. She mumbles my name, pressing her cheek into my hand where I cup her face. Her face scrunches up like she tries to remember something before shaking her head.

"Can't heal me," she slurs, and her eyes close again. Panic rises inside me. Something is seriously wrong.

How high up was she when she fell?

"Sunshine, stay with me, baby. Open your eyes." They flutter open, only focusing for a moment before clouding over again. Fuck.

"Hold me, please?" she croaks, but I put my hands to both sides of her face and pour my magic into her instead. Her eyes fly open. "No." She sounds frantic, grabbing for my hands like she wants to pull them away, but I don't let her.

"Shhh, it's just me. I'm going to fix you up in no time." I try to calm her, my throat tight.

"Don't want you to die, too," she whispers, and her words chill me to the core.

"No." I shake my head at her. "No one is dying here. Do you hear me?" She doesn't respond, her eyes closed.

Is her chest still moving?

My hold tightens on instinct like that can keep her here.

I shake her, yell at her, and my breath stutters when her eyes fly open again. I'm not ready to let her go. I'm not sure I ever will be.

Her eyes are unfocused, and one of her pupils is blown wide.

Bleeding in her head.

I push my magic into her, focusing on her brain and the blood vessels in and around it, repairing the damage. I'm eternally grateful to the healing master at the palace for drilling me on every part of our anatomy.

Her eyes are still open and on me. Her brow is damp with sweat, and her whole body is shaking, like the healing is taking as much out of her as it is from me.

Exhaustion rises while I soothe the swelling and help her body get rid of the blood that pooled in her skull.

Then I check the rest of her. Her eyes are closed by then, her whole body wracked by shivers. I pull her into my arms, holding her close. I'm drained.

"Sleep, sunshine, everything else can wait," I whisper into her hair. Her breath deepens, but her body doesn't stop shaking. I pull her even closer, using my body to warm hers and create a cocoon of air around us. It holds off the smoke and the cold, and for the first time since I realized she was missing, my body relaxes, too. I watch the smoke thinning out, my gaze blurry with exhaustion.

They contained the fire.

I must have fallen asleep because the next time I open my eyes, it's dark around us. Daeva is a soothing presence behind my back, her wing sheltering us.

"*Good, you're awake,*" she chirps, though her worry settles into me with every word.

"*The fire?*" I ask her.

"*Contained hours ago. Rest, you need it,*" she tells me. I'm still weak, and when I try to reach for my magic to check on Ara, I find it nearly depleted. That's never happened before.

Ara is cuddled into me, sleeping peacefully.

I wasn't too late this time.

This time, I didn't bring death but life. Maybe there is a balance to everything, after all.

"*Don't want you to die, too.*" The memory of what she said whispers through my mind. *"Can't heal me."* What had she meant by that? Why had she fought me when I started healing her? Had she simply been confused?

When Ara mumbles in her sleep, I lie down again, tucking her into me to keep her warm. She feels fucking perfect in my arms.

I let myself slip back to sleep, safe in the knowledge that Daeva will guard us with her life.

CHAPTER THIRTY-FOUR
TATE

When I wake the following morning, I can hardly move. Ara wrapped herself around me like an octopus. It seems like she deemed me far more comfortable than the stone floor. Her head is settled on my chest, her arm and leg wrapped over me.

Not that I'm complaining.

"Finally. I'm starving here," Daeva mutters and hops up. Blinding sunlight washes over me since Daeva's wing is no longer cloaking us, and I throw an arm over my eyes to shield them, cursing.

The sun is already high in the sky. No wonder Daeva is hungry. My stomach growls at the thought of food, but I ignore it.

Even though my position is hardly comfortable, I don't want to move. I watch Ara's head rise and fall with every breath I take, and my fingers play with the strands that have come loose from her braid. Her hair is so soft, and even with the dust, it's nearly glowing in the sun. When my gaze wanders back to her face, I find her watching me.

"Good morning." I smile.

"Good morning, I..." She looks around, her eyes traveling over the cliff and the trees, then she pushes herself up and looks down at my body beneath her. "Sorry for ... um ... claiming your body like that."

"Did I complain?" I ask, drinking her up with my eyes while subtly checking for any signs of discomfort or lingering effects of her fall.

She sits up fully now and stretches, looking around. I instantly miss her warmth.

"What happened?" she asks.

I sit up as well, swallowing a wince. My body does not appreciate the night on the hard and cold stone floor.

I recount my side of the events. Her eyes grow wider and wider while I talk.

"Fuck, sunshine, you scared me. You were barely alive when I found you and kept drifting in and out of consciousness." I shake my head, cold all over from just thinking about it. "But all is good now. I got to you in time and healed you."

"What?" she shouts.

I'm confused. What is her problem?

"Never, do you hear me, never heal me when I'm unconscious! Promise me," she urges.

I shake my head, not understanding.

"Please." She looks at me with big, pleading eyes. "Please promise me."

"What if you would die otherwise?" I ask.

"Then I die." She shrugs like it's even a fucking option.

"Are you fucking kidding me?" Anger swirls up fast and vicious. "You want me to stand by and let you die?" I shake my head at her. The thought alone rips me apart.

What kind of person does she take me for to ask something like that?

Louis bleeds out right in front of me while they hold me down. I do everything they ask, promise them fucking everything and more, and still...A knife slits Leo's throat and his father's while I thrash against my capturers. Maybe if I had said something different...if I hadn't given in...or had given in faster...

"You think I could watch you die without lifting a finger?" I roar. "I'm not a fucking monster!"

"You'll die too," she yells. "It's not you who is the fucking monster here." Her breath hitches. She squeezes her eyes shut and clasps a hand over her mouth. Tears roll down her cheeks, and she dashes them away angrily.

"I don't...I can't...I'd rather die than be the cause of your death," she whispers and bites her lip, visibly fighting for control. I can't stand it.

I pull her into my arms. Harsh sobs shake her body like she will break apart at any moment, and I tighten my hold.

"Shhh, sunshine, you're killing me here." I rest my cheek against her hair.

Fuck, I would promise her nearly anything.

I continue holding her even after she has gone quiet.

"You probably noticed the scars," Ara says, and I perk up. "I was never healed, and being a wild child, I had a lot of wounds and a few broken bones," she rushes out in one breath, gulping in another. "My family always said it was to teach me to be more careful."

My body goes rigid at that.

I'm going to fucking kill them.

"No, no, that came out wrong," she says. "My mother is a healer, and it pained her to never be able to do anything for me."

"What?"

"Um..." Ara clears her throat. "Let me start from the beginning. When I was three years old, I ran out after my brothers—like I said, I have four of them—and while Luc and Ben played in the gardens, I went after Dar and Ian. No one noticed right away." She starts kneading her hands. "They are a bit older and were competing with each other at the obstacle course used to train the recruits." She laughs nervously. "Not the best place for a three-year-old."

At least that explains why she's so fucking good on an obstacle course.

"My brothers found me unresponsive at the foot of the course, and they panicked. Dar scooped me up, and they ran to our mother. She set some broken bones, then started pouring her healing magic into me, but my wounds weren't healing, and maybe she panicked too. Either way, she wasn't monitoring her energy levels.

"By the time my father arrived, my mom was too weak to stop. He pulled her away and carried her out of the room to sever the connection. Otherwise, I would have killed her. No one ever healed me—until you." She looks at me, her eyes vulnerable and pleading.

It doesn't make sense. Why would a grown healer not be able... unless—no, that is ridiculous.

My mind races. There has to be another explanation.

She called herself a monster. And that is what cursed ones are, but...*could I have been so wrong about her?*

I let her go and take a step back. Pain flashes over her face before she looks away. She walks over to the cliff—the growing distance between us more than just physical. Panic surges through me at her walking away from me.

"I'm not going to harm you." Her voice sounds bitter and wobbles on the last word. She's facing away from me, giving me no chance to read her.

"Ara, look at me!"

She shakes her head.

"That's not ...fuck, you can't just tell me something like that and expect I'll go on like nothing happened." She stays as she is, her arms wrapped around herself, her head bowed. I'm not even sure she heard me.

I grip my hair. She handed me her life without so much as a warning. I know what I'm supposed to do. I grew up with the knowledge. It was engraved into my brain during the time I trained as a healer, but...

She lifts her head, and her shoulders move with a deep breath. She turns to face me. Her face is full of quiet acceptance.

"Could you make it quick, and maybe...could you tell everyone I died in the fire?" Her request is quiet and calm, her head held high, but her breathing is too fast, too shallow, and her bottom lip trembles.

Denial settles like a massive boulder in my gut, threatening to bring me to my knees. My vision swims. I shake my head. She can't mean what I just heard.

"Please, my family...they, they only tried to protect me." She holds out her dagger, waiting for me to take it.

I try to swallow past the feelings lodged in my throat while I take it from her, my fingers numb. She looks down at the dagger, then back up at me.

I shouldn't feel that conflicted about this. I grew up with the absolute certainty that cursed people are evil. But Ara?

"My dad gave it to me when I was ten," Ara whispers. "I always keep it sharp, just in case..."

The meaning sinks in and rips me apart. She grew up with the knowledge that one day, someone would end her life simply for who she is.

I'm not going to harm you. Her words drift through me. She's not even trying to fight me on this. Why isn't she trying to get out of this? Taking my life instead?

"Why aren't you fighting me?" I ask, my voice hoarse, my eyes searching hers.

She shakes her head.

"It's alright...I always knew it would come to this... " Her voice breaks. "I'm glad I met you. I'm glad I kissed you." She gives me a watery smile. "Despite everything."

The pieces of me she aligned vibrate, ready to burst apart again. My chest is so raw that every breath hurts. Suddenly, her face takes Louis's place, then Leo's. It's her blood pouring out, her eyes full of pain and then going empty. Darkness threatens to pull me under.

"Why aren't you fighting me?" I yell, angry now that she gives up so easily.

"The first time you healed me..." Her voice is soft and quiet. "I was devastated at the thought that I had to kill you to get away unnoticed." She shakes her head again. "I won't do it."

"And I can't kill you." The words burst out, and I realize they're true. I can't do it.

"I won't let you hand me over." She shakes her head, determination settling over her face. "I won't." She lunges for the dagger in my hand, and ice-cold fear grips me. Not for me, but for her.

I whip the blade out of her reach, then twist and pin her to me with my other arm. My body shakes with the realization of what she just tried to do. That she nearly stole her life after placing it in my hands...just when I decided to keep it, to keep her, no matter the costs.

I slide the dagger into a free loop at the back of my belt and wrap my second arm around her, holding on to her. She tugs and wriggles, but I have her pinned.

Losing her in that accident yesterday would have killed me. Losing her like this would have annihilated me.

"Let me go." She stomps on my foot, and I hiss. "If you don't let me go, I will drain you," she threatens, and calmness settles over me. I made the right choice.

"No, you won't," I tell her.

"Are you sure about that?" she taunts, and I realize it's not me who needs persuasion but her.

"Yes, it's not who you are," I say, and she snorts in disbelief. "Why did you step between me and the lightning?" I challenge her.

"Because it would have killed you," she grunts while she lets her full weight sit on my arms by pulling up her legs. If she thinks I'll let her fall, she can wait an eternity.

"And you knew it wouldn't harm you?" I ask.

She snorts again. "I know fucking nothing unless you count the things told in all the stories and..." She pauses. "And we weren't always hunted... and the dragon said... it's magic."

"That is why you met with him." I groan.

She nods and finally stops struggling.

"Fuck, I'm sorry, sunshine." I tighten my hold on her

She leans her head against my chest, looking up at me.

"It's alright," she sighs. "What are you going to do now?"

"Nothing," I tell her, and my lips twitch because it's an exact repeat of our conversation after I found out about her ruse. Ara relaxes into me, and I lean my cheek against her temple.

"Why was I able to heal you?" I finally voice the question that has been haunting me the whole time.

"Everyone's magic... feels different, and when I hold mine back..." She shrugs. "It works."

I remember her trembling, the sweat, her exhaustion. It costs her to do so.

"That's why you wanted me to stop if you are unconscious." I realize.

"Yes." She nods.

Shit, that woman's conscience is humbling.

"I'm sorry, Ara." My voice is rough.

She shrugs. "It's fine." She laughs humorlessly. "After all, it's not easy to be faced with the damn monster under the facade."

I turn her in my arms so I can look into her eyes.

They are red and full of doubt, her lashes and her cheeks still wet. And despite everything she just told me, I have never met anyone more beautiful, inside and out.

I don't just care for her. I love her.

She didn't just wriggle into my heart. She owns it.

This incredible woman, who not only doesn't know how to be cautious but will be hunted if anyone finds out what she is, broke down all my barriers and made herself comfortable as the center of my world.

Her recklessness, her vulnerability makes her the embodiment of my worst nightmare, and still I can't regret falling for her.

"You're no monster," I tell her.

ARA

Tate's eyes. They are so tender, so tormented, so raw. Like the storm so often brewing in them broke and let me glimpse the devastation left behind. It captivates and terrifies me.

"You're no monster," he says.

How can he be so sure of something I'm not even sure of myself?

"I might still become one." I voice the doubt that has festered in me since the day I found the mark on my skin.

"Forget what some stories say. What do you *know*?" Tate challenges me.

"Nothing," I tell him.

"See, that is not true," he disagrees. "You know that you can control it. Otherwise, we both wouldn't be here. You know that you can choose to harm or to protect, like when you stepped in front of me. We both know you saved me that day. You are nothing like the monsters in those stories."

"Yet," I add glumly, but I let his words replay in my mind and realize that maybe I had it wrong the whole time.

What if my curse isn't hiding and biding its time, waiting to take over... but more like a weapon? Something I can wield to harm or to defend, just like Tate said. And he's right. I *am* in control. Even nearly frozen solid and tempted by his warmth, I haven't given in.

He tips my chin up so I have to meet his eyes again.

"I believe in you," he states firmly, and the way he says it lets warmth rush through me, washing away the last cold tendrils of doubt. "But what is far more important is if you believe in yourself."

"Yes," I answer, and I'm surprised that I really do. A smile spreads over Tate's face, so brilliant I can only stare, but he sobers quickly.

"Now that I know, I promise I won't heal you while you are unconscious, but I need you to promise me to never choose your own death so carelessly again." He shakes his head at me. "The moment you lunged for that dagger...fuck, sunshine, I would rather walk the mists than experience that ever again."

He looks so haunted. I want to reassure him so badly, but I can't.

"I owe it to them, Tate," I say softly. "To my family."

"So you are willing to die for them, but not live..." He breaks off and turns away. "Never mind...Daeva is on her way, and we need to get back anyway."

"They sacrificed so much for me." I try to make him understand.

"Ara, I see those things differently. I think we all make our decisions, and we are not responsible or indebted to others just because they happened to make the right one. I will not pressure you into making the decisions I think are the right ones. It's your life. I just beg you not to throw it away too easily, okay?"

I nod, stunned by his sudden outburst.

Tate falls into a broody silence after that.

"Are you close to your family?" I ask Tate, and I'm relieved when he turns to me instead of ignoring me.

"I consider Jared and Nan, his mother, my family, so yes. Otherwise, it would be a no." He gives me a small smile. "How was growing up with four brothers?"

"Mine take overprotectiveness to a whole new level," I grumble. "One of the reasons I'm so good at climbing. It was easier to climb out than convince them to let me go out."

"So they scared off all your admirers?"

"Believe me, every guy ran the other way as soon as they knew who I was," I answer dryly.

"Cassius, too?"

"Joel?" My eyebrows jump up. "What do you mean?"

"Were you ever... together?"

I snort, and his mouth twitches. "I had a crush on him, but he always treated me like a sister," I tell him. That answer is met with silence, and for the hundredth time, I wish he was easier to read.

"So if it isn't Cassius, is there someone else?" Tate's question sounds casual, but my stomach suddenly feels like one of the birds did a nose dive.

I grin.

"Centurion Kyronos, are you working up to asking me out?" I tease, while Daeva lands right next to us, raising a cloud of dust. I close my eyes to shield them, and a shiver runs down my back when I open them, only to find Tate right next to me.

"If you accept an afternoon ride on Daeva as a date, I am." He shrugs, but his gaze is intense. "Otherwise, you would have to wait until after Picking."

I grin up at him.

"I do accept," I say, and my words turn into laughter when Tate simply picks me up and lifts me onto Daeva's back. He gets up behind me, and the way his body presses against mine causes heat to spread through my veins and tingles to race over my skin. His chest is warm and solid behind me, and I let myself relax into him. I look at him over my shoulder.

"I have been accused of getting others into trouble, so consider yourself warned."

He snorts.

"Tell me something new. And who says that I don't like trouble?"

CHAPTER THIRTY-FIVE
TATE

The next two weeks are pure torture. With Ara coming closer to Picking and me being on long patrols twice, we don't see each other for days, and then only while passing in the hallway. We are limited to superficial conversations and easy smiles again, when all I want is to be alone with her.

I curl my fingers into tight fists and try to relax my jaw before I crack a tooth or two while I watch Ara spar with Ilario. Keeping my distance is not easy, and standing over here watching her laugh triumphantly because she just managed to pin him to the mat is fucking torture.

Her eyes fly over to me, and our gazes lock. I have no idea how she does it, but she always senses me, no matter how sneaky I am. I give her a small smile and a nod before leaving the room.

We just got back from our last weeklong patrol flight along the coast. The same one Ara accompanied us last time, and I'm exhausted. But I had to see her before I could even think of rest.

Ever since she told me just how much she's risking here, I'm worried when I'm gone for long stretches of time. As far as I know, Foley hasn't made a move, but I don't doubt he will. From what I heard, he holds a grudge, and I've caught him glaring at Ara more than once.

Three days until Picking starts, and then she will be up on that mountain for five days. I try very hard to ignore what could go wrong in those five days and instead concentrate on the fact that in little over a week, Ara will be a rider, and nothing is keeping me from her then.

So I have to ensure no one notices anything between us—not that there is anything to report.

I walk down the corridor toward the sleeping quarters. All I want is a shower and my bed. Since it's afternoon, the hallways are still empty. All runners have classes, and most riders are either on patrol or training.

I hear hurried steps behind me coming closer, and I glance over my shoulder but turn when I see who is coming after me. Ara.

I nearly topple over when she flings herself into my arms without warning. My arms catch her on instinct, and I let myself enjoy the feeling of having her in my arms for just a second.

"I missed you," she breathes into my ear, and I groan. Is she trying to kill me here?

Even though it pains me, I put her back down gently and step back.

Just a few more days, I remind myself.

She looks confused, but she has to know this is madness, right?

"Sunshine, I—" I'm interrupted by approaching steps. Two riders from the eastern division round the corner.

Fuck. I take another step back and school my features into my usual mask.

"Thank you." I nod. "Get back to class, Summer," I tell her before

I continue my way to my room, unbearably turned on and frustrated at the same time.

And the more I think about it, the angrier I get with Ara for doing something so reckless. What if the riders had come just a few seconds earlier? It's no secret that the eastern division has her on their shit list. What if word had gotten back to Foley?

I'm too agitated to sleep now, so after the shower and a change of clothes, I drag my weary bones to the weight room in hopes of releasing some of my restless energy.

ARA

I'm hurrying back to sparring. Tate's rejection is still a hollow burn in my chest. What the fuck was that? A marble statue would have shown more enthusiasm at seeing me. Maybe he changed his mind?

I push back into the hall only to find everyone still engaged in what they had been doing before. Calix is sparring with Mariel, and Arkwright is pointing out mistakes in a runner's defense while the rest of our class is sparring, watching others do so or sitting at one of the benches waiting for their turn.

My eyes meet Livia's, and she gives me a derisive grin, her eyes traveling from me to the door and back. But there is no way she knows where I have been.

I turn my back on her and make my way over to Mariel and Calix instead.

Geography passes in a blur, and thankfully, we are done with classes after that. I made my decision. I can't go on like this. I need to know.

"Are you coming with us to the common room?" Mariel asks me, but I shake my head.

"I'll see you later." I turn and leave before anyone can ask me where I'm going or my nerves get the better of me.

I march over to the sleeping quarters and up the stairs past our floor until I reach the one our division's leadership occupies. The corridor is empty. I stop in front of Tate's door, taking a deep breath. I can still leave.

I need clarity.

I raise my hand and knock.

This is madness.

I knock again.

The door is flung open, and I find myself facing Tate's chest—his very carved, very bare chest. I swallow and drag my eyes up until I meet his. His eyes are wide.

"Sunshine?" he whispers, and just like that, I want to fling myself at him again.

He is not playing fair.

I clear my throat.

"Can I come in?" I ask and can't help but let my eyes wander over him again.

Steps echo down the corridor, heading in our direction. Tate pulls me into his room and closes the door softly, before he strides to the middle of the room as if to put space between us.

Tingles race through my body when I realize for the first time we are truly alone... in a room... with a key... and a bed.

Heat explodes low in my belly, trickling down. Tate turns to me, his body taut with tension, and my fingers ache with the need to touch him, run them over the swells and dips of his muscles, and feel his smooth, warm skin.

For the first time, his face is unguarded, and I don't need to ask the question I came here for.

He wants me.

He knows my darkest secret, and still, he wants me.

The realization shocks me, and I take a step back. As if the tension ties him to me, Tate follows.

"This is such a bad idea," he growls, his voice low. Heat pulses through me.

He is right. My mind knows that, but my body disagrees.

There is a fire in his gaze and... hunger. I bite my lip, and he groans.

"Now is your chance to run, sunshine," he rumbles while he slowly prowls toward me, giving me time to slip through the door behind me.

"I can't fight this any longer." He shakes his head, keeping up his slow advance.

I just watch him come closer, my heart racing.

"Then don't," I tell him, my voice husky with need.

His hands land on the door next to my head, and he closes his eyes, resting his brow against mine.

"I'm trying to do the right thing here, sunshine." His chest is rising and falling with his breaths. "But you make it impossibly hard."

"That's because I don't want you to do the good and noble. I want the bad and wicked and—"

His mouth crashes down on mine, swallowing my last words and the moan clawing up my throat.

Thank the gods... he's done fighting.

I bump into the door behind me, and Tate's hand slides from my jaw to the back of my head, cradling it. His other arm hooks around my waist, pulling me to him. The warmth of his body seeps into me, and I melt.

I bury my hand in his hair, my nails scraping over his scalp, and I revel in the shudder running through his body.

I thought our kiss in the library was hot, but this...I bite his bottom lip, and his groan runs through me like liquid fire. His need is hard, pulsing evidence between us, and I need ... I ... closer.

I push off the ground and wrap my legs around him, humming in approval, when my throbbing ache meets the ridge of his cock.

"You are playing with fire, sunshine," Tate warns against my lips before his mouth travels down my throat. "I'm just a breath away from fucking you right here against this door."

"Maybe I think it's worth the risk," I whisper. Tate freezes at my words, then tries to pull back. I drop my head to his shoulder with a groan.

TATE

Her words have the same effect as a bucket of ice water, making me instantly aware that this could fuck up everything for her. I try to pull back, but Ara clings to me, letting her head drop to my shoulder with a groan.

"Shit wording," she grumbles, then kisses my neck. "Ditch whatever noble thought caught up to you," she demands and nips my earlobe before pulling back and looking me straight in the eye. Her lips, swollen from my kisses, stretch into a wicked smile.

She is magnificent.

"Please, Tate, I want you." Need slams into me, nearly making my knees buckle.

"Fuck, are you trying to kill me here?" I groan.

"No, simply trying to get you out of your head." She chuckles. I groan again, trying to hold on to the last scrap of my control. "Look at me," she demands, and I do. How can I not, when for weeks now I haven't been able to see anything but her as soon as she enters a room?

Her hair is a mess from my hands tunneling into it, her lips are swollen, her cheeks flushed, her eyes heavy with want, and her clothes rumpled.

"If they catch me coming out of your room like this"—she looks down at her body—"they won't care if we went that far or not, so we might as well take what we need." Her reasoning makes sense in a twisted kind of way, or maybe it's just that I so badly want it to make sense.

But right or wrong is forgotten when her next words shred the last bit of my control.

"I need you, Tate," she whispers into my ear, her breath playing against my skin, and I'm lost.

Who am I kidding? I was lost the second I opened the door, and she looked at me like I was the cake she compared me to weeks ago, or even the moment I found out who she was and her skin pebbled for me.

I rock into her, and her needy whimper is like a gust of wind to smoldering embers.

"This has to go. Now," I demand and tug her shirt up while she lifts her arms. Her shirt lands on the floor next to us, and she looks up at me. The trust on her face lets warmth flood my chest, waking a tenderness I never felt before. I tuck a strand of hair behind her ear and trace her braid.

"Can you let it down?" I ask.

She nods, smiling, and I duck in, needing to feel that smile against my lips while Ara gets to work on her braid.

I explore her mouth, reveling in her taste and the feeling of her against me. My finger traces circles against the silky skin of her lower back, and her hands falter. Then she pulls back, gasping.

"How am I..." She breathes. "Supposed to do anything that needs coordination, with your hands and mouth on me?"

"I can stop," I say and give her a wicked smile before I trace her collarbone with my tongue.

Goose bumps spread over her skin.

So damn sensitive.

"Don't you dare." She gasps, making me chuckle.

Her hair falls around her like a golden veil, the soft strands tickling my chest and shoulders.

I will never get enough of her.

The thought should frighten me, but it doesn't. She's the sunlight that ended my winter, and the past weeks proved she's safer with me than without me, so I'm not letting her go.

I bury one hand in her hair, the way I've wanted to since I saw it trailing down her back at the tavern.

"You are perfect," I say and watch her eyes go tender. Our mouths find each other in another kiss softer, gentler, this time more savoring than demanding.

"Are you sure about this?" I ask when I come up for air.

"Yes," Ara answers with truth in her voice. My heart accelerates with anticipation, and I walk over to my bed with Ara still in my arms.

A knock on the door makes us both freeze. I rest my brow against Ara's, willing whoever is in front of this door to go away.

The knock sounds again, and I groan.

"Go away, I'm sleeping," I shout, hoping the person will take the hint.

"Centurion, open the door," a male voice demands. At the formal address, Ara and I look at each other in shock.

"Fuck," I hiss, setting Ara down gently. I grab my shirt, pulling it over my head, and Ara dives for hers.

The knock sounds again.

"Um...one minute," I shout, looking frantically for a place to hide Ara, but there is nothing here to hide.

I go over to the door and take one last look at Ara, checking that she isn't visible from the doorway. Then I place a shield of air right behind me, guarding her and muffling every sound she makes before I slip out the door, closing it behind me.

I come face-to-face with Deputy Commander Foley.

Despite probably looking like a mess, I don the cool mask I'm used to wearing.

"Yes, sir?" I say, keeping still while his gaze wanders over me.

"Did I interrupt something?" He smirks, and my blood runs cold.

"I was sleeping, sir."

"Are you sure you weren't doing something ..." He leers at the door behind me, and the thought of him looking at Ara like that has my temper flaring up. "Or should I say someone else?" He looks back at me, and maybe he sees the threat in my eyes because he takes a step back.

"I have no idea what you're talking about, sir."

"So you want to tell me I won't find anyone when I inspect your room right now?"

"No one, sir," I bluff.

"Very well, then you won't mind me having a look, will you?" He smiles, his eyes full of triumph.

Fuck. He knows.

CHAPTER THIRTY-SIX
ARA

I sit up on the roof, braiding my hair up and straightening myself out. The city is a rug of glittering lights beneath me, and the wind cools my heated cheeks. I send my thanks to Tempos, the god of weather and wind, that it isn't raining. I hightailed it out of Tate's window as soon as he was through the door.

That was close, too close.

If I wait until Tate is alone, would he be interested in resuming where we left off? Or will he send me off like a lost puppy because his conscience got the better of him again? Does he even deem whatever this is between us worth the trouble?

I bite my lip. He affects me in ways no one ever has, and I'm not used to overthinking every little decision. It drives me nuts.

It's only three days until Picking, and tomorrow will be rough. Maybe I should just...wait it out? Thinking of all the things I haven't told Tate yet makes that option very appealing.

Coward.

I'll concentrate on tomorrow first. My brother's visit will make it an...interesting day. I make my way along the roof and down the path I have taken once before. My landing is more graceful this time, so I knock softly against Joel's window minutes later.

"Again? Are you serious?" Joel scowls at me when he opens the window. He hauls me in before I have the chance to move myself. "Look at you." He gestures at me, and I look down at myself. My clothes are rumpled, my braid surely anything but neat, and I push a few loose strands behind my ears. My lips still tingle and are surely swollen from Tate's kisses.

"What did you do this time? Climb out of someone's bed?" he asks in exasperation. He probably means it as a joke, but it's too close for comfort, and I wince. His eyes widen.

"Are you serious?"

"I think you asked that question before, and we surely agree I'm the least serious person you know. So thanks again." I smile at him, turning to the door, but Joel is faster and steps in my way. What is it with men and doors today? Images of Tate hovering over me flit through my mind, making my cheeks warm.

"Oh no, not so fast. Who is it?" Joel crosses his arms.

I look down at my feet. I'm hoping to avoid the conversation, especially since I don't know exactly what Tate and I are.

"You sneaked out, so you couldn't leave through the door." He pauses. "Please tell me he's not married?"

I glare at him. How can he even think I would go there? He raises his hands.

"Okay, not married, got it." He considers me like the answer is written somewhere on my skin. "Why did you sneak out then? Unless...you were not supposed to be there." He swears.

We are getting too close, too fast.

"Leave it, Joel," I warn. "It's not your business."

"He's a rider, isn't he?" he asks.

Why can't he leave it alone already?

I keep my face as blank as possible.

"Is it someone from my squadron? I'll kick this guy's ass for putting you in such a position."

The corner of my mouth twitches at the thought of Joel trying to kick Tate's ass and again Joel notices it.

"You think I can't take him? Why would you think, unless...No!" His eyes get even bigger. "Tell me it's not Kyronos."

"It's not Kyronos. There, I said it," I deadpan.

"Motherfucker, I can't believe..."

"Ah no, Joel, I'm not your mother. That would be really weird, don't you think?" I can't help it. Humor is my way of dealing with things, and angry people are simply hilarious.

He points his finger at me, trembling with anger. "Don't you dare joke about this. Kyronos? Are you fucking kidding me?" he roars.

"How about you shout a little louder? I think there are still people left who didn't hear you." I pick some dirt from under my nails and give him my best bored expression.

"Didn't I tell you to stay away from him?"

I nod, shrugging. "Not good at following orders, remember?"

"Then what are you doing in the fucking military?"

"At the moment, it seems like I'm snagging myself a beautiful..."

Joel throws his hands up. "I don't want to hear it!"

"Sheesh, relax. I was going to say a beautiful, magical bird." I wink at him. And I see one side of his mouth twitch.

There, we are getting somewhere.

He heaves out a breath. "He is going to hurt you, Ara, and then I will get in all kinds of trouble for beating up my centurion. Not to mention, he's kind of intimidating. Couldn't you choose someone less scary?"

I laugh at that. "He isn't scary. He's sweet and considerate and damn sexy." Joel makes a face at that.

"Are you sure we're speaking about the same guy? From what I know, he's a cold, heartless bastard who fell in disgrace..."

I'm the one throwing up my hand this time.

"Don't talk about him like that. I like him, so deal with it, and if I get hurt, it's no one's fault but my own." I huff out a breath. "Also, while I love you like a brother, Joel, I do, you still don't have the right to tell me how to live my life. So leave it. Okay?"

He huffs out a breath. "I still don't like it," he grumbles.

TATE

The moment I see the open window, I want to sag with relief.

She is fine.

Foley looks into my closet and even peers under my bed, visibly disappointed when he doesn't find anyone. When he crosses to the window, I hold my breath, hoping Ara is already out of sight.

"Isn't it a little early to sleep with an open window?" he asks.

"Is it? I think it's perfectly fine, sir."

"Remind me, where are you from again?" he asks, clearly fishing for information.

"North of here, sir." He looks at me expectantly, but I'm not going to offer any more than that.

"Hmm, I see. Getting a lot of snow up there this time of the year, right?"

"Some areas do, sir."

He grinds his teeth, inspecting the room like he could have missed something.

"Well, my information seems to have been wrong. I won't keep you any longer. Tomorrow is a big day, after all." He nods at me and strides to the door. He's about to open it when he zeros in on the healing kit on my desk. I always keep an extra in my room in case Ara needs it.

It isn't against the rules, but most keep their healing kits with their pack.

"Healing, hmm, such a precious gift. Where did you train?"

With the best fucking healers our country has to offer.

I spent a lot of time at the healing quarters of the palace after the attack, trying to work off some of my debt until my father had me banned.

"With the healer my family frequented, sir."

"Hmm. Very well, maybe you should help out in the healing quarters now and then."

"I will do that, sir." I nod. "Good night, sir."

"Good night, Centurion." And then he's gone.

Damn Foley to the mists and back.

Ara would still be in my bed if he hadn't knocked.

CHAPTER THIRTY-SEVEN
TATE

W̲HERE IS A̲RA?

Nearly her whole squadron passed us in the hallway after lunch, but she hasn't been with them. I let my eyes wander over the people crowding the atrium, hoping to spot her. A group of runners help with the arrangements for the general's visit, but I don't spot her anywhere.

The sun stands high and chases away all the shadows. A group of riders approaches their birds, harnesses and saddles slung over their shoulders, carrying swords and bows. The northern division got the short straw and is doing patrols today.

Jared and I sit on a bench with our backs resting against the building behind us. We're enjoying the sun on our faces and relaxing after finishing a nice long run around the perimeters.

My thoughts are constantly on Ara. And how could they not after yesterday? But since I haven't seen her all day, I'm starting to worry that she's avoiding me again.

Today has been hectic around here with all the ado about the general's visit, who will arrive within the hour.

Could we just have missed each other?

I draw my legs in, so the boy barreling past me with a rake doesn't stumble over them.

Heaven forbid the gravel isn't where it's supposed to be.

I wonder if Darren Blackstone looks anything like his father. I was fond of the old general. He was a cordial man with good humor and a big heart, and I was shocked to hear of his death two years ago.

He used to bring his family when I was little since his wife and my mother were childhood friends. But the visits stopped. So I haven't seen any of the younger Blackstones for quite a few years. They were dark-haired, like their father, weren't they?

The general's laughter at my pranks had been what swayed my father to a more lenient punishment more than once, and I came up with plenty until my parents granted me my wish to drag poor Jared along after I nearly burned down the ballroom.

I smile, remembering Jared's face when he accompanied me for the first time. Despite us growing up together, he had been speechless at the splendor conjured up to impress other kingdoms.

"What are you smiling at?" Jared looks at me questioningly.

"Just remembering your face when I dragged you along to a function for the first time. I can't remember what it was..."

"Man, the food. I had never seen anything like that. Makes all of this seem rather unimpressive, huh?" He looks at the bare stone walls around us. Everything is nearly sparkling with how clean it is, but there's no decoration in sight. He looks at me. "You aren't worried?"

I shake my head. "I haven't seen Blackstone in years. I don't think he'll recognize me."

"I guess it comes rather handy now that you look more like your mother. Fred wouldn't have had a chance to deny his lineage."

I chuckle. My brother is the spitting image of my father, with his blond hair and blue eyes.

"We'll have to drink on that later." I look around. "Where is everyone?"

Jared chuckles.

"She took on at least three errand jobs. I bet we won't see her until dinnertime."

I look at him. "Who?"

Jared grins. "Don't tell me you wanted to know where our flight is or our first years are." He laughs at my face and slaps my back.

Okay, he got me there. Why would she run around all day instead of joining the festivities?

I realize I must have mused that out loud when Jared looks at me with one raised eyebrow. I shrug and focus on numerous flights of first years and second years going through drills, preparing for the show later. I'm grateful they decided to show off the academy students and leave us in full service out of it.

We all endure a rather uninspired speech. Legatus Janus talks about Darren Blackstone's rising star in the military, and Blackstone weathers it stoically with a polite smile.

Drills and flying maneuvers are executed for his entertainment before the formalities are abandoned in favor of a quite festive atmosphere during the feast.

When all of us, especially Blackstone and his staff, are wined and dined, the whole fuss finally winds down.

Sanders beckons all centurions and squadron leaders to him and looks thrilled to give us the opportunity to mingle, shake hands, and address questions with the general and his staff.

That is how I find myself face-to-face with Darren Blackstone.

He's smiling and thankfully doesn't show any sign of recognition when I meet his eyes.

His eyes are an unusual greenish-blue with golden specks, and he looks familiar. But that is no surprise. I knew his father quite well after all.

His gaze moves over my shoulder, and I see surprise flash over his face.

"Joel?" Blackstone's face splits into a wide grin, instantly making him seem younger and much more approachable. Cassius steps next to me, and they hug, clearly glad to see each other.

If Cassius knows Blackstone that well, the chances are high that Ara knows him too. This would explain why she took on all those errands and also confirm my suspicion about the circles she grew up in.

Who is Darren Blackstone to Ara?

The clearing of a throat right next to me pulls me out of my trance, and I realize I have been staring at Blackstone. I return to my flight, but my mind wanders off instead of listening to the conversation around me.

My gaze comes back to Blackstone and Cassius, who stand not far from us, talking and laughing. Cassius seems strangely on edge.

Curious, I keep an eye on them and step a little closer.

"Did you know my sister is here as well? Nearly half of our old group in one place." Darren Blackstone laughs, but Joel pales, perspiration beading on his forehead.

"What..." He clears his throat. "What do you mean?"

Blackstone eyes him carefully. "Still not over her?" He pats Cassius's shoulder. "I always thought you would have ended up together if she hadn't been promised to the crown."

They are speaking about Tamara Blackstone, then. The girl I was betrothed to since we were kids. So my brother inherited not only the throne, but my bride as well, it seems.

I don't remember much more than a little blond girl playing with us in the gardens. I remember that she kept us on our toes with the chore of having to keep an eye on her.

Cassius waves him off.

"I'm fine." He looks around, wincing when he catches my eye, sending me a strained smile. His gaze flies back to Blackstone, and he clears his throat.

"What do you mean she's here?"

"Oh, she's visiting our cousin. I think she needed to get away for a while." Blackstone seems troubled and in thought before his eyes snap back to Cassius.

"I will drop by there as soon as I'm out of here. Would you care to accompany me?"

"Well, that would be great, but unfortunately..." Cassius raises his hands in an apologetic gesture. "No free evening for me." Which I know to be bullshit, even without my gift. Our whole division is free tonight.

"Are you sure? I bet I could put in a good word for you," Blackstone inquires, raising an eyebrow.

At that moment, Arkwright makes his way over to them, saving Cassius from having to answer.

Has to be tough being around the girl you love, knowing she will never be yours.

"Summer?" Blackstone asks, and my attention snaps back to them.

"He is on errands today, but that boy is astonishing in the obstacle course," Arkwright praises. "And quite funny with his silly quirk."

Blackstone's eyebrows rise. "How so?"

"He climbs like he's flying through that obstacle course. And I laughed about his habit of touching the ground before he starts, but it seems to work for him."

"Really?" Blackstone's tone sounds intrigued, but a storm is brewing in his eyes. "That boy wouldn't be by any chance blond and slender, would he?" he inquires.

Arkwright's eyebrows shoot up. "You know him?"

"Oh, I might." I see the muscles in Blackstone's jaw twitch. "But sometimes it's hard to say who you really know, isn't it?"

His eyes zero in on Cassius.

I'm sure now. Blackstone knows Ara. So she grew up on or around the Blackstone stronghold. Maybe her dad was part of the general's staff?

Fortress Blackstone is only half an hour by bird from our capital, where I grew up. And the general and his staff spent a lot of time at court.

I search my memory for anyone high-ranked with the last name Summer, but come up empty.

Damn that woman and her secrets.

CHAPTER
THIRTY-EIGHT
ARA

"I heard they want to put on a show for Dar's benefit." Joel is walking down the corridor with me. He waits for my response.

I grin. It's funny to think of celebrations in my brother's honor when the man I know hates standing in the spotlight. Though he's probably used to it now since it's been two years since he took over from Dad. I bunch up my brows, frowning at the thought that there is this whole other side of my brother I barely know. I have never seen him in an official setting.

Suddenly, there is a distance between us I never noticed before. Like my lies widened a crack to a canyon.

How will he react when I come clean after Picking?

"All the more reason to stay away," I mumble.

"I heard they planned some easy competitions and wanted the five best for each category." He eyes me from the side.

Despite trying to hold back, I cornered Arkwright's attention on the obstacle course. I enjoy climbing too much. I often forget to stick to the mediocre performance I have been aiming for. "They probably planned to show off your squirrel act as well," Joel continues.

"Too bad," I say dryly, thinking of the drama that would have caused.

"Arkwright won't be happy is all I'm saying," Joel interjects.

"Yeah, but Dar seeing me would be worse. And it's not like I'm off twiddling my thumbs," I counter.

"True," Joel says. "I'll try to slow Darren down a bit, but I'm not sure it will work."

"Thank you, Joel." I spontaneously hug him.

I took on the errands of three other runners, earning me a favor from each and a busy day that, unfortunately, makes it impossible to enjoy the general's visit.

A damn shame.

"It's the best I can hope for," I tell him while I ease back. I send him one last smile before I set off toward my first destination, whistling.

The first chore of the day isn't one at all. I'm helping out at the Aeries coop, which houses the Strixes. I help to cart in food for the young Strixes, who aren't yet able to fly. It's a bloody business, and I have to temper my guilt at sending rabbits and other small prey into their boxes, knowing what awaits them. The Strixes have to eat something too after all.

Being around the birds afterward, cuddling and caring for them makes up for it, though. Their blue eyes are like glowing orbs against their dark plumes. They are incredibly fluffy and incredibly affectionate since they are used to humans. Their magic is a soft flame, and I'm glad I have enough control over my curse to pet them without worrying about drawing from their magic.

After the Strixes, I make my way to the weapons chamber. A grumpy old man greets me and snorts derisively after running his eyes over me, clearly not impressed with my stature. I don't take it personally, given that I'll probably cart around weapons with a combined weight of a Rukh or more in the next hours. When I smile and shrug, he fights a smile.

His face is wrinkled and his hair gray, but his posture is straight, his shoulders broad, and his arms thickly muscled. And after clambering up and down ladders, as well as sharpening and polishing weapons, I know why. I arrange and sort for hours and decline the offered lunch break, fearing I might run into Dar if I head into the main building.

Keeping up my smile and not complaining earns me the weapon master's begrudging respect. Work becomes easier from there on since he starts talking about his life and recounts funny stories from his time as an active rider.

Soon, everything sparkles and shines and is back in its best working condition. He claps me on the back with a smile. My arms are three times their weight, but I made a new friend.

I walk back to the main building, staying in the shadows while crossing the courtyard. Despite it being a detour, I take the route through the sleeping quarters instead of through the main hall. I went through too much trouble to stay out of Darren's sight. I won't risk running into him now.

The way to the library is familiar, and the corridor is even more deserted than on every other day, but I'm still relieved when I step through the high wooden doors and into the scent of dust, paper, and leather. I'm pretty sure there is no risk of running into my brother in here.

The library is silent around me and seems empty, apart from the librarian who greets me at the main desk.

He shows me a stack of books waiting to be returned to the shelves, and I get to work. Many of the librarians and runners who help with this have some kind of gift that enables them to put books back onto the high shelves without needing the giant ladders, but since I'm not that fortunate, I'm once more climbing up and down, this time with books in my arms.

My muscles are starting to protest, my movements much slower than earlier in the weapon's chamber, and I dread tomorrow.

I'm on top of the ladder, stretching and leaning over to put a big leather book back when the world does a slow turn around me. I wobble and curse, tightening my hold on the rung of the ladder, my knuckles turning white.

I close my eyes and concentrate on holding on, breathing deep and slow until the world steadies again.

Missing lunch, the constant work, as well as a sleepless night, are starting to take their toll, it seems.

"Are you all right up there?" a voice asks, and I groan. Trust me to nearly faint and fall off a ladder when someone is around to witness it.

"Yeah, I'm great." I keep my eyes closed, wishing whoever was down there would leave.

"Doesn't look like it to me."

"How do you know I'm not simply enjoying the air up here or the view?" I quip.

The man laughs. I open my eyes and find him looking up at me, his laugh infectious. I haven't seen him before.

I slowly make my way down the ladder, letting my weight rest against it while I go, my legs still unsteady. A dragon will freeze solid before I ask this stranger for help.

A cool breeze on my back alerts me to the fact that my shirt is creeping up. I groan when I realize it got stuck on a nail poking out from the ladder. Grumbling, I try to free it one-handed. When that doesn't work, I balance my weight against the ladder, trying to get it free.

One minute, I am up on the ladder trying to tug my shirt free; the next, I'm falling, blinded by a shirt that is now halfway over my head. I brace for impact, but two hands grab my waist and stop my fall.

I tug my shirt down, my face hot, and look up at the stranger who kept me from face-planting and is currently doing his best to stifle his laughter.

"Thank you," I mumble.

"Oh, I thank you. That was far more entertaining than all the shows they put on for us today." He grins, flashing two dimples.

He has unruly dark blond hair and piercing blue eyes, and since he seems to be here with my brother, that is my cue to get going.

I shake my head at him, my cheeks still flaming.

"I didn't mean to embarrass you, but what man doesn't enjoy an angel falling into his arms?" He sends me a wink. I roll my eyes at his cheesy line, making him laugh again.

"Not good?" he asks.

I shake my head. "Definitely room for improvement," I state and laugh when he acts deeply wounded.

"How about I hang around and practice?" he asks.

I hear the pounding drum in the distance.

Damn, is it that late already?

I curse colorfully, making the man's brows rise in astonishment. I grab the little cart the books have been on and shove the two books left on there into the next opening, not caring that it's not where they belong.

My new acquaintance chuckles while watching me.

"Sorry, I'm late!" I toss over my shoulder, not waiting for an answer before I hurry back to the desk.

I race to my room, which is thankfully empty, and retrieve the dress from the bottom of my pack, the same one I wore on my trip to the tavern with Sloan. I pull my shirt over my head, loosen the wrap, and tug on the dress instead. The pants stay since the dress is long enough to hide them, and it'll make climbing more comfortable.

Within minutes, I'm out the window, thankfully catching a guard's break right away. After scaling the fence, I take off in a run.

I'm panting and puffing by the time I reach Sloan's house. I unravel my braid and glance down to check my appearance. My dress is still rumpled from being stored so carelessly, but I can't do anything about that. Running my fingers through my hair, I take a moment to catch my breath, then I knock.

Please let Darren not be here yet.

Sloan opens, and I instantly know something is wrong. She bites her lip and doesn't meet my eyes. My gaze flies past her, and my brother's face comes into focus. *Shit.*

Dar probably looks composed and cool to most people, but I see the slight twitch in his left eye and recognize the set of his mouth. He's pissed.

Shit. Shit. Shit.

My stomach plummets. He knows.

My first urge is to turn around and run. Run as fast as I can and then hide until he gives up looking. Only I know he won't. He would simply wait at the academy until I showed my face, and that would be even worse.

"I guess you want to..." *yell at me.* "...talk to me, right?" I ask.

I receive a stiff nod, and this only confirms it. I'm so deep in trouble it's not even remotely funny. *Fuck.*

Darren turns and walks down the corridor to my uncle's study. *At least he doesn't yell at me in front of everyone.*

Sloan catches my arm when I pass her.

"I didn't tell him. He already knew when he got here," she hisses.

I give her a small nod and a reassuring smile, trying to hide the nerves beneath. I believe her, and I'm thankful for everything she did to help me.

The open door of the study comes closer, looming in front of me like a trap about to go off.

Two more days. I would only have needed two more damn days.

I close my eyes, taking a steadying breath before I square my shoulders and step through the door. Time to dance to the music I came up with.

I have never been in my uncle's study before, and I take my time to inspect it. Anything is better than facing Darren.

It's a good-sized room with high ceilings and bookshelves, giving it the feeling of a small library. One side is occupied by a big chunky desk in dark wood, while the other side has a seating arrangement of two armchairs and a small couch, all dark leather and facing the open fireplace that is currently heated by the dancing violet and blue flames of magical fire. My uncle is my mom's brother and shares her coloring. My eyes are on the family portrait that shows him and his wife with my two cousins, Sloan and Bastian.

The silence around us is heavy, and Dar's eyes burn holes into my back. Once I can't take it any longer, I turn to face him. He leans against the desk, not attempting to mask his disappointment or anger.

"I'm sorry?" I offer, shrugging sheepishly.

"Are you now?" Dar's voice is calm, but his eyes, so much like mine, are not. "What exactly are you sorry for, Ara?" I flinch. He never calls me Ara. I've been his little sparrow for as long as I can remember. "For risking your life so carelessly? For going behind our backs? For getting yourself into deep trouble by lying about your identity? Or is there more I should know about?"

"For most of it," I offer. "But I had a good reason. I—"

"You could be dead," he bellows. "I could have had the report of your death on my desk without even knowing what lies in front of me. I could have signed off on your execution for identity fraud without knowing it." His voice catches on that last sentence, and I swallow, my throat suddenly tight. "Did you think at all about what that would have done to me, Ara?" I see the hurt in his eyes, and my stomach plummets. I disappointed him. Again.

"Maybe it would be better if I were gone. For all of you." I shrug, looking at the floor. I raise my gaze when he doesn't answer.

My brother stares at me, his mouth agape in horror.

"What the fuck are you talking about?" He shakes his head like he can't believe what he heard. "Please tell me you're joking. Say it's one of your twisted ways of making fun of me." His voice is hoarse, choked by emotions. My chest tightens, making it hard to breathe.

"I just...I wanted to fix it. I wanted to prove that I'm more than the reckless, helpless girl who always screws everything up." I look at the floor, trying to hide the tears rolling down my cheeks. "All of it was so important to Mom, and then...the markings...I didn't know what to do..." My voice catches on a sob.

Darren curses, and then I'm enveloped in his arms.

"There were all those things changing...and I was so afraid, Dar. So damn afraid of letting you all down." My body shakes with the sobs I try so hard to hold back, and Dar holds on like he's afraid I'll vanish otherwise.

"So afraid I would become one of those figures of the stories...but I learned to control it, Dar, I really did." I look up at him through my tears and find his face wet as well.

"You should have come to me with all of that," he says.

"I planned to, but then Ian sounded so disappointed, so disgusted, because I made one of my stupid jokes and..." I hiccup, my throat tight again, remembering my brother's words.

I don't want to dispose of another body.

And words I never allowed myself to voice tumble over my lips.

"I am always this burden for you, this dark cloud overshadowing your lives." I fight a breath down my rigid chest. "All of you have given so much...and no matter what I do, I'm constantly disappointing you... And Dad..." Another sob wracks my body.

"Don't you dare put that on yourself." Dar sounds furious.

I shrug. "But it is. He took that position because of me, to protect me. He would have never been at that bloody battle otherwise, and now you..."

"Now you are just full of yourself." Dar taps my chin and shakes his head at me, which earns him a watery smile. He pushes me back a little and makes me look up at him.

"I never knew you carried all that around, little sparrow. I'm sorry I didn't see it." He shakes his head ruefully and pulls me back into his arms. "You are our light. The day you and Ben were born, you wrapped every one of us around your little fingers. Then the day we found out—"

"The day I nearly killed Mom, you mean," I mutter.

"Don't start," he growls. His chest vibrates with it under my cheek. "You were a baby. It was not your fault. Nothing that day was your fault. We should have watched you better. Mom should have known better. But..." He shrugs. "All of us panicked. You looked so pale, so broken when I picked you up. All of us were petrified. Ian and I were so sure we killed you that day." He shakes his head. His eyes are haunted like he can still see all of it. "We felt so guilty for it and were so careful with you because we never wanted to relive that again. You never disappointed us. You drove us nuts, though." He huffs out a laugh.

"I made your life hell, didn't I?" My voice is muffled, my face buried in his chest.

He chuckles. "That you did, but so much more fun as well. I can only speak for myself, but I know the others don't feel different, little sparrow. I never resented you for what you are and never once wished you weren't around."

"But..."

"No buts about it. Everyone who knows you is aware that there isn't a bad bone in your body. Quite clearly, you would rather die than hurt us. So stop doubting yourself and stop shoveling all that guilt onto your shoulders. Especially for the things you had no say in." Breathing becomes a little easier, and I take a stuttering breath.

Darren ducks his head, seeking my gaze. "Dad made his own choices, and that is what killed him. None of this is on you." He shrugs. "Maybe he did take that position to have the power and say to protect you, but you can't be sure he wouldn't have ended up there anyway. He was a warrior long before you came along, and the chances are good he would have been at that battle no matter what." He wipes the tears from my face. "They offered him that position because he was bloody good at it. The same reason I was offered to take over after him. And yes, you have been on my mind, you always are, but you are not the sole reason I took on that position."

"I just feel so...I don't want you to have to protect me all the time," I mutter. Darren laughs at that.

"That is my job. That is our job as your big brothers." He grins when I grumble at that. "Now I'll go back to the academy, clean up your mess, and in a few days, I'll take you back home."

"But—" I start.

"No, little sparrow, that part is not negotiable," he says, his face stern. My stomach sinks. If I can't convince him, all of this will have been for nothing. But can I even do it? Can I go through with Mom's plan now that I've met Tate?

CHAPTER
THIRTY-NINE
TATE

Today, Picking started, and I'm miles away on patrol duty, scanning the forest beneath me for signs of movement. I lingered endlessly in the dining hall the night of Blackstone's visit, hoping Ara would show, but she never did. We left for patrol early the following morning, and despite hovering in the hallway like a creep, I didn't see her then either.

Our flight isn't on watch duty for Picking until the very last day of it, and the thought of Ara going through that right now makes it hard to think straight. I'm not sure I could have stayed away if we hadn't been on patrol, so maybe there is something positive to this.

"She is strong and fierce," Daeva reassures me. But we both know that isn't a guarantee that Ara will survive it.

They drugged the runners at dinner the evening before, blocking known gifts if present to level the chances, and then placed them up on Mount Albión at one of three drop-off areas. The runners have to show their skill by surviving in the rough environment of the mountain and finding their way to the collection point. That gives the birds up there time to evaluate them and choose a rider if worthy.

I couldn't even tell her good luck.

We will arrive back the night before Picking ends, which is still three nights away, and since the area we patrol is too sparsely populated and too rough in terrain to justify outposts, we'll camp out in the open.

"She'll do fine," Jared offers, together with a bowl of stew. He's the one cooking tonight.

"Who?" Zaza asks behind me.

"Uh...Daeva did feel a little off earlier today," I lie.

"You make me sound weak," Daeva complains instantly.

"She is not happy about me saying that," I relay to the others, which makes them chuckle.

"Yes, I'm not happy because you tell lies about me to cover up Jared's mistakes. Tell him to keep his mouth shut, or I will come for him." Since Zaza is still next to me, laughing about something Jared said, I spare him the threat. The way Zaza looks at my best friend while he serves the next rider makes me pause. Is that longing in her eyes? I remember Zaza's comment to Ara about the men in our division. Maybe I should make my best friend talk about things for a change.

I walk over to the trunk of a big fallen tree and sit down, my thoughts wandering about a day's ride northeast to Picking and Ara.

I hope you play it safe, sunshine!

Exhaustion helps me to fall asleep despite my worries. I start awake after a much too familiar nightmare, only it had been Ara bleeding out in front of me this time. I scrub a hand over my face, trying to reassure myself that it was only a dream, but since she isn't safe within the walls of the academy, but out in the open just like me, it's not that easy.

I sit up. The night sky is bright with stars above me since we skipped erecting tents to save time in the morning. The next part of our route is always the worst. The winds in this part of the mountains are tricky and exhausting for our companions.

The night is quiet, and the sleeping forms around me should be reassuring with the birds huddled close by. But instead, there is a tension I can't shake. Like someone is watching.

Daeva blinks at me when I get up, so either it's her turn to keep watch or I woke her with my nightmare.

A rustle between the trees has me snap to high alert. Maybe it hadn't been just the nightmare that woke me. The mist crept up to our camping area during the night. It's not even three steps away from me now.

I shudder and peer into the misty veil, trying to make out anything out of the ordinary. Despite my attention, I don't see the shadowy figure until it steps out of the mist right in front of me.

I step back, reaching for the dagger at my leg and letting my magic flow to the surface.

"Don't," the figure threatens, leveling his taut bow right at my heart. "And tell your bird to stay put, too."

"You heard him," I tell Daeva, and her ire washes down our bond, heightening my own. I grasp for the air around him. As soon as I have a hold on the arrow, I can move.

"Don't," the low voice warns again even though I haven't moved a muscle.

Can he feel my magic?

I can't get hold of the arrow. It's like something is shoving me back, like the air within the mist doesn't listen to me.

"You won't get away with killing me," I tell him, switching to Daeva's view to try to make out his face. The long dark cloak he wears seems to melt into the mist around him, hiding his features completely. If it hadn't been for his voice and size, I wouldn't even have been sure he's male.

"Oh, I'm well aware that killing you could start a war we are not ready for." The stranger chuckles. "And I'm sure she would never forgive me. So you are safe for now."

"Yes, Daeva would hunt you down," I say, switching back to my own view. He looks at my bird.

"Yeah, she doesn't look too happy either." His head turns back to me. "Listen, I'm only approaching you because you are asking the right questions. There is a lot more going on than you know, and this isn't the time to get into it. But I need to warn her. You need to warn her. There are people after her and after you. She has to stay vigilant and can always count on us for help. We'll always take her in."

"Who are you?" I ask.

"Tynan of the mist court, or the titans, depending on how fancy you prefer it." He takes a little bow, all of it without moving his arrow even one finger away from its mark. "I tried to warn her, but she ran... to you—and since I know what you did for her..." He pauses, his gaze turning to the mist, but his bow stays on target. I have to give it to him. He has control. "Tell her to leave a message in the book she dropped or to whisper my name into the mist, and we will contact her. Don't let her walk into the mist alone."

A rustle to my far left draws my attention. Boko turns but settles again.

"What are you talking about?" I ask, turning back, but the space next to me is empty. He vanished as quickly and silently as he came, the mist licking at my feet but slowly drawing back. What the fuck was that about?

"You heard that, too, right?" I ask Daeva.

Thankfully, she confirms. Otherwise, I would have thought I dreamed all of it.

"Do you think he was talking about Ara?" I ask Daeva.

"Unless you faced a dragon for someone else, I'm pretty sure he was. Did she ever run to you?" she asks in return. I'm about to negate that when I remember our encounter in the library.

I never asked her why she ran through the library in total darkness.

Fuck. Had someone chased her, scared her? Nearly reached her within the academy walls? And how had she known where to find me? How did the stranger know she ran to me?

It's safe to say I don't find sleep that night, and my worry about Ara shoots up to astronomical levels.

I can't wait to get back because if he was talking about Ara, he warned me that someone is after her, and she's currently unarmed and up on a mountain that is challenging all on its own.

ARA

I WAKE UP ON A COOL STONE FLOOR. ALONE.

"I guess dropping us off in flights would have been too much to ask," I grumble while I get up, dusting myself off and taking in my surroundings.

I know where I am even though I don't know the room I'm currently in. If you can call it a room at all since it has no ceiling, the four tall walls opening to a barely lit sky above me.

Picking has begun.

There had been moments in my argument with Dar that I hadn't been sure I would even get here. So there is a little satisfaction mixed in the trepidation when I look around. I have to be in the old ruins, and I'm suddenly glad Professor Riku made us memorize all those maps in geography.

The ruins are on the southern side of Mount Albión. The room around me is empty, a few weeds and moss growing in the cracks along the walls. There is only one doorway, so I don't have much choice but to start walking.

Whenever they told us we would be tested, I hadn't thought getting out of a labyrinth would be part of it, but this is exactly what it feels like. I huff out a breath while I eye the two doorways in front of me.

I use the sunlight for orientation, but since I don't know the structure of the building or where the exit is located, that isn't much help.

Somehow, I envisioned Picking being more about flying and finding my way through the wilderness instead of being abandoned in a strange building.

At least the rules are easy: survive and don't leave the mountain unless you are ordered to. Well, I can do that, I hope.

My body aches from the night on the hard stone floor, which makes me think of the last night I spent on a hard floor... in Tate's arms.

Concentrate.

I have been stripped of all my weapons, leaving me with only the helmet on my head and the shield placed next to me, which makes me a little anxious.

At least nothing has attacked me yet.

I meander through one room after another, and my thoughts start wandering again, this time back to my conversation with Dar. We got into a bit of a disagreement after he declared he would take me home.

But he couldn't take away the marking on my arm, which is now a wriggly line longer than the span of my hand. Dar had to agree that it wouldn't go unnoticed forever. He freaked out about the promise to the dragon, though. I wince, just thinking back to that. He was also not amused that I slipped past the guards so easily, so there'll be changes.

The building is eerily quiet around me, and the fact that I haven't met any runners yet freaks me out a bit. I should have run into someone by now, shouldn't I?

When steps come in my direction, I'm already so on edge that my first instinct is to run and hide. I don't question it and scramble up the wall beside me. It provides me with the perfect view to watch the birds circling overhead while I wait for whoever might come into sight.

Some of the birds are with riders, some without, and I'm sure I'm making a fool of myself, but rather that than...what?

What am I afraid of?

It's not like anyone is going around killing runners.

But I still hold my breath when the steps come closer, and Livia comes into view accompanied by a rider. The small hairs on my neck rise, and a shiver runs down my back. Riders are not allowed on this mountain during Picking unless they pick up a body.

They walk past me and in the direction I came from. A rumbling roar in the distance has me appreciating the wall I'm sitting on even more.

Maybe Dar's worries have been more substantial than I gave him credit for. Up until now, I mainly worried about not getting picked or falling to my death if a bird deemed me unworthy, but now...

"You are not taking this seriously enough," Dar's words ring in my mind like a warning bell. Okay, I get it now. I am no longer laughing at all the safety precautions he tried to jam into my brain that night.

When the building is once more silent around me, I hurry on.

My thirst far outweighs hunger by the time the midday sun burns down on me. I grimace at the salty, metallic taste while my tongue slips over my dry, cracked lips. My gaze catches longingly on the green of the tree line whenever I'm up on a wall. I haven't seen Livia or the rider again, but since none of the runners passing me so far have been from my flight or squadron, I didn't bother making myself known.

At least half the day has passed by the time I make it out of the buildings, and the sun is already declining. My feelings are torn when I look over the large open space in front of me. I'm glad to leave the death trap of stone, but I have to cross that to reach the other ruins farther down the mountain slope.

I tightened my hold on the dagger I found in one of the rooms. I have no choice. If I stay here, I will not only get the sunburn of my life but also die of dehydration before the week is up.

I set out in a sprint, and just when I reach the first crumbled walls, a deep roar prompts me to spin to my right. The biggest damn cat I have ever seen emerges from the tree line. It probably shouldn't surprise me, considering the size of the birds found in these mountains, but still.

I back away slowly and cower down behind a wall, hoping the beast can't scent me.

Shit. Shit. Shit. What now?

The size of the dagger in my hand is ridiculous compared to that creature.

My muscles are tight and rigid with tension, and I hardly dare to breathe. I stay as still as possible, my own heartbeat drowning out every sound around me.

My grip on the dagger is so tight that my knuckles turn white. A stone skitters over the ground behind me, and a hand lands on my shoulder.

I whirl around, swiping out with the dagger.

Someone jumps back, making a sound of surprise.

"Easy, Gray, or you will hurt someone."

Calix's smiling face fills my view when I look up.

"I thought you were going to kill me," I tell him.

"And I thought we were over the trust issues by now." He chuckles.

"I didn't know it was you...obviously." I roll my eyes.

"So I haven't somehow made it on your bad side, then? I'm relieved to hear that." He grins. Calix leans past me, his eyes searching our surroundings. "It's gone."

I lean back against the wall, sighing. With the adrenaline gone, I suddenly feel weak and tired.

Calix eyes me. "You look like you could use some time out of the sun," he says. "Follow me."

He heads straight for a crumbling building with some parts of its roof left. I follow him on slightly wobbly knees, glad he found me and I have survived the first day so far.

I let my gaze wander over him. He somehow got his hands on a sword, which is now dangling by his hip, and he moves with ease so he doesn't seem injured.

I'm relieved... working together as a team will make surviving this week a whole lot easier.

The inside of the building is blissfully cool after the sun's glare, and that isn't even the best of it. Calix hands me a waterskin filled to the brim. The water tastes slightly metallic, but it's cool and the most delicious drink I have had in forever.

I nearly drain it before I catch myself and look at Calix apologetically.

He laughs. "It's alright. There is a stream right after the tree line starts. We can get more."

"Thank you," I tell him.

"That's what friends are for." He sends me a crooked smile.

"Where did you get the waterskin?"

"I hid it by wrapping it around my leg." He smirks.

"Sneaky." I grin at him. "And the sword?"

"I found it." He eyes my dagger. "And it seems that was not the only weapon lying around. Did I miss something in class while we were talking about Picking?"

I shake my head. "I can't remember hearing anything about that either." In combination with the way Livia was looking for something, accompanied by a rider, it left a bad taste in my mouth.

CHAPTER FORTY

ARA

I wash my face in the stream Calix mentioned, relishing the cool water on my burning skin, and we fill up his waterskin. Yesterday was a slow start, but today is better so far, especially since we haven't encountered any surprises.

Maybe I have been a little hasty there, I think, when I hear voices ahead of us, and I give Calix a sign to stay back. Ever since I saw Livia with that rider, my inner voice has been telling me to be careful.

Calix might be good at this outdoor stuff, but he's awful at creeping around. He grimaces but complies.

The ground under my feet slopes upward into a small hill, and the voices come from behind it. I stick close to the trees. It's already getting dark, making it easier not to be seen.

I get down on my hands and knees, wincing when a stick burrows into my knee. I'm sore from two nights on hard stone floors, but I do my best to ignore it, crawling forward until I see what, or better, who is beneath me.

It is none other than Livia and the four runners she always hangs out with. I'm glad for my precautions now.

They sit around a magical fire, the violet and blue flames throwing eerie shadows on their faces and bodies.

Of course, Livia found a way around the magic ban.

"He won't walk out of here alive," Livia declares, and the others chuckle. I'm stunned. Not that I put it past her to kill another runner, but unlike Assessment, when behavior like that seems to be ignored, leadership does not condone something like that during Picking. Too much went into training us to have us then die uselessly due to murderous contestants.

I slowly crawl backward.

"He seems to have crossed quite a few people the wrong way," Livia continues.

"I can't believe they even offered to pay you for this," another voice said. "When will we meet them?"

"Once I have found him."

Oh great, Livia kills or intimidates for money now? Talk about making your passion your trade. But despite my grim humor, my gut twists. I have a bad, bad feeling about this.

I get back up when I am far enough away and hurry off in the direction I left Calix. A hand grabs me. I whirl around, my dagger aiming where the other person's body has to be, but I meet steel instead.

"I'm happy to see you too," Mariel's voice hisses. I relax.

"Dammit, Mariel, I nearly killed you."

"Not even close." She giggles.

"Then she's in good company, I'd say," Calix grumbles.

"She tried to kill you, too?" Mariel asks, humor in her voice.

I huff. "You can't sneak up on someone out here and not expect to get a knife for your trouble. Gods, you two, am I the only one paranoid about someone wanting to kill me?"

"Yes," Calix answers, while Mariel says, "No."

"Let's get out of here. Livia and her minions are over there planning someone's demise. So I'd say we should walk a while before making camp."

We walk until there isn't enough light left, and we stumble repeatedly. We pick a spot with soft ground for our camp, and after two nights on stone floors, it feels like heaven. Calix pulls out the rest of the meal we shared for lunch, and we split it between us. Not enough to be filled, but we aren't going hungry either.

We later lie on our backs in the small clearing we found, facing the sky bright with stars.

"Do you think many runners have bonded already?" Mariel asks.

"Hard to say." I shrug. "But did you see the Rukh circling us? He kept close for quite a while."

"Yeah," Mariel answers. "I pray to the gods that one of them picks me. Could you imagine going through the last three months for nothing?"

Calix's breathing next to me is slow and even, hinting he's asleep already.

"We'll be fine," I tell her and wish I could believe it, too.

What if birds don't bond with cursed ones?

I push the thought away and nudge Mariel instead, jerking my head in Calix's direction. She looks over at his sleeping form and giggles when he grunts.

"Have you told him yet?" she asks.

"No, I'm afraid it will change things between us."

"Eh..." Mariel waves her hand like she's trying to get rid of flies. "He is not the person to hold it against you."

"True," I agree. "But you know how he is..."

"With every female but me, you mean." Mariel sighs, and I wonder if that is regret in her voice. But the moment passes, and Mariel switches the topic back to the most obvious one.

"So what bird do you wish for?" she asks.

"I don't know." I sigh. "Probably Strix or Rukh. They are the most common ones, and it's not like I have the intimidation vibe Night Ravens seem to go for." I shrug.

"Well, you are pretty badass, like when I grabbed you earlier."

"You laughed." I deadpan.

"Well, I knew you wouldn't hurt me once you saw it was me," she explains.

"See? Not intimidated," I counter.

"Okay, okay, intimidating is not the word I would use to describe you. More like cute and fun and a little reckless?"

I snort at that. I sound like a freaking puppy.

"That is a good thing, you know," she rushes to explain. "And because you totally are badass under all that sunshine, it works in your favor because people tend to underestimate you." She smiles at me.

I frown.

"And you are mysterious and sexy and…" she hurries on.

I laugh. "Cute and fun, got it. You can rest your case now…"

Mariel gives me a worried look but relaxes when she sees I'm not mad. How could I when sunshine is a nickname I'm very fond of now?

"Are you sure we're still walking in the right direction?" Mariel asks after a while, and she has a point. I, for my part, am not sure. I look at Calix, but his expression tells me he isn't either.

"How about I get up there real quick and see where we're headed?" I point at the cliff next to us with heaps of massive boulders at its foot.

Calix snorts. "Real quick? Well, go ahead. We don't want to spoil your fun."

I grin at him.

"Be careful, okay?" Mariel asks, and I lift my eyebrow.

"Are you doubting my abilities?" I ask.

"Nope. Just be careful," she repeats. I hand her my shield and clamber up on one of the boulders. It's only when I'm out of sight that I get rid of my helmet as well. It will only hinder me, and I very much doubt I will run into anyone up there.

I really should tell Calix.

The sun is high in the sky, and the stone is warm beneath my fingers. It's nice. The wind whips through the few strands that came loose from my braid as I scramble up the face of the cliff. The world falls away beneath me, and my horizon broadens the farther I climb. I haul myself over the edge and take a moment to admire the view while simultaneously searching for clues. Everything I would need to make this moment even more perfect would be a set of wings and maybe a certain centurion at my side.

The spires of buildings peek over a slope to my left, and a sliver of blue—a glimpse of the sea—is right next to it.

If Telos is over there, I recall the map we studied so rigorously over the past few weeks and use the city, along with the mountains around me, to orient myself, *then we have to head that way*.

We aren't far off course. I memorize the trees we have to head for, then make my way down.

I pick up my helmet and place it back on my head before I jump from one big stone to the next.

Pain rips through my ankle, and I cry out. I kick my foot reflexively and dislodge the snake that bit me, its body flying off and falling between the rocks, but not before I see the blue belly. *Shit*.

"Are you okay?" Calix and Mariel shout. I peel back my pants, my eyes fixed on the two puncture marks on my skin.

I curse.

"Gray?" Calix shouts.

"I'm fine." Or at least as close to it as I can be in this situation. I move my ankle gingerly, wincing at the pain and the swelling that is already starting.

I hope my curse will eliminate the poison since bluebellies are part of the magical creatures, but that means I can't tell the others what happened without revealing what I am. Dammit.

"What happened?" Calix asks.

"Um...I twisted my ankle," I tell them.

"Can you walk?" Mariel asks. I take a few steps and find the pain manageable.

"Yeah, I'm fine."

Their doubtful gazes land on my swollen ankle, but it actually looks worse than it feels. I refuse their offers to look at it, and we take off in the direction of the collection point.

The pain spreads while I walk, climbing up my leg and sliding down into my foot. After a while, I start limping, and by the time the sun sets, every step is like walking on incandescent coals. My whole leg is swollen by now, and the cloth of my pants rubbing over my skin is torture.

A stream runs past our campsite, and I don't hesitate. I roll up the legs of my pants and step right into its icy flow. The pain instantly becomes more bearable.

I'm unbelievably tired, and since my appetite is gone, I only nibble on a small piece of the rabbit Calix caught earlier. Thankfully, the others are tired too, so we all lie down after that.

The pain radiating from my leg is so intense that it wakes me, and I can't stay still a second longer. Instead of giving in to crying, I get up and hobble to the stream. Before I reach it, I fall to my hands and knees, heaving up the contents of my stomach.

Dying would be a damn blessing right now.

I crawl the rest of the way to the water, plunging my leg in, not caring that I get my pants wet in the process. Then I just sit there, waiting for the pain to subside and trying to think of anything but the walk that awaits us in the morning or the fact that no bird has tried to approach me yet. Some have been around, and both Calix and Mariel reported they felt nudges in their mind. But nothing for me so far.

I stay in the water until my leg is numb, then I walk back to my sleeping friends, trying to get some rest as well.

The following morning, I'm feverish, and my whole body hurts. I'm tired and cranky, which earns me raised eyebrows, but no one says a thing. I have to excuse myself three times before noon, secretly dry heaving behind bushes.

I'm starting to worry that I was wrong with my assumption about the poison.

Is this what dying feels like?

It takes a while before I get the idea to search my body for traces of magic. As soon as I concentrate on it, I detect it. The poison moves through my body. It's everywhere. Minuscule orbs of magic slide through my blood while my gift is on the hunt, snapping them up one after another. It's a slow process.

Nonetheless, it gives me hope, and I make more of an effort to hide how miserable I am. I also make sure we camp next to a stream again.

The next night, my nightmares of the lightning wielder are back. His sizzling power is cooking me alive. I writhe in pain, my skin taut and itchy with heat. The agony makes me cry out until Mariel shakes me awake. Her hand is cool on my skin.

"You're burning up," she says, concern audible in her voice.

"Oh, that's probably because of the nightmare." I brush it off. She looks at me dubiously but doesn't push it...yet. Calix slept through it all, so at least I don't have to argue with him, too.

I'M STILL FEVERISH IN THE MORNING.

"You look awful," Mariel declares.

"I didn't sleep too well." I shrug. I wobble a little when I get up. Mariel steadies me and scowls when she realizes my temperature is still too high.

"Spill it, now," she snaps.

"Something might have bitten me when I came back down the cliff," I mumble. "But I feel better already."

"Well, you don't look it," she tells me. I'm still woozy and slightly sticky from sweating all night. "Let me help you wash in the stream. Maybe you'll feel better after that."

It's a logical suggestion, so I don't protest when Mariel helps me to the water, supporting my weight. Calix offers to carry me, but we both wave him off. I still haven't told him, and helping me to undress is not the way I intend to do it.

Once I sit in the cold stream in my undergarments, Mariel returns to Calix to keep him occupied.

A Rukh drops down out of nowhere and snatches Mariel before soaring off. I jump up, startled, but her shrieks already turn into laughter.

They circle above us, and I hold my breath when Mariel is thrown into the air, but her bird catches her. He picked her. My laughter of wonder turns into a shriek when I lose my footing and tumble into the stream. I come up spluttering and cursing only to find Calix right next to me.

His eyebrows jump up in surprise at seeing me. I guess I don't have to agonize over how to tell him the truth any longer.

"What the fuck?" he asks, his eyes big when they land on mine.

"Uh...surprise," I say sheepishly.

"You can say that again. What the fuck, Gray?" he says, and I see the hurt starting to seep in.

"I told you my brothers didn't know I was here, and well, I thought I would draw less attention if I pretended to be one of the guys, and then I simply didn't know how to tell you, and...are you very mad?" I rush all of this out in one long breath, desperate to make Calix see that I never intended to lie to him. I try to walk over to him but stumble again. This time, Calix plucks me out of the water and sets me down on solid ground next to the river.

"I need a minute," he tells me. "You are fine here by yourself, right?" he asks, and when I nod, he walks away.

My teeth chatter a bit while I hop up and down on one leg in an attempt to get a little drier and warm before I slip back into my uniform. After days of wearing it, it feels even more disgusting on my clean skin than before.

Would it have been so bad to let us take a pack with spare clothing?

In the time of my confession and my hopping, Mariel's Rukh twirled through something that looks a little like a dance. It's a female, easily recognizable from the lighter coloring, and her movements are mesmerizing. I can't help but look up again and again. My breath catches a few times when Mariel slides, but she always manages to hold on.

The pattern becomes smoother and more relaxed until the Rukh circles down, landing softly close to where I'm waiting next to Calix, once again fully dressed.

Mariel's smile reaches from one ear to the other, her whole body radiating happiness. She jumps down and rushes to us first, hugging me, then Calix, laughing and crying and babbling all at once.

"I'm so happy for you!" I tell her.

"You have no idea how incredible this feels," she gushes. "Suddenly, I'm so much more, and the thoughts and images and all the impressions and…"

"I know," she suddenly cries out, turning to the Rukh, clearly not talking to us anymore. She rushes over to her, cooing at and cuddling her bird. It takes a moment before she turns back to us, but she still seems distracted.

"I'm sorry. I didn't introduce you. This is Tempest, my Rukh."

She laughs at that incredulously. "My Rukh, can you believe it?" She turns back to the bird. "Yes, beautiful, I'm yours too. Of course, I'm yours." And again, she's lost to the rest of the world.

"Okay then, I guess Myrsky wasn't joking when he said we would be distracted for the first few days," Calix rumbles next to me, watching Mariel and Tempest with an expression I can't quite decipher.

"Get out of here, you two," I tell Mariel.

"Huh?" She looks at me and obviously hasn't heard a word I said.

"I said get out of here, enjoy the next hours in peace, and we'll see you back at the gathering place," I tell her. Calix nods next to me.

"You don't mind?" she asks, but I can see she wants nothing more than to get going.

"Of course not." I roll my eyes. "We all knew this would happen."

The two don't waste another minute, and Tempest is airborne as soon as Mariel sits on her back.

They will head back to the same camp we are headed to but will reach it in minutes instead of hours or days. They won't have anything to do but get acquainted until Picking is over.

Calix and I wave after them until they are out of sight.

"So it's just us now," Calix sighs. "Let's hope we have that in the next few days as well."

"Of course we will," I tell him in a cheery voice. I'm sure a bird will pick him, but I doubt the same is true for me. There have still been no attempts to contact me.

"Calix, I really am sorry." I address the other problem, pangs of guilt flipping through my stomach. "I would have told you earlier, but you like to flirt, and I just wasn't sure you could treat me like a guy after you knew," I say. He looks at me for a moment before he bursts out laughing.

"You're right," he says. "I probably would have flirted with you at one point, and that would have started all kinds of rumors, wouldn't it?" He's still chuckling.

"So we're good?" I ask.

"Yes, Gray, as long as you're still the same and still my friend, we're good."

"Of course I am," I tell him while a massive weight slides off my shoulders.

CHAPTER FORTY-ONE

ARA

The following day brings what I predicted, a bond mate for my best friend. It was a little different from Mariel's bonding yesterday, just like Myrsky says. Every species has its rituals. Now Calix stands in front of me, the sunlight accentuating the frown lines on his brow.

"Are you sure?" Calix looks at me and back at Aella, his newly bonded Strix, torn.

It is normal for newly bonded riders and their birds to be lost to the world around them for a few hours. Your souls will intertwine. It's like suddenly there is this new part of you, and it's completely normal to explore it. You'll need this time to solidify your bond. Professor Myrsky's words come back to me, and I remember the distracted way Mariel behaved.

"I'll be fine." I wave him off. Thankfully, I feel much better today.

"See you at the gathering point." I smile, but I doubt I will reach it on wings.

Maybe birds steer clear of cursed ones.

"Here." Calix hands me his waterskin. "Be careful, okay?" He hugs me before he rushes back to Aella like a kid on the solstice. I'm happy for him.

They take off and spiral higher and higher until they are gone from sight. Only then do I let my shoulders slump.

I failed.

It's the last day of Picking, and not one bird has shown interest in me. What now? Is going along with my family's plans even an option? The thought of not marrying a stranger is pure relief, but leaving all of this behind, leaving Tate, makes me sick.

Even if you had bonded, it would have come to this.

I don't have time to wait for next year. My markings are creeping down my arm already, and it won't be long until someone sees them.

The day isn't over yet.

I'll have to make my way to the gathering point, even if it's on foot. So I take a deep breath, pull my shoulders back, and head off into the woods.

I haven't gone far when snapping twigs alert me to someone's presence. I twist around, and there stands Livia.

"Now, who do we have here?" Livia sneers at me. Great, just the person I don't want to see. "I've been looking for you, you know."

This is not good.

"Why? Forgot your name again?" I sound much braver than I feel.

I look around, and my heart pounds when I see two people looming behind her. One is a rider, and the other isn't.

My blood runs cold.

I search for a way out while I try to keep the trembling in check. I'm much stronger than I was a day ago. The poison is finally gone from my blood, but I'm very aware of how weak I still am.

My hand wanders slowly to the dagger at my side while my eyes take in the other man accompanying her. A stranger. Something about the mismatched armor he wears rattles my memory.

"You'll get what you deserve, you little misfit. Not so brave without your big strong friend, are you?" Livia mocks me, stepping closer. "That is the one you were looking for, isn't it?" she asks, pinning me with her gaze.

What?

"Let me get a closer look," the stranger says, stepping up to me. He reaches for my helmet, but I take a step back.

The rider behind them fidgets. "You don't need me here, do you?" he asks, and Livia chuckles.

"No, we got this," she says. Without another word, the rider turns and walks away.

Well, no help from him then.

"Don't be shy," the man croons, making Livia chuckle again. He jumps forward, pushing me hard, and I stumble into a tree behind me. Before I find my footing again, he grabs the helmet, lifts it, and throws it to the side.

Livia gapes at my hair. Her eyes widen, then her whole face contorts in fury.

"You bitch." She backhands me, but I dodge the fist she follows up with. I sweep my tongue over my lip, taking in the coppery taste and the slight sting, while I get my arms up to protect my head. She swings at me again, and I kick, aiming at her knee.

"Don't take my rejection so hard, Livia. I'm just not into girls." I have no idea why I taunt her when she already looks ready for murder, but her enraged scream is satisfying.

The man steps back, crossing his arms like he settles in to watch a show. Whoever he is, he obviously doesn't care if either of us gets hurt.

Livia comes at me again and again, and it doesn't take long until I'm winded. She's good and not worn out by battling poison like me. Her fists find their targets more and more often, and I'm tempted to draw my dagger. But if I do, she will, too, and a blade will do much more damage than her fists. So I refrain.

Our fight moves us onto a clearing. That I don't have to watch out for trees is the only positive thing about my current situation. There is a small fire set up and it looks like someone spend some time here.

They waited for me.

Livia keeps hurling insults and accuses me more than once of murdering Gorgon. Since that doesn't get a rise out of me, she spouts allegations about me fucking Calix, Joel, and Tate, and gets quite creative with it, too.

But I stay quiet, not because I'm so smart and above it, but because I'm simply out of air. My legs feel like jelly, and my heart gallops like it wants to burst out of my chest. I'm exhausted.

She pushes me, and I stumble back, my hand grabbing for her and latching on to a necklace around her neck. I fall back, and the chain snaps, landing in the grass beside me when I land on my ass.

"She's all yours," she hisses, glaring at me but addressing the man.

"Well, thank you for softening her up a little," he says with a smile while he steps up.

"Make her suffer," she demands, and the man chuckles, sending a chill down my back.

"Oh, I intend to." He looks down at me. "Get up." Magic flows over me, compelling me to get up. Fuck. His gift is influencing.

I expect my curse to rise like a wave, but instead, it's only a trickle. It stops his gift, but when I look for it, the normally big ball of coldness inside me is no more than a grain of rice.

The poison must have drained it.

I rise to my feet, and for the first time, I'm truly scared. His magic presses in again, and the curse flickers. I never thought I would see the day I dreaded being without it, but I do. Without it, I'm not only weakened but also vulnerable to his magic. Shit.

"Stand still," he commands, and this time, I'm compelled to do as he says.

Shit. Shit. Shit.

It goes against everything in me, but I hold my curse back. I will deplete it completely otherwise, and who knows when I'll need it.

"And if anyone sees us, you will tell them you want this. You want me." The memory of the only other person I encountered with this gift pops up, and I shudder inwardly while my body stays still as the man commanded.

I'm not helpless. I only wait for the right moment. I repeat the words over and over to stifle the panic crawling up my throat.

"Well, that is handy," Livia declares, startling me. Somehow, I thought she had already left. She steps closer and slaps my face with so much force that my head would have turned if the man's gift hadn't held me in place.

Pain explodes in my cheek. She smiles, grips my shirt, and tears it down the middle. "Look at that, you are a whore, and now you look like it, too." She steps so close that her breath brushes my ear when she whispers, "You deserve everything that comes for you."

Her gaze darts to the man standing next to us, then back to me. "I would love to stay and watch him torture you." She grins. "But some have been picked, so my bird is waiting, and I have to get to the gathering point before I'm late." She walks away but stops and turns back again. "Oh, and Deputy Commander Foley sends you his regards. Have fun," she chirps before heading into the forest, leaving me alone with the stranger.

TATE

W<small>E</small> <small>CIRCLE ABOVE</small> M<small>OUNT</small> A<small>LBIÓN</small>. I<small>TS SNOWY PEAK</small> concealed in a cloud, but my focus is much farther down anyway. I'm using Daeva's view to inspect every moving shape down in the forest and every huddled form on the back of a bird, looking for Ara, but I don't see her.

"Have you heard of anyone bonding her?" I ask Daeva, but she answers in the negative. Either she hasn't bonded yet or Daeva simply didn't hear about it. I hope it's the latter.

While we continue circling, I see a rider ascending from the forest below. He doesn't have a body with him, which is strange, and I try to ignore the nagging dread coming over me.

Foley wouldn't send a rider to kill her, right?

"Her friend just arrived at the gathering," Daeva informs me. Whether she's talking about Calix Ilario or Mariel Tethys, they must know more. I want nothing more than to turn around and demand answers, but I can't since I have to stay up here.

"Can you ask his bird about Ara?" I beg Daeva, and her conscience turns away from me while she does as I asked. We glide over the gathering place, and I bite my tongue, waiting for her answer.

"Freshly bonded are worse than chicks," Daeva grumbles. "When they left, she was well, she says." She relays some images, and the coloring and distortion, next to showing Ilario, tells me they are his bird's view. Ara looks thin and fragile with a sheen of perspiration on her brow. Fuck, she must have been sick or something.

"Only a few more hours and you can dote on her all you want. She's upright and walking. That looks good enough for me," Daeva lets me know.

Damn straight I will look after her. She will be a rider by the time she gets back and, therefore, no longer off-limits.

What if she doesn't bond?

The thought pops into my mind without warning, and dread pools in my stomach. I don't know the answer to that. We never talked about that possibility.

What if she decides to leave?

We keep circling, but I get more and more anxious. Why isn't she bonded yet? Why has no bird snatched her up?

CHAPTER FORTY-TWO

ARA

The man walks back and forth in front of me while I look straight ahead at the forest, which taunts me with the hope of escape.

Who is he? And what does he want?

As if he heard my questions, he starts to talk.

"I saw you, you know." The man laughs cruelly. "He attacked a dragon for you. How very heroic." He stops in front of me. "How about I add a little tragedy to your love story?" My stomach drops, but I don't react, not that I could have without giving myself away. He runs his hands over my shoulders, pushing the ripped shirt down my arms before he traces my scars. Inside my head, I scream and rage at him to take his hands off me.

"What do you think"—he looks at me, contemplating—"if I offer you up all bloody and weak, will he sacrifice himself to rescue you?"

His assessing gaze runs over me, and I want to cover myself. But I keep my curse in check and stay as still as he commanded.

My mind scrambles for a way out of this, for something to defend myself with. But the only weapons around is the knife he took from me. He starts running a blade up and down my arm, scraping lightly without causing real harm...yet.

"He didn't like the dragon cutting you, but he does seem to like scars," he muses. He sneers while he traces a long scar running down my arm—a sword practice accident when I was fourteen. I imagine slapping his hand away.

"Let's add some for him to admire." He runs the dagger along my collarbone next, softly at first, increasing the pressure gradually until it bites into my skin. I gasp at the pain, clenching my teeth to keep from screaming. I will not give him that satisfaction.

The trickle of blood is warm on my chilled skin, and the cut burns long after he stopped, but I can't see it, so I try my best to ignore it.

Think, Ara.

"I waited for you at the base, and you didn't disappoint. The way he held you when you got back. Just think how fascinating it became when I found out that the female visitor never left, but a Grayson Summer never returned the evening before."

He circles me, and I probably would have flinched every time the cold steel touches my skin if his magic hadn't prevented me from doing so. The next cut draws a quiet hiss from my lips.

"It seems the prince has a weakness for you."

Prince?

He must see the confusion in my eyes because he laughs. "Oh, he didn't tell you, did he? It's rather tragic, I guess." He chuckles, clearly enjoying this. His talking buys me time to think, but I have a hard time ignoring him when he talks about Tate.

I glare at him, and he laughs.

"He won't stop me. You won't save him. Accept it." He says it like it's a fact and shakes his head when I keep glaring.

I will not accept that.

"Playing hero is a very ungrateful role, or have you seen anyone thanking your dear prince? He resigned to save the day and earns nothing but hate." My heart squeezes painfully for Tate and everything he endured. No wonder he kept anyone at arm's length.

Then another thought strikes, and I'm stunned. He resigned... that means Tate had been the crown prince, so unless we are talking about another country here...

I was betrothed to Tate for half my life?

The man keeps talking, but I don't hear anything over the ringing in my ears. Hope unfurls in my chest and determination. I will go along with my family's plan, but the original one. He has given up so much, but I won't give up on him. I want Tate, and I will find a way to make it happen, but first, I have to get away.

"And now you will help me settle his debt," he ends, but I'll be damned if I do.

I let my eyes roam, looking for anything to take him down.

There is the fire, but he's much heavier than me, and I'm not sure I'll manage to push him that far. My gaze catches on the stones surrounding the fire.

I wait until he's behind me before I lunge for them.

"You bitch." He tackles me from behind, landing on me and knocking the air out of my lungs. My fingers are just short of reaching the stones. I stretch but lose focus when he slams my face into the ground.

A blinding pain explodes from my nose outward, the sickening crack telling me more than I want to know. His full weight on my back and his hand pressing my face into the dirt makes it hard to breathe.

I buck and wriggle, trying to throw him off, but it's no use.

"You are a lively thing, I give you that. Maybe we should have a little fun before I hand you over. What do you think?" I stiffen, panic bubbling up inside me.

No.

"How did you manage to get out of my bind?" he muses. "Do you have a protection spell hidden somewhere? Don't worry, I'll find it."

He gets off my back, and I throw myself forward, blindly grabbing for a stone. My fingers graze the coals, leaving stinging burns. The pain gets even worse when my hand closes around the hot stone, but I don't let go.

He flips me around, and I swing. My arm vibrates with the impact, but my eyes still water so badly, I'm not sure where I hit him. It's enough to make him back off, though, and I scramble back, nearly falling into the flames in the process. I throw my weight to the side, trying to scramble to my feet, but the bastard is on me before I can. His hands clasp around my throat.

He squeezes. I'm still winded from my fall, and it doesn't take long for dark spots to dance over my vision. He kneels over me, pressing and pressing, waiting for me to pass out.

No.

I pull my leg up as hard as I can. It's a little awkward and without much force, but the aim is perfect. He howls with pain, clutching his crotch.

Air floods my lungs, and I take in as much as I can get. My throat burns and scratches with every inhale, but my vision starts clearing. Crawling, I drag myself away from him, my legs too weak to get up just yet.

I'm slow, but I'm glad about every bit of space between us. Something glints in the sunlight, and I turn to it, crawling as quick as I can.

Please be something sharp and pointy.

But it's the medallion I ripped from Livia's neck during our fight. She didn't pick it up. There is a flame etched into its surface, and I realize that is how she got her hands on the magic flames despite the regulations. I grab it and start to get up when a roar sounds behind me.

A boot hits my side, sprawling me onto my back. My attacker is back on me, straddling me, smashing my head into the ground repeatedly.

I shove at him, but he doesn't let up. My view starts to get wonky, and the throbbing in my head intensifies with every hit. My fingers scrabble with the clasp of the medallion, fighting to open it.

"Barely alive." He grunts, smashing my head into the ground. "Is plenty... for an exchange." My head hits the ground after each exclamation. "No need... to survive." Spittle hits my face. He's past enraged.

He will kill me.

Finally, the medallion flips open. I can't see it and don't have much room to move. I just hope it touches his clothes somehow.

I wish for him to go up in flames, but it takes two more impacts before he notices the flames crawling up his body.

He jumps up, his hands batting at the flames. But magical fire is much harder to extinguish.

The flames spread, and the glow of the flames is visible despite the world spinning around me. He screams, then he takes off, leaving a trail of flames behind him.

I don't care where he runs as long as it's away from me. My eyes close.

I need a minute.

TATE

Smoke starts billowing up from the forest below, and by the time I realize it's not just a campfire, a chunk of the forest is already ablaze. Even without seeing the flames up close, the speed at which the fire spreads makes me suspicious. This is too quick for a regular fire.

"Get the message out," I tell Daeva.

"Already did. Others saw it, too. Someone is flying for the academy already."

"We head back," I decide.

I need to know Ara is safe, and we have to mobilize everyone who can help fight the flames and establish a plan for containing it. Daeva doesn't object and takes a sharp turn.

By the time we get back, blue and violet flames dance between red and golden ones. We set down, and I don't waste time before heading for the rider, who documents all the newly bonded riders coming in.

Gods, I hope I am wrong.

"Is anyone unaccounted for?" I ask, my eyes drifting over the list in his hands, trying to find the name I'm looking for.

"A few, sir."

"Who?"

Please don't say it. Don't say it.

"Vaccari, Godwin, Summer..." He goes on, but I don't hear anything else.

Of course, she's in this fucking inferno.

Why is she so adamant about getting herself killed?

"Thank you." My voice is so eerily calm, I don't recognize it as my own.

I can't think. I can't fucking breathe, and still, my voice betrays nothing.

My eyes are on the smoke, the dark gray veil spreading while I watch. The chances of someone surviving this are very slim, but riders are still coming in.

Vaccari strides toward the rider I just left. There is still hope that Ara will land any second now, too.

She can do it. Some part of me knows it's wishful thinking. But damn do I want it to be true—need it to be true.

My mind replays pictures of how I found her at the foot of the cliff, barely alive. I healed her and beat the odds. I can do it again.

But for that to work, I have to get my hands on her while she's still breathing.

My eyes wander over the groups of riders, sorted by squadron. It doesn't take me long to find squadron four of our division. Ilario's big frame next to Mariel's bright red hair is a dead giveaway, but I can't find *her* anywhere.

The riders commanding elements gather closer to the fire, and I make my way over to them. We split the area into four quadrants, one for each division. The other centurions and I assign parcels to the riders present to get the fire under control.

I take the area right next to the gathering ground since there's no way I'm leaving here without knowing Ara is back.

I throw myself into the task, cutting off the air and smothering the flames faster than they can pop up. The quicker we have it under control, the faster I can go look for her. The natural flames succumb at once.

The magic flames are harder to kill, but I don't give them a chance, concentrating on one small part after another, slowly working inward. The fire wielder to my left and a water wielder to my right are doing the same.

Daeva circles above, keeping an eye out for Ara while I work. I try my best not to let my worry for her consume me, but the words of the stranger from a few nights ago keep circling in my head.

There are people after her and after you.

And then I do something I haven't done in years. I pray to every god and goddess who might listen.

I simply don't know what I'll do if she's gone.

CHAPTER
FORTY-THREE
ARA

When I blink my eyes open, the heat threatens to overwhelm me.

What happened?

I sit up, and the world turns around me in slow circles. My head throbs, and I have no idea where I am or how I got here.

Fire and smoke are all around me. I'm not even sure if it's night or day because all I see is the light of the flames and the darkness of the smoke.

I rise slowly and nearly fall over twice before I manage to stand.

My vision swims and shifts, and I stumble, landing on my hands and knees again. The impact jars my body and intensifies my headache. I'm violently ill, not that my stomach contained much that could make a reappearance.

This is bad, really bad.

I must have hit my head. I know the signs and have had a concussion before.

I close my eyes, but that makes the dizziness worse.

Think, Ara, think.

Fire crackles and hisses around me, the heat and smoke making it hard to breathe.

I have to get out of here.

Tate's face flashes before my eyes, my brothers', and those of my friends.

I close my eyes again, concentrating on the magic around me. If someone gifted is close, I should be able to find them.

Ghostlike veils of magic shift around me, fueling the flames. I stretch farther and farther until it feels like my awareness will snap back at any second because I stretched too far. I reach out just a little more, and there, a small flicker. No... more than one, and one of them I recognize—Tate.

If I reach him, I'll be fine.

I zero in on him and him alone, and then I start walking. My slow progress is made even slower since I can't walk in a straight line. Burning bushes and trees make me take detours again and again.

The flames around me are mostly violet and blue, but there are some in gold and orange as well. The heat of the magical flames probably ignited the other ones.

I wrap my curse around me, and while it does nothing against natural flames, it protects me from the magical fire. I pull the coolness around me, making sure it coats me from the soles of my feet to the tip of my braid.

My skin already bears witness to the heat. It's red and tender to the touch. The heat intensifies the burn. My throat and eyes are raw like someone washed them with sand, and my head pounds in rhythm with my frantic heartbeat.

I'm shaking. It's just a small tremor, but combined with the exhaustion washing over me, it can't mean anything good. I have never used my curse for such a long period, and I'm not sure what will happen if I do. But I can't let it go before I'm out of here. I shudder at the thought of flames devouring me alive.

Some small parts of my skin are slick with sweat, but the moisture evaporates nearly faster than I can build it. The stifling heat seems to get worse by the minute.

My walk is unsteady, more of a stagger really, and if it hadn't been for Tate, I would have lost my orientation long ago. I stumble on past flaming walls and the fiery remains of a once proud forest.

If I reach him, I'm safe.

Repeating it over and over keeps me going, but my progress becomes slower and slower.

I'm so focused on the shimmering warmth of Tate's power that I nearly miss the magic signature coming from behind. It's spunky and sparkly, and it's so much more than anything I've felt before. No... I have encountered magic as mighty as this before, I realize, but only once—the dragon. This one feels different, though.

I whirl around, but I'm only met by more flames.

What is that?

I stumble, curse, and nearly go down, my shield slipping for a second, which earns me a burn on my right leg. I hiss.

Who am I kidding? I will never get out of here alive.

"Don't you dare give up now! Not after I chose you," a voice thunders. It's male, demanding, and shooting through me like a golden flame, surrounding me, caressing me, igniting a spark in my center right next to the scrap of coolness that becomes steadily less.

There is a presence next to me, above me, surrounding me, burrowing deep into me where it mingles with my very existence.

I cry out as the sensations flood me. My already unsteady view splits up, my mind jumping back and forth between the sight in front of me and another one.

A blackened, half-naked woman wobbles, her skin reddened and blistered. She looks around, then up, blue-green eyes glowing in a soot-smeared face, the mouth agape in shock.

That's me.

The constantly changing view on top of my already twisted one causes me to double over, dry heaving, my hands clutching my thighs in support while I fight to stay upright.

Feelings, thoughts, and memories that aren't mine assault my mind, and my vision gives out. I thrust my arms out for balance.

Mighty claws curl around my arms. I lose the ground beneath my feet and nearly my grip on the curse when I'm flung through the air. I tumble. Flames and clouds of smoke dance around me.

I close my eyes. It's too much, all of it.

I land on something moving and soft, my fingers grabbing hold of something that feels like feathers. My eyes fly open, trying to focus on what is right in front of me, under me. The gold and red, the yellow and orange look like fire but feel like feathers. There is a pulsing, whooshing sound, like mighty wings.

Wait, those are wings, with feathers made of fire and trailed by smoke.

"How else am I supposed to fly?" the same voice from before asks, sounding amused.

The heat recedes the higher we get, leaving me with a comfortable warmth where I'm touching the feathers and the cool caress of the wind on my heated face.

I am riding on a fucking Phoenix.

And he's speaking to me, which can only mean—

"Happy you are on board. But I can hear you, you know? And I'm not 'a fucking Phoenix.' I'm Solaris."

How do I answer? I ask myself.

"Just like that is fine," Solaris answers.

"You can hear my thoughts?" I'm not sure how I feel about that.

"Loud and clear, by the way, you might want to do something about that obsession. I'm not listening to you mooning over that human all day."

"I'm not—" Why am I defending myself? "Keep out of my thoughts if you don't want to know what I'm thinking about." I huff. The world still twists and turns around me, and I'm slipping.

I tighten my grip but lose it again when Solaris caws in protest. My vision narrows, and I fight to stay conscious.

"*So we are really...*" I try to initiate a conversation, hoping it will keep me awake a little longer.

"*Yep, I'm stuck with you now as long as I get you some help soon. You trust this Tate?*" he asks.

"*With my life,*" I answer while a buzzing fills my ears. My pulse pounds through my body, and my vision goes black. I concentrate on the feathers between my fingers, clinging to them with my mind, but I'm slipping again.

"*Nothing else will do.*" I hear Solaris say before he demands, "*Hold on.*" He descends, the sudden movements turning my stomach. The air around me is suddenly much cooler. Voices shout. Then there is nothing.

CHAPTER
FORTY-FOUR
TATE

A FLAME SHOOTS OUT OF THE DARK SWIRLS OF SMOKE. No, not a flame, a bird, a *Phoenix*. I look at it in awe. The images don't do it justice.

The Phoenix is majestic and raw. Its power is like a physical blow, and its presence captures everyone's attention. My eyes are so focused on the flaming creature that, at first, I don't realize someone is sitting on the Phoenix's back, a huddled figure, lopsided and blackened by soot. Or maybe it's just the stark contrast between a uniform and the brilliant light of the Phoenix's flaming feathers.

Relief slams into me when I recognize her, and it turns into horror seconds later when she slides sideways.

No, no, no.

I'm sprinting toward the fiery bird, but I'm too far away.

She falls, her body hitting the ground in a slumped heap like a castaway rag doll.

The Phoenix gives off a screech that reverberates in my bones—distress. I duck to evade the Phoenix's flaming wings, which are still spread wide after he dropped to the ground. He caws, but I don't pay him any mind, my gaze fixed on Ara's still form on the ground.

She lies close to the burning tree line. The heat of the fire sears my face, making my skin taut, short of cracking. Blisters line the exposed skin of her arms and back. She's only dressed in her pants and her wrap, soot darkening her skin, and I can't see her face and stomach since she's face down.

I sweep her up in my arms, sucking in a breath at how hot her skin is on mine. Cuts, bruises, and burns cover nearly every surface of her skin. I have no idea what hell she went through, but nothing will touch her now that I have her.

I cradle her close to my body and rush away from the heat.

Healing her right away would have been ideal, but she's unconscious. The promise I made drives me insane even though I know why it has to be this way.

She is in my arms and still breathing. Everything is going to be alright.

The Phoenix looms in front of us, his wings still wide, his movements agitated.

He keeps everyone away.

Riders start to gather in front of him, and I stay back, forming a cocoon of cool air around us to have some relief from the heat.

"Can you get us?" I ask Daeva.

"*You have to move farther out, or I'll risk my wings catching fire.*" There is a pause. "*Solaris can take you if you can hold your shield around you until you arrive.*"

"Solaris?" But I realize it has to be the Phoenix's name before she answers. "Please thank him for the offer, and I mean no offense, but I think you would draw less attention."

"*I'll get you. Twenty steps farther out, and I can pick you up.*"

"Okay."

I duck under Solaris's wings, made a little more awkward by

carrying Ara, and I'm instantly flanked by Jared and Cassius. Calix and Mariel come running, too.

Cassius speaks up next to me. "We have to get her to the healers." The words remind me that she cannot see a healer under any circumstance. My eyes flit to Calix, but since he doesn't show any reaction concerning Ara being very visibly a woman or Cassius's slipup, he knows.

"Get back to the others and not a word to anyone," I bark at them. "I got this."

Jared is a quiet support next to me, sending them off when they try to follow despite my orders.

Daeva lands, Zephyr right behind her, and I reluctantly hand Ara over to Jared to get into the saddle before he hands her back to me.

"I'm right behind you," he assures me. I nod, and we take off.

"Land right in front of the housing quarters," I tell Daeva.

"Solaris will follow us," Daeva informs me.

"Arguing against it won't help, will it?" I ask.

Daeva clicks her beak, and the agitated movement of her head lets me know Solaris doesn't seem to be a fan of my suggestion. But what did I expect? He bonded with Ara, so I would be very surprised if he's someone who always listens and plays by the rules.

About ten minutes later, Daeva lands in the academy courtyard, and I'm already out of the saddle and moving before Zephyr lands behind me. I'm pushing through the door to the sleeping quarters when Jared catches up to me.

"That is not the way to the healing quarters," he observes quietly but doesn't try to stop me.

"She can't see a healer." My voice is clipped. My thoughts running in circles. She didn't wake up, and I am not even sure if it's her pulse or my own that vibrates through my body. I can't let anyone near her while she's unconscious, but what will I do if she doesn't wake up?

Can I try to heal her nonetheless?

I hurry up the stairs, taking two steps at a time. We haven't encountered anyone so far, and I hope it stays that way.

"Are you sure about not seeing a healer?" Jared's voice is full of doubt, and I don't blame him. Every moron would question my decision without all the information.

I send him a look that stops him from trying to convince me otherwise. Instead, he releases one long breath.

"That bad, hmm? I've never seen you so in knots about a woman before." He lifts his hands when I glare at him. "Just saying."

Fortunately, the building is empty; everyone is out at the fire or the gathering ground celebrating the new riders. I charge into my room and make sure Jared locks the door behind us.

Now I can only hope no one saw us and that she wakes up before anyone comes looking.

Jared watches me like I have lost my mind, and I'm very close to doing so.

Next to my worries, I'm also bombarded by Solaris, courtesy of my darling Night Raven. I get it, but if anyone is supposed to tell us anything, it's him. He's connected to her. He can slip into her mind, not me.

He currently sits on the roof right over my room, keeping watch, and I have to say I was astonished to see that he can douse his flames. His feathers are now coal black, with glowing lines running through them like embers, glimmering and pulsing but barely visible in bright daylight. His eyes are black as well, rimmed by gold, the same tone as his beak and talons.

I only know this because I slip into Daeva's view occasionally to check on him, and she sits up there too, eyeing him warily, probably because of whatever he said to her.

I cross my room back and forth, watching Ara like a hawk. Waiting for her to open her eyes, twitch, do anything that tells me she's still alive.

Who has seen Ara's fall? The answer is easy: everyone. The Phoenix emerging out of the fiery inferno behind him drew everyone's attention. So the question is rather how soon will someone come looking?

She has to wake up.

Ara lying on my bed is a cruel joke, considering she was so very alive the last time we were here together. I trail a finger softly over her cheek. Her skin is reddened here as well, but at least not blistered like her arms.

My arm is sticky with blood where her head rested, and I pray it's no more than a cut.

That I can't do anything before she wakes up is killing me. I continue pacing, my gaze searching out her face again and again.

"You want to tell me what is going on?" Jared leans against the door, his eyes flicking from Ara's still form to me and back.

"I can't tell you her secrets. Or at least not this one." I busy myself by getting my emergency kit out of the wardrobe.

Maybe I can't heal her, but I can start treating her wounds the non-magical way. I motion Jared over, and he holds her head while I look at the wound. It's hidden beneath her braid, so I loosen it, unraveling the partly golden and soft, partly dark and stiff strands to get a clear look. Her hair flows over my lap in soft waves, and I revel in their silky texture while I work my way to her scalp.

"Something happened between you, didn't it?" Jared's eyes are on my fingers caressing her hair, and I know he's wondering how much of the time I sneaked off I spent with her. Seeing the long strands of gold between my fingers reminds me of the evening at the tavern, of the moment when she hid her face by burying it in my neck, jolting my whole body awake.

"Holy mists, you let her in, didn't you?" Jared asks.

I work my way through the last part of her hair, which is matted to her scalp and sticky with blood.

Flakes of dried blood come off and stick to the wet coating on my fingers, caking them, crumbs falling into my lap.

I tell him of the encounters he didn't know about. He chuckles when I tell him how I caught her coming out of Cassius's room and nearly killed him for it. Recounting it, I realize I never had a chance to stay away.

I don't tell him about the curse. My trust in Jared is blind and complete, but the more people know about it, the bigger the threat to her.

Jared leaves to find out what is going on outside while I stay next to her, lost in thought. I cleaned away the soot on her skin and the bloodstains, so only the cuts, bruises, and burns remain. The cut on her scalp is superficial. Head wounds often look worse than they are.

I catch myself playing with the strands of her hair again. It's clean and dry, thanks to my magic, and currently fanning out over my pillow.

I changed her into one of my shirts, leaving her other clothes folded on the bedside table. Not because they are salvageable but because it gave me one more thing to do. Now, nothing is left but waiting, and it's driving me insane.

I watch her chest rise and fall. Her eyelids flutter occasionally, but I don't get my hopes up anymore. The first time it happened, I thought she was waking up, but she seems to be dreaming.

I nearly lost her today.

I still might, and the reaction this triggers inside me scares me.

Jared comes back, and nothing has changed.

"Everyone believes Summer to be in the healing quarter. So we are good for now," he tells me. "Just know this could get ugly. Cassius already demanded an update from me as soon as I showed my face. Calix demanded answers, too." He looks at Ara. "Your girl sure knows how to pick her friends."

I savor the sound of those words.

My girl.

The hours go by, and Jared has gone out to check the status and said he would bring some food as well. Not that I'm hungry. I contemplate asking Jared for help as soon as he's back, but how can I explain that he needs to separate us if I exhaust myself? Who will protect her when I am out, and Jared watches over me?

What if she wakes right after, and I depleted my gift for nothing? Also, even Jared will start to ask questions at some point.

I'm ripped out of my gloomy thoughts when Jared hurries into the room and slams the door shut behind him, turning the lock immediately.

"Shit, man, I have no idea who your girl is, but this is about to get ugly," he declares breathlessly.

"What do you mean?" I push away from the wall I leaned against for the past hour, stalking over to him.

"I have no idea what he's doing here, but I just passed General Blackstone. He was hurrying toward the healing quarters, demanding updates on Summer. That guy looked pissed."

"Shit." I run a hand over my face, looking at Ara's unresponsive form on the bed. "I think they know each other."

"No shit, I figured that one out already. But who is she to him?" Jared looks at me like I have the answers to that.

"Fuck if I know," I mutter. I guess there is still a whole lot I don't know about her.

"Sooner or later, someone will remember they saw you leaving with her," Jared warns.

"Let's hope it's later." I sigh.

Jared doesn't leave again after that update. Both of us lean against my desk, talking in hushed voices, my eyes flitting to Ara regularly, checking if anything has changed. Worry presses so hard on my chest that I'm sure I will suffocate if there isn't a change soon.

A loud knock on the door has us straightening. Jared and I exchange a glance before we both look at Ara's still form. The door handle jiggles, but the door is locked.

The knock sounds again. A twisted kind of déjà vu overcomes me. What wouldn't I give to go back to the last time someone knocked on my door while Ara was in here? This is so much worse.

"No one knows we're here, right?" I whisper to Jared.

"I'm not sure. I haven't seen anyone, but there is still the chance someone saw me coming here." His eyes are as worried as I feel.

The sound starts again, a pounding now instead of a knock.

"Open up right now, or I'll kick in this door," a male threatens from outside. He sounds familiar.

I sigh and move to the door. Jared positions himself next to me so the open door will hide him from view. He gives me a nod, indicating he's ready for whatever or, better, whoever waits on the other side. I look at Ara one last time before I turn the key and open the door.

CHAPTER FORTY-FIVE
TATE

I come face-to-face with Darren Blackstone. I close the door behind me, using the moment to get a protective shield in place.

"Is Summer here?" he asks, and I have to give it to him that even in all this, he uses the right name without pause.

"I don't know what you're talking about."

His eyes flare. "I know you left together."

"Whoever told you that?"

"Now listen to me, you little shit, you will open this door right now, or your career is over," he threatens, his voice cool and calm. I shrug.

"If you want through that door, you'll have to get through me first."

"Gladly. Do you want to die quick or painful?" The way he looks at me tells me he means it.

The door behind me opens, and Jared sends me a frustrated glare as soon as he realizes I've trapped him behind my shield. Blackstone looks even angrier when he notices it, too.

"You will let me to her right now, or gods help me, I will rip you apart with my bare hands," he growls.

"Only if you promise you won't take her to the healers," I tell him. "Otherwise, I will fight you."

This takes him by surprise, and his mouth opens slightly.

"You know?" So Ara lied when she said she never told anyone before.

Jealousy burns through me. Blackstone is a good-looking man, with his intimidating physique, dark hair, and blue eyes, but he's surely ten years older than her.

If he used his position to get his fingers on her... I will destroy him.

"You know?" I echo his words.

"Clearly, I don't know," Jared pipes up from behind me. "Gods, Tate, can we discuss this inside before someone else comes along and demands to know, too?"

Blackstone and I stare at each other until I give a small nod and take the shielding off the door. Blackstone rushes past me and through the door, falling to his knees next to Ara's lifeless figure.

He pulls her into his arms, and Jared clasps a hand on my shoulder to hold me back.

"No." Blackstone's voice sounds choked. He buries his face in her hair. "Little sparrow, don't you dare die on me." He pulls back and strokes her face with such tenderness that I think I'm going to burst. He loves her. My heart twists.

"Is she your lover or something?" Jared asks the question burning through me.

Blackstone's head snaps around, and he sends Jared a glare.

"She is my sister, you sick fuck."

Holy mists, his sister?

Jared's stunned expression tells me he didn't expect that either.

After that outburst, the tension in the room lessens noticeably, and for the first time since I brought her here, a flicker of hope lights my chest.

I explain my plan of healing her as soon as she wakes up, and it takes some convincing, but finally, Blackstone agrees to leave her in my care.

"I'll keep everyone off your back, but you will get me as soon as she wakes up," Blackstone demands, then explains where to find him. I gladly agree. He's visibly torn about leaving but then straightens. His face relaxes, and I would never have guessed he cares at all.

"Impressive," Jared comments while Darren Blackstone leaves and closes the door behind him. "And here I thought you were an anomaly."

I only grunt at that, settling back against my desk, watching Ara.

She has to wake up.

ARA

Everything hurts, but that means I'm still alive, right?

I notice the scent—Tate. I relax. I'm safe.

Steps move from next to my head to my feet and back again. He paces. Whatever got me here has to be bad.

I strain my brain for information, but I only remember talking to my brother. No, that can't be right... Why would I be with Tate if I had been talking to my brother? There are other memories, snippets: a forest, a snake, fighting, panic, a man sneering at me.

And there is another scent, much fainter than Tate's and less pleasant—the fire at the mountain, smoke. But that was weeks ago. Why am I smelling smoke now?

Concern floods me, but it's not my own; it's someone else's.

"You'll be alright," a voice reassures me in my mind.

In my mind?

My eyes fly open with a startled gasp, but I close them again when the room dances above me. My head pounds, and I'm queasy.

I try again, and this time, Tate is leaning over me, but his face is double, and the versions swim into each other, making the nausea even worse.

My whole body hurts so bad.

I don't want to sit up, but I'm afraid I will be sick any minute, so I try only to fall back, whimpering.

"Don't move, sunshine." Tate's voice is soothing but worried. "You did take quite a fall, and I don't even know what you went through before that."

Fall? Have I fainted or something? Gods, I hope not.

"Fall?" My voice is a croak, my throat parched.

What the heck did I do?

"You don't remember?" His voice is grim.

I start to shake my head, but that makes my nausea and pain even worse, so I stop.

"Can I start healing you? Please, just a bit?" he asks.

"Okay." Damn, my voice does sound bad, all hoarse and raspy, and speaking hurts. "Could you start with my head?" I really would prefer to get out of this without throwing up at his feet.

"Yeah, that is a great idea," he says, and the mattress dips with his weight, his soft touch settling on my brow seconds later. Glowing golden warmth floods my body in a rush, like he pushes all he's got at me at once.

He's scared I will fall asleep again.

Because of the sheer might of his magic flooding me, I expect my curse to retaliate with a vengeance, and it does rise, but weakly.

What the fuck happened?

The pounding in my head recedes, and when I open my eyes, it's without the double vision.

Relief is written all over Tate's face when my eyes meet his. His magic shifts inside me, trailing over my spine and my organs like it's searching for injuries.

"It feels like your magic is poking around, searching through me." It slips along my hurting throat, soothing it. My voice still sounds awful, but the pain is gone.

"You feel that?" He stops, looking at me questioningly.

"Yeah," I croak. He still looks so haunted that I want to cuddle and comfort him. I start to sit up, grinding my teeth, when my body screams in agony. But at least the world no longer tilts around me.

"What are you doing?" Tate snaps. His hands land on my shoulders, pushing me softly back down, but he snatches his hands away when I wince in pain. Anguish flits across his face, and I growl in frustration.

"I need you to hold me," I tell him.

"I need to heal you first," he replies.

"How about you heal me while holding me?" I ask. Tate looks at me, and for a second, I think he'll refuse, but then he nods with a small smile on his lips.

He gets rid of his boots and discards his weapons before climbing onto the bed next to me, close but not quite touching me. I huff out a breath. That won't do at all.

I bite my cheek to keep from crying out while I turn until my head rests in the dip below his shoulder, my hand resting on his chest. I sigh, relief washing over me even though my skin hurts wherever my body presses into his. The tension leaves his body, and I smile to myself. So it does comfort him to have me close.

His arm, the one I trapped beneath my body, moves slowly, pushing up my shirt until his fingers touch the skin at the small of my back. His other hand cradles my face. His magic slips into me again, and I sigh.

"I think I can get used to being healed like this," I whisper, and his body rumbles with laughter beneath me.

"Fine with me." He chuckles. "As long as it's me healing you."

"Possessive, are you?" I tease.

"You have no idea," he answers, his lips brushing over my forehead, his arm pulling me closer. I get lost in the moment, his body and scent wrapped around me, his magic under my skin. I feel safe and cared for like I never have before.

And like always, when I'm close to him, I want him. If it weren't for my current weakness, I would have pounced.

I must have drifted off to sleep at some point because the next thing I notice is how Tate carefully tries to detangle himself from me. I make a sound of protest, tightening my hold and wrapping my leg over him.

I hear a groan and a chuckle behind me. Tate's hand caresses my cheek before he tries again.

"Relax, Blackstone, I only healed her." Tate's voice is a grumble under my cheek.

"Oh, that is what you call it these days?" Jared's teasing voice answers.

"Shut up, Jared." Again, I feel Tate's voice more than I hear it.

"Kyronos, if you don't get your hands off my sister right now, I will break your pretty face," my brother growls.

Wait, what?

The blissful state of half asleep dissipates while I try to make sense of it all. What are Tate, Jared, and Dar doing in one room?

Where am I?

My eyes blink open, and my gaze lands on Tate's face right above me. His eyes are fixed behind me, though.

I study his face, noticing his ruffled hair, the shadows under his eyes, and a few dark streaks on his cheek and brow. He looks exhausted but beautiful, nonetheless.

My heart squeezes when I remember the haunted look he wore earlier. I stop my perusal of his face at his lips and watch them move, the conversation around me only a buzz in the background.

His lips are so close. I lean in and nibble at his full bottom lip, startling him. He looks down at me, stopping mid-sentence, and I seize the opportunity and push closer, slipping my tongue into his mouth, twirling around his, tasting him.

I groan, or maybe it's him. Either way, he kisses me back, and I wrap my arm around his neck to pull him closer, angling my head to go deeper.

"Ara." My name is wielded like a whip, reminding me that we are not alone.

Dammit.

Reluctantly, I pull back, smiling at the dazed expression on Tate's face. Then I sit up and turn to face my brother.

"What the fuck, Ara?" Dar barks, irritation visible on his face but relief, too. His eyes dart to Tate behind me, promising violence, and I nearly laugh at that. Somehow, Tate doesn't seem to be the guy easily intimidated by my brother's antics.

"Just expressing my gratitude." I shrug, trying to keep a smile from splitting my face.

"Oh, in that case," Jared says, "I did help too, you know." His eyes sparkle mischievously. Twin growls erupt from my brother and Tate, both so similarly threatening I burst out laughing, and Jared joins in.

At his unhappy expression, I scramble out from under the cover and launch myself at my brother, who catches me like he always does. His strong arms hold me close.

"You scared me there, little sparrow," he grumbles into my hair. And my heart bursts with love for my softy of a brother who always has to play the cold and hard one.

"You know what they say: pests are hard to kill." I make light of the situation, but it doesn't have the desired effect.

"It was pretty close this time, little sparrow. And not the first time, from what I heard." His gaze wanders over my head before coming back to mine. "I want you to come home with me."

I wriggle out of his hold at that, huffing out a breath and taking a step back to get some space between us before he simply throws me over his shoulder and takes off.

"I don't want to go home yet, and it's not like I can either. I made the vow, Dar." He waves away my argument like it's nothing.

"I'm serious," I insist.

He shakes his head. "You know I can solve that problem in a heartbeat. I want you home. I want you safe."

"And what about what I want?" I ask. When he shakes his head in exasperation, I feel like a child all over. "You can't make me, Dar." I realize I chose my words poorly as soon as his face hardens. He hates being told he can't do something as much as I do, and in the heat of the argument, I forgot something important: he's the commanding general, and I'm a rider, part of his forces now. So he has total command over me.

"Oh, you will soon realize I can make you do a lot of things," he says, a clear warning ringing in his voice. Dammit.

"I'm sorry, Dar." I wrap my arms around him, and he stiffens for a second before he relaxes and his arms come around me. I push to my tiptoes and kiss his cheek.

"How about you arrange for me to have a few days off, and I come home with you so we can talk about everything in peace?" I suggest. "Giving both of us time to cool down a little. We could even have a family meeting about it."

I know I have him when he sighs at that. Of course, he jumps at the chance to hear everyone's input before making a decision.

"Okay." A smile tugs at the corner of his mouth.

"That sounds actually like a very grown-up suggestion." He pauses. "I'm impressed. We will leave in three days. I have a few things I have to take care of first." He takes my face in his hands and bends down to kiss my brow.

"I'll clear everything with Legatus Janus. Now rest, little sparrow." He looks behind me. "Preferably in your bed. And I will see you in three days."

I nod.

He sends a warning look over my shoulder at Tate, whose presence hovers two steps behind me, then nods at Jared and leaves the room.

I release my breath in a sigh.

"Impressive," Jared comments. "I did hold my breath there for a second." He smiles, his eyes flying to Tate and then back to me. "I'll leave you to...talk things through. Glad you are fine, Ara." He gives me a wink before he leaves the room, too.

I'm painfully aware of Tate behind me, but something in the tense silence makes me almost afraid to turn and face him.

What is he thinking? Has he taken my offer of coming home for a break as giving in? Does he think it's that easy for me to walk away from him?

Strong arms wrap around me, pulling me into his chest, and I melt into him, drinking in his strength before I turn in his arms.

"I'm sorry. I didn't know how else—" His lips stop my apology, ghosting over mine in a featherlight kiss.

"I know, sunshine. You did everything you could." His lips meet mine again, more demanding this time. "I thought I lost you today," he breathes. "The moment I realized you were in that inferno." I crinkle my brow in confusion. *Inferno?*

"Which reminds me. I need a name?" he growls.

"What are you talking about?"

He frames my face with his hands, all serious now.

"Someone attacked you, hurt you. And in case that person survived the fire, I need a name to remedy that."

He watches me, waits for an answer, and I rack my brain, but there is nothing. *There has to be something.*

"I ... I don't know." I stare at him, and he must see the panic, the helplessness in my eyes because he pulls me into his chest, holding me tight.

"Shh, it's fine. Give it time. It'll come back to you."

"Let's talk to Calix and Mariel, and maybe that will—"

"Yes, we'll do that, but later. Right now, I need to hold you, kiss you, feel you right next to me." My body heats at his words.

Gods, this man is everything. I rise up on my toes and bring my lips to his in an attempt to get closer. Our kiss turns hungry and desperate, but to my disappointment, he lets it slow down again to sweet and light kisses, not nearly enough to sate the hunger he roused.

I pout, and he chuckles, sweeping me up into his arms.

"You were on the brink of death a few hours ago. Rest, sunshine. Sleep, get your energy levels back up, and then I'm all in for whatever you want."

I'm still grumbling while he tucks me in close to him. His warm body at my back relaxes, his arms safe and reassuring wrapped around me, keeping me close. He places a kiss on my temple, and I simply melt, a huge yawn sneaking up on me.

Okay, maybe I could do with a little sleep first.

The next thing I know is Tate kissing me awake at the crack of dawn. My hands snake up before I open my eyes, my fingers hitting the smooth leather of his uniform.

What?

That is not what I hoped for. I blink my eyes open, and he grins down at me, fully clothed, his hair still wet from a shower.

"What are you doing up and dressed?" My question sounds exactly like the accusation it's supposed to be, and he smiles.

"I already got a new uniform for you since the other one was ruined anyway. I hope it fits. I had to guess the size since the other one was always a little big." He leans down and kisses me again. "I have to leave. You have an hour until formation, and I have a division leader meeting in a few minutes."

"No," I whine, too tired to be embarrassed about sounding so needy. It earns me another long kiss and a groan before Tate hurries out the door, probably a little late by now.

A full day is in front of us, but gods help me, tonight, I will make sure that man ends up in my bed, or rather I in his. As far as I know, single rooms are out of the question until at least the second year.

"We have to work on your shields first," a voice grumbles in my

mind. It's the same one I remember from yesterday, right before Tate healed me.

"Who are you?" I ask tentatively.

"*If I hadn't seen and felt the state you were in, I would take offense at that,*" he tells me. Now that I concentrate on him, I can sense him too, more vicious than Tate's warmth, and my mind seems to stretch on where it once ended, a swirl of color, thoughts, and emotions only separated by a thin veil.

"*Are we...are we bonded?*" Even my thought carries my disbelief.

"*At least you are fast to catch on. Now that your head is no longer a scrambled mess, let me introduce myself again. I'm Solaris. I'm a Phoenix of the line of Sa...*"

"*You are a Phoenix? I'm bonded to a fu—*"

"*If you call me a fucking Phoenix again, I will roast you alive,*" he snaps with indignation, making me chuckle despite his threat.

"*I'm sorry.*" I bite my lip, trying to contain my giddiness.

I did it. I'm bonded. I'm bonded to a Phoenix.

My body is still sore, but I don't notice it over my elation. I shower and dress, grinning from ear to ear and talking to Solaris through all of it. It's like I've known him for years, but I could listen to him talk all day.

CHAPTER FORTY-SIX
TATE

I don't have to feign shock when Ara comes to formation in the skyrider uniform. She timed it perfectly. Nearly all riders are present, but leadership is still missing.

Holy mists, does she look good in leather armor. The dark gray leather hugs her curves, leaving little to the imagination, and I'm not the only one who can't keep his eyes off her. I fight the urge to hit a few of my fellow riders, who are undressing her with their eyes.

Her golden hair flows down her back, brushing the curve of her ass, nearly glowing against the contrast of her uniform. She makes my mouth water.

Her hips sway while she sashays up to me, and I have a hard time keeping my gaze locked on her face.

I swallow, trying to cool the fuck down before I spontaneously combust. When she draws closer, I hook my thumbs in my belt in an attempt to keep my hands off her.

"Do you mind if I say a few words before we start?" She smiles at me with a mischievous glint in her eyes.

"Should have seen it coming," I murmur, allowing my eyes to wander over her once. I bite my lip, fighting the smile that wants to split my face, and shake my head at her, gesturing to go ahead.

She steps in front of me, facing our division. The rustling around us tells me she has the attention of the whole Aerie, but that doesn't seem to bother her. My fingers itch with the urge to pull her into my chest, to claim her publicly as mine. But even though she spent the night in my bed, we haven't even talked about that yet.

"Hey, everyone. I'm Ara. You knew me as Grayson before, and I thought I'd save you and myself the repetitive questions. I hid between you guys because it was easier to go unnoticed that way. My family didn't want me to join the skyriders, and dressing as a man seemed the most practical way to keep them out of my hair until they couldn't stop me anymore." She smiles, letting her eyes wander over to her squadron, her flight. "Some of you have become very good friends, and I just wanted to say I'm still me. I just have a different cover, and I'm sorry for deceiving you."

"Damn, Gray, you want to tell us we had..." Calix swept his gaze appreciatively up and down her body. "All of that under us while training on the mat and didn't know?" He whistles. "That's fucking cruel, girl." I debated whether to kick his ass as an example, but I shouldn't have worried.

"Well, at least I can tell you now that your moves have room for improvement." Ara smirks, and everyone laughs. Calix clutches his chest theatrically as if she wounded him, but then his face splits into a smile.

She turns to me, and her smoldering look lets me know I'm not the only one fighting for control here. She winks, turns, and walks to her place in formation. There is a beat of silence before the whispers start. Many eyes are glued to her on her way back.

I don't know what Blackstone said to Legatus Janus, but while he welcomes the new riders in our ranks and even singles Ara out for being the first Phoenix rider in decades, he doesn't mention her lying about her identity.

I slowly relax. Not that I thought they would execute her while being bonded to a phoenix but I feared repercussions nonetheless.

"I guess it does pay off having brothers in high positions, huh?" Jared nudges me while we make our way to the strategy meeting. I raise an eyebrow at him. "At least if you know how to wrap them around your finger. You have to work on that second part, you know. It would make your life much easier."

"I'm not so sure about that. The easier part, I mean."

"It works for Ara. Granted, you are lacking a few assets, very fine assets..."

"Jared," I warn.

"What? I'm only saying that she has a very fine—"

"Don't finish that sentence," I growl.

"Alright, alright, relax." He laughs, clearly enjoying winding me up. And I only now realize how effective those implications are concerning my...concerning Ara.

Ara sits only a few rows in front of us during the strategy meeting, joking and laughing with Mariel and Calix next to her. She bumps into Calix, her hair trailing over his arm that rests on the back of her chair. My fingers itch with the need to touch her.

I reach for her with my magic. A tendril of air slides up the side of her neck, then caresses her cheek. She shudders, and I suppress a grin when she shoots me a quick look over her shoulder.

"*Claim her as yours and be done with it*," Daeva grumbles in my head, and damn do I want to follow her advice.

"*We haven't talked about it.*"

"*Then talk to her. This is insufferable,*" she snaps.

I have to agree. Right now, I'm even jealous of the air I command, since it gets to touch her while I can't.

She is mine, and I want everyone to know it.

Jared looks over at Ara and her friends and then at my twitching fingers.

"Relax, she kissed you in front of her brother," he says. "And she didn't take me up on my offer either, so it wasn't only to piss him off."

I grin at the memory.

The hours pass in what has to be the slowest countdown in history. I don't even have the chance to get my hands on her under the pretense of sparring because the freshly bonded riders spend the whole day with their birds.

ARA

"I shouldn't have left you." Calix shakes his head, looking guilty. Mariel nods.

"That is absurd, don't you dare feel guilty about that." I glare at both of them. I used dinner to quiz them about what happened during Picking, but neither knows anything about an attack.

"The way you looked, when Kyronos rushed you out of there..." Calix shakes his head again.

"We were so worried. Cassius was pacing the common room like a madman while you were in the healing quarters." Mariel raises her eyebrows. "Anything you want to tell us there?" she teases.

I groan. "He is my twin's best friend, and we grew up together, nothing more." I shake my head at her.

"Wait, you have a twin brother?" Mariel perks up. "Do you look alike? Why do I only now hear about that?"

I laugh. "Oh, you would love Ben. But I told you I had four brothers."

"Yeah, but that doesn't answer my question. Does he look like you?"

"Ben is me in taller, broader, and male," I smirk, and Mariel's grin widens.

Calix groans. "Now you've done it. Mariel, he is infantry. You wouldn't go for an infantry guy, right?"

I laugh at my friends while they start bickering. I feel the lightest I have in a long time. I don't have to pretend to be Grayson anymore, my family knows where I am, and I'm still here, I'm alive and bonded, and then there is Tate. Life is pretty damn good right now.

I'm still joking with Mariel and Calix, and we are on our way out of the refectory when Tate strides over to us. A thrill shoots through my body when our eyes meet. His gaze falls to my shoulder, and I'm suddenly aware of the arm Calix has thrown over Mariel and me. Tate's face is stoic, but his eyes narrow the slightest bit. I can't even blame him. If a girl had her hands on him, I would go ballistic.

I shrug Calix's arm off and take a step toward Tate, unsure how to approach him. Despite sleeping in his bed last night, we haven't talked about this.

"Summer, follow me." Tate's voice is cool and clipped, but there is fire in his eyes.

"Sure." I smile at him while my gut twists in a mix of need and nerves. I tell my friends I'll see them later while Tate turns around and strides down the hallway without looking back.

Okay then.

I hurry after him, but my steps falter when his voice suddenly caresses my ear.

"You better hurry up, sunshine, because otherwise, I can't guarantee anything."

My eyes fly up and meet his where he stands at the end of the hallway, cool as the Ice Coast, watching me with a nearly imperceptible smile on his lips.

Heat explodes in my core, and his eyes glint with a mix of humor and male satisfaction, when my steps quicken. He knows exactly what he's doing to me.

"I'll be gone for the next...hours," I tell Solaris while I'm hurrying down the corridor next to Tate. The Phoenix makes a sound resembling a snort.

"*I'll leave you alone,*" he tells me, and the veil between us thickens until it's a smooth wall. He shut me out. Perfect.

Tate opens a door to our right, pulling me into it, and I barely have time to register that we are in the same storage room Joel pulled me into all those weeks ago before the door locks behind me.

Then all I notice is Tate.

His body presses into mine, pushing me back against the door. His hand cradles my head before it can collide with the wooden surface. His lips are on mine, before the surprised "umpf" fully left my mouth, and holy mists, his mouth. His kiss is demanding, possessive, and so unbelievably sexual I'm igniting like a Phoenix.

I drown in sensations: the hard planes of his body pressing into me, his lips on mine, his hand in my hair, the soft rasp of his calloused fingers on my skin, his scent, his taste, his magic curling all around us. My senses are flooded by him, and I want more.

"Sunshine," he groans when we both come up for air, panting. "You are driving me fucking insane. Do you have any idea how hard it was to keep my fingers to myself today? Whenever you are in the room, I can't look away, and just thinking of being close to you has me instantly hard." He lets his brow rest against mine. "Watching you walk around in this uniform and, even worse, your hair trailing over Ilario's skin instead of mine...I...Fuck, I need you."

Sparks of heat shoot through me at his words and stoke the pounding fire in my core, fanning the embers he started by kissing me awake in his bed this morning. The gaze he sent me before formation fueled those flames, and the soft caress of his magic during the strategy meeting poked them. Then there is the way he marched over to me after dinner, his whispered demand, and the way he drank in my reaction.

I'm on fucking fire and his stormy golden eyes watch me burn. I pull his mouth back down to mine, linking my arms around his neck. His arms tighten, pulling me impossibly closer, anchoring me in this inferno of desire.

He acts like I'm his first breath after a deep dive, like he needs me for survival, like I'm essential to his soul. I slide a hand into his hair and draw a low, rumbling groan from his throat by scraping my nails over the base of his neck and up his scalp.

"We need to talk," Tate breathes against my skin, and I hum my agreement. He is right, but talking is the last thing on my mind right now.

I pull his lips back to mine, and every thought of talking is forgotten. My hands roam over his body, but there are too many layers covering it.

Something rumbles behind Tate, and he picks me up, only to place me seconds later on the small table I could have sworn had been stacked with boxes before.

He doesn't step back, but stays where he is, standing between my legs, our bodies deliciously aligned. The way he looks at me makes me feel beautiful, powerful and precious all at once.

"Such a convenient gift you have," I murmur.

"Oh, you haven't seen anything yet." He grins down at me, cradling my face with both hands, when I suddenly feel a finger trailing down each of my arms. I jerk in surprise, and he laughs. A mischievous, naughty laugh that has my stomach flipping over.

He places teasing kisses on the corner of my mouth, my brow, then my eyelids when they flutter closed, before his mouth travels along my jaw and down my throat.

"Please tell me I can peel you out of this uniform because since you sauntered up to me this morning, I can't think of anything else," he mumbles against my skin, sending shivers down my body, and intensifying the heat at the apex of my thighs.

"Yes, but only if I get your glorious body naked in return," I whisper, and his lips curve against my skin. His fingers immediately start undoing the buckles of my uniform.

"Do I detect there a fondness of my body?" he teases.

"It is hardly my fault that you look so incredibly lickable," I reply and chuckle when he groans.

"Sunshine, how the fuck do you expect me to hold on to my sanity when you say things like that?"

"I told you once before. Maybe I—" He cuts me off by placing his hand over my mouth.

"Holy mists, woman," he growls. "It's bad enough I dragged you in here because I couldn't wait a second longer. Let me at least take my time with you."

I nip his palm and, when he pulls it back, trap his thumb with my teeth, running my tongue along the pad of it.

"You live to torture me, don't you?" He groans, and I giggle, but it ends in a gasp when he lifts me, and my bare ass meets the table seconds later.

"Now, let's see how long it takes me to make you beg," Tate rumbles, sinking to his knees in front of me. My eyes widen and the throbbing in my core intensifies at his words, at the sight of him kneeling at my feet with a devilish smile on his face.

He takes off my boots one after the other, and then shimmies my pants down my legs while raining teasing kisses on the inside of my calves, my knees, my thighs.

He helps me out of my tunic and my undergarments until I'm bare in front of him, while he is still fully clothed.

I had sex before, but nothing like this. The way Tate admires and worships every inch of my body, the looks he sends me, I bet I could come from that alone.

Every touch of his hands, his lips, his tongue, his magic sends fire through my veins until he finally settles where I need him most.

"May I?" His breath ghosts over my throbbing core, and I squirm.

"Yes," I breathe. "Oh please, yes."

"Well, that didn't take long." He sends me a wicked smile. "And I didn't even start yet." And then his mouth is on me.

I gasp his name, and he hums in approval, sending sparks shooting up my spine.

A day's worth of stubble scratches against my sensitive skin while his tongue caresses me.

I have heard about this. It's impossible to grow up between men without hearing...a lot, but holy mists, I never thought it would feel this good.

I gasp.

I'm so aware of him by now that every little touch is sensory overload, and I'm caught somewhere between the need to arch into him or pull away. My eyes flutter close, and my world narrows to the sinful things Tate can do with his mouth, his firm grip holding my legs apart, and the tension swirling in my gut.

He sucks my clit hard, and my hand flies to my mouth, trying to muffle the scream clawing up my throat, but Tate catches my hand and pulls it back down.

"Don't you dare, sunshine," he growls against my sensitive flesh. "No holding back. I want to hear what I do to you!" His voice, his words send shock waves through me, heightening the tension impossibly more.

"But we are..." I start and end in a moan when he sucks my clit again. He fucks me with his tongue, then slides it up over the sensitive bundle of nerves again and again.

And just like that, I'm too far gone to think about anything as mundane as where we are right now. I'm lost in the sensation, chasing after the high that lures me.

My whimpers and moans mixed with nonsensical half sentences fill the room, while the crest comes closer and closer.

I arch into him, and stars explode behind my eyes as the tension shatters into waves of pleasure rolling over me, dragging me under, sweeping me away. My inner muscles clench and unclench, desperate for something to squeeze around.

I'm a shuddering, panting, limp mess sprawled out over the table when Tate pulls me up against his chest. His gloriously naked chest.

I have no idea when he got rid of his uniform, but damn, do I approve.

"So fucking beautiful," he rumbles before he claims my mouth in a hungry kiss, and I can taste myself on his tongue. "I could watch you come all day."

"Wish granted," I mumble against his lips, making him chuckle.

"Oh, I'm far from done with you yet."

But I already know since his throbbing hardness presses against me, demanding attention.

"I have this for you." He slips a chain over my head, and I recognize his magic instantly. "I know the regular ones probably don't work on you, and I thought maybe..." His magic settles over my womb, and it doesn't need more than a calming thought to stop my magic from unraveling it.

"You made that for me." I beam up at him. "Thank you." He looks adorably relieved at my reaction.

His healing training must have been extensive if he can even do contraceptive charms, and once more I wonder about his past and why he didn't become a healer. But now is not the moment for questions.

I pull him down for a hungry kiss and widen my legs, inviting him.

"Tell me what you want," Tate whispers against my lips, and I grin at him wickedly before I obey.

"I want you to fuck me, Tate," I say, and my grin widens when his cock twitches at my words. "I want to feel you slide into me, stretch me, fill me..." That is as far as I get before his mouth claims mine again, and then he complies, pushing into me in one hard thrust.

I groan into his mouth, panting around this sudden overwhelming fullness, struggling to adjust while pleasure surges up my spine.

Tate releases my lips.

"Fuck, are you good?" he asks, searching my eyes.

I nod, and even this slight movement causes me to clench around him. He squeezes his eyes shut.

"Fuck, sunshine." He groans, visibly fighting for control, resting his head against mine, his chest heaving. I run my fingers through his hair, reveling in the sensation of our connection. He looks at me, and the fire in his eyes, the need for me written all over his face, has me swallowing.

"Brace your hands on the table," he orders, and when I do, he starts to move. Slow, powerful thrusts that have sparks running through me.

"You feel so fucking good," Tate mutters in my ear, and the pleasure in his voice makes mine burn brighter. I moan in pleasure, and he drinks the sound of my lips.

His lips, his fingers, his magic trail over me. He caresses my back, my hips, my throat, my breasts, and I gasp when he pulls one of the aching peaks into his mouth.

Tension coils with every thrust and drag of him inside me, building up higher and higher while Tate increases the tempo.

My thighs tremble, and I know I'm getting close. Tate's hips snap faster, his sounds of pleasure mixing with mine.

"Come for me, sunshine."

His growled demand pushes me over the edge. I yell his name. Lightning surges through me, releasing in an explosion of pleasure while I clamp down hard, rippling and throbbing around him. The wind whips around us, rattling the boxes and maps, catching in my hair, the strands lashing our skin and my eyes fly open. Tate's eyes are on me, his expression caught somewhere between awe and shock.

"Fuck. Ara," he groans my name while he pulses inside me. His head falls to my shoulder, and I hold on to him while he continues to shake.

The wind slowly dies down, and only now in the quiet aftermath do I realize where we are and that we have been by no means quiet.

My gaze flies to the door.

"You think I would share this moment with anyone?" Tate growls into my neck, and I smile.

He shielded the room. Now that my senses slowly return, I can feel his magic all around us. I run my fingers through his hair, resting my head on his shoulder, and wait for my body to stop trembling. To say that Tate blew my world apart would be an understatement, and by the satisfied smile on his face, he knows it.

"I'll just stay like this for...a year or two before I move again," I mumble into his skin, and his body vibrates with his silent laughter.

"No," he disagrees. "I have different plans, and you already agreed," he murmurs, and I soon learn that he's taking my granted wish seriously and that regeneration and healing are basically the same thing.

We do make it back to his room, eventually.

CHAPTER
FORTY-SEVEN
ARA

I STAND AT THE WINDOW AND LOOK OUT INTO THE DARKNESS. I'm dressed in nothing but one of Tate's shirts. Rustling behind me makes me turn. Tate is sprawled out on his stomach, the moonlight painting silvery highlights on his glorious back rising in slow intervals. He's out cold. It's no wonder, after the way we spent the best part of the night.

A nightmare woke me—not the lightning wielder this time, but Tate looking at me with disappointment and disgust in his eyes. I don't have to be one of Egin's priestesses to interpret that dream.

My mind is running in circles, preventing me from falling asleep again. I thought about reaching out to Solaris, but I think the colorful images and the slow trickle of thoughts mean he's sleeping, and I don't want to wake him only because I can't sleep.

Tate was right last night when he said we needed to talk. But we didn't, and now my worry about his reaction is eating me alive.

He hates lies, and I kept this from him.

I know exactly which would have been the right moment to speak up: when he asked me if there was someone else. I should have explained it to him then.

I contemplate not telling him at all, to simply sort out this mess and tell him afterward, but who knows what will happen at home?

My family could prevent me from returning, and above all, he deserves the truth.

"Ara?" Tate's voice is gravelly with sleep. "What are you doing over there?" He looks at me questioningly, his hair adorably tousled, his eyelids heavy with sleep. He sits up, turning to me, and I drink him in. My heart constricts just looking at him.

I smile. "Thinking."

"Come back to bed," he says, lifting the blanket, and I go to him without hesitation. He pulls me into him, my back nestled to his front. "Holy mists, you are ice cold. How long have you been standing over there?"

I shrug and wriggle closer to his delicious heat. I didn't even realize how cold I was until my skin came into contact with Tate's. I fidget again.

Maybe I should just tell him now?

"If you keep that up, I promise you won't get any sleep soon," Tate warns. He hardens behind me, and I wriggle again, intentionally this time. He groans.

"Now you are asking for it," he accuses, and is spot-on with that assumption. I giggle while I rub against him. "Alright, I thought I did a good job relaxing you, but it seems I still have work to do," he whispers while he pushes up and over me, dazzling me with a sleepy and wicked smile.

The heat in his eyes makes my body melt. Gods, the things this man makes me feel, it would be frightening if it didn't feel so damn good.

He grips the bottom of the shirt I wear, his tantalizing fingers trailing over my ribs and the sides of my breasts while he pulls the fabric up. I come up so he can tug it over my head, before falling back to the bed.

I simply watch him doing my best to memorize the way he looks at me, just in case he never looks at me like that again.

"What?" he asks. I run my fingers up his body, reveling in the shudder that runs through him. "What are you thinking?" His voice is all raspy and heavy with desire, making my breath hitch and my body tremble in anticipation.

"How about I show you?" I wrap my legs around him and roll us over so I'm straddling him now. He's glorious. I kiss my way up his body, lingering when I encounter the mark on his chest. He stiffens for a second when my finger follows the pattern but relaxes again when I lean down and kiss it.

I can only imagine how much hatred he has endured because of it, and I wish one day he will confide in me and tell me what position he gave up to earn it.

I hope he knows that in my eyes, it shows strength to choose his path instead of taking the one laid out for him. But it also reminds me that we still have left so much unsaid.

Guilt bubbles up at the thought that I haven't told him about my betrothal yet. I no longer plan to go through with Mother's plans, not now that I have him, but still...

I will tell him... tomorrow.

I kiss the scar on his neck next, and he stiffens again. I decide that I will keep doing this until he understands that I love all parts of him, even the ones he doesn't.

Love?

My stomach somersaults, and I stiffen. I'm trying to deny it, but just looking at him makes my heart flip in my chest again.

Panic constricts my lungs, making it hard to breathe.

What if he doesn't want me after I tell him?

Concern crinkles Tate's brow.

"What is it?" he asks, his gaze searching my eyes. I force out a smile.

He will understand. He won't back down because of a faceless man my parents picked, right?

Even if it's the crown prince? A little voice taunts me, and I panic.

I can't lose him.

So instead of answering him, I take the coward's way out and distract him, distract us both by feeding the insatiable need between us, and it's only later, when I lie on his chest, our heartbeats a pounding rhythm between us, our breaths quick and labored that my thoughts return.

I love him.

"You certainly are good for my ego," he teases, kissing the top of my head.

"Oh, I was sure I was stroking something else," I quip, making him chuckle again. I love this light and playful side of him, the way his eyes twinkle. Gods, what would I give to stay at this moment with him forever.

Somehow, the realization that I love him makes what I have to tell him even worse. I shudder.

Instantly, Tate's magic settles over us, warming me, and I bite my cheek to hold in a sob.

"Better?" he asks.

I nod, my face buried against his chest.

How the fuck am I supposed to tell him?

CHAPTER FORTY-EIGHT
TATE

I look down at her, snuggled up against me in my bed. She's perfect, and it's still hard to believe that she's here, next to me, safe and bonded, and mine. I smile to myself.

Mine.

We never did talk, but her actions were loud and clear.

Dawn is painting the sky a pale gray, and I'll soon have to get up. Maybe I'll skip the extra training just this once.

I brush a lock out of her face, marveling at the fact that I have the right to do so. She stirs, snuggling closer, burying her face at my shoulder. I kiss the top of her head, and she shifts again.

Her eyes blink open, zeroing in on my face, and she smiles sleepily.

"You are fucking perfect," I whisper and brush my thumb over her cheek.

"I could get used to your face in the morning, too," she murmurs, her voice still heavy with sleep and squeals when I tickle her ribs for that smart comment. My lips silence her.

"You will get us caught." I shake my head at her playfully and tug her closer.

"Worried about your reputation?" Ara flashes me a devilish grin before she goes in for another kiss.

"No, only for the life of anyone who makes the wrong comment." My voice is gruff, and I steal another kiss. I'm not lying. I'm sure I will fly off the handle if someone talks shit about her.

"You are cute," she says, tracing the outline of my face.

I smile down at her, shaking my head at that ridiculous statement. Only she would ever describe me as cute.

"The next days will be hell." She pouts and looks so adorable doing it that my grin widens.

"Just tell your brother no and stay," I suggest even though I know it isn't an option.

"I can't. There is so much I need to speak to them about, so much I need to take care of." She sighs. "I pushed everything out of my mind, not thinking past Picking, and now that with you." She looks up at me. "I really should clear up... some things." There are nerves in her eyes, and she opens and closes her mouth a few times as if unsure if she should continue. "Actually...I have to tell you something," she finally rushes out.

Suddenly, I'm sure I don't want to hear it.

She sits up, and the bedsheet pools around her waist. My shirt looks ridiculously big on her, slipping off one of her shoulders. I want to lean in and kiss the bare curve, but my eyes are drawn to her twisting hands.

My heart rate spikes, and I fight the urge to grab her, to make her forget whatever it is she's about to tell me.

Instead, I sit up as well and, grabbing her chin softly, bring her gaze back to me.

"Tell me."

She swallows and wraps her arms around herself, her smile missing. Now she's scaring me.

"You know that I didn't tell my family I came here." She starts, and I nod, waiting patiently when she stops and bites her lip.

"Part of why they let me go, let me stay away for so long and never questioned it, is that I turn twenty-one next month." She takes a gulping breath, her eyes flicking down to my hand, still holding her chin, and hurries through the next sentence in one long breath. "At that point, the betrothal agreement will come into effect."

It takes a moment for my brain to catch up, but then my thoughts come to a screeching halt.

"You are promised to someone?"

That can't be.

I make her look at me, search her eyes, and hope I misunderstood. But she nods.

She fucking nods. I release her.

Anger boils up in my chest, nearly choking me.

"You are promised to someone else and didn't tell me?" My voice is dangerously soft. She knows me well enough by now to wince.

How could she let this happen? Was this no more than her last taste of freedom?

"How could you?"

Hurt and betrayal want to rip me apart.

"I don't plan to marry him," she says.

"Oh, and that makes it better?" I snap. "You should have told me!"

"I know! I left all of that behind when I came here, and then that with us just happened, and I...I didn't know how to tell you... without losing you." Her eyes look dangerously bright. She looks down. "Please don't be angry."

"Oh well then, tell me how I should feel when the woman...I..." *love...* The word burns in my throat while I swallow. "I... fucked all night casually mentions that she's another man's woman and about to be married."

"I'm not," she cries out. "I don't even know him. I only met him once as a child. Our parents made that agreement." She snatches my hand like she wants to hold on to me. "I will not do it, Tate. I won't." Her eyes plead with me to understand.

On some level, I do get it. I grew up with all this bullshit, after all. If I hadn't given up my position as crown prince, I would be in the same position. Arranged marriages are common not only for wealth and political power but also to keep the magic flowing strong.

"Who is it? Do I know him?" I growl. Cassius's face flashes before my eyes. But she said she doesn't know the bastard, so it can't be him.

"You are leaving for Argona, right?" I barrel on. I still have power there. I have connections. Maybe I can persuade whoever it is to negate the agreement. Scare them into it, if necessary. I can—

"The heir of the crown." It's barely a whisper, but she might as well have kicked my feet out from under me.

Another piece of the puzzle clicks into place... It had been in front of my eyes since I knew Blackstone was her brother, but I was so occupied with worrying for her life that I simply didn't connect the dots.

My friends call me Ara.

Ara is a nickname...and Summer isn't her family name...

"You're Tamara Blackstone?"

Shit, it all makes fucking sense now. How she isn't intimidated by rank and titles; how she's fucking perfect in handling even the most arrogant prick. Her exceptional swordsmanship...She was raised by a general and among warriors, probably playing with swords instead of dolls. She was raised to be a queen, my queen.

Ara—no, Tamara Blackstone—nods, and my heart splinters into tiny, jagged shards, threatening to gut me alive.

She was supposed to be mine, but now, she's my brother's.

THANK YOU FOR READING FEATHERS OF ASH AND HOPE! Continue Tate and Ara's story in Trials of Embers and Trust, Book 2 of the Flameborn Series.

If you enjoyed Ara and Tate's story so far and would like to read more, sign up for my newsletter to receive exclusive bonus scenes as well as information about upcoming releases and more. Your email address will never be shared, and you can unsubscribe at any time.

And while this journey isn't finished and there is much more to come, I would be forever grateful if you take the time to leave my book an honest review and share your thoughts so others may discover this story.

Thank you so much,

K.J. Altair

Acknowledgments

It all started with writing a market scene for another story when Ara strode onto the page, dressed like a boy. She helped the main character out and accidentally got kidnapped for it. Let me tell you, Tate was not amused—but that is another story—and it somehow just spiraled from there.

Suddenly, all these ideas and scenes popped into my head, and dialogue full of banter played through my mind. I wrote the ideas down, determined to work on the story another time, and before I knew it, I had 30,000 words worth of notes. Well, you hold the result of that in your hands right now.

But until a rough first draft becomes a final book, it takes heaps of polishing, and there are a lot of people who helped me get this book to where it is now.

Because of them, this story became far better than anything I could have created on my own. For that, I'm immeasurably thankful!

But before I get to the actual writing part, I want to thank the people who endured me through all the ups and downs of this journey.

First and foremost, I want to thank my wonderful husband, who encouraged me to leave my career in medicine and dive headfirst into writing.

While I was off fighting fictional battles and chasing plot twists, you tamed the kids, made the time, and only occasionally questioned my chaos, so this book truly wouldn't exist without you. Thank you for being the best husband a woman can wish for! You are and always will be my inspiration for all the book boyfriends I create, and I'm forever grateful for the miscommunication that started our story. Love you, babe!

I also want to thank you, my beautiful girls, for all the times you waited patiently until I finished scribbling down my ideas before answering your questions and solving your problems. You are the best!

Thank you to my fantastic critique partners. Austynn Cull, I learned so much on the way and truly enjoyed all the calls we spent discussing our respective worlds and the problems dragon riders and skyriders face. Sean King and Alyssa Castor, thank you for your feedback and views on what I created; seeing my writing through different eyes was immensely helpful.

To my wonderful group of beta readers: Bassey Blessing, Tyesha Nauslar, Olga Sikaki, Rebecca Treadway, Aleighsha Parke, Chantelle Kerr, and Elle Maguire—thank you for stepping into this world with me, for your time, your insights, kind words, and encouragement. Every one of you had an eye for something else, and in combination, it was exactly what I needed.

A special thank you to Rebecca Treadway and Chantelle Kerr— you went above and beyond, and this book carries your fingerprints in the very best way.

Another heartfelt thanks goes to my dear editor, Jenny Sims of Editing4Indies. You put on the final sheen and helped me catch all the little spots so the story can truly shine now.

Thank you to all my awesome book besties on BookTok for your excitement and support; you are incredible.

Then there are my amazing ARC readers. I'm so grateful you took the time to read this book early and share your honest reviews with the world. Since reviews are incredibly important to indie authors like me, I can't thank you enough for taking the time to let others know about this book! Thank you!

And last but absolutely not least—thank you, dear reader, for actually reading this book (instead of just buying it for the pretty cover and letting it live on your TBR forever ;) Yes, I know the problem). Seriously though, where would any story be without someone to read it? So, thank you for walking beside Ara and Tate, for giving their journey your time, your heart, and your imagination. I had an absolute blast writing it, and I hope you enjoyed it just as much.

Love,

K.J. Altair

About the Author

K.J. Altair is the author of *Feathers of Ash and Hope*, a **New Adult Fantasy Romance** filled with slow-burn sizzle, high-stakes adventure, and forbidden love. Ever since she learned to read, books have been her constant companions and—apart from her husband and kids—she loves nothing more than getting lost in another world.

When she's not writing, she can be found devouring novels (especially fantasy and romance), indulging in dark chocolate, or traveling and enjoying the magic of the real world.

Follow her on: Booktok, Bookstagram, or Goodreads, and join her newsletter to stay up to date on new releases and more.

- tiktok.com/@kjaltair
- goodreads.com/kjaltair
- amazon.com/author/kjaltair
- instagram.com/kjaltair
- threads.net/@kjaltair

Made in the USA
Middletown, DE
06 October 2025